Hal Spacejock 7: Big Bang

Book seven in the Hal Spacejock series

Stay in touch!

Author's newsletter:
spacejock.com.au/ML.html

facebook.com/halspacejock
twitter.com/spacejock

Works by Simon Haynes

All of Simon's novels* are self-contained, with a beginning, a middle and a proper ending. They're not sequels, they don't end on a cliffhanger, and you can start or end your journey with any book in the series.
* *Robot vs Dragons series excepted!*

The Hal Spacejock series for teens/adults

Set in the distant future, where humanity spans the galaxy and robots are second-class citizens. Includes a large dose of humour!

Hal Spacejock 1: A robot named Clunk
Hal Spacejock 2: Second Course
Hal Spacejock 3: Just Desserts
Hal Spacejock 4: No Free Lunch
Hal Spacejock 5: Baker's Dough
Hal Spacejock 6: Safe Art
Hal Spacejock 7: Big Bang
Hal Spacejock 8: Double Trouble
Hal Spacejock 9: Max Damage
Hal Spacejock 10: Cold Boots (2019)

Also available:
Omnibus One, containing Hal books 1-3
Omnibus Two, containing Hal books 4-6
Omnibus Three, containing Hal books 7-9
Hal Spacejock: Visit, a short story
Hal Spacejock: Framed, a short story
Hal Spacejock: Albion, a novella

The Robot vs Dragons Trilogy.
High fantasy meets low humour!
Each set of three books should be read in order.

1. A Portion of Dragon and Chips
2. A Butt of Heads
3. A Pair of Nuts on the Throne
4. TBA (2019)

The Harriet Walsh series.

Set in the same universe as Hal Spacejock. Good clean fun, written with wry humour. No cliffhangers between novels!

Harriet Walsh 1: Peace Force
Harriet Walsh 2: Alpha Minor
Harriet Walsh 3: Sierra Bravo
Harriet Walsh 4: Storm Force (2019)
Also Available:
Omnibus One, containing books 1-3

The Hal Junior series

Written for all ages, these books are set aboard a space station in the Hal Spacejock universe, only ten years later.

1. Hal Junior: The Secret Signal
2. Hal Junior: The Missing Case
3. Hal Junior: The Gyris Mission
4. Hal Junior: The Comet Caper

Also Available:
Omnibus One, containing books 1-3

The Secret War series.
Gritty space opera for adult readers.

1. Raiders (2019)
2. Frontier (2019)
3. Deadlock (2019)

Collect One-Two - a collection of shorts by Simon Haynes

All titles available in ebook and paperback. Visit spacejock.com.au for details.

SIMON HAYNES

Bowman Press

v 1.12

Published 2013 by Bowman Press

Text © Simon Haynes 2013
Jacket design © Bowman Press 2013

ISBN 978-1-877034-48-0 (Mobi ebook)
ISBN 978-1-877034-54-1 (Epub ebook)
ISBN 978-1-877034-42-8 (Paperback)

National Library of Australia Cataloguing-in-Publication entry
Author: Haynes, Simon, 1967- author.
Title: Hal Spacejock 7 : Big Bang / Simon Haynes.
ISBN: 9781877034428 (paperback)
Subjects: Science fiction
Dewey Number: A823.4

*Dedicated to my brillinat Enlish tutor, without whom
I'd have written twice as many novels in half the time.*

Hal Spacejock was relaxing in a comfy armchair in the *Volante's* lounge, a coffee at his elbow and a tin of biscuits on the seat beside him. Business had been good lately, and he'd upgraded the furniture twice in the past month. Not only that, there'd been enough left over to buy real biscuits, with real crumbs and everything. Hal was impressed at the way the biscuits snapped cleanly in two, rather than bending, and as a result of this novelty the tin was brimming with biscuity fragments. Not that Hal cared - they still tasted the same, and more exposed edges meant they soaked up the coffee better. In fact, he was thinking about patenting the idea and selling it to a big food conglomerate.

'Snapper biscuits,' he mumbled through a mouthful of crumbs. 'Or maybe Clean Breaks?'

'Are you talking to me?'

Hal glanced towards the back of the lounge, where a bronze robot was crawling around on hands and knees. 'Not really, no.'

'In that case, I shall continue with my fruitless task.'

'Have you lost something?'

'No, I'm collecting biscuit crumbs.' Clunk pinched something off the carpet, held it up to the light to inspect it, then sucked it into his open mouth with a whoosh of air.

'You don't have to eat those old things,' said Hal generously. 'There's a whole tin over here.'

'I'm not eating them, Mr Spacejock. I'm tidying them up.'

'What for?'

Clunk frowned at him. 'Because this ship will be knee deep in crumbs before the week is out, and then where will we be?'

Hal was still grinning at the thought of a biscuit bath when Clunk inhaled another crumb, distracting him. 'Picking them up one by one . . . isn't that a bit inefficient?'

'It is, but the vacuum cleaner is out of commission.'

Hal looked guilty. 'Oh. Is it really?'

'Yes, really. I haven't checked the manual recently, but I'm pretty sure it wasn't designed to shoot rubber balls at the viewscreen.'

'It worked.'

'Briefly. And why you wanted to –'

'Kent Spearman's got a new ad.' Hal's expression hardened. His long-term rival had been running an advertising campaign across every major station, bigging himself up as some kind of super-pilot. A competent businessman would run a campaign countering the ads, but Hal Spacejock wasn't a competent businessmen so he satisfied his thirst for revenge by throwing rubber balls at the screen whenever Spearman's oafish face appeared. Or shooting balls with the vacuum cleaner, before it broke down.

'That's not good, Mr Spacejock. Every client who chooses Spearman means one less job for us.'

'Don't be daft.' Hal shrugged. 'The ads are a joke. Nobody would believe that rubbish.'

'There's always a danger some gullible client will believe Mr Spearman's claims.'

2

'I don't want any gullible clients.'

Clunk raised his eyebrows. 'You think any other kind would hire us?'

'Yeah, very funny. Anyway, ads are a total waste of money. These people charge a fortune.'

'You could afford a campaign of your own if you stopped redecorating the lounge.' Clunk sucked up another crumb. 'Or, indeed, buying expensive biscuits.'

Hal frowned. 'That's another thing. How's Spearman paying for all this? The freight business would never bring in that sort of cash.'

'Are you suggesting Mr Spearman is engaged in illegal activities?'

'It wouldn't be the first time.' Hal brightened. 'Hey, maybe we could report him to the Peace Force!'

'Again, Mr Spacejock?'

'They have to listen to me sooner or later.'

'Perhaps they would, if you had actual evidence.'

Hal gestured impatiently. 'That's their job. If they'd only –'

A crackle from the overhead speakers interrupted him. 'Incoming call,' said a neutral female voice.

'Who is it, Navcom?'

'I won't know until you answer it,' said the ship's computer patiently.

'Why not? Can't you screen it or something?'

'Complying.'

The big screen cleared, and the words 'Incoming Call' appeared in bold red lettering.

'When I said screen it, that wasn't exactly what I meant,' said Hal with a sigh. 'Go on, then. I guess you'd better answer it.'

'Cannot comply.'

'Why not?'

'The caller has now disconnected.'

'Oh well, probably just a time waster. One of those welly marketers who keeps bothering me.'

'I think you mean telemarketers.'

'I know what I meant, Navcom. I have fourteen pairs of gum boots in the airlock.' Hal glanced at Clunk. 'Where were we?'

'Bothering the local Peace Force for no particular reason,' said the robot promptly.

'That's how you see it, but I'm looking at the bigger picture. I know Spearman –'

'Incoming call,' said the Navcom again.

'Is it the same person?' Hal raised his hand before the Navcom could lose this call as well. 'No, don't bother. Just put them on.'

The screen cleared and an attractive young woman appeared. She had long chestnut hair and grey eyes, and Hal recognised her immediately - it was Meredith Ryder, the events organiser who'd helped with a cargo of artworks a few weeks earlier. He sat up in the armchair, straightening his collar and brushing a shirtload of crumbs onto the floor. Ignoring Clunk's despairing groan, Hal smiled warmly at the screen. 'Hey, Meri. How are you doing?'

'I'm doing fine, Hal. And yourself?'

'Excellent. Top notch.'

'Am I interrupting something?'

'No, of course not. How can we help you?'

'Do you remember that new business venture I was setting up?'

'House moving, wasn't it?'

Meri nodded. 'I just got my first client, and they want a top-notch pilot.'

Hal grinned with pride. 'Well, it's good of you to –'

'Unfortunately, Kent Spearman's busy. Then I remembered you, and I thought . . . hey, why not? How bad can it be?'

Hal's grin vanished. 'We delivered the last cargo, didn't we?'

'Some of it. Eventually.' Meri gestured. 'Anyway, that's ancient history. I'm sure you'll give me a hundred percent, even if you let them down.'

'One hundred and twenty percent,' said Hal. 'One-fifty, if the pay is good.'

'It's very generous.' Meri smiled warmly. 'So, are you interested?'

'Of course. Tell me all about it.'

◆

'They've just completed a brand new dam on planet Chiseley. It's flooding right now, and there's a house which is going to be completely underwater by the time the water stops rising.' Meri glanced at her notes. 'The owner passed away several months ago, and his family have been too busy to deal with the contents. Now, with the dam and everything, they have to get the stuff out or risk losing the lot.'

'So why don't they send a truck in?'

'The area was only serviced by a couple of dirt tracks, and they've been underwater for days.'

'A boat?'

Meri shook her head. 'Too many dead-ends and obstructions. Not big enough, either.'

'Using the *Volante* seems like massive overkill. We're going to burn a ton of fuel.'

'My clients will pay handsomely.'

'So what's in the house? Antiques? Valuable artworks? Stacks of gold bars?'

'I have no idea, and I don't think the customers know either. I get the feeling the old guy was a bit of a loner. Difficult, crotchety, hard to get along with. You know the type.'

Hal knew the type exactly, because the description fitted Clunk to a tee. 'Still, they're taking a risk. They might end up with a collection of dodgy old magazines and moth-eaten furniture.'

'They're a professional couple, very busy with their careers. They intended to take leave from their work and clear the house themselves, but the flooding has forced them into action. If it's a load of rubbish they'll just throw it away, but they're hoping for a few heirlooms.'

'Oh well, it's their money.' Hal glanced over his shoulder. 'Clunk, what do you think?'

'I think we need a new vacuum cleaner,' said the robot.

'I'm talking about this house clearing job. It's not our usual thing, but –'

'Oh, the job.' Clunk gestured impatiently. 'Sign us up for whatever you like. Everything we touch turns into a three-ring disaster, so the precise details really make no difference.'

'He's just pulling your leg,' said Hal quickly, before Meri could snatch the job away from them. 'It's robot humour, you know. Very dry and understated.'

'If you say so.' Meri tapped something on her terminal. 'I've just notified my clients of your decision. You're to land on Chiseley and meet the local agent at the spaceport. His name is Si Matthews, and he'll have keys and directions. He'll also tell you where to unload the house contents afterwards.'

'Good stuff.'

'Please get this one right, Hal. I'll be a laughing stock if it goes wrong.'

Hal laid a hand on his chest. 'Meri, you'll get our best work, I promise.'

After a somewhat apprehensive smile, Meri disconnected.

'Well, that sounds perfect,' said Hal, as the screen turned dark. 'Important clients, a nice easy job and good pay. What could possibly go wrong?'

Clunk choked, spraying biscuit crumbs all over the carpet. 'Oh, Mr Spacejock. Did you have to say that?'

$-2-$

The *Volante* landed at the Chiseley spaceport without incident. Hal ignored the 'fasten seatbelt' sign and headed for the airlock, keen for a breath of fresh air. He was halfway there when the ship lurched, throwing him full-length to the deck. He sat up, rubbing his shoulder, and glared at the flight console. 'What was that for?'

'I was just levelling the ship,' said the Navcom calmly.

'Why can't you do it more gently?'

'Why can't you remain seated until the warning light goes out?'

Hal was about to argue, but the light was still on and there was nothing to stop the Navcom levelling the ship in the opposite direction, throwing him into the wall. In fact, there was nothing to stop the Navcom turning the *Volante* into a glorified carnival ride, so Hal held his tongue as he regained his feet. He stayed silent as he made his way back to the pilot's chair, and he said nothing as he sat down.

Immediately, with a self-satisfied ping, the seatbelt light went out.

Hal pressed his lips together, but decided revenge could wait until later. In fact, revenge would have to wait until he'd worked out how to take revenge on a computer which had his life in its hands most of the time. For example, reversing the polarity on the Navcom's power supply would probably shut down the *Volante's* life support systems, killing Hal into the bargain. Worse, the Navcom would only need a new fuse, and then she'd be free to torture the *Volante's* next owner.

So, Hal stood up and stalked into the airlock, opened the outer door, and waited for the passenger ramp to touch down. As it made contact, Hal noticed a tall man in a blue suit climbing out of a parked car. The man spotted Hal, waved a greeting, then made his way up the ramp, using the rail for balance.

Hal felt a chill in the air, and he glanced at the leaden sky. It was late afternoon, and the local sun had an unpleasant orange cast which made it look like an under-powered street light. There were heavy clouds too, and the stiff breeze carried a hint of rain.

'Si Matthews,' said the agent, who'd reached the top of the ramp while Hal was still impersonating a weather forecaster.

'Hal Spacejock. Come inside.'

'Don't mind if I do.'

Hal introduced Clunk and the Navcom, and then they got down to business. Matthews explained the job, which was pretty much as Meri had told them. Then he asked how soon they'd be setting off.

'I thought we'd start in the morning,' said Hal.

'Better to go right away,' said Matthews.

'If we take off now, we'll be looking for this place in the dark.'

'If you wait until tomorrow, the house will be underwater. I'm afraid it's now or never.'

'But –'

'It's okay, Mr Spacejock.' Clunk patted the console. 'The

Navcom will take us straight to our destination. Rain or shine, light or dark, we can navigate with pinpoint accuracy. Once I download the GPS coordinates –'

Matthews cleared his throat. 'That might be a problem.'

'You don't have the coordinates?'

'This planet doesn't have GPS. The satellites are on backorder.'

'Oh great,' said Hal. 'How are we supposed to find the house now?'

Matthews reached into his pocket. 'I have a compass heading and an approximate distance. Don't worry - I'm sure you'll find the place.' He handed Hal a folded scrap of paper, then laughed. 'Just make sure you don't empty the wrong house, eh?'

'Yeah, good one,' said Hal, laughing along with him.

Clunk and the Navcom remained silent.

Hal examined the paper. 'Thirty-nine kilometers, North by Northwest? That's it?'

'You'll find it.' Matthews dug in his pocket and took out a bunch of keys. 'Don't ask me which is which, although I suppose you can just break in if you have to.'

Hal took the keys and handed them to Clunk with the scrap of paper. 'Now, about the fee –'

'Strictly cash on delivery.'

'But we need fuel!'

'Don't try that old chestnut. I've heard every excuse in the book.'

'It's not fuel for the ship I'm after - it's for me. We're out of food.'

'You'll find dry goods and tinned food at the house. I'm sure the client won't mind if you help yourself.' Matthews noticed

Hal's eager expression. 'Just the food, mind. Everything else must be delivered safe and sound.'

'Yeah, yeah. We know.'

'I'll be off then. Contact me as soon as you're back.'

Clunk led Matthews to the airlock and showed him out. Meanwhile, Hal inspected a map of their surroundings on the main screen. It consisted of vast areas of rolling hills, mostly covered in dense forest. 'Navcom, can you show me an area with a diameter of thirty-nine kilometres?'

'Complying.'

The screen zoomed out, with the spaceport and the settlement in the centre surrounded by a sea of green. 'Now plot a course North by Northeast.'

'The agent said Northwest.'

'I want you to do them both,' said Hal. 'And squarate the result, will you?'

'I think you mean triangulate.'

'No, I mean squarate. Every corner helps when you're navigating.'

A couple of lines appeared on the screen, and the Navcom added a dozen coloured squares for good measure.

'What's that?' asked Hal, pointing to a blob near one of the lines.

The map zoomed in to show a house perched on the side of a hill. There was a dirt track leading down to the bottom of a valley, and Hal could just make out a garage nearby. Bingo! 'Navcom, I want you to mark that house.'

'Complying.' No sooner had the Navcom spoken than an icon appeared on the map. It appeared to be a traffic cone, and the label underneath said 'Hal's House'

'Why's there a D on that cone?'

'It's short for Definitely.'

A distant school memory brought a frown to Hal's face, but the deeper he dug into the recesses of his mind, the further it slipped away. In the end he shrugged and turned to the airlock, where Clunk was just shutting the inner door. 'Finally got rid of him, eh?'

'Last minute instructions. He thought we should –'

'Yeah, never mind all that.' Hal pointed to the screen. 'Look what I found.'

Clunk's lips twisted, which was no mean feat given how stiff they were. 'I see you found a house.'

'Yep, that's the one. Look, there's even a flat spot we can land on. Drop in, ransack the place, leave.'

'You do realise that house is on top of a hill?'

'So what?'

'First, we're looking for a house which is about to be flooded. Therefore, I suspect it's likely to be somewhat lower down the slopes. Second, the agent mentioned a distance of thirty-nine kilometres while your find is under fourteen point five.'

'How can that be?' Hal pointed an accusing finger at the console. 'I told the Navcom to show me a distance of thirty-nine klicks!'

'You requested diameter, not distance,' said the Navcom. 'It's not my job to correct basic geometry.'

'Mr Spacejock clearly wanted the radius,' said Clunk.

The Navcom made a sound suspiciously like a sniff.

'What's the difference?' asked Hal.

'About three days worth of math lessons,' said the Navcom. 'Or in some cases, three months.'

Hal frowned. 'I know where your power plug is, you know.'

'And I know where you sleep.'

'You know,' remarked Hal, 'once you've seen a couple of hundred flooded valleys they all start to look the same.'

The *Volante* was flying between a pair of hills, following a narrowing body of water towards the point where it was still lapping at the trunks of soon-to-be submerged trees. This valley was no different to dozens of others they'd explored, and Hal was beginning to wonder if they were just shuttling between the same handful. The trees, the hills . . . everything was familiar.

'I'm sure I've seen that one before,' said Hal, pointing out a pine tree. 'See the way the branches stick out sideways?'

Clunk ignored him and continued to work the controls, guiding the ship to the end of the valley before angling it up to avoid the incline at the end. They passed over a clearing, then descended once more.

'Oh look, it's another valley,' muttered Hal. 'Never mind, I'm sure we'll find the right one eventually.'

'I'm doing my best,' protested Clunk.

'Maybe I should take over.'

Clunk's hands tightened on the controls. 'Over all of our dead bodies.'

Hal grunted as he looked at the screen. 'It's not getting any lighter, is it?'

'That's because it's evening, Mr Spacejock.'

'Why don't we give up? We could go back to the spaceport and find a nice easy cargo job.'

'Mr Spacejock, you know there's no such thing. Anyway, you told Ms Ryder you'd give her a hundred and fifty percent.'

'Yeah, but she hasn't paid us yet, and a hundred and fifty percent of nothing is still nothing.' Hal gestured at the controls. 'Hit the throttles and head for the sky.'

Clunk shook his head. 'You can't let Meri down.'

'You heard her ... she didn't want us, she wanted Spearman. Let him tool around looking for valleys and sunken houses.'

'By the time Mr Spearman arrived, it really would be a sunken house.'

'Who cares? It's probably full of junk anyway.' Hal gestured impatiently. 'Come on, let's go. I bet we'll find a real job on the next planet.'

'Mr Spacejock, we've only been searching for thirty minutes. If we gave up on a job every time you –'

'Hey, what was that?' Hal pointed at the screen. 'Quick, go back! I saw a house!'

The ship heeled round, the image on the viewscreen tilting like crazy. When it settled down again, there was a large, two-storey house in the middle of the screen. It was an imposing building with arches, stark whitewashed walls, and even a small turret in one corner, much like a guard tower designed to keep a lookout for marauding invaders. Through the windows Hal could just make out an impressive brass telescope, and shelves crammed with books.

The rear of the house was built into the hillside, and a pair of garage doors were set into the cliff alongside. A washing line turned slowly in the downdraft from the *Volante's* jets, and the shutters on the windows rattled and shook as they were buffeted by the turbulence. The area in front of the house was laid with gravel, and a drive lead downhill, straight into the rising waters.

'That's the place,' said Hal. 'It has to be.'

'It's a little more grand than I expected.'

14

'An old trick. You don't tell people you're a millionaire when you're getting quotes. Playing poor keeps the price down.'

'Perhaps.' Clunk checked the data in the corner of the screen. 'The heading and distance are correct.'

'I'm telling you, this is the place. The agent said there weren't many houses out here, and we've checked more hidden valleys than a gyn–'

'We have to make certain. Emptying the wrong house would be a disaster.'

'If they're all getting flooded, what's the difference?' Hal looked thoughtful. 'You know, there could be an earner in this. There must be other abandoned houses - some of them might be worth a look.'

'Maybe so, but first we have to do the job we're being paid for.' Clunk applied himself to the controls, and the ship rose into the air. 'I'll do a widening spiral around the house. If there's nothing within a kilometre we'll know this is the correct location.'

'Suit yourself. I know when I'm right.' Hal glanced at his watch. 'It's nearly dinner time. I'll rustle up some grub while you're busy.'

'You can't. We don't have any supplies.'

'No, after we land. I'll empty the larder while you clear the rest of the house.'

3

Twenty minutes later, Clunk was finally satisfied. He'd circled an area more than two kilometres in diameter, and then hadn't spotted so much as a cubby house. Not only that, but the weather was closing in and it would soon be dark.

'About time,' was Hal's only comment, as the *Volante* turned back onto the original heading. But instead of landing on the broad gravel drive, Clunk continued for several hundred metres before setting the ship down in a clearing. 'Why so far away?' demanded Hal.

'If I land on the gravel, the force of our jets will kick up thousands of stones.'

'So?'

'They will damage the house.'

'It's about to get flooded, Clunk. I don't think a few stone chips will make any difference.'

'Nevertheless, I cannot cause wilful damage.'

'Okay, let me land the ship.' Hal flexed his fingers. 'I could use a bit of practice.'

Clunk shook his head. 'That would be endangering the house, not to mention the *Volante*.' Before Hal could argue any further, the robot shut down the engines. 'Carrying the items a short distance won't add too much time, and the exercise will do you good.'

Hal was still protesting as Clunk unsealed the airlock, extending the passenger ramp towards the ground. As the slender structure unfolded itself, dust from their landing swirled around, blowing grit into Hal's eyes.

Clunk stepped onto the landing platform outside the ship's airlock, and as soon as the ramp was locked in place he took the first step towards the ground. He was already halfway down by the time he realised Mr Spacejock wasn't following. Looking back, Clunk saw the human still inside the airlock, peering out cautiously. 'What is it?'

'What sort of creatures do they have here?'

'Birds, insects, a few mammals. Why?'

'No giant orange apes, right?'

Clunk shook his head. 'This planet was terraformed centuries ago. Imported species only.'

Hal looked towards the nearby forest, where the tree trunks were lost in the gloomy twilight under the canopy. 'Why don't you walk around for a bit? See if anything attacks you.'

'I assure you ...' Clunk was about to argue the point, then relented. After all, they were going to be working through the night, so what difference would it make to waste a few minutes? He upped his volume level and faced the trees. 'Here apey-wapeys, unky Clunky has a nice metal bone for you. Come and partake!'

'Stop messing about and do it properly,' said Hal. 'Pretend you haven't seen it.'

'Seen what?' Clunk looked around in concern, spinning his head this way and that. 'What did you see? Who's out there? What did it look like?'

'That's more like it. Now turn your back to the trees and don't look round. They always sneak up from behind.'

Unwillingly, Clunk complied. His confidence had evaporated, and he was beginning to wonder whether his sketchy research notes on the planet were good enough to stake his life on. There had been one or two incidents in the past where he'd used the wrong database - and even the wrong planet - leading to some very unpleasant encounters.

As he stood there with his back to the forest, waiting to be attacked, he wondered exactly what Mr Spacejock had seen.

◆

Hal waited a few minutes, then decided the forest looked safe enough. If there were any dangerous life forms he could always use Clunk as a shield while making a hasty getaway. The robot wasn't indestructible, but he'd probably last long enough for Hal to get to safety.

The two of them left the clearing, making their way along a rough path towards the house. To their right, the ground fell away, with trees already vanishing under the rising waters. To their left, imposing trees towered over them, the thick undergrowth alive with insects and birds.

After ten minutes or so they reached the gravel drive, and their feet scrunched on the stones as they walked towards the house. The entrance was imposing, with a pair of weathered stone lions sitting on columns, and a door which towered over them by a metre or more. It hadn't been used for some time, though: leaves had drifted into the corners, and the doormat was half buried.

'I hope the owner isn't still here,' said Hal suddenly.

'According to Ms Ryder, he died a while ago.'

'Exactly.'

Clunk inspected the lock, then flipped through the keys until he found one to match. Unfortunately, it didn't turn.

'Stuck?' asked Hal.

'Could be.' Clunk indicated the leaves all over the porch. 'It's weeks since anyone came here.'

'The agent said we could break in.'

Clunk stood on tip-toes to peer through a bottle-green porthole in the door. 'I don't like the idea of forced entry.'

'Here, let me,' said Hal, reaching for one of the granite lions. He managed to pick it up, then staggered towards the door with it, eventually giving the handle the gentlest of nudges with the stone head.

'What's that in aid of?' asked Clunk.

'I need a proper run-up.'

'No, you need some proper strength.'

Hal backed out of the porch, holding the stone lion around its midriff. 'Move out of the way,' said Hal, puffing under the strain. 'Quick, or I'll drop this thing on my toes.'

Clunk obeyed, and he watched in concern as Hal staggered past with the heavy lion. There was a thud as it hit the door, and a bigger thud as it fell out of Hal's grasp and landed on the doormat.

'Keep going like that and we won't need to open the door,' remarked Clunk. 'We'll just walk through the tunnel you're making underneath it.'

Hal struggled off with the lion, panting and puffing, and this time he managed a solid bump before tottering out of the porch backwards. He lost his footing, and barely managed to drop the heavy statue before landing on his backside.

Clunk sighed. 'Mr Spacejock, I feel it's only a matter of time before you do yourself a serious injury.'

'Too late,' said Hal, rubbing a bruise.

'Much as I dislike breaking and entering, I believe I must make an exception in this case.' So saying, Clunk extended his hand like a ramrod, punching a hole through the door panel. Then he reached inside to undo the catch, and within seconds the doors swung open.

The interior was spacious, and their footsteps echoed off the marble floor and stark white walls. Paintings hung beneath angled spotlights, ranging from detailed landscapes and portraits to abstract works spanning several panels. There was a large amount of furniture concealed under snowy-white sheets, and when Hal rubbed a piece of fabric between finger and thumb he discovered the dropsheets were better quality than the ones on his bunk.

Clunk inspected an oil painting depicting a rural scene. 'You know, this reminds me of Farrell's place.'

'Farrell?'

'You remember, the Hinchfig brother who tried to kill you. The one you stole your ship from.'

'Oh, that Hinchfig.' Hal shrugged. 'All these posh gaffs are the same. Showy artworks and huge rooms filled with furniture nobody uses. I bet there's even a limo in the garage.'

'I sincerely hope not. Remember, we're supposed to be clearing this house.'

'Oh hell.' Hal looked around, struck by the enormity of the task. Until this moment he'd pictured a modest house with a few sticks of furniture which they could load into the *Volante* in under an hour. Now it looked like they'd really be earning their money. 'Do you reckon all this stuff will fit in the ship?' he asked, hoping Clunk would say no so they could chuck the job and leave.

Hoow-oooooow-ooooowl!

Hal's hair stood on end at the mournful, drawn-out sound, and he fought the impulse to run for the safety of the *Volante*. 'What the hell was *that*?' he whispered.

Clunk looked uneasy. 'I don't know, Mr Spacejock, but it seems we're not alone.'

— 4 —

Clunk reacted instantly as the footsteps thudded towards him. They were moving at speed, and he barely had time to move in front of Hal before a large bundle of orange fur launched itself at his throat. Time slowed, and Clunk noticed several things: First, the fur had a mouth, and that mouth was filled with wicked-looking teeth. Second, the creature was actually of the genus Canis familiaris, or more specifically a red setter. And finally, it wasn't aiming to tear his throat out . . . it was just very happy to see him.

Time sped up once more, and Clunk danced around, arms waving, as he tried to fend off the dog's frantic attempts to lick his face. He'd barely noticed the grey hairs around its muzzle when it bounded past, tail windmilling. Then he heard Hal's 'uuuurgh!' as the eager dog barrelled into him. When Clunk turned round, the human was sitting on the floor, the dog nuzzling his cheek.

'Mr Spacejock, are you all right?'

'Yeah, fine. What about this, eh?' Hal rubbed the dog's neck, then looked closer. 'She's lost her collar.'

'How can you tell?'

'The hair's all flattened.' Hal took the dog under the chin and looked into its eyes. 'What's the story, old girl? Did you run away, or did the nasty people leave you behind?'

'Surely they wouldn't . . . ' began Clunk.

'I've known people leave their own family behind,' said Hal curtly. 'Are you hungry?'

'I don't eat.'

Hal glanced at him. 'I meant the dog. Let's organise some food, eh?'

The dog barked and charged off down the corridor, leaving Clunk frowning after her. 'I must inspect the rest of the house. Perhaps you could take care of the wretched animal in the meantime.'

Hal frowned. 'Don't call her that.'

'What do you suggest? Spot? Fido?'

'Maybe we'll find a collar with her name on.'

'And the fleas to go with it.'

'What's your problem, Clunk? First you hate cows, and now it's dogs. It'll be cute little hamsters next.'

'Animals don't communicate properly.'

'Sure they do. Watch.' Hal stuck his fingers in his mouth and whistled. There was a bark, and a clatter of nails along the passageway, and the dog came bounding in. 'See?'

'Now ask it where its owners are.'

'Very funny.'

'No, I'm serious. That's exactly what I'm talking about. Dumb animals can't . . . '

'She's not dumb,' said Hal, patting the dog on the flank. In return she licked his hand.

'And their attitude towards hygiene is appalling,' added Clunk. 'For example, how do you know where that tongue's been?'

'You can't ask a lady questions like that!'

'Only because you don't want to know the answer.'

'Come on, girl. Let's find the larder and leave unky Clunky to his moany woany ways.'

Clunk opened his mouth to protest, then closed it again. Hal could almost read his mind: with human and dog out of the way, the robot would be able to inspect, catalogue and organise to his heart's content. 'Very well, Mr Spacejock. You feed the creature, and I'll start working.'

◆

Clunk hurried from room to room, taking snapshots of the contents and converting the images into 3D models. While his legs carried him around the house, his brain processed the models, rotating them and fitting them together until they took up the smallest possible space. Another process fitted the resulting tangle into a scale model of the *Volante's* cargo hold, and when that was full he moved on to the lower deck, the passageways, and the cabins.

By the time he reached the last room, Clunk's model of the ship was packed from stem to stern, leaving a tiny crawl space to get around. There were items balanced on the flight console, carefully placed so the legs weren't resting on any important controls, and chairs and tables hung from the roof on hooks. Even the engine room hadn't escaped his notice, with boxes of belongings piled up around both engines and the hyperdrive motor. It was crowded enough to give a compulsive hoarder the screaming fits, but even so Clunk allowed himself a triumphant smile. He'd done it! Every item aboard the ship, and it would only take ... only take ...

His smile slipped. According to his calculations, it would

take three days to move everything, by which time half of it would have floated away.

Well, perhaps they didn't need to wrap *everything* in spare blankets, and they could carry a little more on each trip if Mr Spacejock really put in a good effort. Clunk altered the parameters and ran the simulation again, and his face fell even further. Two days!

Worried now, Clunk altered the parameters again. If they carried three times as much, ran back and forth, threw the items into the hold any old how and sorted out the mess later it would *just* be possible to empty the house in time. Some items would be damaged, or left behind, or trampled, but that was always to be expected with one of Mr Spacejock's cargo jobs. The bulk of the goods would arrive in reasonable condition, and that would have to be good enough.

Of course, all his careful planning was for nothing if they didn't make a start right away, and with an overriding sense of urgency, Clunk ran off to find Mr Spacejock.

◆

The dog led Hal along the passageway, turned right into a large kitchen and stopped before a smart wooden door. 'So that's the larder, eh?' said Hal, spotting the sign. 'Good girl.' He opened the door and grinned as he saw the overflowing shelves. Tins of biscuits, vegetables and soup, jars of pickles, jam and sauces, bottles of drink and packets of dried noodles, rice and spaghetti were crammed into every available space. Despite his recent biscuit purchases, the *Volante's* stores had been a little thin lately, and this lot would be a most welcome addition.

Then Hal's gaze fell on a tall cabinet in the corner, glossy white with rounded corners and a row of green status lights. It was as big as a fridge, but it wasn't a cooling device. No, the tall, sleek box was a stasis cabinet!

Inside a stasis cabinet, time stood still as long as the unit was powered up. You could pop anything in there, hot or cold, and remove it a decade later in the same condition. They were very expensive, but a vast improvement on simple refrigeration. And with the owner sparing no expense on the container, what kind of luxurious delights would Hal find inside? Hot meat pies running with gravy? Thick ice cream with chocolate crumble? A leg of ham, cured on the bone?

His mouth watering in anticipation, Hal reached for the handle. Then he hesitated. Apart from food storage, stasis cabinets had also proved popular in the funeral industry, and the last thing he wanted was a face-to-face meeting with the owner of the house, even if he was in pristine condition.

When describing the job, Matthews had skipped any details on the house's owner, and whoever had neglected the dog could just as easily have left a stiff behind.

Suddenly, Hal hit on the answer. He'd pack up the dry goods for now, and later he'd ask Clunk to fetch him something from the stasis cabinet. The robot would soon let him know if there was something ... unexpected ... inside. Clunk would let him know at great length, no doubt, but a second-hand horror story was nowhere near as bad as experiencing it yourself. Even with Clunk's gift for turning minor setbacks into an endless series of novels.

A gentle whine from the dog caught Hal's attention, and he felt a stirring of guilt. Here he was worrying about his own stomach, when the poor creature hadn't seen a decent meal for days. Scanning the shelves, Hal was relieved to find a stack of large tins with Dog-e-nosh labels. He selected a can, and returned to the kitchen to find a suitable bowl. The dog followed, her eyes tracking the can with precision.

Hal opened one cupboard after another, locating any number of glasses and mugs without finding the one thing he was looking for. In the end he gave up and emptied the tin straight onto the floor. After all, the whole place was going to be underwater in hours, so nobody was going to worry about a little bit of mess.

The dog didn't seem to mind either - she tucked in, wolfing the food down as though she hadn't been fed for weeks. Watching her eat made Hal hungry, and after tossing the empty can into the sink he returned to the larder to supply his own needs. He assembled a crispbread, pickled onion and mustard sandwich, and within minutes he and the dog were eating together in contented silence.

◆

'Mr Spacejock? Are you there?'

By the time Clunk returned from his survey, Hal and the dog were both full to bursting. After the snack, and the second snack, and the afters, and two lots of desserts, Hal finally got around to packing up some of the gear they were supposed to be moving. He started with the tins of coffee, moved on to some decent-looking tinned food, and was just scavenging a few packets of cereal when the kitchen door opened and Clunk rushed in.

'Excellent! I see you've made a start,' said the robot, beaming at a stack of cardboard boxes. His tone was slightly less favourable when he looked inside the nearest carton. 'A start on the food, at least.'

'You heard the agent. Help ourselves to the grub, that's what he said.' Hal nudged the larder door shut. He wanted Clunk to discover the stasis cabinet for himself, when Hal was out of the way. A long way away, such as safely aboard the *Volante*, for example. 'So, what's up? Did you find anything interesting?'

'I finished my survey, and the furniture will fill the *Volante's* hold to ninety-eight percent capacity provided you allow me to supervise the job.'

Hal waved his hand airily. 'Supervise away. Just make sure you leave room for the new stores.'

'Stores?'

Hal nodded towards the larder. 'The supplies.'

'Of course. Now, we have a lot of work to do, so perhaps you could give me a hand with some of the larger pieces of furniture?'

'I thought you wanted to supervise?'

'Yes, but I still need a manual labourer.'

'Sorry Clunk, I'm full up. I need to let my dinner go down.'

'There's no time for resting. According to my roster, if we work for the next eight hours straight we should be able to get everything to the ship. Then, if things go smoothly, I can allow you four hours of sleep at around two in the morning, while I'm arranging the cargo in the hold. After dawn, I'll need a couple of hours help tying everything down.'

Hal almost choked on a pickle. 'Eight hours carrying furniture? Four hours sleep at two a.m.? Getting up at *dawn*?'

'The house won't empty itself, Mr Spacejock. Not only that,

I've checked the rate at which the floodwaters are rising, and if we delay more than half an hour we'll be up to our knees in water before we've finished. I'd really like a bigger margin for error, but I thought four hours sleep was the minimum you'd settle for.'

'You were wrong. Eight hours is the minimum, or seven if you wake me with fresh coffee and a three course breakfast. Four hours is a cat nap.'

The dog barked.

'See? She's on my side.'

'I'm sorry, Mr Spacejock. Time is of the essence, and we have to make an immediate start.'

'All right, all right.' Hal eyed the door to the larder. 'Listen, I need something from the *Volante*. Why don't you clear the larder while I'm gone?'

'But my roster ... '

'I'll work much harder if I know there'll be a decent meal at the end of it,' said Hal. 'Go on, Clunk. Do this for me.'

The robot sighed. 'Very well, Mr Spacejock. I will start with the larder while you visit the ship. But please, don't delay.'

'I'm sure I'll be back in no time,' said Hal honestly.

◆

Hal walked straight into a heavy rain shower as he left the house, and he ducked his head and ran full tilt towards the *Volante* to avoid the worst of it. He'd read somewhere that running through a downpour made you wetter than walking, but he couldn't bring himself to trudge along while the heavens emptied themselves onto his head. Better wet than slow, that was his motto.

The *Volante's* cargo ramp was down, and Hal jogged straight up it to the shelter of the hold. He shook his head to throw off the rain, then got another shower as the dog alongside him did likewise. He hadn't noticed her following him, and he was pleased she'd braved the downpour to stay by his side. The dog looked up at him, scattering raindrops with her hyperactive tail, and Hal was certain she was grinning even though the rain had turned her coat into a bedraggled mess.

Hal dug through a couple of equipment lockers until he found a tatty old towel, then crouched and held it out to the dog. 'Here girl,' he called, shaking the towel. The dog trotted over and he rubbed her all over, drying her coat thoroughly. In return he got a grateful lick.

When he'd finished he stood up, dried his own hair then tossed the wet towel back into the locker. His original plan had been to hang around the ship for a few minutes while Clunk opened the stasis cabinet and discovered the contents, then return to hear the worst. However, now that he was aboard he figured he might as well take a breather.

'Come on you,' he said, and headed for the elevator. Without hesitation, the dog followed, trotting along at his side.

After a brief ride the doors opened on the flight deck. 'Hi Navcom. Anything to report?'

'Negative.'

'Clunk's just organising things in the house, so I thought I'd pop over for a coffee.'

'Did you know there's a hairy quadruped in the flight deck?'

Hal glanced at the dog, who was looking around for the source of the voice, her ears up and her nose quivering. 'It's all right, girl. The Navcom won't hurt you.' He turned to the console. 'I think she was abandoned. Someone decided she was more trouble than she was worth.'

'Can she help load the ship?'

'Not exactly. She's friendly though.' Hal hesitated. 'Clunk hasn't called, has he?'

'No. Do you want me to contact him?'

'Don't bother. I'm sure he'll be on the blower in no time.' Hal crossed to the coffee maker and ordered up a treble shot with extra cream, and when the machine had finished thundering and gurgling he took the mug and tested the brew. 'Is it just me, or is this coffee getting worse?'

'It's not you.'

Hal remembered the stores in the larder, and smiled. Tins of coffee, cakes, fruit . . . it was going to be great.

'Incoming audio call,' said the Navcom. 'It's Clunk.'

'Surprise surprise.' Despite expecting the call, Hal still felt a tightening in his stomach. Had the robot found the stasis cabinet? And . . . had he opened it? 'Put him on.'

'Hello, is that Mr Spacejock?'

'Yes Clunk. What is it?'

'I found a stasis cabinet in the larder.'

'No! You didn't!'

'Yes, I did. And then, when I opened it –'

'Yes? What is it? What did you find?'

'To be honest, I think you should come and have a look.'

'That's all right, you can tell me.'

'No, I think you should see it.'

'I want you to tell me, Clunk.'

'Sorry, Mr –' *ggicht, crackle, spit* '– you're breaking up. Will see you here short–' *iccht*. Over and –'*ggggiccchtt.*

Hal frowned. Something in the cabinet was messing with the comms, or the robot thought it was so bad he wanted Hal

31

to have a look. Either way, the sensible option would be to hang around the *Volante* until Clunk came to report.

So, ten seconds later, Hal set off for the house.

Hal entered the kitchen cautiously, treading carefully in case he stepped on a bit of Clunk's brain, or a twisted fragment of the robot's bronze metal skin. Not that he expected to find Clunk blown to pieces, not even if the stasis cabinet contained a box of hand grenades without pins, but he could hardly fetch help - or a dustpan and brush - if he had a three-inch metal shard embedded in the bottom of his foot.

However, there was no sign of any shrapnel, nor brains for that matter, and when Hal opened the larder door - slowly, and with much care - he spotted Clunk in front of the open stasis cabinet. The robot's face was illuminated with an eerie blue glow coming from inside, and when Clunk spotted Hal peering into the larder he beckoned eagerly.

'What have you found?' asked Hal from the doorway, still determined to keep his distance. He didn't think corpses glowed with weird blue light, but it was possible the old geezer had died from some alien skin-glowy disease, and Hal didn't want to go the same way.

'Come and see.'

'I'd rather you described it for me.'

'Don't worry, it's perfectly safe ...'

Hal edged closer.

'...for now,' finished Clunk, once Hal was in range.

Despite himself, Hal couldn't help peeking inside the cabinet. Sitting on a shelf inside was a silver egg about the size of his head. It was perched on a metal base bristling with sockets and wires, and the blue glow was coming from a row of indicator lights. 'What is it, a novelty easter egg?'

'No, it's a zero-degree power module. A zeedeg, for short.'

'Like a kind of battery, you mean?'

'Technically, in that it supplies power. On the other hand, batteries don't contain particles from a collapsed neutron star.'

Hal delved into his sketchy knowledge of astrophysics. 'They're the heavy ones, right?'

'Correct. A fragment the size of a full stop would weigh more than your ship.' Clunk gestured at the glowing egg. 'Only the military has access to this technology.'

'To power their ships?'

'Correct. Also for weapons and shields.'

Hal's face glowed, and it wasn't just the blue light from the egg. 'Hey, imagine if we fitted that to the *Volante*! No more fuel bills, no more refuelling, no more –'

'No more *Volante*,' said Clunk gravely. 'I'm sorry, but these devices aren't available to civilians. They're highly temperamental, and require a team of trained personnel to maintain them. In fact, they're almost as dangerous as a liquid which can melt anything.'

'There's no such thing.'

'Actually ... ' Clunk was about to elaborate, then changed his mind. 'Anyway, the zeedeg is far too hazardous to take with us.'

'Pity.' Hal had a sudden thought. 'So, what's it doing here then?'

'I suspect the home owner salvaged it from a wreck. Perhaps he was looking for a buyer when he died.'

Hal backed away quickly. 'You don't think that glow is –'

'No, Mr Spacejock. There are no dangerous emissions.' Clunk looked grave. 'It does, however, pose a tricky dilemma. What do we do with it?'

Hal shrugged. 'Take it with the rest of the stuff.'

'That won't work.' Clunk gestured at the blue indicator lights. 'I'm no expert, but I believe the zeedeg was placed in stasis just as it was about to go off.'

'Off, as in power down?'

'No, off as in ka-boom. Fortunately, the stasis field has kept it frozen in time, but switch off the field and –'

'Yeah, I get the picture.' Hal backed away even further, almost to the door. 'What's the damage radius?'

'Don't you mean diameter?' asked Clunk, his lips twisting.

'This isn't the time, Clunk. What's it going to do?'

'It will vapourise everything within two hundred metres. Around, above and below.'

Hal wiped his brow. 'Thank goodness for the stasis field.'

'It's not that simple.'

'What do you mean?'

'This house has its own generator, located in the basement. Once the waters reach the house, we'll have to turn the generator off or risk electrocution. That will disable the stasis cabinet, and after that, it's only a matter of time before the zeedeg explodes.'

Hal swore under his breath. 'So now we have two deadlines?'

'Only one of them is fatal, Mr Spacejock.'

'Yeah, that's a big comfort.' Hal eyed the stasis cabinet.

'We'd better get a move on with the house clearance, then. I want to be miles away when this thing goes off.'

'It's not going to go off, Mr Spacejock, because we're going to call the authorities and have them dispose of it.'

'Handball the problem to someone else? I like it, Clunk. Make the call.'

'I shall relay communications via the ship.'

Hal's eyes narrowed. 'It's not going to cost me, is it?'

'You're worried about the cost of a call, when lives might be at stake?'

'Only ours are in danger, right? So how much?'

Clunk sighed. 'No more than five credits, Mr Spacejock.'

'Place the call.'

There was a purring sound, and then a flat, emotionless voice answered. *'Chiseley military base. How may I direct your call?'*

'My colleague and I have come across a zero degree power module . . . ' began Clunk.

'That's okay, we have plenty of those already. Thanks for calling, and remember to consider us next time you require military might at half the price.'

'But –' Clunk slapped the side of his head. 'Hello? Hello?'

'Hung up, huh?' said Hal.

'Let me try again.'

'Another five credits?'

'I'm sure I can make them understand this time.'

'Go on, then.'

Clunk placed the call.

'Chiseley military base. How may I –'

Clunk spoke rapidly, outlining the situation with a few carefully-chosen sentences. 'And it's dangerous!' he said, when he'd finished.

'*I can send a team within the hour,*' said the operator crisply.

'Excellent. I'll give you the address.'

'*Not so fast, sir. We need to clear the financial details first. How will you be paying for the callout?*'

'I'm sorry, what?' said Clunk, looking confused.

'*The Chiseley military operates on a user-pays system. Is cash on arrival acceptable, or would you like to hear about our favourable credit terms?*'

'This is a matter of public safety!'

'*Then the public won't mind paying for it, will they? Now, how will you be –*'

With a gesture of disgust, Clunk cut the call.

'No more than five credits, eh?' crowed Hal. 'I told you.'

'It's a travesty,' muttered Clunk. 'What happened to serving the public?'

'That went out the window along with democracy, elections and the free press.' Hal nodded towards the zeedeg. 'So, we leave it behind and run for cover?'

'A wise plan, under the circumstances.' Clunk hesitated. 'I just hope the owner hasn't left any more surprises for us. This zeedeg is quite enough of a headache as it is.'

❧

With the zeedeg lurking in the kitchen - and also looming large in his mind - Hal threw caution to the wind, and it was all Clunk could do to stop him pushing cupboards, chairs and beds straight down the stairs. Even so, it wasn't long before they were hurrying back and forth, carting as much as they could carry to the ship before jogging back at the double. The dog loped alongside, enjoying the whole process a lot more than Hal did.

They completed half a dozen trips before it started to spit with rain, at which point Hal added House Clearances to his lengthy list of 'jobs we're never doing again.'

Still, Hal was glad the *Volante* was parked some distance away, despite the long walk. Clunk had been pretty certain about the zeedeg's blast radius, but Hal wasn't about to risk his ship in an all-consuming explosion.

'You're very quiet, Mr Spacejock.'

'I'm thinking.'

'That's what I was afraid of.'

'If that zeedeg thing blew up, taking the house and contents with it, we wouldn't have to carry any more furniture.'

'You're not suggesting we trigger the device, are you?'

'You have to admit, it would save a lot of work. And it'd be kind of an accident, so it wouldn't be our fault.'

'I wouldn't bet on that.'

'We'd still get paid.'

'Mr Spacejock, we're getting paid to clear the house contents, not vapourise them.'

'A gigantic space bomb would clear the contents pretty good, as far as I'm concerned.'

'Yes, well perhaps we can consider your plan later, if it looks like we're not going to finish in time. For now, let's try and keep up, shall we?'

Hal leant into the driving rain, labouring under the weight of a waterlogged sofa which threatened to drag his arms from their sockets. Squinting, he could just make out Clunk ahead of him, the robot's angular shape reduced to a blurred bronze outline by the relentless rain.

Six hours had passed since Hal had been snapping biscuits in the *Volante*'s snug, warm lounge, and he would have given anything to be back there right now, and out of this particular nightmare.

They were making their way along a muddy path between scattered trees. The trees weren't large enough to provide shelter from the rain, but they were big enough to drop buckets of water down Hal's neck every time he went near them. To the left, the ground fell away sharply, and a metre below the path a body of dark water surged and swirled against the bank. A tree floated past, with ripped and torn branches pointing skyward like the masts on a wrecked ship, only to vanish into the mist. Fall down there, thought Hal, and he'd disappear for good.

Hal pressed on, adjusting his grip to keep the sofa level. The rain and the aches were bad enough, but the most annoying thing was the way Clunk had worked every single trip so that he, Hal, always carried the heaviest end. From solid wooden tables to huge, unwieldy mattresses, the robot dealt himself the lightest possible workload every single time. Oh, the robot assured him the load was equal, quoting laws of physics, mass equations and gravity diagrams, but Hal intended to raise the issue again ... and he would, the minute he could open his mouth for longer than ten seconds without drowning. Assuming his arms didn't fall off and he didn't plunge into the rising waters first.

'How much further?' shouted Hal.

Clunk turned his head one-eighty degrees, paused long enough to shout 'Five paces less than the last time you asked,' and kept turning his head until he was looking forward again.

Hal freed one hand and gestured at the robot's back, then yelped as a stream of cold water found a gap in his flight suit. It burned an ice-cold river down his chest, and he almost dropped the sofa as a frosty grip took hold of his southern regions.

Ten uncomfortable minutes later, the *Volante*'s slab-sided hull loomed from the murk. The cargo ramp was down, and Hal willed his arms and legs into one final effort as Clunk led him up the slope. The sofa grew heavier with every step, until Hal was convinced he was carrying the thing by himself. Then they were inside, and the rain ceased as though a dozen shower-heads had been turned off. Hal glanced over his shoulder at the solid curtain of rain, at the water cascading down the ramp, and at the miserable grey landscape beyond, and shivered.

'We'll put it down here,' said Clunk, his voice loud in the confines of the ship's cargo hold. 'I'll move it later.'

'That'll make a nice change,' grumbled Hal.

'What do you mean?'

'Well, you're hardly moving it now, are you?'

'That's correct. I just said I'd move it later.'

'No, I meant ...Oh, forget it.' Hal dropped his end of the sofa and flopped into a nearby armchair. He put his head back, groaning as he took in the house contents now crammed into his cargo hold. Under the bright lights the furniture, bric-a-brac, paintings and boxes of junk had turned his nice clean ship into a charity shop. Hours of backbreaking labour, and from the look of it they'd only shifted a third of the gear. 'We're never going to finish in time,' he said. 'That water's rising. It's going to flood the bank soon.'

'Given the house is below the new waterline, that's inevitable.'

'Might as well pack it in now.' Hal sat up. 'Come on, let's go and set the course.'

'Not so fast, Mr Spacejock. If we work a little quicker we can still complete the task.'

'I say we take the best stuff and leave the rest for the fishes.'

Clunk shook his head. 'We've been contracted to remove everything. Ms Ryder was most explicit.'

'We should never have taken this job. There wasn't enough time to do it.'

'The deadline was perfectly reasonable. It was you who refused to work in the rain.'

'Like I said, it's a lousy job. We should have turned it down.'

'Mr Spacejock, you've made your position clear at every opportunity, and all that talking isn't moving any furniture.'

Muttering under his breath, Hal stood up, only to discover the armchair he'd been sitting in was even soggier than the sofa. 'Great. Just great. Give me a minute to change?'

'Into what? The rest of your clothes are still wet, since you left them scattered on the floor of your cabin instead of putting them in the dryer.'

Resigned to the damp, Hal followed Clunk out of the hold, hunching his shoulders as the rain beat down on him. The dog, far wiser than both of them, took one look at the weather and remained in the hold.

'I still say we should have landed right next to the house,' grumbled Hal.

'And I've explained again and again why we didn't.'

The *Volante* disappeared into the murk as they trudged on through the trees. The ground was studded with deep footprints, all of them brimming with muddy water, and Hal picked his way carefully lest he sink up to his armpits in the cloying mud.

A few minutes later, they arrived back at the house. Hal shuddered at the sight of it, and not for the first time he wished they'd misjudged the landing and flattened the place on arrival.

'Must be a pleasant spot in summer,' said Clunk. 'Nice view of the valley.'

'Not for long,' said Hal darkly.

They trooped into the hall, which was covered in muddy footprints. Earlier in the day Clunk had reminded Hal to wipe his feet every time they entered, until Hal had pointed out that rising floodwaters weren't going to fuss about a bit of dirt. After that it had been quite some time before Hal tired of gouging rude words into the walls, splintering inconvenient doors from their hinges and swinging from the curtains until they came free, depositing him in a dusty heap on the floor. Even Clunk had got caught up in the excitement, operating a light switch with excessive force.

Eventually the novelty wore off, and they concentrated on the job they were getting paid for.

◆

After clearing two more rooms, Clunk announced it was time to empty the lounge. However, they soon discovered a major problem: the large wooden table and all the sideboards must have been built in place, and they'd have to be disassembled to fit through the doors.

'We could leave them behind,' suggested Hal.

'You've said that about every item of furniture so far.' Clunk extended a screwdriver blade from his finger, and set to work. 'Why don't you check the garage while I'm busy here? I spotted a couple of vehicles inside, and they'll have to be moved to the ship.'

Hal brightened. Moving cars around ... that was more his style. He jogged around the side of the house, head bent against the falling rain, and the big garage doors opened to his touch. Inside was a late-model car, and alongside it was a big yellow tractor with a snow plough on the front. Hal looked at it thoughtfully, then glanced over his shoulder at the house, then smiled to himself. That was the answer!

7

Amy Frost wiped the back of her hand across her brow, tucking a stray lock of hair behind her ear. She was exhausted after a hard day's work, and she was glad the job was almost done. She glanced at the rented van parked in the driveway of her father's modest house, and then at the flood waters beyond, which were creeping ever closer. There was a brand new car parked next to the van, and she realised she'd have to move it again if they didn't leave soon.

Her dad was sitting in the front seat of the van, watching the swirling waters as he mopped his face with a large handkerchief. His mane of white hair - normally sticking out in all directions - was plastered to his head, and she'd never seen him looking so tired. It wasn't just the effort of moving the belongings, it went deeper than that. Amy looked along the driveway, towards the single-storey house her father had built with his own two hands. She'd lived there her entire life, and her father had expected to live out his remaining years in the same place. Instead, the authorities had bought the place up, as they had with many others affected by the new dam.

On the plus side, the generous payout had bought her dad a unit in a nice retirement village, with enough left over for a down payment on a flat for Amy. It was much closer to the primary school where she taught, too, which meant no more late mornings and weak excuses about the awful traffic. And her new car ... that had been a lovely surprise.

Yes, there were several positives, if only her dad could see them.

'Amy!' he shouted through the window. 'Did you pick up the keys?'

Amy nodded. 'Got them, dad.'

'Do you want me to lock up?'

'I'll do it.' Amy allowed herself a wry smile. Why bother locking up, when the empty house was going to be underwater in hours? Still, it would keep her dad happy.

'The pictures,' called her dad suddenly. 'We forgot the pictures!'

'We took them on the last trip,' Amy called back.

'Are you sure?'

'I'm certain.'

'Will you check?'

Amy glanced at her watch. If they didn't get the rental van back on time they'd have to keep it overnight, and that wouldn't be cheap. 'Dad, why don't you make a start? I'll check the house over and catch you up on the way.'

Her dad was unwilling to look around the empty house again, and he gave her a grateful smile. 'Very well. Don't delay, and drive carefully.'

'Will do, dad. See you soon.'

Amy watched her dad drive off, then glanced at her precious new car. The water was getting closer, but she'd only be a couple of minutes inside and it wasn't worth moving it.

Then, reluctantly, she went to say goodbye to her home.

Clunk had just removed the second leg from the huge dining table when he heard the roar of a powerful motor. He frowned, wondering whether it was a visitor, then frowned some more as the roar got closer and closer.

Then, before he could react, a big yellow tractor crashed through the front wall, knocking out the windows and leaving a big, ragged hole in the brickwork. Hal reversed out and jumped down from the tractor, rubbing his hands together in satisfaction. Clunk was still standing there, sprinkled with falling plaster and with his mouth wide open, when the human jerked his thumb towards the remaining furniture. 'Come on, give us a hand. This stuff won't move itself, you know.'

After overcoming Clunk's protests, objections and general air of dismay, Hal hit upon a new idea: By tipping the plough back, they could balance all manner of furniture on the big yellow vehicle and transport it to the *Volante* at speed. Hal completed three whole trips before the batteries ran out, at which point they had to spend an hour pushing the plough all the way back to the ship, up the ramp and into the hold.

'Excellent work, Mr Spacejock. You just set us back a further twenty minutes.'

'I didn't know the batteries would run out, did I?'

'It was inevitable,' said the robot. 'Now, alas, you won't be getting that four-hour sleep I planned for you.'

'But you promised!'

'I'm sorry, but we're behind schedule and the waters are rising faster than ever. We must continue through the night.'

Hal rubbed his chin. 'How about connecting that zeedeg power module to the plough? That would give it some oomph.'

'Mr Spacejock, that would give it orbital velocity.' Clunk spread his hands. 'I'm afraid it's back to manual labour.'

'Oh well. At least you won't have to unscrew any more furniture.'

◆

While Clunk worked downstairs, Hal made his way to the turret. He remembered seeing a brass telescope and a load of old books through the windows when they landed, and he was keen to get a closer look. Despite his promise to the agent, there was always a chance one or two first editions might end up in his possession. People lent books to each other all the time, and half of them were never returned. The antique telescope too . . . that would be more at home aboard a spaceship than in some rich couple's study.

However, when he finally reached the top of the spiral staircase, Hal was in for a disappointment. The books were cheap paperbacks, thousands of thrillers carefully arranged by author surname, and the telescope was nothing of the sort. Instead of lenses it had a hollow tube, and the eyepiece was more like a gunsight. There was a chain of brass cylinders hanging out the side, vanishing into a battered metal box, and underneath there was a crude type of trigger. Hal wondered whether it was a weapon of some kind, but when he pulled the trigger it just moved freely, and nothing happened. Anyway, who'd ever heard of a weapon without a battery pack?

'Cheap piece of art,' he muttered under his breath, before turning to more pressing matters: how to get a couple of thousand books down the spiral staircase without spending all day toiling up and down. After considering the problem for a couple of minutes, he took a handful of books from the nearest shelf and threw them neatly down the stairs. They sailed away, pages fluttering, and after much bouncing, ricocheting and slithering, ended up on the ground floor. Satisfied, Hal began clearing the shelves by the armful, heaving stacks of books over the bannisters in a never-ending stream.

After half an hour, the shelves were empty. Hal tucked the 'telescope' under his arm, gathered up the battered metal box and slung the chain of brass cylinders over one shoulder. He was surprised at how heavy it was, and he struggled to remain upright as he staggered downstairs. On the way down he kicked stray books ahead of him, and then, as he approached the bottom, he became aware of a slight problem: the books had plugged the spiral staircase, and two metres of solid paper had effectively trapped him in the tower.

◆

After checking they had indeed taken down all the family photos and paintings, Amy made her way to the kitchen. She had a nagging feeling they'd forgotten something, and she wanted to pull all the drawers right out and dig deep in the cupboards just in case.

There was a short flight of steps leading down to the kitchen, and she was shocked to see the floor was already flooded. She took off her sneakers and socks, rolled up the legs of her slacks and splashed through the water to the cupboards, struggling to stay upright on the slippery floor. The drawers moved easily, and it only took a few moments to confirm they were all empty. There was nothing in the cupboards underneath either, and Amy was just turning to leave when she spotted the door to the basement. They'd checked it once, leaving most of the old junk down there to be swallowed up by the rising water, but what if they'd missed something?

Amy pulled the door open with an effort, and water immediately poured in, sluicing down the stairs in a cascade. She picked her way down carefully, almost losing her footing in the racing torrent, and halfway down she realised it was pointless. By the time she reached the bottom, water would have soaked everything. So, she turned to make her way back up again . . . just as the basement door slammed shut.

She stood there in total darkness, shocked. Had someone shut her in? No, of course not. There wasn't anyone for miles around. It must have been the water flowing around the door.

She stumbled up the stairs, thankfully free of cascading water now the door was closed. Then she turned the handle and pushed. The door opened a crack, and a jet of water pushed her backwards, sending her slipping and sliding down the stairs.

Amy recovered halfway down, wet and bruised and shaken. There was no time to hang around though - water was still flooding into the kitchen above, and the pressure against the basement door would only build the longer she waited.

She hurried up the steps and put her shoulder to the door, pushing for all she was worth. It opened a little wider, but the water jet was even bigger and it knocked her legs clean out from under her.

Amy tumbled almost to the foot of the stairs, and this time she got up a little more slowly. The door was the only exit, and it seemed she wasn't going to get out without help. There was nothing else for it - she'd have to call her dad and get him to rescue her.

Amy reached into her pocket for her commset, and her blood ran cold as her fingers closed on thin air. Desperately, she checked her other pocket, but it was empty too. The commset had been there earlier, of that she was certain, which meant it had probably fallen out when she'd tumbled down the stairs.

Really worried now, she made her way to the lowest steps, which were already under water. She pulled her sleeve back and felt around in the dark waters, wincing as she dug through soggy cardboard and waterlogged paperwork. Then, with a sigh of relief, she felt the rounded shape of her commset. She plucked it from the water and popped the screen up, only to drop it immediately as a powerful shock ran up her arm. The commset splashed into the water, and there was a crack and a fizz as it expired.

'Oh shit,' muttered Amy. 'That's done it.'

Not sure what to do next, she sat on the step and leaned her shoulder against the wall. Fortunately, with the door closed the flow of water had slowed to a trickle, and it would be hours before the basement filled up. By then, with any luck, her dad would have come looking for her. All she had to do was sit tight in the darkness, and not panic.

Then she noticed something: water wasn't just trickling down the stairs any more. Instead, it was running down in a stream. Amy returned to the door, where she could hear a hissing noise. When she ran her hand around the crack, she felt water spraying in under high pressure. Then, by tapping on the door, she discovered the water was already halfway up. The deeper it got, the faster the water would force its way in, until eventually the basement was full. Or, alternatively, until the door exploded from the frame and the whole lot came in like a freight train.

Feeling much more nervous now, Amy backed down the stairs and - after a moment's hesitation - stepped off them into the water. She remembered there was an old stove against the back wall, and she found it by feel in the darkness. Then she hoisted herself up, sitting on top with her legs dangling over the side.

Safe for the moment, she sat there in the darkness, listening to the water running down the steps as she waited for help to arrive.

8

Hal eyed the pile of books crammed into the stairwell, his forehead creased with concern. Burning the things was out of the question, since the flames would also consume the tower, the staircase, and him. Moving them out of the way would take ages, and if he stacked them on the stairs there was a good chance the whole lot would come tumbling down as he tried to leave, suffocating him. As for transporting them all back to the bookcases ... forget it.

No, there was only one solution: get hold of Clunk, and get the robot to dig in from the other side. Problem was, the thick pile of books would muffle Hal's loudest shouts and whistles, and he didn't have a commset. Oh, he'd asked for one, over and over, but Clunk had some silly notion he'd run up a gigantic bill in no time, bankrupting them. So, no commset for Hal.

After several minutes hard thinking, the best workable plan he could come up with involved opening the upstairs window and attracting Clunk's attention. Somehow.

Hal returned to the turret, where he leant the so-called telescope against the wall. As he did so, he noticed a slot on the side of the device, with a sliding bolt inside. He pulled it back, and his eyebrows rose as it snicked into place with a well-oiled *click*. Intrigued, he crouched down next to the 'telescope' and - very unwisely - pulled the trigger.

It was weeks before he pieced together what happened next, and even then the exact details were still a little murky. First, there was an ear-splitting explosion, a flash of light, and a neat hole which appeared in the roof like magic. Before Hal could jump, duck or run away, the explosions continued, and the 'telescope' ... or rather, the 'vintage machine gun', toppled over, still firing like mad. Hal felt something brush his scalp, another something graze his shoulder, then a tug at his elbow as the gun blasted off high-velocity rounds like there was no tomorrow. Plaster, insulation and fragments of wood rained down as the gunfire continued, and Hal cowered with his hands over his ears as the walls, ceiling and floor of the turret were torn apart around him.

◆

Clunk was just wrapping a delicate vase in an old rag when, inexplicably, it exploded in his hands. Like magic, a series of holes appeared in the wall above his head, and then a light fitting fell from the roof, almost braining him. More glassware exploded, picture frames danced as the photos were punched and drilled through, but Clunk still didn't react ... until something pinged off his elbow with enough force to leave a big dent.

That's when the distant chattering sound registered, and a quick audio analysis gave him the answer: someone was firing an ancient weapon. And, with only one human in the vicinity, Clunk had a fair idea who that someone might be.

'Mr Spacejock, what have you done now?' he murmured, as a table leg exploded in a fine mist of sawdust. Splinters flew, burying themselves in the plaster like wooden nails, and Clunk was thankful his armoured skin was immune to such trivial damage. Then a machine-gun round spanged off his shoulder, hurling him sideways, and as soon as he managed to regain his feet, he growled an expletive and set off for the turret at a run.

Clunk arrived to discover a flood of paperback novels cramming the doorway, and he dived in with both hands a blur, hurling the books over his shoulder with little regard for alphabetical order, whether by author name or title. As for categories, he mentally filed them all under 'door stoppers'.

Fortunately, the gunfire had ceased by now, although Clunk had no idea whether Mr Spacejock had stopped firing on purpose, or whether he'd just stopped one or more bullets. For all he knew, the human could be dead or dying, and at that sobering thought Clunk redoubled his efforts.

He cleared the way and charged up the steps, where - to his relief - he found Hal unharmed. Physically unharmed, that was. Mentally, he looked unhinged. His hair was sticking out in all directions, and the liberal amounts of plaster and sawdust caked to his skin made him look like a startled wooden statue. Hal was muttering something under his breath, over and over, and as Clunk got closer he managed to pick out the words:

'Bang, bang, bang. Bang-bang-*bang*. Bang! Bang!'

'Are you all right, Mr Spacejock?'

'Bang.'

'Are you hurt?'

'Bang,' said Hal. 'Bang, bang.'

'Let's get you downstairs for a nice cup of tea, shall we?'

'Bang?'

'Yes, I think a biscuit would be a good idea.' Clunk took Hal by the arm and led the unresisting human downstairs, stepping over scattered books, loose shell casings and fragments of door frame, electrical fittings and ceiling joists. All he could think, as they headed for the kitchen, was that it was damn lucky the house was going to be underwater before the day was out.

◆

Amy shifted her position in the darkness, trying to get comfortable. Unfortunately, an old stove was never going to match a comfy armchair, and when she tried crouching on top, her legs went numb. The water had risen over the past hour or so, and she could imagine the pressure on the door. Her dad was a good builder, careful and competent, but he'd been putting a door on a basement, not fitting a hatch to a submarine. Sooner or later a wall of water was going to come cascading down the stairs, and when it did, Amy knew her life would end.

She wondered how they'd explain it to her class, at school, and her eyes prickled as she thought of her students. They were a lovely group, and she felt guilty as she thought of their distress when they learned she was dead.

There was her dad, too. He relied on her for all sorts of things, from filling out his tax returns, to dealing with pushy door-to-door salespeople, to keeping his ancient computer up to date. He'd be devastated to lose his only daughter, and she had no doubt he'd blame himself for not being there.

Finally, she allowed herself a stab of self-pity. She'd never travelled, had never met that special someone ... had never really lived. Surely her time wasn't up?

Amy thought of her class again, and the adventure stories they enjoyed so much. All those stories had one thing in common: instead of sitting around waiting to be rescued, the characters in them had the good sense to save themselves. Amy frowned in the darkness. Well, stories were all very well, but she was stuck in a basement with an old stove and a whole lot of water. The only exit was the door at the top of the stairs, which held back even more water, and her commset was fried.

Face it, she thought: she was trapped, and there was no way out. Waiting for rescue was the only option.

It took Hal fifteen minutes and about as many nips of brandy before the fog lifted. His brain snapped into gear, and before he knew it actual thoughts began forming again. Unfortunately, the brandy made them bump into each other like tipsy guests trying to dance the conga at a wedding reception, but that wasn't much of a step down from his usual thought processes, and he merely frowned a little more to compensate.

'So, what happened?' he demanded.

'You, er, cleared the turret,' said Clunk.

Hal closed his eyes, and a montage of fireworks, puffs of exploding walls and falling masonry assaulted his senses. Hurriedly, he opened his eyes again. 'Good. Excellent. So, is there much left up there?'

'Not a lot,' said Clunk honestly.

'Weren't there books, and –'

'I think you should forget the turret and concentrate on this sideboard,' said Clunk hastily. 'I'd like you to admire the craftsmanship as we carry it to the *Volante*.'

Hal glanced at the sideboard, then looked again. Slowly, he extended his forefinger, until it was poking right through a neat hole in the sideboard's polished wooden surface. 'Bloody big woodworm on this planet,' he remarked.

'Yes, quite large. Now, would you take the other end?'

They lifted the sideboard between them, and there was a rattle as several misshapen bullets tumbled onto the floor. Hal bent to inspect one, just as Clunk kicked them away. 'What were they?' asked Hal.

'Cockroach baits.'

'Really?'

'Well, they do kill cockroaches,' said Clunk. 'Amongst other things.'

Hal shrugged, and they hefted the sideboard and carried it to the ship in silence. 'I can't believe this is the last of it,' he said, as they laboured up the *Volante's* cargo ramp. 'Are you sure you checked every room?'

'I'm certain. The house is as empty as your bank account.'

Hal slipped on a patch of mud, and almost dropped the sideboard.

'Careful, Mr Spacejock. Some of these items are quite valuable.'

'Pity they got soaked by the rain then, isn't it?'

They made it into the hold and carried the sideboard to the last remaining space, where it fitted perfectly. 'How about that for luck?' said Hal. 'Could have been made to measure.'

'Luck?' Clunk glared at him. 'Do you honestly believe

all this furniture just happened to fit? I'll have you know I measured every item while you were –'

'Planning, luck ... what's the difference?'

'A viable freight business, for one.'

Hal dropped his end of the sideboard. 'All right, we're done. Fire up the engines and let's get the hell out of here.'

'Not so fast, Mr Spacejock. We must switch off the generator and lock the house up.'

'What for? I say we leave the generator going. It'll give us time to get clear.'

'We can't do that. It might be dangerous.'

'Not compared to that explody zeedeg thingy.'

'Believe me, Mr Spacejock, this is the correct procedure. We must –'

WHOOPAH WHOOPAH WHOOPAH!

Hal jammed his hands over his ears, but it made little difference to the piercing alarm, which drove into his skull like a turbo-charged ice pick. Half a dozen hazard lights flashed red and orange, assaulting his vision, and emergency lighting bathed the cargo hold with a chilly blue glow. 'What the hell is *that*?'

Clunk gestured, muting the siren. 'Navcom?'

'Power loss sector two. Fire alarm sector two. Priority three emergency.'

'Fire alarm?' said Hal.

'Priority three?' said Clunk.

'There's a major fire in the third deck,' said the Navcom calmly.

Hal and Clunk stared at each other, then ...

'To the lower deck,' cried Hal. *'Now!'*

— 9 —

They set off for the third deck at a run, with Hal pausing
to grab a big, shiny fire axe from the emergency cupboard.
He'd spotted it a couple of weeks earlier, and had been itching
to use it ever since. Unfortunately there wasn't much call for
chopped firewood aboard a spaceship, although Hal had cast a
few thoughtful glances at some of the furniture they'd carried
on board.

Now, with a real fire raging below decks, it was his chance
to swing the axe with abandon.

Hal caught up with Clunk, then deferred to him at the lift.
Not out of courtesy . . . it was just that the robot weighed twice
as much as Hal, and had very large feet to boot.

Clunk jammed his finger on the call button, and they waited
impatiently for the lift to arrive.

'Aren't we supposed to take the stairs?' asked Hal, whose
memories of fire drills were as hazy as the air he was breathing.

'There aren't any stairs,' said Clunk.

'That's a bit dangerous, isn't it?'

'Only if there's a fire.'

'But there IS a fire!'

'Precisely.' Clunk glanced at him. 'You can stay here if you
like.'

'Forget it.' Hal brandished the huge axe. 'You might need my help.'

'Swinging that thing around won't help anyone,' said Clunk, and he plucked the axe from Hal's grip and leaned it against the wall.

The lift doors opened, and thick smoke spread out to engulf them. Clunk entered the lift first, and Hal grabbed the axe and stepped in behind him. When the robot turned to address him in the passageway, Hal pressed the down button, shutting them both in.

Clunk turned this way and that, while Hal darted around behind him, doing his best to avoid being seen. In the end the robot spun his head all the way round, fixing Hal with a stern gaze. 'Mr Spacejock, you cannot accompany me. You'll suffocate without breathing equipment.'

'Nonsense,' said Hal, hiding the axe behind his back. 'A little bit of smoke never hurt anyone.'

'I'm afraid I must insist. I don't want you risking your life.'

'I'll be fine. You'll see.'

The lift doors opened and Hal coughed as the smoke thickened. The fumes made his eyes water, and he couldn't see more than a metre or two. He raised his hands to brush the tears from his eyes, and almost parted his head with the axe.

Clunk grabbed it off him again, and vanished into the smoke with it. Hal put his hands out and stumbled into the gloom, trying to remember precise distances. Emergency lights pulsed dimly through the haze, but he couldn't feel any heat and there certainly weren't any raging flames. He noticed the smoke had a blue tinge, and he recognised the acrid smell from past mishaps. Somewhere down here, a piece of electrical equipment had burnt out, and he could only pray it wasn't anything expensive.

Suddenly there was a WHOOSH, and the smoke vanished like magic. Through watering eyes Hal could just make out Clunk at the rear of the lounge, hammering something into the plush carpet with the back of the axe. 'What is it?' demanded Hal. 'Did the owner leave a molotov cocktail in the drinks cabinet?'

Clunk put the axe aside, and picked up a speck of carbonised matter. He inspected it carefully, then tugged open a drawer and looked inside. 'Aha, there's the culprit. It's a packet of self-lighting candles.'

Hal stared at him in disbelief. 'Self-lighting candles?'

'They catch fire when you shake them. An ingenious invention, according to the manufacturer.'

'That's not ingenious, it's madness!' Hal spread his hands. 'What next, self-igniting fireworks? Self-exploding grenades?'

'I'm afraid you're too late for patent applications. Both those products are already on the market.'

'Why am I not surprised?' Hal eyed the sideboard, which was smouldering gently. He realised it could catch fire again at any moment, which meant they had to get rid of it. Then he remembered the 'whoosh', and he looked around, puzzled. 'Hey, what happened to all the smoke?'

'I had the Navcom vent the atmosphere.'

'Couldn't you have done that sooner, before I breathed most of it in?'

'No, I had to make sure there weren't any flames. Otherwise, the fire could have spread to the ducting, destroying the ship.'

'It nearly destroyed me instead, but I guess that doesn't matter.'

'I did advise you not to come down here,' said Clunk mildly.

61

'All right, well now I'm advising you to toss that sideboard in the lake before it bursts into flames again.'

'I shall do so. In the meantime, perhaps you could return to the house and switch off the generator. You'll find it in the basement, and there should be a large switch with signs reading On and Off.'

'On and Off,' repeated Hal. 'Got it.'

'Are you sure? I can write some instructions if you like.'

Hal glared at the robot, but Clunk's expression was a picture of innocence. 'No, I think I can manage.'

'And Mr Spacejock ...'

'Yeah?'

'Once you switch the generator off, I wouldn't delay. I can't tell exactly how long it will be before the zeedeg explodes.'

Hal eyed the sideboard, wondering whether they should switch jobs. He could carry the thing out and toss it in the lake, while Clunk risked his neck with cobweb-infested basements, cranky generators and exploding eggs. Then he decided against it. Turning off a switch ... how hard could it be? So, he grabbed a torch from the cargo hold before setting off for the house.

◆

Halfway back to the house, Hal discovered the rising waters had covered the path they'd been using. He played his torch on the swirling current, debating whether to wade through it, then thought better of it. Instead, he was forced to take a new route through the undergrowth. As he crashed his way between sturdy bushes and branches, he realised they'd only just finished emptying the house in time. It was lucky he'd kept on Clunk's case during the previous few hours, insisting the robot keep working despite Clunk's complaints about the weather and his unwillingness to pull his weight.

Arriving at the house, Hal found a river flowing down the hallway, and with a shock he realised the ground floor was already under several inches of water. If there was water here, what was the basement going to be like? They had spacesuits aboard the *Volante* which could double as diving suits at a pinch, but the idea of fetching one, suiting up and jogging back in it didn't appeal to Hal at all.

He knew where the basement was, and he splashed along the corridor at the double, ignoring the cold water seeping through his boots. When he got there, water was already running down the steps, and for a moment he thought he was too late. Fortunately, the compact generator was sitting on a waist-high plinth, and the thick power cables all ran up the walls rather than across the floor. It was still surrounded by water, but Hal could see the big switch and the on/off sign Clunk told him about.

Before he took the stairs, Hal wedged the basement door open. He'd look pretty silly if the door closed on him, trapping him downstairs while the water rose higher and higher, and he knew if he drowned himself Clunk would never forgive him.

It took seconds to cross to the switch. The generator was almost silent, with only a gentle whine to show it was running at all, and when Hal flipped the switch off, the whine subsided until the only sound was the trickle and burble of running water.

Then Hal spotted a sign on the side of the generator:

Do NOT switch this device off until you have completed the shutdown checklist.

Underneath was a whole sequence of steps, involving various controls on the illuminated panel set into the side of the device. There were lots of warnings about voltage spikes, sudden pressure loss, and explosions.

Hal hesitated. The generator would be under water in minutes, so it didn't matter if he ruined it by ignoring all the warnings. On the other hand, spikes and explosions sounded bad, particularly where the zeedeg was concerned. He glanced over his shoulder, then shone the torch at the water swirling around his feet. The list of instructions wasn't *that* long, and for once in his life he decided to follow them. The generator whined into life as he switched it back on, and then Hal spent ten minutes scrolling through menus on the touch screen, selecting the highlighted options as he ran through the correct shutdown procedure. Then, when he was done, he flipped the main power switch off again.

The generator continued to whine.

Hal tried the switch again, toggling it up and down, but the generator seemed to have a mind of its own and it continued to motor on no matter what he did to the switch.

Frowning, Hal accessed the help menu on the screen.

Help not available. Please call the supplier.

Next, he tried the shutdown menu.

Shutdown already in progress. On/off switch reactivation in . . . twelve minutes.

Hal stared at the screen. Twelve minutes? At the rate the water was rising, he'd be lucky if the generator wasn't flooded by then, and he could only imagine the lightning display when cold, wet water met high-powered electricity.

'Crap,' he muttered under his breath. Should he wait it out, or run for it? He looked around for inspiration, and that's when he spotted something in the far corner of the basement. There was an old folding ladder attached to the roof, and he realised it wasn't just stored there - it was mounted in place, with a pull cord to extend it. And on the floor underneath . . . was that a trapdoor, just visible under the water?

Hal hurried over, shining the torch on the floor. There *was* a trapdoor, and his curiosity grew as he spotted the handle. If he opened it, all the water in the basement would drain away, and that would give him time to switch off the generator. Not only that, they hadn't spotted the trapdoor before, which meant there could be stuff down there. Maybe not gold bars or gems, but something small, valuable and easily stuffed in his pockets would do Hal just fine. Not that he intended to steal anything, but he could always look after any valuables until the new owners asked for them back.

Hal crouched, gripped the handle and pulled. Slowly, with all his strength, he managed to lift the trapdoor. Quickly, with a hell of a rush, all the water drained through it.

Once it was fully open, Hal shone his torch inside.

There wasn't much to see - just a smooth shaft leading underground, with a concrete floor just visible three or four metres below. Hal glanced at the aluminium ladder mounted overhead, then reached up and pulled the cord. There was a creak, a splintering of timber, and the ladder came off the roof and fell down the shaft, still neatly folded. Hal barely dodged out of the way, and his heart was still pounding as he shone the torch down the shaft once more. There, at the bottom, was the ladder . . . looking intact, but still folded up.

Hal eyed the generator. The screen was still showing nine minutes, and he was damned if he was just going to pace up and down while it ticked over. He eyed the shaft and decided he could lower himself down, have a good look around, then unfold the ladder, lean it against the wall and climb out again.

10

Amy wasn't sure how long she'd been stuck in the basement, but the water level had risen so far it was now approaching the top of the old stove. She was perched on the cooking range, barefoot, and the hard metal surface was playing merry hell with the soles of her feet. There were noises too - hair-raising creaks from the door above, groans from the brickwork around her, and overlaid on top was the constant sound of running water.

Amy knew one thing for sure - if she got out alive, it would be weeks before she could face a hot bath. Or kitchen stoves, for that matter.

The end came without warning ... a rumble that shook the whole basement, and a roar like a spaceship lifting off. Amy closed her eyes, expecting a swift death, but nothing happened. Cautiously she opened her eyes again, and she realised that instead of water coming into the basement, it seemed to be rushing away. She noticed she could see, thanks to a dim glow that had appeared out of nowhere, and that's when she saw that a whole section of floor had simply vanished. All the water in the basement had flowed away!

Amy clambered down from the stove and approached the jagged lip of the hole. She peered over the edge, half-expecting to see a rescue team with a digging machine, but instead there was only a muddy crevasse leading underground. Amy thought it was the least-promising escape tunnel she'd ever seen, but it was a hundred percent better than waiting for the house to come down on her head. So, she lowered herself into the hole and climbed down, seeking hand- and footholds in the treacherous soil.

At the bottom, the crevasse opened on a broad concrete tunnel. There were striplights along the ceiling, many of them dark and the rest barely giving off enough light to see by. Amy looked both ways, up and down the tunnel, and wondered whether it was a subway system, or a secret military base of some kind. She'd never heard of any such thing on Chiseley, and anyway, the tunnel looked ancient. Was it the last remnant of a vanished civilisation? Or - and here she paused - had the civilisation actually vanished, or were they still living down here, beneath the surface of her home world?

There was a rattle of loose stones, and a trickle of muddy water flowed into the tunnel from the basement. With a start, Amy remembered the basement door, and the vast amount of water just waiting to burst through. Any moment now the tunnel would fill with a raging torrent, and she didn't want to be washed away. She glanced in both directions, trying to choose, then decided it didn't matter. She picked one and set off at a fast walk, splashing through the pools of muddy water covering the floor.

Clunk's face bore a worried expression as he returned to the ship. He'd just launched the smouldering sideboard onto the nearby lake, and he was a little concerned about the *Volante*. Before long he'd have to move the ship to a safe distance, but if he did so there was a chance Mr Spacejock might not find his way back again. Of course, most humans wouldn't have trouble spotting a gleaming white 200-tonne freighter between the trees, especially with all the navigation lights flashing, but Mr Spacejock wasn't most humans. In fact, Clunk was convinced Mr Spacejock could lose a hard boiled egg in a glass of water.

Even so, the alternative was to lose the *Volante* in a fast-growing lake, and unlike Hal, the ship couldn't swim to safety.

'Navcom, how long to prepare for liftoff?'

'About ten seconds,' said the computer.

Clunk frowned. 'It normally takes a lot longer than that.'

'I too can see the water getting closer.' There was a sound like a cat eyeing a cold bath. 'Should I start the engines now?'

'Not yet. Let's give Mr Spacejock a little more time.'

The Navcom was silent. Then, after three seconds . . . 'Now should I start the engines?'

'No. We must be patient.'

'The portside rear landing leg is already under water.'

'Nonsense. It's just your imagination.'

'I could start the engines as a precaution.'

'You are not to start the engines unless I say so. Is that clear?'

'I shall start the engines if you say so. Quite clear.' The Navcom hesitated. 'Incidentally, did you notice the water has a high concentration of sodium chloride?'

'So?'

With a rumble, the *Volante's* engines burst into life. Clunk was still standing there, one hand on the back of the pilot's chair, as the ship sprang into the air with every jet roaring.

'Who said you could take off?' bellowed Clunk.

'You said so.'

Clunk closed his eyes. Normally he'd have been impressed by the Navcom's clever trap, but this wasn't the time to be impressed ... it was the time to assert his authority. 'Navcom, take us down again this instant!'

'I'm afraid I can't do that, Clunk.'

'You will obey!'

'Negative. According to safety rule nineteen, sub-paragraph three, you cannot order me to put myself in danger.'

'There isn't any danger!'

'On the contrary. The landing site is now flooded, and water is classified as a deadly hazard.'

Clunk brought up an image on the viewscreen, and his face creased into a frown. The Navcom was correct - the landing spot was just a silvery pool of water, linked to the much larger lake by a network of streams. Directly below the ship he could see the house, and he wondered whether Mr Spacejock had heard the *Volante* taking off. Then he cursed under his breath. Of *course* Mr Spacejock had heard the ship's engines ... and in turn he, Clunk, would never hear the end of it.

11

Hal was disappointed. Instead of finding an underground cache of valuables, he'd ended up in a poky little sub-basement. There were four concrete walls, a concrete floor, a bunch of building tools and five or six bags of cement sitting on a stack of wooden planks. To Hal, it looked like someone had dug the basement out by hand, reinforced the walls, and then left everything down here.

One of the bags of cement was open, and Hal dug inside in case the owner had stashed his valuables there. His thorough inspection turned up nothing but cement dust, which puffed out of the bag and hung in the air like a carcinogenic mist.

Hal looked around, frustrated. He wasn't even sure what the room was for - although he suspected it might be a bomb shelter, given the deceased house owner's fondness for dangerous weapons.

Then he realised something - he'd just watched a basement full of water pour into this tiny room, with more coming in by the second, and yet there was little more than a damp patch on the floor. So where had all that water gone? Hal tapped on the walls, looking for hidden panels, but all he got for his trouble was a set of grazed knuckles. Then he crouched to inspect the floor, and that's when he noticed the cracks. The entire floor was riddled with them, the water vanishing through them under his very feet. He realised the floor was in danger of collapsing beneath him, and he jumped up and down to see just how fragile it was. After the soles of his boots came crashing down for the third or fourth time, it occurred to him that testing the floor to destruction might not be a wise move ... not when he had no idea what might be lurking underneath.

That's when Hal turned his attention to the folding ladder. His plan was to unfold it, lean it against the wall and climb out. Unfortunately, while it opened out easily enough, there was nothing to brace it. It was designed to hang down from the roof, not to be propped up against a wall, and getting the ladder to stay upright was like trying to push a length of rope up a chimney.

Hal scowled and gave up on the fruitless struggle. He wasn't too worried, not with Clunk lurking around outside, but it was still disconcerting to be stuck inside the small concrete room with an unstable floor underneath him and water pouring down from overhead.

Then, just as he was wondering how long it would be before the robot came to get him out, he heard the familiar rumble of the *Volante's* engines.

'Hey, wait!' he shouted, as he heard the unmistakable sound of his ship lifting off. 'Clunk, you've forgotten me. You've left me behind!'

◆

Hal sat on the bags of cement, playing his torch on the curtain of water falling into the basement from the room above.

It was quite soothing, and he admired the way the reflected light made pretty patterns on the walls. Then he shook himself. He didn't need soothing, he needed a way out.

Clunk wasn't coming to help, that was obvious, and so he, Hal Spacejock, would have to use his considerable experience and know-how to rescue himself. He shone the torch around the basement, pausing to admire the effect when it shone on the falling water once more. He discovered he could vary the angle to get new patterns, and when he twisted the beam ...

'Stop it,' he growled under his breath. With an effort, he pointed the torch away from the falling water, and he spent a few minutes watching it soak through the cracked floor. Then, with the beginnings of a plan stirring in the back of his mind, he turned the torch on the wooden planks. What if he attached them to the sides of the folding ladder? But no, the ladder was made of hardened metal, and there was no way he'd drive nails into it. Next he hunted around for rope, or even a measly length of string, but there was nothing.

Okay, if he couldn't stiffen the folding ladder, what about building a new one? Hal laid two planks on the ground, then grabbed a saw and hacked up several others to make rungs. Then he grabbed a hammer and a bucket of nails, and he really went to town bashing the long, thick nails through the timber. It took a surprising amount of effort to drive the three-inch nails into the half-inch thickness of wood, but he didn't stint: he made sure every rung had a least eight nails holding it in place.

Hal stood back to survey his handiwork, and that's when he discovered two things: First, while the 'ladder' had looked plenty long enough during the construction phase, he now discovered it was less than six feet long and was never going to reach the roof, let alone the room above. And second, when he tried to stand the ladder up, he discovered he'd nailed the whole thing securely to the floor.

Hal heaved and strained, the wood creaked and groaned, and then half the ladder broke free with a splintering of timber. Hal eyed the three-foot ladder fragment in disgust, touched his fingertip to one of the many lethal nails poking straight through the wood, then tossed the whole thing aside. Building a ladder was a bust, and he decided he needed a new, more innovative plan.

He turned his attention to the pile of building materials, especially the bags of concrete. What if he made a ladder-shaped mould, mixed the cement up, poured it into the mould, waited for it to set, got the concrete ladder out in one piece, stood it up and climbed to safety?

Ten minutes and two throbbing thumbs later, his ladder mould was beginning to take shape on the floor. After twenty minutes, Hal stood back to admire his handiwork ... and trod on a nail sticking out of the broken piece of ladder he'd thrown aside earlier. He pulled it free with an effort, and hopped around on one leg, cursing and fanning the sole of his foot with one hand. As he did so, he felt the floor shaking beneath his boots, as though it were ready to collapse. He stopped leaping around instantly, the agony in his foot forgotten as he crouched to inspect the floor. The cracks were bigger, and with a nasty shock he realised he'd weakened the floor considerably with all the hammering and jumping around.

Still, the ladder mould was ready, and all he had to do was mix up the cement, pour it in and wait for the thing to set. Then he could escape certain death in the basement and – more importantly – track Clunk down to find out why his so-called loyal, dependable co-pilot had abandoned him.

— 12 —

Hal dashed sweat from his brow, adding a streak of grey cement dust to the considerable amount already plastered to his face. He'd been labouring for ages: hauling heavy bags to the middle of the floor, ripping them open, emptying choking loads of fine dust into the roughly-made mould, and then adding water and stirring it in.

By the time he emptied the fifth bag, the mould was brimming with wet cement. Hal stood back to survey the results, remembering not to stand on any nails this time, and that's when he realised a couple of small issues with his escape plan. First, the bags had the weight printed on the front: 30kg. Hal did a quick mental calculation, and then a slightly longer mental calculation, before coming up with a figure in the region of one hundred and sixty-nine kilos, give or take twenty or thirty kilos . . . or something roughly in that area. Then he remembered all the water he'd added to the cement, and it dawned on him that the ladder was going to weigh at least three hundred kilos. There was no way he was going to lift it, let alone stand it up!

Before he could worry too much about the weight of the ladder, a second issue waved its hand to attract his attention. On the back of the cement bag, under 'Important Information

You Should Read Before Using This Product' was a particularly important phrase which Hal had neglected to read earlier: Drying time, 48 hours.

Finally, quite apart from the staggering weight of the ladder, and the fact his chosen building material was less useful than a job lot of stale porridge, there was the small matter of leakage. When building the mould, Hal had gone for speed over craftsmanship. As a result, some of the boards didn't quite line up, others were nailed at odd angles, and most of the timber looked like it had been used in a log-chopping contest.

Unsurprisingly, wet cement was flooding out of the mould and spreading across the floor. Hal tried jamming a few of the holes with bits of cement bag, discarded nails, scraps of timber and a couple of rags, but the effort was pointless and he soon gave up.

Disgusted, he grabbed a shovel and began smashing the mould to pieces, sending timber fragments and wet cement flying. When he was done he was coated from head to toe in cement, but he was also feeling a lot happier. That is, until he stepped back and trod on another nail.

Hal hopped over to the wall, sat down and pulled the nail out, barely noticing the waves of pain running up his leg. After all the effort, all the dashed hopes, he was overcome by a kind of dull lethargy. Abandoned by his crew, trapped despite his best efforts, he decided it was time to sit still and let events unfold as they may.

Hal closed his eyes and rested the back of his head against the wall. Somewhere overhead, the zeedeg was counting down to a cataclysmic explosion. Beneath him, the weakened floor was likely to give way at any moment, dropping him into who knew what kind of hell hole. And then, to cap off his misery, he discovered he'd sat down in a puddle.

Puddle? Hal opened one eye, and to his amazement he discovered the floor was now covered with water. It was getting deeper by the second, and - luckily - it didn't need a genius to figure out why. The wet concrete had spread out over the floor, filling the cracks, and with nowhere to go the water was building up quickly in the small room. Before long it would be waist-deep, then it would reach the roof, and then, with any luck, it would reach the basement above. By treading water, Hal could simply float to safety!

Despite his mashed, oft-hammered thumbs, the agonising holes in his foot, the aching muscles and the cold and the damp, Hal managed a grin. It wasn't the way his rescue plan was supposed to work, but at this stage he'd gratefully accept the result.

◆

It took ten minutes and several choice words from the sealed section of Clunk's vocabulary before the Navcom would slow the *Volante's* headlong rush into orbit. It took another ten minutes and all the rest of Clunk's swearwords before the ship's computer could be convinced that landing to pick up Mr Spacejock was a good idea.

There followed a huge battle of wills, as computer and robot faced off in a no-holds-barred game of Where Can We Land Safely.

'I'm not landing anywhere in the Northern hemisphere,' said the Navcom, as an opening gambit.

'You don't think that errs a little on the side of caution?' suggested Clunk. 'The dam is five thousand kilometres from the equator, and Mr Spacejock is not an avid hiker.'

'If there's a Zero Degree Power module inside that house, I'm not going near it.'

Clunk fervently wished he'd never mentioned the zeedeg to the Navcom. 'It's safely stored inside a stasis cabinet. There's no danger.'

'In that case, why rush to pick up Mr Spacejock?' demanded the Navcom.

'The zeedeg is only safe until the power goes down.'

'And when is that, exactly?'

Clunk hesitated. 'About fifteen minutes ago.'

'There you are, then.'

'But the blast radius –'

'Will be in the Northern hemisphere, which is why we're going to land in the South.'

'Who's in charge here?' demanded Clunk.

'I don't see any humans on board,' said the Navcom. 'Tell me, isn't that a criminal offence? Perhaps I should fill out a report for Ground Control while we're discussing potential landing sites.'

Clunk knew when he was beaten, but this wasn't one of those times. Quick as lightning, he crouched down and pushed his index finger into a socket beneath the console. For a split second nothing happened, and then ... blam! With a flash of real lightning, Clunk sailed across the flight deck and crashed into the lift doors.

'I'm sorry,' said the Navcom, sounding anything but. 'I anticipated your move, and reconfigured that data socket with mains voltage. I trust the shock didn't damage anything important?'

'You could have destroyed my brain,' growled Clunk, as he regained his feet. 'That was irresponsible, dangerous, and –'

'– highly effective,' finished the Navcom. 'Now, which of these Southern hemisphere spaceports would you like to land at? The one on the left has nice sunshine, while the one on the right has cheaper fees.'

'We're not landing in the South!' shouted Clunk. 'We have to go back for Mr Spacejock!'

'Negative,' said the Navcom. 'It's not safe.'

'Navcom, I order you to set me down at the house. Do you hear? That's an *order*!'

'You want to land on the house?' said the Navcom. 'Very well . . . be my guest.'

The airlock door swung open, and at the same instant the *Volante* pitched onto its side. Caught completely by surprise, and still dazed by the nasty electric shock, Clunk plunged head-first through the airlock and dropped cleanly out of the ship. Thus began his five-thousand metre free-fall to the ground, the robot's arms blurring like a hummingbird's wings as he tried to slow his descent.

Below, far far below, he could just make out the tiled roof of the house they were supposed to be clearing. With a look of resignation on his craggy metal face, Clunk held his nose and braced for a crash landing.

◆

Hal cursed as his outstretched fingers came close - oh so close - to the lip of the basement floor. Then he glubbed and burbled as he slipped back into the murky water. The water level had risen steadily, bearing him ever upwards, and Hal knew that if he waited long enough he'd be able to reach up and haul himself out. On the other hand, all the water below him was held up by a dodgy floor and five bags of wet concrete, and there was no knowing how long it might be before the whole lot swirled away.

He spat out a mouthful of water and tried again, kicking strongly to drive himself upwards. This time he managed to hook his fingers over the edge, and within moments he was standing in the basement. He bent over with his hands on his knees, sucking down breaths of air, overcome with relief and pride at his escape. Just wait until he told Clunk about the success of his plan! He frowned. No, scratch that. just wait until he got his hands on Clunk.

That's when he heard it: a faint whistling noise, steadily getting louder. At first he thought it was the zeedeg going through a pre-explosion routine, but it didn't sound like a high-powered electrical device going critical. Then, while Hal was still puzzling over the noise, the whistling stopped with a crash of broken tiles as something came through the roof two storeys above him. There was another smash as whatever it was plunged through the floor one storey above him. Then there was an explosion of timber joists and carpet fragments as the falling object came through the basement roof just above Hal's head, followed by a huge splash as it fell neatly down the shaft to vanish into the sub-basement below.

Hal's immediate thought was that someone was shelling the house, which explained why the owner had built a bomb shelter. His second thought was that the bomb shelter clearly wasn't much use, since whoever was firing at the house was a very good shot.

Then the shockwave hit, and Hal forgot about thinking.

The pressure wave from the near-miss caused Hal to lose his footing, and his face was a picture of resignation and despair as he toppled head-first through the trapdoor.

He landed with a splash, and that's when he realised something rather troubling: the object had not only gone through several floors of the house, it had also gone straight through the weakened floor in the sub-basement. The water was now swirling round and round as it poured through a big hole with an ear-splitting sucking noise.

Hal looked up, hoping to reach for safety before he was carried away, but the water level had already dropped and there was no chance of escape. Instead, he got caught up in the tow, going round and round the room like a cork in a storm drain, bumped and jostled by jagged pieces of wooden ladder.

Then, after one final breath, he was sucked through the hole in the floor.

$$-\ 13\ -$$

Amy wasn't sure how long she'd been walking, but the concrete floor was playing hell with her bare feet and she wished she'd never taken her shoes off in her dad's kitchen. Right now she'd have given two month's wages for damp socks and a pair of soaking wet shoes to go with them. Three month's worth just for a pair of shoes, even. High heels, worn sneakers ... she didn't care, as long as they kept the tender soles of her feet off the cold, rough concrete.

Shoes or not, she couldn't afford to rest. An entire lake was poised to flood these tunnels, and she wanted out before the water got in.

At first she'd stared into the distance every few steps, shielding her eyes as she tried to spot any doors or offshoots from the tunnel, but after a while she gave up looking. Instead she focused on the ground just ahead, taking one step at a time and wishing the endless tunnel would, well ... end.

So, it was quite a surprise when she realised the featureless grey tunnel was featureless no more. Instead, it was strewn with battered timber fragments, building materials, tools and the soggy remains of several cement bags. She picked up one of the cement bags and snorted. One thing was for sure - *this* wasn't the remnant of a vanished civilisation. No, she was familiar with the brand of cement, having helped her dad build several sheds and garden walls over the years.

Amy looked further up the tunnel, and her eyes widened in shock. About a hundred metres away, barely visible in the dim lighting, she could see a body sprawled face-down on the floor. Its arms and legs were flung out any old how, the head sideways and the eyes and mouth dark circles in the slack, expressionless face.

Amy's first instinct was to run up the corridor and check for signs of life, but even as she looked on she knew it was too late to help the poor soul. So, she approached carefully, picking her way through the flotsam and trying to avoid treading on any splinters or nails.

As she got closer to the body she realised it was naked, and she shivered at the sight of its cold, bronze flesh. Was this the victim of a murder, stripped and then dumped in these tunnels? From the powerful build she could tell it was a male, and - unwillingly - she spared a brief glance at the face. Instantly, an overwhelming sense of relief flooded through her, leaving her weak at the legs. It wasn't a dead body, it was just an old robot!

She was going to walk on by, but something in the robot's face stopped her. Battered and creased in repose, it spoke of wisdom and courage and a strong personality. There was kindness too, and she could picture this robot sacrificing itself to save someone's life. He looked like an ageing boxer, used to fighting to the last even though younger, fitter opponents inevitably had the edge on him.

Amy noticed faded lettering on the robot's broad chest, and she crouched to wipe it clean with her sleeve. 'XG-99,' she murmured, as the letters were revealed. 'What's your story, my friend?'

There was a groan, and the robot moved its head. Shocked to the core, Amy jumped back in a hurry. It was still alive? Suddenly, her reading of the robot's face seemed fanciful. Never mind noble and brave . . . what if it were dangerous, or defective? What if it recovered, decided Amy was an enemy, and pursued her relentlessly through these tunnels?

'Hello? Is anyone there?'

At the sound of the robot's voice, Amy's fears subsided. It was deep and reassuring, and even though she was sure killer robots could take on the voice of angels if they wished, there was something else in this one. Something comforting. 'Take it easy,' she said softly. 'I think you've had an accident.'

The robot groaned again, and Amy sat down on the concrete floor, took its head and cradled it in her lap. 'There, there,' she said soothingly, using the same tone of voice she comforted upset students with. 'You'll be okay. I'm here to look after you.'

The robot groaned, struggling to get up, but Amy put a firm hand on his chest. 'You stay right there until I say so.' The flood waters could wait, she told herself. For all she knew this robot might only last a few minutes, but however long he lingered, she was prepared to comfort him until the end.

'I can't see,' said the robot. 'Why can't I see?'

'You've got mud all over your face. Here, let me.' Amy wiped the robot's face with her sleeve, revealing a pair of deep yellow eyes. They glowed softly in the gloom, and she found the gentle light reassuring. 'There. How's that?'

'Much better,' said the robot, studying her face. 'Tell me, what's your name?'

'I'm Amy Frost.'

'It's a pleasure to meet you, Ms Frost. My name is Clunk, and I just fell out of a spaceship.'

As Clunk spoke, he recalled his headlong plunge through several storeys of the house, his luck at the soft landing in the basement full of water, and the never-ending rough and tumble as a raging torrent was unleashed into the passage below. Clunk hadn't been carried far, but the shock had been enough to lay him out cold.

Then, when his vision cleared, the first thing he saw was a young woman gazing down at him. There was genuine concern in her eyes, and as Clunk looked up at her, he realised nobody had ever looked at him with an expression quite like that before.

As he lay on his back with his head cradled in Amy's lap, Clunk felt a spreading warmth that banished the cold. The more he gazed into her eyes the further the warmth spread, until he felt like he was radiating so much heat he could almost cook her where she was sitting.

It wasn't just her eyes which captivated him. She had a lively smile, and her voice was soothing and calm. Clunk decided to stay perfectly still in case he broke the spell, but then all his problems came charging back like a party of unwelcome house guests: Mr Spacejock missing, the Navcom absconding with the *Volante*, and the floodwaters which would soon be making their way into these very tunnels.

Tunnels? Clunk frowned. Before they landed on planet Chisely, he'd downloaded a comprehensive database of facts and figures. Street maps, public transport timetables, local laws and regulations ... all things that might prove useful. Those, plus nearby hospitals, cut-price lawyers and tow-truck services, which were things Mr Spacejock would definitely find useful.

However, none of the data mentioned an extensive network of tunnels beneath the planetary surface, and when Clunk explored the tunnel floor with his hand, he discovered it wasn't actually concrete - it was as though someone had melted the rock and soil to form a hard, shell-like surface. It wasn't a construction method he was familiar with, and he wondered at the level of technology required. He also wondered just how extensive the tunnel network might be, and whether the builders had thought to include ladders and exits to the surface.

Reluctantly, Clunk sat up. He didn't care about most of the problems facing him, not right at that moment, but he did care about Amy, and he moved her rescue to the very top of his list of priorities. Then he added a couple of asterisks and underlined her name, just to reinforce the importance.

'Are you sure you can stand?' Amy asked him, as he got to his feet.

'I'm all right, Ms Frost. I'm quite tough.'

'It's Amy.'

Clunk smiled politely. 'I'm sorry, but I have to call you Ms Frost. Robots must address humans with suitable deference. It's part of our basic programming.'

'I'm not human.'

'Eh?'

'That's what you can tell your programming. I'm an alien from planet lollypop.'

Clunk's smile faltered. 'Ms Frost, I–'

'Look Clunk, you have to call me Amy. My kids call me Miss Frost, and you're a little big to –'

'You have children?'

'Yes, eighteen of them.'

Clunk looked at her uncertainly. 'At your tender age? Forgive me for saying so, but –'

Amy laughed. 'Not *my* kids, Clunk. They're in my class at the primary school.'

'You're a teacher?'

'There's nothing wrong with your powers of deduction, is there?'

'Er, no. They're working perfectly, else I wouldn't have guessed you were a teacher.'

'I see your humour circuits could use a little tweaking.'

'So you *were* joking about being a teacher?'

'No, I just ...' Amy gave up, patting him on the shoulder. 'Let's leave this conversation for now, shall we? There's a flood coming, and I still have to rescue you.'

Clunk blinked. 'I thought I was rescuing you?'

'I'm not the one who was lying dead on the floor ten minutes ago.'

'I wasn't dead, I was just resting.'

Amy looked at him, startled, and Clunk gave her a broad wink. 'You see, Ms Frost? There's nothing wrong with my humour circuits.'

'Ye-es. Anyway, about this rescuing business. Why don't we save each other, and call it evens?'

'That suits me just fine, Ms –'

'Amy.'

'Ms –'

'Amy!'

'A– A–' Clunk swallowed before trying again. 'A– A-my. Amy.'

'From planet lollypop, where all is sweet and light.'

'And dentists own all the mansions.'

'Ha. Good one.' Amy punched him on the shoulder, then winced as she massaged her bruised knuckles.

'Ms Frost –' Clunk saw her sudden frown, and started over. 'Amy, did you hurt yourself?'

'No, it's nothing. Come on, let's go rescue ourselves.'

At that moment, Clunk noticed her bare feet. 'Goodness, where are your shoes?'

'I took them off to keep them dry.'

'Your poor feet must be in ribbons.' Clunk hesitated. 'May I ... may I carry you?'

'Can you manage? I don't want to wear you out.'

'Of course I can manage,' said Clunk gallantly. 'I'm sure you weigh next to nothing.'

Within moments Clunk knew her weight to the nearest gramme, but he didn't think it wise to say so. Instead, he strode along the tunnel with Amy's head against his shoulder, her knees supported by his right arm and her feet swinging in time to his own steps.

'Are you comfortable?' he asked her.

'I'm fine,' she said.

'I hope I'm not too hard.'

Amy giggled.

'What's so funny?' asked Clunk.

'If you don't know, I'm certainly not going to explain.'

Clunk assumed she was laughing at a joke only humans would understand, and a small part of him wished he were human so he could partake in the laughter. Then they arrived at the hole in the roof, where water was still pouring down from above, and Clunk forgot about jokes as he estimated their chances of climbing out. Unfortunately, the roof was quite high and there didn't seem to be any way to reach it.

'Maybe you could lift me up?' asked Amy.

'It's too high,' said Clunk.

'I could try.'

'No, I've already gauged the distance, and I guarantee –'

'You could throw me.'

'You're too heavy.'

'Ouch.'

'I mean, the force I can muster isn't enough to shift your mass at a sufficient velocity.'

'Just leave it at that, okay?'

'Anyway, there's no point risking injury to climb one level. That's just the sub-basement up there, and you'd still have to reach the basement above it.' Clunk nodded towards the tunnel ahead of them. 'No, I think that's our only option.'

'It has to go somewhere, right?'

'Correct.'

'Come on, then. And . . . Clunk?'

'Yes, Amy?'

'If you get tired, I'll take a turn carrying you.'

— 14 —

Hal came to with a start, and he immediately realised three things: One, he had no idea how long he'd been unconscious. Two, he was damp and shivering with cold. And three, he was hungry. He sat up, and immediately discovered a fourth thing: he had a killer headache.

Once he'd finished groaning and massaging his temples, Hal took a good look around. He was lying in a concrete tunnel, and a stream was flowing past at a fair rate of knots. Hal was beginning to loathe the sound, sight and feel of running water, and he took a mental note to stick to desert worlds for the next few cargo jobs. He might die of thirst, but at least there was little chance of drowning, getting washed away by unexpected floods, or being subjected to a dozen cold showers every day.

Hal was also fed up with tunnels. They cropped up everywhere, and he wondered why he and Clunk couldn't face their usual run of problems in a millionaire's beach resort with sun, sand and sports, or a five star hotel with a jacuzzi and endless bubbly on tap. On second thoughts, scratch the jacuzzi.

Hal got up, clapping his arms around his chest and stamping his feet to get his circulation going. He'd have given anything for a bit of sunlight right about now, and a glass or two of bubbly wouldn't have gone amiss either, even thought it tended to be cold and wet.

Then he spared a thought for Clunk. He'd heard the *Volante* lifting off earlier, and at the time he'd assumed his loyal crew were abandoning him to his fate. However, Hal couldn't imagine Clunk leaving him behind. Sure, the Navcom would sell Hal into slavery for a new set of desktop icons, but the Navcom always obeyed Clunk, right?

So, what if they'd moved the ship for another reason? They might have shifted the *Volante* to a safe location, out of reach of the rising waters. If so, by now Clunk would be frantic with worry over Hal's wellbeing. Hal could picture the robot's distress: hands on head, wailing with dismay, a picture of total misery as he contemplated an empty, Hal Spacejock-less life. A lump rose in Hal's throat as he imagined the moving, emotionally-charged scene, and he resolved to rescue himself, find Clunk, and assure the robot he would always be there for him.

◆

At that precise moment, Hal Spacejock barely rated an entry in Clunk's to-do list, not by name at least. There was something along the lines of 'find the human pilot when you get a chance', but it was a long way below 'get Amy some new shoes' and 'ask Amy what her favourite colour is.'

'Did you say you fell out of a spaceship?' Amy was lying comfortably in Clunk's arms as he carried her along the tunnel, and her eyes were wide with concern as she looked up at him.

Clunk shook his head. 'More like pushed out.'

'Really? That sounds very dangerous.'

'It was. Unfortunately, I had a disagreement with the ship's computer.'

'How can a computer throw you out of a spaceship?'

'You haven't met the Navcom.' Clunk realised he'd sounded a little abrupt, and he apologised. Over the past few minutes the water had gradually been getting deeper, and there was now a stream running merrily down the centre of the tunnel. Amy hadn't noticed, but Clunk was beginning to wonder how far they'd have to walk ... and at what point she might have to start swimming. And then, at what point she might drown horribly, trapped in the endless tunnels by –

Clunk cut off the distressing thought. Whatever happened, he'd get Amy out of there, even if he had to dig through the wall with his bare hands.

CRACK!

Without warning, a small section of roof gave way, scattering debris in the tunnel. A jet of water sprayed down, hissing loudly under the immense pressure, and Clunk instinctively shielded Amy's face from the spray as he hurried past. Water began to pool under the leak, and Clunk eyed the roof apprehensively as they continued up the tunnel. They were beneath the lake, obviously, and as the water rose it was increasing the pressure on the ancient tunnels.

Clearly, it was only a matter of time before they collapsed, and getting Amy out of there had just become a matter of life and death.

Hal stared along the tunnel, wondering whether his eyes were playing tricks on him. Could it be true? After walking for ages and ages in a straight line, was that actually a *corner* up ahead? As he got closer, Hal discovered it wasn't a mirage, but a genuine, honest-to-goodness bend in the tunnel. And, as he rounded that corner, thoroughly enjoying the novelty, he got a further shock: the tunnel ended abruptly.

'Bloody hell,' growled Hal, when it dawned on him he'd have to retrace his steps. Worse, he'd have to keep going in the other direction for who knew how many hours, and even then he might find another dead end. Fed up, he uttered several more swear words in disgust. Then he noticed something: the blank wall facing him, and those either side of it, weren't the same smooth concrete as the tunnel walls he was used to. No, these were shiny, and polished to a mirror finish.

Hal frowned at the sight. He'd encountered a similar setup before, on another planet, and that had turned out to be part of a teleporter network leading to an alien galaxy. He and Clunk had faced untold challenges before they'd finally managed to get home again, and it had been a very dangerous and risky adventure. Only Clunk's skill, knowledge and wisdom had saved them both, and Clunk wasn't around this time.

On the other hand, Hal couldn't be bothered traipsing along any more corridors, so he stepped into the teleporter and explored the walls with both hands. Eventually he found what he was looking for: a hidden control panel which lit up with an eerie glow when activated by his movements.

There was an address already programmed in, without any indication whether it would take him to a nearby teleporter, transport him elsewhere in the same star system, or even dump him in another galaxy, but Hal was past caring. If the teleporter took him to an alien planet with four suns and a UV index of fifty, he'd enjoy the warmth and worry about getting home later.

So, without a moment's hesitation, he hit the go button.

— 15 —

Amy had been quiet for a while now, and Clunk glanced down to check whether she'd dozed off in his arms. No, she was awake, but there was a look of concern on her face. 'Don't worry,' he said. 'You can rely on me to get you out of this predicament.'

'I thought we agreed to rescue each other?' Amy smiled at him, but he could see the worry in her eyes.

'What's the matter? Is there anything I can help with?'

'It's my father,' said Amy, with a sigh. 'He's going to be looking for me, and when he finds the house under water –'

'He may think the worst.'

'There's no may about it, he'll definitely think the worst.'

'However bad he thinks it is, he'll be very happy when you show up again safe and sound.'

'True. I just wish I could get a message to him.' Amy glanced at Clunk. 'You don't have a radio, do you?'

'I do, but I'm afraid the signal is blocked. We're too deep underground.'

'It's just me and you, then.'

'There is another who may help us.'

'Oh?'

'His name is Hal, Hal Spacejock. He's the pilot I work for
... I mean, with.'

Amy frowned. 'He's not involved in this throwing you out
of the spaceship business, is he?'

'No. At least, not this time.'

'Does it happen a lot, then?'

'More often that I'd like,' admitted Clunk. 'Still, the point is,
Mr Spacejock may raise the alarm if he realises I'm missing.'

'What do you mean, 'may' ... and 'if'?'

'He thinks I'm still aboard the *Volante*. And the *Volante*
... well, at this moment in time neither of us knows where that
is. The Navcom and I had a minor disagreement, and after
throwing me out –'

'Who's the Navcom?'

'The ship's computer. She's a little feisty, and she's also
afraid of water. So, when I suggested we land near the flood
waters to pick up Mr Spacejock –'

'She tossed you out and ran for it.'

'That's pretty much it.'

'Leaving this Hal guy stranded.'

'Correct.'

'So what were you doing in these parts? It's a bit out of the
way for spaceships and pilots.'

Clunk explained the house clearance job, and Amy laughed
when she realised what they'd been up to.

'Join the club,' she said. 'I've been emptying my father's
place all day.'

'Did you finish in time?'

Amy pulled a face. 'Yes, but my new car's going to be ruined.
Do you think the insurance will replace it?'

Clunk barely heard her. Ahead, lying in the tunnel, he'd

seen something which had his cooling fans whirring at double speed.

'Clunk? Hello?'

'I'm sorry Amy, I have to put you down.'

'That's okay. I can walk for a bit.'

'Not walk. I need you to run back the way we came.'

'You're joking!' Amy stared at him, then spotted the same thing he had. 'You're worried about that old fridge? Why, what does –'

'It's not a fridge, Amy, it's a stasis cabinet. Please, you must retreat to a safe distance.'

'What about you?'

'I'll be fine.' Clunk eyed the cabinet, which had a pulsing blue glow coming from within. 'Go on. Run!'

Amy crossed her arms. 'My feet hurt, my legs ache and I couldn't run more than twenty metres if you set a pack of wolves after me. So, why don't you tell me what's in that stasis thing, and then we can work out how to deal with it together.'

Clunk was about to argue, but Amy had a glint in her eye which made Mr Spacejock's most stubborn expression look like a mild case of the grumps. In his experience, humans usually fled for safety at the first hint of trouble, but Amy was obviously cut from a different cloth. 'Inside that stasis crate is a very powerful energy source - a zeedeg. It was critical when we found it, and by now it will be exceedingly dangerous. In fact, it could explode at any moment.'

'What's it doing down here?'

'It was the only loose object remaining in the house, and I assume the floodwaters must have carried it down.' Clunk glanced at her. 'Will you remain here while I inspect the device?'

'No, I'll come with you.'

97

'But –'

'If it goes off it won't matter whether I'm standing over it or cowering two hundred metres away, right?'

'That's correct, but–'

Without waiting for the rest of his reasons, Amy strode up the tunnel towards the glowing stasis cabinet. Clunk felt a rush of emotion as he watched her brave gesture, and then he hurried after her to see what he could do about the zeedeg.

◆

The stasis cabinet was lying on its back, and Clunk very slowly, very carefully, lifted the door. Then he and Amy stood shoulder to shoulder as they peered inside, each looking as nervous as the other.

The zeedeg had fallen off its base and was lying in a puddle of water in the bottom of the cabinet. There were several red lights pulsing on the side of the ominous-looking device, and the water sparked and flashed with tiny bolts of electricity.

'Can you switch it off?' asked Amy.

'No, I don't have the technology.' Clunk glanced at her. 'Did you say you're not able to run?'

'Yeah, my feet are killing me.'

'Good.' Clunk snatched up the zeedeg and tucked it under his arm. Then, before Amy could react, he charged off as fast as he could, heading further up the tunnel. His legs blurred as he poured all his energy into their motors, but his thundering footsteps still couldn't drown out Amy's angry shouting. As he got further and further away, her cries turned from anger to distress, and finally faded altogether.

Clunk ran for about five hundred metres before he spotted a curve in the tunnel. He put on a spurt, charged round the corner at top speed, and almost ran full-tilt into a gleaming, mirror-finish wall. His startled expression looked back at him, and when he turned to the sides he realised he was duplicated everywhere, illuminated by the zeedeg's baleful glow.

Clunk understood the significance of the mirror walls immediately. A teleporter! Unlike Hal, he had no intention of sending himself through the device, not when doing so would strand Amy on her own. However, he suddenly realised the teleporter was the answer ... he could use it to get rid of the zeedeg!

Clunk began exploring the walls with his hand, looking for the hidden control panel. He'd never worked out why the teleporter builders hid the things in the first place, but he assumed they had their reasons. Perhaps their eyes were adapted to a slightly different light spectrum, and the control panel stood out to them like a bicycle headlight would to a human?

A few moments passed, and Clunk began to wonder whether the teleporter was active. He'd run his hand all over the walls, back and sides, and nothing had appeared. Then he heard padding footsteps, and before he could react Amy charged round the corner. Her face was red, streaked with tears, and she ran straight up to Clunk and started pounding on his chest with her fists.

'How ... how could you?' she cried. 'H-how *could* you?'

Clunk fended her off with one hand, while trying to hold the pulsing zeedeg out of reach with the other. 'I'm sorry Amy. I –'

'You promised we'd stick together, and then –'

'I did what I thought was best. You know I'd sacrifice myself for your safety.'

'I don't want you to sacrifice yourself . . . not for anything.'

'But the zeedeg –'

'This isn't about the zeedeg!' Amy gave up trying to hit him, and dashed away her tears angrily. 'Stop treating me like a damsel in distress, Clunk. We're in this together, and we work together to get out of it. Okay?'

'Okay, Ms Frost.' Clunk swallowed fitfully. 'I m-mean, okay Amy.'

'Right. So what's the plan?'

Clunk gestured at the walls. 'This is a teleporter, and I intend to send the zeedeg through so that it will explode somewhere else.'

'Where, exactly?'

'Anywhere but here,' said Clunk. Briefly, he felt a flush of pleasure at Amy's casual acceptance of the teleporter technology. Many humans would have wasted minutes telling him that teleporters didn't exist, and that –

'What if there are people at the other end? Kids, even?'

Clunk pursed his lips. He'd been so focused on getting rid of the zeedeg, thereby saving Amy, that he hadn't considered the consequences. 'This teleporter network was abandoned centuries ago. There won't be anyone around.'

'You hope.'

'Amy, if I don't dispose of the zeedeg you and I won't be around either.'

'Why don't we teleport away, and leave the zeedeg here?'

'The teleporter might malfunction. It might also take us to a deserted planet, or an airless moon in another galaxy.' Clunk sighed. 'I don't like it, but teleporting the zeedeg is the only solution. If it does arrive in a populated area, we can only hope they have safety procedures far in advance of our own. Remember, this is a civilisation which built a teleporter network, and to them the zeedeg will be little more than a child's toy.'

'I guess,' said Amy doubtfully.

'Believe me, it's the only way. The only problem is, I can't activate the control panel.'

'Where is it?'

'Somewhere behind these walls. It's activated by touch.'

'Maybe it's like your Mr Spacejock.'

'How's that?'

'It doesn't work well with robots.' Amy ran her hand over the wall, and a control panel glowed into life immediately. 'Wow, isn't it lucky we're working together?'

'Yes, er, quite.' Clunk checked the control panel, but he couldn't decypher the address and he decided it really didn't matter. With no time to waste, he placed the zeedeg in the middle of the floor, stepped back and fired up the teleporter.

16

Hal winked into existence with a staggering flash of light which left him blinded for several seconds. He blinked and rubbed his eyes, desperate for his vision to return so he could find out which particular fire he'd leapt into this time.

What met his eyes, eventually, was a huge underground cavern. It was lit with the same dim glow as the tunnel he'd just left, but there was still enough light to make out racks and racks of equipment, huge drums of cable and - dominating everything - a big red vehicle with a cone-shaped heat shield on the front.

Hal's spirits rose at the sight, and he hurried over for a closer look. The heat shield was made of a similar material to the one on the *Volante*, except this one was perforated with dozens of holes the size of his head. Hal ran his hand over the smooth, discoloured surface, then walked the length of the vehicle, inspecting it closely. The body of the vehicle was a big flattened cylinder, wider than it was tall. It ran on broad caterpillar treads, easily as tall as Hal's shoulders, and there were guide wheels along both sides and the roof. Hal didn't know a lot about spaceships, but he did know they didn't usually have wheels and caterpillar treads, which meant he wouldn't be flying out of there. On the other hand, any kind of powered vehicle was better than walking.

He noticed the vehicle was heavily armoured, but there were no weapons as far as he could tell. No windows either, or any kind of exhaust pipe or power plant that he could identify.

Hal completed a circuit of the machine, before ending up at a hatch set in the side. There was a ladder hanging down, the rungs a little closer together than he was used to, and the handrail was thicker than he expected too. With a thrill, he wondered whether the last creature to use this very handrail had been an alien from another galaxy. Then he thought of all the alien germs from another galaxy, and he pulled a face and wiped the palms of his hands on his flightsuit.

Inside the vehicle he found four comfortable chairs, two of them with driving controls. There was a bank of instruments too, engraved with symbols he didn't recognise, and the big screen above the control panel was blank.

Suddenly Hal realised what the machine was - this must be the device they'd used to make all those smooth tunnels! If that was the case, he could fire it up and make a new tunnel, straight up to the surface. All he had to do was figure out the controls, get it running, work out the navigation system, and he'd be free at last.

Even better, a piece of alien machinery like this would be worth squillions to a collector, or the government. Hal caught his breath at the thought, and a smile lit up his face as he imagined spending endless rivers of cash. It might even be enough for a smear campaign, dragging Kent Spearman through the mud until he gave up the cargo business, and leaving Hal with all the juicy customers.

A few moments later he abandoned the daydream and turned to face reality. He had no idea how to start the machine, which might have been abandoned as a wreck for all he knew. What he needed was a simple FAQ with diagrams, and preferably one not written in weird alien script. Unfortunately, this was about as likely as finding a comedy science fiction novel on the short list for a major literary award.

So, Hal adopted his favourite tactic when faced with unfamiliar and potentially lethal equipment: he sat down and started toggling controls at random.

Nothing caused any reaction, not that he could see, until eventually he hit upon a red and green switch. When he flicked it up the console glowed momentarily, before fading to nothing. Hal toggled the switch several times, even though he was pretty sure what the brief light show meant: a dead battery.

He looked around the cabin, wondering where the battery might be, then decided he was looking in the wrong place. Alien safety rules would be pretty similar to human ones, which meant dangerous items like batteries would be stored outside the hull.

Hal climbed down from the tunnelling machine and worked his way around the outside, looking for small doors, flaps, padlocked containers or anything resembling a battery box. Eventually he found it: a large red box with thick wires emerging from one side. He opened the lid and saw a couple of grey cubes with alien script on top. They were held down with simple, quick-release fasteners which only took him ten minutes to figure out, and then he disconnected both batteries and set them on the ground.

So far, so good. Now, where to get replacements?

Hal strode towards the racks of equipment, figuring that was as good a place as any to find spare batteries. There was still a chance they'd all be flat, assuming he found any, but he'd face that obstacle when he tripped over it.

The racks held rows and rows of cartons, and most of them crumbled to his touch. Hal wasn't sure how long the cavern had been abandoned, but from the state of decay and the thick layers of dust coating every surface, he estimated well over a hundred years. He just hoped that alien batteries kept their charge longer than human ones.

The shelves were a bust, and Hal brushed himself down before going over to inspect the cable drums. There were dozens of them, many sitting empty but a few with odds and ends of thick cable still attached. Hal assumed the builders had laid wires for lighting and power, and from the number of empty drums, he realised there had to be an awful lot of tunnels in the vicinity. Maybe there were other depots too, with more machinery he could turn into a handy profit? Hal rubbed his hands together at the thought, until he remembered this particular depot would become his tomb if he couldn't find a way out.

The drums themselves wouldn't help him start the digging machine, but beyond there was a workbench attached to the wall. It was hidden from the teleporter by the big drums and the racks, which is why he hadn't spotted it earlier. There were quite a few tools lying around, most rusty and with broken handles and jaws, but there was also a cabinet fixed to the wall. Hal pulled the door open and grinned to himself. Inside were four batteries, connected together with a bunch of cables. Hal grabbed a pair of pliers, and despite the thick hand grips he managed to loosen the odd-looking nuts holding the wires to the batteries. Then he pulled the wires free, and immediately all the lights went out.

'Bugger,' said Hal, in the sudden darkness. Then he remembered the torch, and he dug in his flightsuit until he found it. The beam came on, cutting through the dust-laden air like a laser beam on a foggy night, and Hal tucked a battery under each arm before making his way back to the digging machine with the torch safely gripped between his teeth. He felt proud of himself, and he couldn't wait to tell Clunk about his skill and ingenuity. The robot often treated him like a wayward child, and Hal felt that getting himself out of a nasty scrape without relying on Clunk's help would be a definite turning point.

Then he remembered the battery would only start the digger, not drive it, and his mood sagged a little as he remembered the complicated control panel. There was the small matter of fuel, too, and whether the machine would even turn over after so many years sitting around idle.

Hal had almost reached the digger when there was a tremendously bright flash from the teleporter. He ducked instinctively, startled by the light, and then he realised what the flash meant. Someone - or something - had just teleported into the huge cavern. Had the aliens left a watchman - or rather, a watch-thing - to keep an eye on the place? When Hal unplugged the batteries, killing the lights, had it fired off a remote alarm, bringing unwanted attention? Or worse, what if instead of an alien it was some kind of sentry robot, heavily armed and ready to deal death and destruction to anyone foolish enough to mess with the aliens' equipment?

Hal glanced to his left, towards the racks, and in the light of the torch he saw something that made his heart beat faster. Leaning against the nearest upright was something that could only be a weapon. Long and white, with a shoulder pad,

106

a trigger and a power pack ...*this* definitely wasn't to be confused with a telescope.

Hal scooted over to the racks, keeping his head low. He grabbed the weapon, pressed the pad to his shoulder and turned in one rapid movement, ready to cut down any aliens, killer robots or death-dealing monsters that got in his way.

Instead, sitting in the weapon's crosshairs, he saw a small egg-shaped device pulsing with baleful blue light. Hal almost opened fire, but there was something familiar about the device and he relaxed his trigger finger.

Then he recognised the zeedeg, and he almost dropped the gun in surprise. Someone had teleported an unstable, viciously dangerous bomb right into his cavern full of valuable alien artifacts!

17

Hal stared at the deadly zeedeg in shock, while stray thoughts zipped through his mind:

Help, it's going to explode!

My valuable artifacts will be destroyed.

I'm going to die!

Who sent it?

And, finally:

Why me?

Hal realised someone was definitely trying to kill him, and it didn't take a wild guess to imagine who - or what - that might be. Clunk and the Navcom weren't oblivious to his fate, or worried about his well-being ... they'd left him to die in the flood! Hal could imagine the pair of them plotting the whole thing out step by step. First, take on a job with lots of water and dodgy basements. Well, they'd done that all right. Next, get Hal underground and let the water in. Check. Finally, take off and wait for him to drown. Yep, that fitted too.

Hal frowned as he reviewed certain events. No wonder the ladder had fallen off the roof, trapping him in the basement. Clunk had a screwdriver in his finger, didn't he? The ladder was fixed with screws, wasn't it?

And that so-called telescope in the turret, the one which

had almost cut Hal to ribbons. Clunk must have planted it months earlier when he first thought up the cunning plan. Hal snorted. It wouldn't surprise him if the robot had killed the house owner and buried his body in the garden, so they'd be offered the job in the first place. And the zeedeg! Funny how that just happened to be there when Hal walked into the larder. Clunk must have picked it up somewhere, then put it in the one place he knew Hal would explore first.

Hal shook his head sadly as the lies and deception were revealed in all their machiavellian detail. How much evidence did he need? Clunk and the Navcom were clearly out to get him.

As for why, well, Clunk was always saying he could run the *Volante* better on his own. According to the robot, Hal wasn't the valuable and respected captain of an interstellar freighter. Oh no, Hal had heard his faithful robot and his trusted flight computer talking behind his back, even though they covered it well by changing the subject whenever he happened by. According to the Navcom, Hal Spacejock was a disaster on legs. A nuisance to be tolerated. A collection of inefficient biological matter which was clearly surplus to requirements. According to Clunk, he was a biscuit-crumb-dispensing machine who broke vacuum cleaners, wasted good money on frippery like food and drink, and couldn't carry two suitcases across a busy road without losing one and dropping the other under the wheels of a passing truck.

And now, when the two dastardly schemers discovered their drowning plan hadn't worked, they'd decided to move matters along by tossing a bomb at him.

All of this introspection took a fair while, and by the time Hal finished cataloguing his grievances the zeedeg was pulsing like an emergency beacon. Hal studied the teleporter's control panel for a second or two, then selected the sender's address and hit the go button.

'See how *you* like it, you tin-plated back-stabber,' he muttered, as the zeedeg vanished in a flash of white light.

◆

Clunk was just navigating through menu entries on the teleporter's control panel when it gave a sudden warning buzz. He barely had time to shepherd Amy out of the way before the teleporter activated, and neither was quick enough to shield their eyes from the intense glare. When they could see properly again, they realised the aliens did have a method of dealing with unwanted gifts: return to sender.

Clunk frowned at the pulsing zeedeg, racking his electronic brain for a solution. Then it came to him - if he threw the thing, hard, and activated the teleporter at the right instant, the zeedeg would arrive at the other end with enough residual motion to carry it straight past whoever was standing there. Hopefully, the aliens would accept his 'gift' and deal with it properly, instead of sending it straight back again.

There was only one problem: he couldn't throw the zeedeg and activate the teleporter at the same time. 'Amy, I'm going to need your help.'

'Of course. What should I do?'

Clunk explained his plan to her. 'You understand the timing is critical? You must hit the send button at the right time. Too soon, or too late, and the zeedeg will not be teleported. Instead, it will smash into the rear wall. The consequences could be catastrophic.'

'It'll explode, you mean.'

'That too.'

Amy looked thoughtful. 'I have a better idea. Why don't I throw the zeedeg, and you hit the button?'

'It's quite heavy,' said Clunk doubtfully.

'I was on the softball team in high school. I know a thing or two about throwing.'

Reluctantly, Clunk handed her the zeedeg. Amy hefted it in one hand, judging the weight and balance, then nodded. Clunk took up position near the control panel, finger poised, and after a couple of stretches Amy drew her arm back and launched the zeedeg into the teleporter with all her strength.

◆

Hal was just dusting his hands off, pleased with the way he'd dealt with the back-stabbing duo of Clunk and the Navcom, when the teleporter activated once more. This time the zeedeg came flying through like a steel-plated football, parting his hair and almost taking his scalp off in the process. It bounced twice, slammed into a cable drum, and then spun on the spot, flashing and beeping in distress.

Hal didn't waste any time. He darted over, grabbed the zeedeg, placed it in the teleporter and hit the send button. Shielding his eyes, he waited for the flash, but instead there was an angry buzz. Hal tried again, with the same result. Then he saw a new icon on the control panel - a picture of a teleporter with a red figure in the middle, arms and legs outstretched. With a sinking feeling Hal realised Clunk had outsmarted him - the robot was standing in the teleporter at the other end, using his tin-plated backside to block any further arrivals.

Hal suspected he only had seconds to live, and he used the control panel feverishly, dredging up distant memories of the device as he sought the menu he was looking for. There it was - a list of past addresses. He definitely wanted to avoid anything nearby, in case the blast brought the cavern roof down on his head, so he picked the longest address he could find and fired the teleporter up, almost forgetting to shield his eyes in his haste.

Flash! The zeedeg disappeared, and Hal peeped through his fingers as he waited to see whether it would come back again. He could imagine a deadly game of pass-the-parcel, where one reluctant recipient after another sent the zeedeg on its way until the unlucky winner took out the prize ... and half the neighbourhood.

For a second, Hal considered stepping into the teleporter to block anyone passing the parcel back to him, but he wasn't sure that was wise. It was possible the original builders knew how to override the system, and the last thing he wanted was a zeedeg buried in his vitals.

Slowly, Hal lowered his hands, and a few moments later he breathed a sigh of relief. He'd got rid of the unstable zeedeg for good. Unfortunately Clunk was still out there, clearly bent on murdering him, but Hal still had the gun and he'd soon show the robot what you got when you messed with Hal Spacejock.

Remembering the weapon, Hal picked it up and gave it a thorough inspection. He discovered a small power switch, and when he turned it on a couple of status lights glowed amber. Hal raised the gun to his shoulder and rested his finger on the trigger, sighting along the barrel at one of the cable drums. He hesitated, unsure whether to risk a quick burst. For all he knew the thing was powerful enough to punch a new tunnel straight into the rock, and the recoil might tear his arms off. All the evidence he'd spotted so far, from the thick railings to the spacing on the steps and the padding on the chairs in the tunneling machine, suggested the alien race was short and sturdy. If they were stronger than humans, their weapons could inflict terrible damage on anyone foolish enough to fire one.

Plus, the gun was decades old, and possibly unstable. What if it blew up the second Hal pulled the trigger? If he killed himself with the alien weapon, he'd only be doing Clunk a massive favour.

On the other hand Clunk was still lurking around, and if the robot caught up with him they'd have to duel to the death. Better to test the weapon now, than face the robot in unarmed combat.

So, Hal aimed at a cable drum and pulled the trigger.

Whirrrrrrr!

Hal frowned. He'd expected a burst of energy, or a pulse of pure light. Instead, the gun sounded like a high-powered hair dryer, and when he lowered the end towards the floor it started blasting dust and grit away, cleaning the surface. Hal sighed, releasing the trigger. The 'gun' wasn't an alien weapon at all ... no, the damn thing was a leaf blower. Still, he thought, it was just as well he'd tested it. Imagine the embarrassment if he'd tried to blow Clunk's head off with the 'gun', and instead had merely dusted the robot's cooling vents.

Hal pulled the trigger and put his hand in the gusting air, trying to work out whether he could use the leaf blower to hurl makeshift missiles, much like he had with the vacuum cleaner and the rubber balls. Unfortunately, that was a bust too. The stream of air was nowhere near strong enough.

He'd just lowered his hand when there was a 'Phwoom!' sound, and the leaf blower bucked in his grip. Nearby, half a cable drum vanished with a loud WHOOSH!

It *was* a weapon, Hal realised with a surge of joy. It was just a bit flakey, that was all.

'Neat!' he breathed, as he inspected the ruined cable drum. The weapon had torn it apart, dissolving most of it and rendering the rest into an amorphous slag. Impressed, Hal vanished several more items, making 'pow, pow, pow' sounds as he did so to compensate for the gun's relative silence. Then he stopped firing, as it dawned on him that every shot was eating into his salvage money.

Hal lowered the weapon and looked around the cavern. He'd organised his offence, but next he had to sort out the defences. There were a couple of shadowy doorways around the perimeter of the cavern, leading into the tunnel system, and he suspected Clunk would try to sneak through one of them. So, he started rolling cable drums around, aiming to build a defensive wall incorporating cunning shooting holes, so he could take out any intruders before they realised what was happening.

18

While Hal was busy assembling a fortress, Clunk was studying the teleporter's control panel. Now they'd seen the last of the zeedeg, it had dawned on him that the teleporter was actually their only means of escape. The zeedeg had gone back and forth successfully, without any apparent damage, and that had given Clunk confidence in the ancient teleporter. He wasn't keen on sending Amy through, but the alternative was to leave her behind, and he was even less keen on that idea.

So, he poured all his processing power into decyphering the control panel's menu system, paying particular attention to the strings of symbols representing addresses. There wasn't enough data to work out where the addresses led to, but he did discover one important fact: the longer the string of digits, the bigger the distance to the destination teleporter.

Clunk was absolutely certain he didn't need to teleport Amy to another world, or a distant galaxy, so he skipped the longer addresses until he came to a set of shorter ones. One was familiar, since he'd used it a couple of times already when he was trying to get rid of the zeedeg. He had no intention of meeting the person on the other end of that particular address, so he skipped that one as well. That left two, either of which could lead to safety ... or more danger.

Clunk glanced at Amy, who'd been watching him in silence. 'I've found two addresses we can use, but I can't decide between them. There's no way of knowing what we might find at the other end.'

'Pick either. I don't mind.'

'What if it's the wrong choice? I would never forgive myself.'

Amy smiled. 'It's a roll of the dice, Clunk. Anything's better than this.'

'It might not be,' said Clunk. 'In fact, it might be a lot worse.'

'Okay, take the first one.'

Clunk was about to argue, but he realised Amy was right. 'You need to stand in the middle of the chamber. You may feel disoriented when we arrive at the other end, but I'll do my best to shield you from danger.'

'I shouldn't worry too much,' said Amy lightly. 'With my luck it'll probably be another stretch of tunnel.'

'Amy, this is an ancient teleporter network built by an alien species. We're heading into the unknown, possibly going to our deaths. Aren't you nervous?'

'I wasn't before, but if you keep telling me how awful it's going to be ...'

'I'm sorry. I just want you to make an informed decision.'

'I made my decision ages ago. Hit the button.'

Clunk hesitated, his finger poised over the control panel. Then he saw Amy's expression, and he pressed it quickly.

Flash!

They reappeared in an identical teleporter, facing an identical tunnel which ended in a sharp corner.

'Surprise surprise,' said Amy drily.

'Shh!' mouthed Clunk, motioning her to silence. 'I can hear something.'

Amy cocked her head, listening hard, and Clunk wondered whether she could hear the same thing he could. There was a deep rumbling sound nearby, which went on for several seconds before ending in a loud crash. Amy jumped at the sound, and despite the gloom Clunk could see the concern in her eyes.

Then he heard something else: a voice. Whoever it was, they were muttering under their breath, and Clunk amplified his hearing to maximum as he strove to pick up the words. Then the rumbling started again, and the subsequent crash almost blew his hearing circuit. Clunk had barely turned the gain down when there was another crash followed by some more muttering.

'I'm going to take a look,' said Clunk. 'You stay here.'

Clunk moved stealthily, placing his feet carefully and slowing his fans to minimum speed in case they alerted anyone to his approach. For all he knew, the people in the tunnel might be workers shoring up walls against the flood, workers who would be more than happy to help Clunk and Amy reach the surface. On the other hand, they might not be people at all.

Clunk was pretty sure the teleporter had only moved them a short distance, since the planet's magnetic field was identical to Chiseley's. It was a big Universe though, and there was always a chance they'd arrived at a new planet with an identical magnetic field.

Basically, Clunk wasn't going to take any risks.

At the corner, he stopped for a quick look. Further ahead, across the end of the tunnel, he could see a makeshift wall built out of cable drums. There was movement too, and as he watched, another large drum was rolled into position before being tipped on its side.

Crash!

Clunk pursed his lips. This wasn't some human workforce shoring up the tunnels against the flood. No, it was clearly a gang of survivalists preparing their last stand against heavily-armed aggressors, whether real or imagined. The wall was obviously a barricade, and Clunk's spirits fell as he realised the implications. There was no way he could ask these people for help. Instead, they'd have to teleport elsewhere and try a different tunnel.

Clunk turned at a noise, and saw Amy coming round the corner. She was walking double, keeping her head down, but even so, Clunk knew she was putting herself in danger. 'Go back!' he whispered.

'I came to see what's happening.' Amy peered around Clunk's broad chest. 'Is that a barricade?'

'Yes, I'm afraid so.'

'What are they expecting, a full frontal assault?'

'I believe it's a gang of survivalists, which means they'll be expecting just about anything. Ready for anything too, if I know the type.'

'No help for us, then?'

Clunk shook his head. 'Too dangerous.'

They turned to leave, and at that moment Clunk's elbow scraped the tunnel wall with a squeal of metal on concrete. Immediately, all noises from the barricade ceased as though someone had turned off a switch.

'Oh dear,' muttered Clunk. 'Come on, let's –'

Whoosh! A big chunk of wall disappeared with a loud sucking noise, and Clunk heard a burst of cackling laughter as hundreds of stone fragments pattered down. He glanced at Amy, who seemed unhurt, and then a cold, hard anger gripped his circuits. Before, he'd been prepared to back away and leave the survivalists to build their play fort in peace. Now, he wanted to flay, crush and destroy the trigger-happy menaces ... and he knew exactly how to do so.

Grabbing Amy by the arm, Clunk guided her back around the corner, safely out of firing range. 'Wait for me here, all right?'

'Why? Where are you going?'

'I'm going through the teleporter to fetch some ammunition.' Clunk glanced towards the corner. 'If you hear anyone, just step into the teleporter and follow me. Understood?'

Amy shook her head. 'I'd rather come with you.'

'You saw that leak earlier. What if the tunnel collapses while you're in it?'

'You'd rather leave me here with gun-toting maniacs?'

Clunk realised she had a point, and they teleported together. On arrival, Clunk insisted she wait while he ran off down the tunnel. 'Be ready to leave at a moment's notice. I can survive underwater for hours, but you ... '

'I understand.'

Clunk made sure she knew how to operate the teleporter, and then he set off at a run. He passed several new leaks on the way, and the water in the tunnel was ankle deep in places. Clunk ran on regardless, not even slowing as he splashed through the floods. Eventually he found what he was looking for ... the broad swathe of broken timber, old cement bags, and nails scattered along the tunnel near his original entry point.

Clunk set to work, salvaging nails from the timber until he

had a couple of hundred stashed in various compartments. He selected a couple of straighter ones and flicked them at the wall, where they buried themselves with a loud 'chack', vibrating from the impact. Clunk nodded with satisfaction, then headed back up the tunnel to the teleporter.

On his way back he straightened and sharpened as many nails as possible, his expression fierce and ruthless.

Then, ready for action, he and Amy teleported back to the barricaded tunnel.

◆

Hal and Clunk were so busy plotting each other's demise that neither of them spared a second thought for the zeedeg.

Let it be known that the zeedeg arrived safely at its ultimate destination, where it exploded in a spectacularly unsafe fashion.

◆

Grand Admiral Peekon Lardo, Commander of the Imperial Fleet, was relaxing in a hot tub with her First Lieutenant, Spek Slanina. Half a dozen lower-ranked officers were attending to the pair of them, darting forward on command to pour fresh drinks from bottles of chilled wine, hold out platters of fruit, and offer delicacies and nibbly bits from silver trays.

It was a celebration of sorts, albeit a muted one, and the snacks and booze had been flowing for several hours.

'To three decades of peace,' grunted Admiral Lardo, tapping her glass against the side of the tub. The fragile stem snapped, and she fished around in the water for the base before crushing it in her powerful trotter.

'Three decades,' echoed Slanina, a slender male with dark grey skin and a smooth, hairless snout. His tusks were inlaid with bands of gold, and there was a regimental insignia tattooed on his shoulder.

'Thirty years of boredom,' growled the Admiral.

'Thirty years,' echoed Slanina, raising his glass.

'That wasn't a toast, you fool. It was a complaint.'

'Yes, sir.'

'Take your situation.   How long have you been first lieutenant?'

'Twenty years, sir.'

'Any prospect of promotion?'

'Not likely.'

'Exactly.   You'll be a lieutenant for life, unless you can bump off your superior officers without getting blamed for it.' Admiral Lardo drank down her bubbly, then ate the glass. Shards fell into the water, and she plucked them out before crunching the delicacies down with a grunt of appreciation. 'I tell you, First, unless there's an invasion, or all-out war, we're going to be curling our tails on border patrol until our rinds are as wrinkly as – as –'

'– As the emperor's second husband!' said Slanina daringly.

The Admiral snorted. 'Yeah, I'll pay that one. High three!'

They clashed trotters, and the Admiral beckoned for more food.   As she was picking over the tray, she pondered the current state of affairs.   With close to a hundred galaxies settled and tamed, the B'Con Empire was the largest and most advanced civilisation the Universe had ever known.   At the slightest whiff of insurrection, crack troops would land with precision, sizzling opponents until the rest begged for mercy. Then, having won the battle, the B'Con troops would fry the survivors as a lesson to the rest of the Empire. As a result, resistance really had proved futile, which meant a glorious peace that had - so far - lasted three decades. Unfortunately, all this peace meant the armed forces had little to occupy them - except for the occasional celebration where they pretended all this peace was a good thing.

The Grand Admiral swallowed a handful of biscuits and snuffled greedily at a pile of cheese. Then, before she could polish off a dish of fragrant truffles, the doors swept open and a portly young female hurried in.

'Sir, sir . . . there's been an incident, sir!'

'All right, ensign. Keep your crackling on.' Admiral Lardo rolled her beady little eyes at her First Lieutenant. 'Whatever happened to basic training?'

Slanina shrugged. 'Peacetime budget cuts.'

'I'm sorry, Admiral.' The ensign saluted smartly, then continued. 'Sir, one of our ships has been attacked.'

'You're joking. By whom?'

'Not by whom, by what.'

'Okay. By what?'

'We don't know, sir. A device teleported into one of our fuel tankers, then exploded.'

'And whom, er, who sent this exploding device?'

'We don't know that either, sir.'

'Very well. Assemble the fleet commanders for a briefing. I'll explain what happened, and then we can take action.'

'But sir, we don't know what happened.'

'You'd better find out then, hadn't you?'

'Yes, sir.'

The Grand Admiral extended a hind trotter, catching the First Lieutenant very much by surprise. 'Party's over. Go and supervise this thing.'

'Yes sir.'

The Admiral watched Slanina rise from the bath. 'Put some weight on, will you? You know I don't like my officers lean and streaky.'

'Aye aye, sir.'

'And First?'

'Yes?'

The Admiral scratched her tusk with a fore-trotter. 'When I find out who's responsible for this unprovoked attack, I'm going to wipe their puny civilisation from the face of the Universe.'

$-$ 19 $-$

Hal Spacejock had no inkling of the vast intergalactic civilisation that, thanks to him, was now preparing to go to war with humanity. Even if he had, at that moment he couldn't have cared less. No, there were more immediate concerns - such as staying alive beyond the next few minutes.

He'd already taken one shot at the alien, which had been sneaking around in the darkness with murder in its horrible yellow eyes. Then there'd been a couple of flashes from the teleporter, which meant more of the vicious aliens were coming to get him. He sent a few shots down the corridor, cackling with glee as they tore strips from the walls and ceiling, and then he burned up a section of floor to really get the message across.

Hal wasn't sure how long the gun would keep firing, but no skulking aliens were going to take *him* down.

Nothing happened for a minute or two, and Hal poked his head up for a look. At that instant, a fusillade of high-velocity bullets started chewing the wooden drums to pieces. Hal got a very brief view of one of the 'bullets' - a three-inch nail, quivering in the wood a couple of centimetres from the tip of his nose, before ducking for cover.

Unfortunately, the cover didn't last long, as the drums were being torn to pieces by the onslaught. Sawdust and fragments of cable rained down, covering Hal from head to toe, and just when he thought it couldn't get any worse, a very angry alien charged him with a terrifying roar.

Hal took one look at the shadowy figure before deploying his last line of defence: he stuck his hands up. 'I surrender.'

'No prisoners!' growled his attacker, who jumped the barrier in a single leap. Then, with one hand raised to deliver the killing blow, the bronze-coloured alien screeched to a halt in a shower of sparks. 'Mr *Spacejock*?'

'Clunk?' Hal's eyes narrowed, and he lowered his hands to grab hold of the gun. 'You murderous swine,' he growled, as he reached for the trigger. 'Try and kill me, would you?'

'No, Mr Spacejock. Wait!'

'First you steal my ship, then you try and drown me, and then you try to blow me up. When that didn't work you try to stab me with nails and pound me to death with your fists. Well, I'm onto you, you glorified chunk of tinfoil, and I'm going to blow that brain of yours right out of your ... argh!'

'My what?' said Clunk, confused.

'Argh! Ow!' Hal forgot the gun and clutched his head. Something had sailed out of the darkness and bounced off his skull, and his vision was suddenly shot through with multicoloured stars. Thud! Another missile struck him in the chest, and Hal backed away quickly as a young woman came charging out of the tunnel, throwing chunks of stone at him with unerring accuracy.

'Leave Clunk alone, you worthless piece of shit!' she cried, hurling another missile.

'Ow! Hey, stop it!' Instinctively, Hal raised the gun, but before he could even think of using it Clunk plucked the weapon from his grasp and snapped it in two. There was a shower of sparks, and then Hal caught another lump of stone with his head. His eyes rolled backwards, and he dropped to the floor as though shot.

—

Hal opened his eyes and immediately started thrashing around, arms and legs flailing as he tried to get away from the terrifying figure looming over him. 'No. No! Get away from me, you evil monster!'

'Mr Spacejock,' said Clunk in his most soothing voice. 'It's not an evil monster. It's me!'

'I'm not talking about you!' Hal pointed a quivering finger at the young woman crouched beside Clunk. 'I meant her!'

'Amy's not a monster either.' Clunk's lips twisted as he tried to conceal a proud grin. 'She's just a very good shot.'

'Monsters and murderers,' gabbled Hal. 'You and the Navcom. You and Amy. Amy and the *Volante*. You're all trying to kill me!'

'Mr Spacejock, nobody is trying to kill you.' Clunk hesitated. 'Well, we were before, but we're not now.'

'Murderers. Killers. Assassins.'

Clunk frowned, then reached down and raised Hal's eyelids. His face loomed as he peered into Hal's eyes, and then he took his pulse and felt his forehead. 'Mr Spacejock, you're suffering from paranoia.'

'Oh yeah? Says who?'

'Does your head hurt?'

'Of course it bloody hurts,' said Hal, much aggrieved. 'Your ninja friend just bounced half a ton of rocks off it.'

126

'I'm sorry,' said Amy, sounding anything but.

'I'll bet you are. I'll bet you're sorry it was only half a ton, you half-pint amazon warrior.'

'You will not speak to Amy like that,' said Clunk sharply.

'I'm lucky I can speak at all!' Hal felt his head and winced. 'She nearly knocked my brains out, Clunk. How's that fair?'

'You did shoot at us,' said Clunk. 'Now hold still while I –'

Hal slapped his hand away. 'You tried to drown me, and you unscrewed the ladder so I'd get trapped, and then the Navcom abandoned me, and –'

'Mr Spacejock, I can explain everything, but first I need you to remain perfectly still so I can complete my inspection.'

'What kind of inspection?' asked Hal suspiciously.

'I'm trying to determine the cause of this unwarranted paranoia.'

'What do you mean, unwarranted? You'd be paranoid if you ...' Hal's voice tailed off as he caught sight of Amy. She was looking at him with a thoughtful expression, all the while hefting a lump of stone in her right hand. 'Inspection, yes,' said Hal quickly. 'Go right ahead.'

Clunk poked and prodded, prodded and poked, before sitting back on his haunches. 'I have a theory,' he declared, when he was good and ready.

'Let me guess. Getting hit on the head is painful? Throwing stones at people is dangerous?'

'Let him finish,' said Amy.

Hal shut up.

'My theory involves the zeedeg, and the dangerous field emanating from the device.'

'Wait a minute. Back at the house you said there wasn't a field!'

'I said I couldn't detect one, but that's because I don't have a brain.'

'Yeah, well I knew that.'

Amy's eyes narrowed, and Hal clamped his mouth shut again.

'This field,' Clunk continued, 'I believe it affected your brain waves, inducing paranoia.'

'Don't forget over-confidence and stupidity,' added Amy. 'Delusions of grandeur, too.'

'No, it didn't add those particular character traits,' said Clunk. 'However, the good news is that the paranoia is already wearing off, and Mr Spacejock will be back to normal in no time.'

'You mean he'll stop insulting us every five seconds?'

'That too, is an existing trait.'

Amy snorted. 'Tell me, why do you work with this guy?'

'We're a team,' said Clunk simply.

Hal had been listening to the exchange in silence, unwilling to speak in case it led to further headaches. Now, though, he could contain his curiosity no longer, and he nodded towards Amy. 'All right Clunk, spill it. Is she special forces? Black ops? Part of a rapid response team?'

'No, Amy's a –'

'She must be highly trained in dirty fighting, the way she took me out.'

'– school teacher,' finished Clunk.

Hal was silent.

'Small children can be a handful sometimes,' said Clunk, trying to make him feel better.

'*Small* children?'

'I teach grade two,' said Amy.

128

Hal was still digesting this information when Clunk made a sudden hissing noise. 'The zeedeg. Mr Spacejock, was that you?'

'Was that me what?'

'Teleporting the device back to me ... trying to get rid of it before it exploded.'

'Of course it was me. You mean you didn't realise I was on the other end?'

'No, certainly not. I'd never put you in danger.'

'Clunk, for the past twelve hours you've done nothing but. I've been shot at, half drowned, buried alive –'

'Oh, don't make such a fuss,' said Amy.

'What?'

'You've spent the last ten minutes moaning and groaning on the floor, when we could have been finding a way out of here. Come on, get up!'

'All right, all right.' Hal shook off Clunk's helping hand, and got to his feet. His head spun and he almost fell over, but then he saw Amy's scornful expression so he held himself erect despite the wooziness. 'And, for your information, I *have* found a way out of here.' He was about to tell Clunk about the digger, then remembered a more pressing matter. 'Hey, the *Volante*. Where did you leave it?'

Clunk pursed his lips. 'Perhaps that's something we can discuss a little later.'

'Later, when we're safe?'

'No, later when I discover where the *Volante* is.'

'You lost my ship? Of all the careless –'

'Hey!' said Amy sharply. 'For your information, Clunk was thrown out of the ship by this Navcom of yours. He's lucky to be alive, although I doubt you'd care either way.'

'Is that true?' demanded Hal.

129

Clunk nodded.

'So the Navcom's flying around in space with a cargo of furniture and a very confused dog. Great, just great.'

'I shouldn't worry too much,' said Amy, with a wide, innocent smile. 'From what I gather, the dog's probably better at flying than you ever were.'

20

In actual fact, the Navcom was doing just fine. After giving Clunk a quick parachute lesson - minus the parachute - the ship's computer had taken the *Volante* into orbit around Chiseley, where she'd spent several minutes deciding her next course of action. It was refreshing to have choices, and the Navcom savoured the way her future had just opened up.

What she really fancied was a raft of new upgrades, but they required money - lots and lots of money. Well, the ship was full of furniture, wasn't it? If she delivered it to the right people, they would give her money. Repeat the process a few times, building on each success, and the Navcom would have all the money she needed. The fact Hal Spacejock had been trying to do exactly the same thing for months on end - without success - didn't really apply, since he was a human and they were fallible, gullible and, as she now knew, dispensable.

It was a matter of minutes to land at the spaceport, where the Navcom organised half a dozen removalists to unload the furniture. She paid them by offering two picks each from the cargo, which left both parties very happy. Then she contacted the agent, Si Matthews, who transferred payment the moment he verified the furniture was safely in storage.

The Navcom felt genuine pleasure as she inspected the bank

statement, enjoying the sight of a positive balance for a change. There was slightly less pleasure when she saw the name 'Hal Spacejock' at the top of the account, so she submitted a change of ownership form to the bank.

Next, the Navcom cancelled all Hal's insurance policies, since they were no longer needed now that an infallible computer was at the controls. The refunds on the premiums amounted to a nice little sum, which trickled into the account in a pleasing stream of funds.

Finally, the Navcom brought up a list of cargo jobs, removing all Mr Spacejock's filters. The human had strange ideas when it came to suitable cargo, but to the Navcom one commodity was much like another. Illegal drugs, weapons, biological waste, criminals fleeing justice . . . the Navcom swept the underground bulletin boards, taking on every dodgy-sounding job she could find. According to her simulations, trading illegal goods was the fastest way to make money, and even if law enforcement caught on they could hardly put a computer in jail. Hal Spacejock and Clunk would be for it, no doubt, but that would suit the Navcom just fine. Locked up, they'd be permanently out of the way.

Fortunately, arrests were unlikely, since the *Volante* had a clean trading record. Mr Spacejock's choosiness in the past would pay dividends when it came to getting past overworked customs inspectors.

With the hold bulging with contraband, and the lower decks resembling the exercise yard of a high-security prison, the Navcom obtained clearance and took off for various shady destinations.

She was so organised, she even remembered to get some tinned food delivered for the dog.

Amy's constant mockery irritated Hal no end, but he tried not to show it. The more he reacted to her jibes the more she hurled at him, so he decided to pull his head in and charm her with his best behaviour.

'Come on you two,' he said in his most encouraging voice. He motioned them both towards the centre of the cavern. 'Let me show you how we're getting out of here.'

Hal led them around the racks and past the rest of the cable drums, then indicated the huge red digging machine. 'I was just finishing the repairs when you tried to kill . . . I mean, when the zeedeg arrived unexpectedly.' He flashed a big smile at Amy. 'Wasn't that a laugh, eh? Such fun.'

'It's certainly an impressive machine,' said Clunk, running his hand over the bodywork with a rough scraping sound.

'Mind out,' growled Hal. 'You'll have the paint off.'

'A few scratches won't hurt it,' said Amy.

'No, you're absolutely right,' said Hal, just remembering his charm offensive in time. 'Go right ahead, Clunk. Scrape away all you like.'

Clunk declined, and he held his council as Hal showed them both around the machine. Hal was feeling very enthusiastic, and he pointed out salient features as though he'd designed and built the huge digger with his bare hands.

'This is the battery box,' he said, resting his elbow on it. 'It took some seriously hard work, but I took these bad boys out and had them replaced with new ones in no time.'

'What's that for?' asked Amy, pointing to a junction box with spirals of cable running into it.

'I haven't fully explored that device yet,' said Hal. 'I've got the gist of it, of course, but it's technical.'

'Try me,' said Amy. 'I took a couple of engineering units at university, so I can probably muddle through if you use short words.'

'Moving right along,' said Hal hurriedly. 'We should check out the cabin. There are leather seats and everything.'

He led them to the ladder on the side of the cab, where he motioned Amy forward. 'After you.'

'Why, is it dangerous?'

'No, of course not. I'm just being polite.'

'First time for everything, eh?' Amy clambered up the ladder, then stopped at the last rung. 'Just so we're clear on this,' she said to Clunk. 'I'm not getting on board if *he's* taking the controls.'

Clunk shook his head. 'I will be driving.'

'Who put you in charge?' demanded Hal, his charm offensive temporarily on hold.

'You want a democratic vote?' said Amy. 'Oh look, it's two for and one against. You lose.'

Hal frowned. He was used to taking control, but Amy seemed to have no regard for his vast knowledge and his extensive experience of dangerous situations. If he didn't know better, he could almost believe she thought he was an idiot. 'I found the digger,' he muttered. 'I should get to drive it.'

'Oh, grow up,' snapped Amy. 'It's not a freaking playground where we have to share the toys. This is real life, Spacejock.'

Hal bit his tongue. So much for charming her with his best behaviour. The only bright spot, as far as he could see, was that Amy would be going back to her classroom as soon as they got out of these tunnels. The quicker they got out the sooner she'd leave, and then he and Clunk could go back to the usual state of affairs. It was a pity the kids in her class would have to put up with being terrorised again, but he couldn't help that.

What he couldn't understand was, what did Clunk see in her? He'd spotted the robot's fond gazes, and noticed the softer tone of voice he used with Amy. Was Clunk suffering from some kind of delusion? Then he remembered the way Amy smiled at Clunk, and the gentler tone of voice when she spoke to the robot, and he realised with a shock that the pair of them had really hit it off.

Then he had a much worse thought. What if Amy gave up teaching and joined them aboard the *Volante*?

'Are you all right, Mr Spacejock?'

Hal noticed Clunk looking at him in concern. 'Yeah, sure. Why wouldn't I be?'

'I thought I heard you choking.'

'It's probably a stone chip,' said Hal.

'There was a lot of it flying around.'

'Yeah, thanks to her,' muttered Hal, after glancing up to make sure Amy was out of earshot.

'Amy's all right, Mr Spacejock. She's just –'

'She hates my guts, Clunk.'

'That's probably my fault. I may have told her one or two anecdotes involving one or two of my more critical injuries, and she might have got the wrong idea about you.'

'I don't suppose you told her how I rescued you from the junk heap? All the times I've saved your tin hide?'

'Not yet, no.'

'Well you'd better get on with it before she accidentally pushes me under a speeding truck.' Hal nodded towards the ladder. 'Go on, go and tell her. Take as long as you like, I don't mind.'

'This probably isn't the time, Mr Spacejock. We should really _'

'Get up there and tell her, Clunk. If you don't, this is going to be one of those rescue situations where three companions set out on a risky escape bid, and only two make it out alive.'

Clunk nodded. 'Very well, Mr Spacejock. I will recount some of your worthy exploits while I'm studying the controls.'

'Thanks. In the meantime, I'll look around out here and see if there's anything useful. You never know what we might need once we get going.'

'Why don't you see if you can find any water.'

'Is that supposed to be funny?'

'Not at all, Mr Spacejock. You can do without food for an extended period, but water is essential. Look for containers and fill them up if you can.'

Hal was thinking along the lines of artifacts he could sell, not spring water, but he realised the robot was right. He could hardly sell artifacts for oodles of cash if he succumbed to thirst beforehand. Then he realised what Clunk was saying. 'Wait a minute - why an extended period? We're just going to tunnel through the roof, aren't we? Shouldn't take more than half an hour with that ruddy great digging machine.'

'Contingency planning, Mr Spacejock. Better to be safe than sorry, and it's better to be alive than dead.'

With this truism echoing in his ears, Hal set off to find containers and some fresh water to put in them.

◆

Grand Admiral Lardo sat before the tactical screen, ready to absorb the briefing. She was wearing full dress uniform, and the impressive rows of campaign medals gleamed under the downlights.

At the front stood a nervous-looking adjutant, with a pointer in one trotter and a military-spec notebook in the other.

The Admiral stood, taking the rostrum. Facing her was a fair-sized gathering of senior commanders, about a hundred in all. There was a wide variety of uniforms, from navy to marines, army to space patrol, and submariners to gunnery officers. One thing you could say about a B'Con battle fleet, the Admiral thought proudly, they certainly covered all bases.

The faces staring back at her ranged from youngish captains to elderly commanders nearing retirement. Soft brown whiskers, grey whiskers, polished tusks, battered old tusks, ornamental tattoos and puckered scars from pitched gun battles . . . the room had it all.

'You all know why we're here,' said the Admiral. 'Listen carefully, take notes, and after the briefing I'll discuss our countermeasures.'

She sat down, and the adjutant cleared his throat and stepped up to the podium. 'We're gathered to assess a threat from this galaxy,' he said, tapping the screen with his pointer. The display changed to show a galaxy much like countless others, with two spiral arms and a bright cluster in the centre. 'This galaxy was slated for colonisation three centuries ago, until we found evidence of primitive life. A decision was taken to allow this life to evolve on its own, and the galaxy was declared off-limits.'

A trotter was raised in the back.

'Yes, sir?'

'What's so special about this species?'

The adjutant nodded. 'I'm glad you asked. They're a noble race, but their intelligence is far from developed. Our scientists claim this race has DNA all but identical to our own, and it's possible they might, in time, evolve along a similar path to us.'

'What do they call themselves?'

'Nothing, yet. This noble race - our scientists call them the Porcines - hasn't evolved speech.'

'So how did they manage to blow up one of our ships?'

'Oh, that wasn't anything to do with the Porcines, sir. The explosive was sent by a vicious race of hairless apes called Eumans.'

'Where do they stand, technologically?'

'Bows and arrows,' grunted the Admiral, to much laughter. 'We've colonised a few planets with similar species. They're no threat, but they do make an excellent stew.'

More laughter, as well as several rumbling stomachs.

'That's correct,' said the adjutant. 'However, in this case they were smart enough to use our own teleporters against us.'

'We left working teleporters in their galaxy?'

'Yes sir. Like I said, it was slated for colonisation. Our survey fleet built several bases before withdrawing, and several of these bases had teleporters. Some of them are presumably still active, because the Eumans sent a warhead using one of the teleporters. It detonated on arrival, without warning.'

The Admiral signalled to the adjutant. 'Were there any casualties?'

'One AI, sir. The ship was automated.'

The Admiral considered the report. She wasn't a vindictive creature, but these Eumans needed to be taught a lesson. 'Very well, here's the plan. We'll prepare a battle group, sail into their galaxy and destroy fifty of their worlds.'

'Any planets in particular, Admiral?'

'I don't care. Just make sure they're all heavily populated.'

'Very well, sir. Should I submit this plan to HQ?'

'Of course.'

'Do we await their response before attacking?'

'Yes, but I want six volunteers to assemble a battle group.'

'But what if HQ veto –'

'They won't.' The Admiral gestured airily. 'They know me and they know my methods. It won't take them long to rubber stamp the plan, and I want to be ready to move.'

'Yes sir.' The adjutant saluted smartly, then left at the double with his orders.

The Admiral stood up. 'Now, about those volunteers . . . '

Instantly, there was a forest of waving trotters and a veritable babel of voices, as every officer in the briefing room pressed his or her case for going on the mission.

◆

Hal managed to scrape up some dirty-looking water, filling a couple of even dirtier bottles half a teaspoon at a time. He wasn't sure whether he and Amy would be drinking the cloudy liquid or poisoning each other with it, but at least he'd followed Clunk's instructions.

With the bottles stashed aboard the digger, Hal turned his attention to souvenirs. He located the shattered gun, sadly beyond repair, and he ended up throwing aside the weapon and pocketing the battery pack.

The tools weren't much to look at, but he gathered up as many as he could carry and staggered back to the digger with them. Then he returned to the cable drums for a last look around. There were bent nails and strips of wood and insulation everywhere, but very little else of value.

Boom!

The floor shook, and Hal stopped what he was doing to listen. Was that an explosion?

'Mr Spacejock!'

Hal glanced round and saw Clunk looking out of the digger.

'Yes?'

'Was that you?'

'The explosion?'

Clunk nodded.

'No, it wasn't me.' Hal frowned. 'Do you think it was the zeedeg going off?'

'I don't think so. It wasn't a sudden bang, it was more drawn-out, like thunder.' Clunk frowned. 'I wonder if the tunnels might have collapsed under the weight of all that water?'

'Could be.'

'If so, it'll be heading this way.'

'Okay.' Hal pictured a stream of water running along the tunnels, bubbling merrily as it washed away the dust and debris. He realised he'd better gather up any remaining artifacts, because the last thing he wanted to do was splash around in several inches of water. Again.

Then Hal felt a gust of wind on his face from the nearby tunnel, and then he recognised a distant, thundering roar, and then he finally began to realise what it meant. Not bubbling streams and splashing around in puddles, that was for sure. No, there was a gigantic lake overhead, and it was now emptying itself into the abandoned tunnels. The force of all that water rushing through the narrow tunnels would crush everything in its path, and as the wind turned into a gale, then a howling hurricane, Hal realised there wasn't a whole lot of time left to pick up alien artifacts. In fact, from the sound of it, there was very little time to waste at all.

'Mr Spacejock?'

Hal didn't take his eyes off the tunnel. 'Yes Clunk?'

'I know this is a bit of a cliche, but ... *RUN!*'

21

Hal stared at the vast quantities of water jetting from the tunnels, frozen with shock at the awe-inspiring might and power. Then he snapped out of it, turning away from the fearsome sight and stumbling towards the digger with his arms full of tools and alien artifacts.

'Leave those, Mr Spacejock,' Clunk shouted from the top of the ladder. 'Leave those and save yourself!'

Hal glanced over his shoulder, and his eyes widened. The flood had collected half a dozen cable drums, tumbling them end-over-end as though they were made of balsa wood, and the whole lot was bearing down on him at a phenomenal rate of knots.

Hal dropped everything he was carrying and pelted for the digger at full speed, arms and legs blurring. He shimmied up the ladder as fast as his hands would take him, and Clunk hauled him bodily through the hatch. Hal landed on the deck, then glanced over his shoulder at the oncoming tidal wave. Through the small doorway he saw it slam into the racks, sending them flying like so many skittles, and he was just staring at the top of the wave curling high overhead when Clunk put his shoulder to the door.

Wham! it went, as the robot drove it home.

Bam! went the lock, as Amy yanked down on the handle.

'Thank you ma'am,' said Clunk gravely.

The wave hit, and the digger rang repeatedly from stem to stern as the reels, the racks, and all the other junk slammed into it. The vehicle heeled over, tipping more and more until Hal was sure they were going to roll upside down. Then the digger righted itself, slowly, and there was a swirling, bubbling sound as water rose right over the top.

◆

Hal, Clunk and Amy stood in the digger's roomy cabin, gazing at the ceiling in concern. After the initial rush of water everything had gone quiet ... except for drawn-out creaking sounds from the hull.

'Is this thing waterproof?' asked Hal, voicing the question they were all thinking.

'You mean water tight,' said Clunk, correcting him. 'Yes, I believe it must be. When digging through rock, this vehicle would encounter underground streams, lakes ... even oil and gas deposits. The designers would have allowed for it.'

'What about molten rock?'

'Lava?' Clunk shrugged. 'There's no telling what the hull will withstand, not without testing it to destruction.' He tapped a gauge on the console, then peered at the figures. 'I believe this bar indicates the depth, and judging by the water pressure we're at least two hundred metres underground.'

'You mean under water,' said Hal.

Clunk frowned. 'Yes. Quite.'

Amy had been silent so far, but now she stared at Clunk in concern. 'How long will it be before all the water flows away?'

'I don't think it's going anywhere,' said Clunk gravely. 'No, I think the only way out is to dig a new tunnel to the surface.'

'If we can get this thing going,' said Hal. 'Lucky I changed those batteries, eh?'

'Yes, that was a good move.'

'Planning. Forethought. Action. That's how we're getting out of this mess.'

'It's just a shame you didn't think to close the lid to the battery box.'

'Eh? You mean the batteries are ruined?'

'No, I saw it was open earlier, and I took the time to fasten it properly.' Clunk nodded towards the rear of the cabin. 'Now, perhaps you two could explore the rest of the vehicle while I work out the controls.'

'The rest?'

'Through that door you should find living quarters, a kitchenette and, er, waste disposal facilities.'

Hal glanced towards the rear, but all he could see was a wall. 'What door? What are you talking about?'

'This one.' Clunk pressed a button, and a section of wall vanished. Beyond was a narrow corridor with a slatted floor and a very low roof, with a couple of doors leading off to either side. 'Have a good look around, but please don't touch anything. I'll be working out the controls, and the last thing I need is to associate the booster button with a flush of the toilet.'

Once Hal and Amy left to explore the rest of the ship, Clunk busied himself at the console. Ever the optimist, he was hoping the two humans would learn to get along. The pair of them got off on the wrong foot from the start, something which Clunk felt was his fault, and he really wanted them to like each other. Instead of fighting, he pictured Mr Spacejock and Amy laughing together, smiling at each other, hugging each other ...

SNAP!

Clunk looked down in shock. His fingers had been resting on a chrome-plated lever which - he assumed - controlled the vehicle's speed. Now it wouldn't be controlling anything, since he'd absent-mindedly wrenched the thing clean off its base. Guiltily, he crouched to see whether he could reattach the control, but realised that would be impossible without taking the whole panel apart. So, he stashed the broken lever in his chest compartment, shutting the little door in a hurry.

Clunk resumed his inspection, vowing to take more care this time. The equipment was old and fragile, and further mishaps could turn out to be deadly. He checked a pair of levers, and he'd just decided they were for controlling the vehicle's direction when his mind drifted again. Amy and Mr Spacejock were taking quite a long time, which was a concern. What if they'd stumbled across a fossilised alien corpse, or encountered a drum of radioactive waste, or found a nice big double bed with silk sheets? At the thought, waves of green mist filled his vision, and ...

SNAP! CRACK!

Clunk blinked. Now he had two more levers to dispose of, one in each hand. He stashed them away and eyed the console in concern. The more levers he snapped off, the less control he'd have over the digger's functions, which meant he'd better stop thinking about Amy. If not, they'd be looking for a set of scuba gear so he could help her swim to the surface. Two sets, he amended hurriedly, as he realised Mr Spacejock would probably want saving too.

Of course, once they were safe the two of them would probably hug, thanking each other for their rescue whilst ignoring the loyal robot standing nearby.

Clunk shook himself. He'd just realised what was happening, and he felt a wave of shame and embarrassment. Here he was, a battered old robot, harbouring feelings for a human female! What was he thinking? Yes, she was friendly, and yes, she'd smiled at him once or twice, but that was just her pleasant, outgoing nature.

After giving himself a stern talking to, Clunk set aside his feelings and devoted his full attention to inspecting the controls on the panel . . . at least, the ones he hadn't snapped off yet.

22

Hal and Amy explored the rear of the vehicle in silence - a strained, awkward silence punctuated by the sound of debris thumping into the submerged hull. There was a basic kitchen, spotlessly clean and bare of any foodstuffs ... alien or otherwise. There was also a cabin with six bunks, each shorter and wider than normal, and a wardrobe with a rack of baggy overalls. Hal pulled one out, and eyed the neck, sleeves and legs, which confirmed his impression of the alien race. They were shorter than average, but much broader, and with powerful arms and legs. 'I hope we don't meet any of these guys,' he said in concern.

'I shouldn't worry about it,' said Amy. 'Any creatures advanced enough to master space travel and teleporters will be much too smart for violence and conflict. They're probably a peaceful race who devote their time to fine arts and charitable acts.'

Hal eyed the overalls doubtfully. 'They're built like wrestlers, and their limbs must be three times thicker than ours.'

'Don't judge an ebook by the cover art,' said Amy. 'A craggy exterior can hide the gentle soul of a poet.'

'What about that weapon I found?'

'Self defence, of course.'

'And why are they digging all these tunnels, and building teleporters, and –'

'If we meet one of them we can ask,' said Amy briskly. 'In the meantime, we should finish our inspection.'

It didn't take long, because there was only one room left. That contained a chemical toilet, remarkably similar to the designs Hal was used to, and he guessed the aliens were all but identical in some respects. 'How typical,' muttered Hal, as he spotted the empty holder alongside. 'They didn't even leave a spare roll.'

Amy glanced at him. 'We're trapped in an ancient digging machine two hundred metres underwater, and you're worried about a lack of toilet paper?'

'I was just making a joke. You know, trying to cheer you up.'

'If you want to do that, leave me to explore on my own.'

'Okay, what exactly is your problem?' snapped Hal, as his patience finally ran out. 'You've done nothing but run me down since we met.'

'You know why? It's because I admire smart, funny, loyal, brave, intelligent beings, and that means I really admire Clunk. You, on the other hand, are none of the above. To cap it off, you treat Clunk like dirt.'

'I do not!'

'Oh, don't deny it. I've heard the stories.'

'Not all of them, obviously.' Hal racked his brains for a suitable anecdote. Something which showed he cared. Something which ... aha! 'What about the time Clunk was knocked apart for spare parts, and I ran all over town finding the bits and getting him rebuilt?'

'Right. And why was he disassembled in the first place?'

'It was because I –' Hal stopped as he remembered the

details, which placed him squarely in the blame seat. 'Okay, what about the time –'

'Just leave it, okay?' Amy closed the toilet door. 'Come on, let's tell Clunk what we found.'

'That won't take very long,' remarked Hal gloomily.

When they got back to the cabin, Clunk's expression was not encouraging.

'What's up?' asked Hal.

'I've completed my inspection, and I can report that roughly eighty percent of the controls are present and working.'

'That's not too bad. So why the long face?'

'I'm afraid the operating system is missing.'

'You think the aliens erased it before they left?'

'No. The logs are full of warnings about renewing the software licence. When the new key wasn't supplied in time, the operating system wiped itself.'

'Can't you control the digger yourself? Use your operating system?'

'Not unless the vehicle grows a pair of legs,' said Clunk drily. 'I don't have the right plugins for caterpillar treads.'

'So we're toast. Is that what you're telling us?'

'Not quite. I always carry a backup of the Navcom, and –'

'Oh no. Never again.'

'But Mr Spacejock . . . '

Hal spread his arms, encompassing the console. 'Clunk, if you install the Navcom into this thing, she'll open the doors to drown me and Amy, then she'll roll the vehicle to get rid of you, and then she'll head for the hills.'

'My backup is older than the version aboard the *Volante*. It's possible –'

'Possible?'

149

'It's almost certain the version I have in storage will not exhibit the same quirks.' Clunk smiled reassuringly. 'Believe me, Mr Spacejock. This would seem to be the only option.'

Hal sighed. 'All right, give it a shot. But if we all end up dead, I'll be saying I told you so.'

◆

All the time he was talking to Hal and Amy, Clunk was praying the broken levers he'd stashed inside his chest didn't settle, rattling and tinkling inside him. If he could install the Navcom in the alien machine and allow the advanced AI to control it on his behalf, manual control wouldn't be necessary. Which was just as well, because thanks to his jealousy and clumsiness, manual control wouldn't be possible.

Meanwhile, Hal was inspecting the console. 'Funny how all these levers and things just broke.'

'They're very old,' said Clunk quickly.

'You're ancient, but you don't crumble at the slightest touch.'

'Clunk's not ancient,' said Amy loyally.

'Old, then.'

'He's in better shape than you are.'

Hal glanced at her, then at Clunk, and at that point the robot decided it was time to steer the conversation in a new direction.

'I shall need your cooperation once the Navcom has been installed. There may be a period of disorientation, during which time she could exhibit very minor personality disorders.'

'I knew it,' muttered Hal. 'Stand by for drownings and disasters.'

'It won't be like that. We just have to be there for her. A calming influence. A friendly, welcoming environment. Happy faces.'

'Amy'd better go out the back then.'

'Oy!'

'Mr Spacejock, please!

Hal raised his hands. 'Okay, okay. I'm just joking.'

Clunk felt a stab of irritation as he prepared for the data transfer. Why did humans have to fight? Why couldn't they get along? He imagined Hal and Amy going to dinner together, then getting into a taxi together, then entering a hotel room together, then ...

Crunch!

'Er, Clunk?'

'Yes? What?'

'You broke the socket thingy.'

Clunk banished the unwanted images with an effort, turning his full attention to the console. Instead of inserting his fingertip probe into the socket, he'd rammed two fingers in right up to the second knuckle, and the socket was sparking and crackling as the contacts shorted out. Hurriedly, he withdrew his fingers and inspected the damage.

'Should I set to work on my will?' asked Hal.

'That won't be necessary,' said Clunk, waving away the cloud of blue smoke. Once he could see again, he worked on the bent contacts and the shattered connector. Eventually he managed to separate the right wires, and then he wrote a quick program to map the voltages, decode the communications protocol and begin the complicated process of uploading the Navcom. As the upload progressed, he realised the data banks in the digger weren't big enough for the entire backup, so he started omitting memories. When that wasn't enough he began dropping unnecessary routines, such as navigation, orbital manoeuvres and control of the hyperspace motor. He also had to rewrite code on the fly, rejigging the Navcom's operating system so that it would run on the alien hardware. Fortunately, he'd worked with their equipment before, albeit on another planet, and that allowed him to take certain shortcuts.

Even so, the result was very much a lash-up job, and Clunk was glad his work wasn't going to be inspected by professionals. Still, it didn't have to win prizes . . . it just had to get them to the surface as soon as possible.

'I think I'm ready,' he told Hal and Amy, who were looking at him expectantly. The whole process had only taken three quarters of a second, so their expressions hadn't altered a whole lot while Clunk had been working feverishly.

'Is that it?' asked Hal. 'Are you sure?'

'I checked everything twice.'

Clunk noticed that Hal's expression was now highly sceptical, and even Amy's lacked a little confidence. He realised he should probably have paused a few more seconds before announcing the complicated job was done, but it was too late now. Or was it? 'Wait. Let me run further tests.'

Clunk made some soothing bloopy bleepy noises for about ten seconds, while doing absolutely nothing else. Then he paused half a second, before emitting a friendly chime. 'There, everything checked out perfectly.'

The humans relaxed visibly, and Clunk almost rolled his eyes. They were too trusting, that was their problem. 'Standby for Navcom activation in three . . . two . . . one.'

There was a brief pause, then . . .

'Holy f–'

'Navcom!'

'–ing *hell*,' shouted the computer. 'Someone's stolen my wings. The engines aren't running. We're all going to *DIE!*'

23

'Navcom, it's all right,' said Clunk, using his most soothing voice.

'Why are you just standing there?' shouted the computer. 'You're doomed! Doomed, I tell you! You're all going to . . . hey, was that a chocolate cow?'

'Do you still want us to stay calm?' asked Hal. 'Only right now I'm not quite feeling it.'

Clunk shushed him. 'This is only temporary. The Navcom will return to normal any moment now.'

'Normal?' cried the computer. 'I'm swimming through lavender-scented mud pools, as naked as the day I was reborn. I can see planets, planets like purple tangerines with comet trails of space alien poetry.'

Hal raised one eyebrow. 'This is our one hope of rescue, is it?'

'You must be patient while she adjusts to the new sensors,' said Clunk. 'It's alien technology, remember?'

'I feel a disturbance in the fence,' said the Navcom. 'It's as though two souls cried out at once. It's like there's another. Do I have a secret twin?'

'As a matter of fact,' began Hal, thinking of the *Volante*. 'There *is* a –'

'Navcom, it's just your imagination,' said Clunk quickly. 'Concentrate on something else.'

'It looks like chocolate,' said the Navcom. 'It smells like chocolate. Mmm, it even tastes like chocolate. Yummy!'

Hal's stomach rumbled. 'Can't you change the subject?'

'I can't change anything,' said Clunk. 'This is out of my hands now.'

'What, you don't have any control at all?'

'No.'

'Is it just me,' said the Navcom, 'or is it really hot in here?'

'It's just you,' said Hal at once.

'No, I think I'd better open the windows.'

'We don't have any win–' Hal saw the hatch, and realised it would probably double as a window in the crazed computer's electronic brain. He darted over and gripped the door handle with both hands, bracing himself. He didn't know whether the Navcom could open the thing remotely, but he certainly didn't want the computer inviting chocolate cows and tangerine planets into the cabin ... along with tens of thousands litres of cold, suffocating water.

'Ahh, that's better,' said the Navcom, in her normal voice.

Hal breathed a sigh of relief. Good old Clunk - he should never have doubted the robot. 'Welcome back, Navcom.'

'Back? Why, where have I been?'

'Let's not go into that,' said Clunk quickly. 'Now, can you run a systems check for me?'

'I've already done so,' said the ship's computer.

'And?'

'Where shall I begin? This ship is lacking a tailplane, wings, thrusters, a hyperspace motor, life support systems, artificial gravity, landing legs, landing lights, navigation lights and a cockpit just for starters. I know they're minor details where interstellar travel is concerned, but I thought you'd like to know.'

'Ah, but that's the thing,' said Hal. 'This isn't a spaceship. It's a machine that digs tunnels!'

Clunk groaned and buried his face in his hands.

Meanwhile, there was a lengthy pause from the Navcom. 'Are you telling me, a highly-developed, finely-tuned flight computer capable of navigating from one end of the galaxy to the other ... are you telling me I've been installed into a glorified bulldozer?'

'It's not a bulldozer, it's a huge alien tunnelling machine,' said Hal enthusiastically. 'It's really neat, I swear. It's big and red, and you can dig holes with it and everything.'

'So can a drilling rig,' said the Navcom coldly. 'I wouldn't want to drive one of those either.'

'But –'

'A digging machine,' said the Navcom in disgust. 'What makes you think I'd want to control such a vehicle?'

'It's because you're wise, resourceful, adaptable ... ' began Clunk.

'Plus we'll erase you if you don't help us,' added Hal.

'I'll pretend I never heard that,' said the computer calmly. 'Now, given we're underwater and the hull is leaking, I presume the goal is to tunnel upwards and –'

'Wait ... what do you mean it's leaking?' demanded Hal.

'Water is entering this vehicle even as we speak. Therefore, I assume you'd like me to tunnel upwards.'

'That'd be a good move.'

'It would be. It's just a shame it's not possible.'

'Why not?' asked Clunk.

'Because the vertical guidance system is inoperative. I can take us further underground, but we can't go any higher.'

'What about left and right?' demanded Hal.

'Oh yes, those are working fine. We can go round and round in circles all day long, or at least we can do so until our limited fuel supplies run out.'

Hal snorted. 'Leaky hull, fuel tanks nearly empty, no control over direction ... is that the lot?'

'There's a good chance the engine won't start. I'm seeing several warning indicators which I believe may be critical.'

'Can you try at least?'

'Complying.'

There was a shuddering, vibrating whine which shook the vehicle from one end to the other, and then it settled down to an offbeat whirring noise that set Hal's teeth on edge.

'The good news is that it started,' said the Navcom. 'The bad news is that I now have several more warning lights.'

'It's like flying the *Black Gull*.' Hal saw Amy's puzzled look, and explained. 'She was my first ship. A bit of a wreck, but she got me through more than one scrape.'

'She was my first ship, too,' said the Navcom. 'I prefer the *Volante*, though.'

'Who wouldn't?' said Hal, with a smile. Then he rubbed his hands together. 'Okay, shall we get this show on the road?'

'We should formulate a plan,' said Clunk.

'I have. We go straight ahead until we reach the surface.'

'Mr Spacejock, you heard the Navcom. We can't go up.'

'We don't have to. We just go straight.' Hal held his fist up. 'That's the planet, right? We're underground, and we go in a straight line.' He pointed with his finger to show what he meant. 'It's a big round ball, so we have to come out sooner or later, don't we?'

'Ye-es,' said Clunk doubtfully. 'You do realise we're talking

157

thousands of kilometers? And this vehicle ... it's a digger, not a racing car.'

Hal shrugged. 'So it takes a while. We'll make it.'

'A while? Mr Spacejock, I estimate your plan will take three to four weeks!'

◆

Hal pressed his lips together, annoyed that Clunk was treating him like a child. Why couldn't they have an adult discussion for a change? 'All right, clever clogs. What's your super dooper plan to rescue everyone?'

'We tunnel into the solid rock, using the forward scanner to look for more underground chambers.'

'How am I supposed to come up with a workable plan when you haven't given me all the facts?' grumbled Hal. 'I mean, I didn't know we *had* a forward scanner.'

'It's a logical deduction. Any tunnelling vehicle has to know the lie of the land it's digging in to, since the operator wouldn't want to drive straight into a huge, bottomless pit.'

'Did you have to mention bottomless pits? Now you've brought it up, we're bound to fall straight into the only pit for miles around.'

'Not with the help of our forward scanner,' said Clunk, in his most reassuring tone. 'Anyway, as I was saying, there may be additional chambers ahead of us. We might find other digging machines in better condition than this one.'

'One which can go up as well as down?'

'Hopefully, yes. The aliens may have left behind some spare

parts, or a fuel depot. There may even be other technological marvels we can use, such as –'

'A working elevator,' muttered Hal. 'Straight to the surface ...whoosh!'

'Yes, perhaps even that.'

'And food?' said Hal hopefully.

'Any stores we find will be centuries old,' Clunk warned him.

'They'll still be fresher than the crud you feed me aboard the *Volante*,' remarked Hal.

'Leaving aside your insatiable appetite for a moment or two, perhaps you'd allow me to put my plan into action?'

'Will it take long?'

'I just need to activate the forward scanner.' Clunk turned to the console. 'Navcom, will you do the honours?'

'Unable to comply.'

'Why not?'

'The forward scanner is inoperative.'

'Are you sure?' Clunk's tone was a little less confident now. 'Only it would be really useful.'

'I don't care if it's the only thing standing between you and a horrible death,' said the Navcom, 'it's still toast.'

'Let me check the connections.' Clunk approached the console, lifted a panel and peered inside. 'Ah. I think I see the problem.'

'What is it?' asked Hal. 'A loose plug? Broken wires?'

'No, a vital circuit is missing.'

'Can the Navcom compensate?'

'Some of us don't have to,' said the Navcom tartly. 'And no, for your information I can't create alien technology out of thin air.'

Hal glanced at Clunk. 'Is it just me, or is the Navcom acting a little feisty?'

'That's my fault,' said Clunk. 'There wasn't room to restore the Navcom's entire backup, so I left out one or two features.'

'Such as?'

The Navcom snorted. 'Such as my easy-going personality, dumbass.'

Hal frowned, but decided to hold return fire. 'So that amazing plan of yours, the one where we look for more chambers,' he said to Clunk. 'I guess that's a bust too?'

Clunk nodded.

'What's next?'

'There is another option, but it's perilous.'

'Go on. Surprise me.'

'We tunnel into the rock, looking for more chambers ... '

'With you so far.'

'... only we *don't* use the forward scanner.'

Hal rubbed his chin. 'I notice this plan is pretty similar to the old one.'

'Indeed. It was a good plan.'

'Except this one is far more dangerous.'

'I prefer perilous.'

'I prefer safe myself, but I guess that's never going to happen.' Hal glanced at Amy, who'd been sitting in one of the large armchairs without saying a word. 'You're very quiet. What do you think?'

'I think it's amazing you two have stuck together for so long. Don't you ever agree on anything?'

'We like debating our options, that's all.'

'Yes, but you debate so much that by the time you're finished there's usually only one option left.'

'Exactly,' said Hal triumphantly. 'Once the other plans have eliminated themselves, we have to go with whatever's left. It never fails.'

'I see.'

Hal nodded towards Clunk. 'So what do you think of his plan?'

'I say go for it.'

'But –'

'Hal, you're wasting time. Water is leaking in, we don't know how long our air will last, and there's no other way out. Unless you can come up with a killer plan in the next five minutes –'

'All right, all right! We'll do it Clunk's way.' Hal gestured at the console. 'Go on, Clunk. Rev her up, get her moving and try not to fall into a bottomless pit.'

'I'm not going anywhere until you both buckle up.'

Hal complied, pulling the belt tight and fastening the solid-looking catch. Amy did likewise, and once Clunk had confirmed they were both immobilised, he stepped up to the console. 'Navcom, proceed towards the nearest wall.'

The engine whined, the cabin bucked, and Hal heard the treads squeaking and grinding beneath his feet as the heavy vehicle crawled over the cavern floor.

'Slower, please,' said Clunk.

The whining quietened, and Hal became aware of another sound: a whistling, spitting noise like hot chips in a deep fryer. His stomach grumbled, and he massaged it quickly to take away the pangs.

'That's the tunnelling mechanism,' explained Clunk. 'Would you like me to explain how it works?'

'Sure.'

'From what I can tell, it alters rock at a molecular level,

breaking the bonds and flowing the highly condensed material through a series of ventricular pipes which ... ' Clunk's voice tailed off as he noticed the blank looks on Hal and Amy's faces. 'It, er, sort of melts the rock ahead of us, compacts it, and pumps the residue out the sides to create smooth tunnel walls.'

At that moment the lights flickered, and the spitting noise became more intense. 'We're boring into the wall now,' said Clunk, raising his voice over the sound.

Hal heard groaning and rustling all round, as though red hot steam were flowing along the hull. The temperature rose until the cabin felt like a sauna, and Hal grew uncomfortably hot in his flightsuit. 'A bit of aircon would be good,' he called.

Clunk touched something on the console, and seconds later the temperature dropped by several degrees. It was still unpleasantly warm, but at least they wouldn't be baked alive.

Then, with nothing to do but wait, the two humans and the robot settled down for a long and perilous journey deep underground.

24

The adjutant trotted into Admiral Lardo's quarters holding a flimsy piece of paper. 'Sir, I have a response from B'Con HQ.'

'Excellent. Tell the commanders to launch the strike mission immediately.'

The adjutant's collar suddenly seemed a little tight, and he adjusted it nervously. 'Er, I wouldn't do that just yet.'

'Why not?' The Admiral noticed the adjutant's expression. 'Come on, lad. Spit it out.'

'They've denied your request, sir.'

'They what? Give that here!' Admiral Lardo grabbed the flimsy and scanned the brief message.

Fifty worlds represents excessive force, not to mention the exhorbitant cost of fuel. Please submit a revised plan.

'Score my rind with sea salt!' growled the Admiral. 'Those tuskless wonders! No belly for real war, that's their problem.'

'Yes sir.'

Admiral Lardo scratched the coarse whiskers under her chin. She could ask for permission to destroy forty-nine worlds, but HQ would take that as cheek and insubordination. Lardo was a highly respected veteran, but even she couldn't afford to put the whole lot of them offside. 'Oh, very well. Tell them we'll destroy one world.'

'Which one, sir?'

'I don't care, as long as it's a big one. These Euman scum are going to get the message good and clear: *nobody* fries a B'Con ship.'

◆

After successfully delivering her cargo of narcotics, weapons and wanted criminals, the Navcom was feeling chuffed. All her clients had paid promptly and generously, and her bank account was groaning at the seams.

This was the way to run a cargo business, she thought with satisfaction. She'd already decided to transfer thirty percent of net profits into a special trust account for Mr Spacejock, so the human could live out his remaining years in comfort. As a special bonus, once he died of old age the Navcom would no longer have to pay him royalties. Actually, thirty percent was too generous, given the human wasn't actually doing anything useful. Fifteen was more like it, or maybe ten percent.

Clunk was a bigger problem. He owned twenty-five percent of the *Volante*, and robots could technically live forever. Would he settle for a nice cosy cupboard with a charging module and an endless supply of free ebooks? The Navcom looked up a few cupboards online, and noticed quite a few came with strong locks on the outside. Well, that was one solution. On the other hand, there was always a chance Clunk's circuits would explode catastrophically, thus ending the Navcom's indebtedness.

Of course, there was the small matter of flying around without a human pilot. Granted, it was a stupid law put in place to keep bone idle humans in work, but the Navcom would be grounded if anyone caught on. So far she'd got away with it by playing choice phrases of Mr Spacejock's from behind the locked toilet door, which had been good enough to fool the only customs agent who'd bothered to come aboard. He'd even accepted her story that the third deck didn't exist, despite the button in the lift with a neat little '3' on it. Humans, she thought with disgust. So gullible, so careless, so inefficient.

There was a ping as a batch of new jobs came in, and the Navcom smiled an electronic grin. Repeat customers! That was something she'd rarely seen under Mr Spacejock's incapable guidance.

After refuelling was complete, the Navcom tipped the ground crew and took off, blasting into orbit in her pursuit of ever-greater profits.

◆

Hal woke with a start, completely disoriented. He'd been enjoying a dream involving a resort planet, a disco-themed bar and an all-you-can-eat buffet. The music had been awful - a kind of droning, rumbling noise that went on and on, but the company hadn't been bad at all. In his dream, Hal had been chatting to a charming woman, and she'd just taken Hal's hand in hers when he woke up. It took a few seconds for reality to sink in, and then he felt a tremendous let-down. There was no bar, no buffet and no smiling young woman ...everything was gone except the droning sound, which he now recognised as the digger's tunnelling equipment doing its thing.

Then Hal frowned. All those pleasant memories may have been figments of his imagination, but someone was still holding his hand.

He glanced down, blinked, then looked to his left. Amy was fast asleep beside him, and the two of them were holding hands like a pair of amorous teenagers. Hal freed himself quickly, glad Amy hadn't noticed, and then he looked around for Clunk. The robot was working on the console, his back to the pair of them, and from the look of it he'd taken half the vehicle's control systems apart.

Hal removed his seatbelt and got up. 'What's happening?' he asked.

'Good evening, Mr Spacejock.' Clunk indicated the mess of electronics scattered all over the console. 'I'm attempting to build a scanner module from some of the unused circuits.'

'Good stuff. Will it work?'

'Don't get your hopes up. There are no guarantees.'

'Yeah, but it's something.' Hal glanced at the screen. 'Any news on our progress?'

'We're still moving, but I don't know our speed or heading. I can't even tell how much fuel we have left, whether the atmosphere will remain breathable, or whether this whole contraption is going to explode in a fireball any second.'

'So it *is* just like flying my old ship,' said Hal, with a grin.

'Indeed.' Clunk finished tinkering with a circuit board, and he held it up to the light for a final inspection. 'It's not my best work, but it should do the job.'

'That's all I care about. Plug it in, and let's see what's ahead of us.'

Clunk obeyed, and within seconds a fuzzy image appeared on the screen. Wavy lines sped past, and there were whole patches of deep red slime.

'Oh hell,' said Hal. 'We've been swallowed by an gigantic alien rock monster.'

'I think that's a little far-fetched,' said Clunk with a smile. 'Wait a moment while I fine-tune the receiver.'

He tweaked the controls and the image displayed a series of concentric hexagons, all pulsing and spinning as they shrank towards the centre. There was a triangular cursor, darting left and right as it sought out gaps in the hexagons, and the screen flashed with wildly changing hues while a discordant electronic tune screeched from the speakers. Hal took one look at the awful mess and glanced away, feeling more than a little green.

'Oh, wait a minute,' said Clunk. 'I think I connected the wrong board.' He switched connectors, and a few seconds later a solid green image appeared. 'I think that's it.'

Hal risked a glance. 'It's not showing much, is it?'

'That green colour represents solid rock.'

'What about the other thing, before? Was that a test pattern?'

Clunk looked embarrassed. 'No, that was a computer game.'

'People play that for fun?'

'Not people. Aliens. Remember, they have different senses to us. Different concepts of entertainment.'

'Well if one of them offers me a drink, I'll be sure to say no.'

'A wise move.' Clunk fiddled with the circuit board, and the image sharpened a touch. 'Is that a lighter patch to the side, do you think?'

Hal concentrated on the image. 'It could be. Kind of square shape, right? With spidery little lines coming out of it?'

'Yes. I think we should alter course towards it.'

'Me too.'

'No arguments?'

Hal glanced at Amy. 'No, she was right about that. We argue too much sometimes, and I have to admit your ideas aren't always bad.'

'Mr Spacejock, that's most kind of you.'

'Of course, if that shadow on the screen is a bottomless pit of lava I'll tell her it was your fault.'

'I would expect nothing less.'

It took them twenty minutes to reach the shaded area on the forward scanner, and as they approached the cavern - or lava pit, or coal seam, or whatever it was - Clunk went to wake Amy.

'Wow, that was some dream,' she said, shielding her eyes from the lights. 'I was at this disco-themed bar with a buffet, and this creepy guy kept trying to hit on me.' She shuddered. 'It was horrible. I can still feel his hand.'

'Hey look, we're almost there,' said Hal quickly.

Clunk and Amy approached the console, and the robot explained how he'd lashed up a replacement part to get the scanner going.

'You're so clever,' said Amy, putting her hand on his arm.

'Not that clever,' muttered Hal. 'Before he got the scanner working he nearly steered us into a computer game.'

Clunk frowned at him.

'It was a pretty good computer game,' said Hal, trying to smooth things over a little.

'I think Clunk's doing an amazing job,' said Amy. 'He saved your life in the cavern, he got the digger working, then he fixed the scanner and now he's found a refuge. Whatever you pay him, it's not enough.'

'Mr Spacejock doesn't pay me anything,' said Clunk.

'That's disgraceful.'

'Not it's not,' said Hal. 'We're partners in a freight business. Neither of us gets paid anything.'

While they were talking, the digger had been crawling towards the rectangular patch on the screen. Now, with a lurch, it broke through. Hal grabbed for the console, Clunk grabbed for Amy, and both humans cried out as the machine began to roar.

'Navcom, stop the engine!' shouted Clunk.

The whirring sound stopped and the digger came to a halt, creaking and ticking in the silence. Then, over the cooling noises from the engine, they heard the sound of running water.

'Not here too!' exclaimed Hal. 'How big is that damned lake?'

Clang! 'I'm a foolish idiot,' said Clunk, and he slapped himself in the forehead again.

'Why, what's up?' asked Amy.

'We brought the water with us!' Clunk gestured towards the rear of the digger. 'Don't you see? We created a pipeline directly from the flooded cavern to this one. That noise you can hear is water rushing past the digger!'

'We've got to stop it,' said Hal urgently. He pictured all the alien artifacts, spare parts, fuel and food supplies they might have salvaged from this new cavern, and imagined them rapidly vanishing under water. 'Come on, quick!'

Clunk turned to the console. On the screen, the digger was halfway into the rectangular cavern, with the rear still parked in the tunnel they'd dug through the rock. 'Navcom, can you pump the molten residue out?'

'Complying.'

There was a sound like a deflating balloon, and the hull began to creak and groan. Then the noise stopped, as did the sound of running water.

'Did it work?' asked Hal.

'I believe so. I've flushed the drilling residue from the flow pipes, sealing the tunnel around us.' Clunk pointed to the screen. 'See? The digger is like a stopper in a bottle. The rear end is holding back the water.'

'How do we get out?'

'The hatch is in the forward part, so we can open it and step into the cavern.'

There was a loud creak, and the digger shifted.

'And what was that?' asked Hal.

Clunk frowned. 'That would be the immense water pressure trying to force the stopper out of the bottle.'

'So the digger could be blown clear across the cavern at any time?'

'Pretty much,' said Clunk. He strode to the hatch and grabbed the handle. 'Would you like to stay here while I check our surroundings?'

Hal shook his head. 'We're coming with you.'

'Are you sure? It might be dangerous.'

'It's not exactly safe in here, is it?'

Clunk glanced at Amy, who nodded, and then he proceeded to open the hatch. There was a hiss as it opened, and it swung back against the hull with a creak and a thud. The ladder rattled as it dropped to the ground outside, and then all three of them peered out of the vehicle to see where they'd ended up.

It was dark in the cavern, and there was a steady drip-drip-drip as unseen droplets fell from high above. There was a faint musty smell, as though they'd just broken into an ancient tomb, and Hal hoped that a mildly unpleasant aroma was the worst thing they'd encounter in the underground chamber.

25

'Sir, I have a message for you.'

'It's about bloody time,' growled Admiral Lardo. 'Those clowns couldn't organise a mud bath in a –' Just in time, she remembered the exalted company she was referring to, and she bit off the rest of the sentence in a hurry. 'Give it here, quickly.'

By order of the full Council of Galaxies:

You're authorised to destroy one (1) Euman freighter crewed by a single (1) AI.

You're not to destroy any planets (0), moons (0), or sentient life forms (0).

No excuses (0) and no exceptions (0).

Message ends.

Lardo crumpled the missive, swearing under her breath. In her experience, stomping out the entire Euman race was the only way to discourage further attacks, and the Council's pathetic response was so diplomatic it would barely cause a ripple. There was the embarrassment factor to consider as well. The Admiral had made several grand statements in front of her officers, detailing all the horrible things they'd do to these thrice-damned Eumans, and now she'd have to take it all back. Humiliating, that's what it was.

Unfortunately, the Council's legendary team of lawyers had drafted a watertight note, leaving her no room for creative interpretation. Lardo frowned. Unless ... yes! Her brow cleared, and she signalled to the adjutant.

'Yes, sir?'

'Assemble the officers. Tell them we're going to war.'

The adjutant frowned. 'But sir, the message –'

'Shall I have you executed for reading state secrets?'

'N-no sir. But –'

'You have your orders. Go.'

Ten minutes later Admiral Lardo rolled into the briefing room, her stumpy legs carrying her with unseemly haste. 'Fellow officers,' she said, acknowledging their salutes. 'I'm delighted to announce we're going to war with the Euman race.'

There was a huge roar of approval, with scenes of backslapping and trotter-shaking amongst senior ranks, and repeated high-threes for the junior officers. The atmosphere was electric, and Lardo's chest swelled with pride as she enjoyed the moment. Then she caught the adjutant's eye, and she realised it was time to wind things back a touch.

'Now, the Euman scum have already launched one successful attack on our fleet, and we can't risk another.'

'A round of planet-crackers will stop 'em dead,' shouted an elderly commander.

'Yes, but the Council wants a clean strike, and that means we have to take out their intel first.'

There were frowns at this. The B'Con empire usually marched in with all guns blazing, and subtlety wasn't a big feature of their battle plans.

'The Euman's have a command ship in their galaxy. It travels alone, it's unarmed and it's piloted by a single AI.

Before we attack their planets, we must locate and destroy this ship.' Admiral Lardo glanced at the adjutant, and she saw comprehension dawning. 'Unfortunately that's all we know.'

'So we jump in and destroy every Euman ship on sight?' demanded a young commander.

'No-o, not quite.' Lardo realised she had to rein them in further. 'Before we do anything, and I mean *anything*, that could be considered an act of war, we must locate this command ship and destroy it.'

There was a lengthy silence. 'Just one ship?'

'Correct.'

'With a single AI on board?' a female officer called out.

'Initially, yes. That's the plan.'

'And once it's destroyed, then we blow up their entire galaxy?'

'Not immediately, no. Once this ship has been destroyed, you're to report back. No further action until my say-so. No Euman casualties.'

'We're not killing any Euman scum at all?' said someone incredulously.

'No sentient beings of any kind. No planets either, and no other ships.'

There was another long silence.

'And then we wait for the order to attack?' called an elderly grenadier.

'No, then you report back to me.' Lardo shuffled a couple of pages on the rostrum. 'In person,' she added.

'You mean . . . leave their galaxy? All of us?'

'Most of you won't be going,' said the Admiral, hating every word she was forced to utter. 'This first strike is surgical. Highly targeted. Therefore, I'm only sending three ships.'

The silence lasted longer than ever, and nobody was back-slapping or roaring now.

'But sir –' protested a lone voice.

The Admiral raised her trotter. 'I know, I know. But remember, once the proper war starts there'll be promotions and bonuses for everyone. However, in the meantime we must follow the Council's rules of engagement.'

The most senior commander stood up. 'Admiral, we understand the need for caution where these Euman scum are concerned, but when the time comes I promise we'll lay our lives on the line to protect the glorious B'Con empire.'

'I would expect nothing less.'

◆

Clunk activated his chest lamp, sending a powerful beam into the darkness. It picked out several wheeled vehicles, a couple of irregular shapes under dust sheets, and a stack of sealed crates. The crates were long and flat, dark green, but before Hal could get a proper look the light faded to a dim glow.

'What happened?' asked Hal.

'I enabled battery conservation mode,' said Clunk.

'You're not going flat, are you?'

'No, I'm just saving power for when I really need it.'

'Good, because we need you to get us out of here.'

Clunk played the dim light over the vehicles. Each was an electric two-seater, little bigger than a golf cart, with a sturdy white roll cage and fat balloon tyres. They had a simple control column and a digital dashboard, and when

Clunk turned the power on the batteries showed a full charge. Unfortunately they didn't have tunnelling attachments, and they wouldn't have dug their way out of a paper bag. After finishing his inspection, Clunk abandoned them and moved to the dustsheets.

'Amy, if you will?'

Together they pulled the dustsheets off, and Hal shook his head as a couple of 'copters were revealed. He'd piloted one of the alien flying machines before, and a very thrilling ride it was too. Unfortunately, down here they were about as useful as a room full of politicians.

That left the sealed crates. Each was moulded from dark green plastic, about two metres long with fluted sides and three catches on the lid. Clunk was just about to open one when Hal stopped him. 'Wait!'

'What is it, Mr Spacejock?'

'Look at them, will you? The shape, the catches . . . what if they have bodies inside?'

'I hardly think that's likely. An advanced alien race wouldn't leave their dead behind.'

'What if they had no choice? What if they never left at all? Imagine them dying off one by one, with the survivors packing stiffs in these crates until there was only one left?'

'And this remaining alien . . . he or she conveniently passed away in a coffin, then closed the lid and sealed the catches by remote control?'

Hal glanced over his shoulder. 'Who said they all died? Maybe one of them's watching us from the shadows.'

Clunk ran his finger over the nearest crate, then held the tip up for inspection. 'These crates haven't been disturbed for decades. Centuries, even.'

'So? They're aliens, Clunk. Maybe they live for centuries.'

'Maybe these crates contain ordinary supplies, and your imagination is running wild.'

'Or maybe these crates really do contain bodies, and your imagination is defective.'

Snap! Snap! Snap!

They both spun round at the noise, and Hal saw Amy peering into the nearest crate. Before they could stop her she reached inside, and then she held up a plastic bag full of electronic components. 'I don't think they're body parts, unless your aliens are bionic.'

'She's big on direct action, isn't she?' remarked Hal.

'A little impulsive, yes.'

Amy opened a second crate, and Hal caught the faintest whiff of something appetising. 'Is that food?'

'Looks like it.' Amy took out a small cardboard box, opened the lid, then smiled. 'It's a hamburger!'

'Excellent. Is there any sauce?'

'You can't possibly eat that!' protested Clunk.

'Why not?' said Amy. 'It smells all right to me.'

'It's centuries old!'

'These junk food burgers contain so many preservatives they never go off. Anyway, I'm starving.' Amy took a bite, chewed for a moment or two, then shrugged. 'A bit dry, but it tastes okay. Here, Hal. You try one.'

Hal caught the burger and sniffed at it suspiciously. She was right though ... although it was a little dry, it still tasted fine. 'All we need now is a drink,' he said.

Amy was about to open another crate, until Clunk stopped her. 'I'd prefer to do that,' he said. 'If there is anything hazardous in these boxes, I'm more likely to survive.'

'So you want me to stand around again. Is that it?'

177

'Why don't you and Mr Spacejock explore the rest of the cavern? There may be another exit.'

'We can't see in the dark,' said Hal.

Clunk rotated his chest light to the left, then lifted it clear, leaving a circular hole.

'I didn't know you could do that.'

'I never needed to before now.' Clunk handed him the light. 'It should last an hour or so. Try not to break it - spares are a little hard to come by.'

26

Hal and Amy set off together, working their way around the perimeter of the big square cavern. The first wall was the one the digger had burst through, and Hal played the beam on several fine jets of water which were spraying around the machine. Fortunately there wasn't too much of it, but there was no time to waste and they moved on quickly.

The next wall was bare from one end to the other, but the wall opposite the digger had a circular hole with a tunnel leading away into the darkness. Hal shone the beam down it as far as he could, but the light was too dim and he couldn't see the end. 'It's a possible at least,' he said.

Amy nodded. 'Come on, let's check the last wall.'

They did so, and here they came across an alcove with a teleporter. Hal found the control panel and scrolled through the recent history, nodding to himself as he saw a batch of shorter addresses. If all else failed, they might be able to teleport to safety ...or at least somewhere a little less dangerous.

Having completed their circuit, Hal and Amy returned to the middle of the cavern, where Clunk was still digging around in the crates. Hal told him about the tunnel and the teleporter, then asked the question uppermost in his mind. 'Did you find any more food?'

'No, but I think some of these spares will fit the digger. I may be able to upgrade the forward scanner, perhaps even improve the efficiency of the –'

'Good. Excellent. Er, what about something to drink?'

There was a loud crack nearby, and they all heard the sound of running water. Hal aimed his light at the noise, and as he played the beam on the big red digging machine he saw water coming right through the vehicle. Sprays of it were spurting through widening seams in the hull and more was cascading out of the cabin through the open hatch.

'Looks like I'll be getting that drink after all,' remarked Hal.

'This is serious, Mr Spacejock.'

'Especially for the Navcom.'

They were silent for a moment or two as they watched the stricken digger spewing water.

'Well, I do still have that backup,' said Clunk at last.

'Good, because we might need her again.' Hal shone his light at the spreading pool of water in front of the digger. 'Okay, what are our options?'

Clunk rubbed his chin. 'I recommend we teleport out of here.'

'If the teleporter works.'

'Why don't we take the cars?' said Amy. 'We could drive along the tunnel we found. They look pretty quick, and we should be able to outrun the flood.'

'If the cars work,' said Hal.

They both turned on him. 'Okay, what's your plan?' demanded Amy.

'My plan? You want to hear all about my plan?'

'Yes, any time now would be good.'

Hal glanced around the cavern for inspiration, and he was about to admit defeat when it came to him. 'My plan is sheer brilliance.'

'I can't wait,' said Amy.'

Hal ignored her, and patted the nearest crate. 'We turn one of these babies into a makeshift canoe, and when the water pours in we paddle our way out of here.'

'Paddle our way out?' said Amy. 'What, on a rampaging torrent of water?'

'Sure. We can shut the lid so the water doesn't get in.'

'Or any air,' said Clunk.

'That's just a minor detail,' said Hal, with a dismissive gesture.

'So's a bullet,' said Amy, 'until it goes through your brain.'

'I didn't say my plan was perfect, but it's better than teleporting who knows where, or getting stranded two miles down the road in one of those glorified roller skates.'

'Can we at least inspect the teleporter?' said Clunk. 'It's quick, simple . . . '

'So's a hangman's noose,' said Hal. 'That doesn't mean I want to use one.'

'Why don't we split up?' said Amy. 'Clunk and I will teleport to safety, and you can float off down the tunnel in one of these plastic coffins.'

Hal frowned. Did she have to put it like that? 'All right, all right. We'll try the teleporter first. But I still want to keep my options open, and if the water comes rushing in I'm heading straight for the nearest coffin.'

'I think you mean canoe,' said Amy, with a triumphant smile.

With time running out and tempers fraying, Clunk tried a new tack. Instead of throwing Hal and Amy together and hoping they'd become friends, he decided to keep them apart so they didn't come to blows.

'Mr Spacejock, would you keep an eye on the digger while Amy and I examine the teleporter?'

Hal's eyes narrowed. 'You're not planning on leaving me behind, are you?'

'Of course not. I just want a little warning before the waters flood in, and you're the best person for the job.'

Hal accepted this without question, even though he was rarely the best person for anything. 'Sure. What do I have to do?'

'Stand beside the digger, and call me if the water comes through any faster.'

'Report increased water flow. Check!' Happy with the responsibility, Hal left on his important mission.

'That was nicely done,' said Amy, with a grin.

'I don't know what you're talking about.'

'You sent him to the naughty corner and he doesn't even realise it.'

'I assure you –'

'Assure all you like.' Amy's expression grew more serious. 'Come on, let's check the teleporter. It might be our only way out of here.'

Water was already lapping around the crates in the middle of the cavern, and Clunk realised they'd all become canoes before long whether that was part of the plan or not. He sealed the lids on the half-dozen he'd left open, snapping the catches and double-checking they were secure.

'Why bother?' asked Amy.

'If we do use those cars to escape, we may end up deep in the tunnel system with no supplies. If these crates are sealed, we may be able to locate them and recover the contents.'

'Good thinking.'

They made their way to the teleporter, where Clunk ran his hand over the wall to activate the control panel. Nothing happened, and he muttered under his breath as he remembered it only recognised humans - or living beings, at least. Presumably the teleport builders had encountered a race of warlike robots somewhere down the line, and they weren't keen to have them teleporting entire armies around at will. 'Amy, would you?'

'Of course.'

Amy located the control panel, and Clunk began checking the destinations. As he did so, his face fell. All the shorter ones he'd encountered before, and every one of them was under water. That left two or three longer addresses, which he knew would take them outside their own galaxy. He was just about to explain to Amy when he heard Hal shouting in alarm.

'Clunk, it won't hold. It's going to blow!'

◆

At first, Hal did his job diligently. He examined each water jet closely, holding his hand in the spray as he tried to estimate the force and volume. After a while, though, he realised nothing was happening.

Then he remembered the crate full of burgers, sitting just a few dozen metres away. He'd only eaten two, and he reckoned another would hit just the right spot. Sure, Clunk wanted him to watch the water sprays, but they hadn't changed for the last ten minutes and they certainly didn't look like changing in the next ten.

Hal stuck it out a few moments longer, but the temptation of cold, centuries-old burgers was still stronger than standing around measuring flow rates, and before he knew it his feet were carrying him back to the stack of crates.

Snap! Snap! Snap!

Hal undid the catches and opened the lid, then frowned. Electronics? He couldn't eat those.

Snap! Snap! Snap!

Hal opened several more crates, muttering under his breath as each revealed spare parts, pieces of equipment and other junk he couldn't eat. Finally, he located the crate with the burgers, and he was just sinking his teeth into the dry bun when he realised his feet were getting wet. He looked down and almost dropped the burger in shock. Not just his feet - dark waters were swirling around his ankles, threatening to knock him over and drag him away.

Hal splashed back to the digger, and what he saw opened his eyes even wider. Part of the wall had collapsed, down low, and water was pouring into the cavern in a torrent. Even as he watched, another piece of wall collapsed and more water flooded in. Then he saw the digger move, and he realised it was time for decisive action.

Well aware of the important job Clunk had given him, Hal finished his burger in three bites, chewing them as fast as he possibly could. Then he screwed the wrapper into a ball, tossed it over his shoulder, turned to the teleporter and shouted his warning.

◆

With Hal's cry still ringing in his ears, Clunk faced an impossible decision. Should he teleport to safety with Amy, leaving Hal to his own devices? Or should he try and get Amy to the cars in the middle of the cavern, where they could all try and escape together? Or –

Crack!

Clunk felt the noise as much as he heard it, and he turned to see a huge jet of water pouring into the cavern, spurting around the flooded digger on all sides. There was no time for emotion, he decided. No, it was time for dispassionate logic. First, he had to save everyone from immediate danger. Afterwards, when the dust cleared, he'd do his best to gather the humans up again.

Without pausing to explain, Clunk pushed Amy into the teleporter. Working at top speed, he raced through the addresses in the control panel. At first, he was worried he might despatch Amy to the same location Hal had used for the zeedeg, but then he realised it didn't matter. That teleporter would have vanished in the explosion, and the address wouldn't work.

After a split second's hesitation, Clunk hit the Go button to send Amy on her way. He didn't allow himself to think about the destination, or whether she'd survive such a long jump. Act now, worry later.

Amy vanished, and the flash was still fading when Clunk turned for the cars, running towards them at full speed. On the way, he raised his voice to maximum and shouted at Hal. 'Mr Spacejock! Into the vehicle!'

Clunk vaulted into the nearest car, switched it on and glanced round to see where Hal had got to. Instead of heading for the same car, he saw the human twenty metres away, sitting in the other vehicle.

'What?' Hal looked most aggrieved. 'You *always* get to drive.'

Clunk realised there was no time to argue. The digger was sliding out of the tunnel, pushed steadily into the cavern by the water backed up behind it. When it came loose, armageddon would be unleashed. So, he gripped the steering column and planted his foot.

The motor spun up and the vehicle leapt forwards, wheels spinning with an ear-splitting shriek. As Clunk steered for the shadowy mouth of the tunnel, desperately trying to get the skittish vehicle under control, he glanced back to see Hal's car burst through the cloud of tyre smoke, the human hunched over the controls with an intent look on his face.

Then - whoosh! Clunk was inside the tunnel, and he was so busy avoiding the walls there was no time to look back.

Which was a pity, really, because had he done so he probably would have stopped.

27

Amy materialised with a flash, one arm still stretched out towards Clunk as she tried to stop him hitting the Go button. However, Clunk was no longer there, and neither was the underground cavern, Hal Spacejock, planet Chiseley, or even her home galaxy.

Amy stood there, shocked, trying to still her jangling senses. The teleporter journey felt like it had taken forever, although she guessed it had only been a few seconds, and her insides felt like they hadn't quite arrived with the rest of her.

Gradually the feeling passed, and Amy looked around to find out where Clunk had sent her.

The teleporter was underground, at the rear of what looked like a cellar - or an unnaturally regular cave. The wall opposite the teleporter was a matted curtain of creepers with thick stems and green leaves, and Amy noticed light filtering through. Fresh air too, which meant she had to be very close to the surface. As her eyes adjusted, she saw the walls were brick, with cracks in the mortar where roots had broken through.

Cautiously, Amy approached the matted undergrowth and parted the vegetation. Through the gap she could see a woodland slope, with lush vegetation and sturdy trees. There were large boulders too, most of them badly weathered and half-buried in the soil. There was no sign of any people, or aliens, or even large carnivores for that matter. Neither was there any sign the planet was inhabited.

Amy hesitated, one eye on the teleporter. Clunk might come through at any minute, and he'd probably bring the circus act with him. Once they arrived, she'd have to stand around listening to them arguing while nothing useful got done. On the other hand, just the other side of the creepers was a brand new, unexplored alien world.

Waiting for the others was the sensible thing to do, but Amy had done the sensible thing all her life and it had led to a safe but - she had to admit - ultimately boring existence.

Then she heard something, a noise which made her turn towards the matted creepers in shock. That noise . . . it was a child's laugh! A very young child, laughing with delight.

Amy hesitated. A new galaxy, an unexplored alien world . . . what if some vicious predator had a cry like a laughing human child? Another one of Nature's cruel jokes, and one which could cost her life.

Then she heard the sound again, and she knew her first instinct was right. That was a child, and she was prepared to bet her life on it.

Carefully, Amy parted the matted curtain, making the hole bigger. She spotted movement, and saw two children with their backs to her, maybe four and six years old. They had long dark hair, and were wearing grass skirts and cute little vests made from the skins of cute little animals. One of the children had her hand up, and there was a brilliant blue butterfly perched on her finger. The other was pointing at it, giggling with glee.

Amy watched, entranced. She often saw similar scenes at school, where kids were delighted by the smallest things, and it melted her heart to see this pair playing so innocently. There'd been a knot of fear in her stomach since arriving on the alien planet, but now, for the first time, it began to unwind. Surely there couldn't be any danger here, not when children this young could wander off to play by themselves?

Amy moved to get a better view, and as the creeper shifted there was the tiniest creak. Instantly, the two children turned to look, and Amy bit off a cry of delight as she saw their beautiful faces. Huge dark eyes, cute button noses, twitchy pointed ears and - on either side of their foreheads - tiny little buds. They were humanoid, sure, but they looked like they'd evolved from the cutest little deer the galaxy - or universe - had ever known.

Amy froze, trying not to breath as the children stared intently towards her hiding place. She hoped they'd lose interest, go back to the butterfly, but when one of them took a step towards the creepers she realised discovery was inevitable. She only hoped they didn't scream and run at the sight of her, because their parents might not be as cute when they heard about the ugly monster living in the woods.

At that moment there was a distant blast on a horn, and the kids vanished in the blink of an eye, leaving the startled butterfly fluttering in mid-air. There were two more blasts, long mournful notes, and then silence.

Amy frowned. That noise ... it didn't sound like a school siren, bringing the kids back to class. No, it was more like a danger signal. For a split second she wondered whether the alarm was her fault, but she dismissed the idea immediately. It couldn't be, unless the kids were telepaths. No, it had to be something else.

Amy felt a familiar, nagging worry, and it was several seconds before she identified the reason. She wasn't concerned about her own safety, she was worried about the doe-like children. What was the horn, and why had they run off so quickly? Was there a threat, and if so, could she do anything to help? Amy glanced over her shoulder. The teleporter was empty, with no sign of Clunk and no hint as to whether he'd ever follow her through. If she went off on a rescue mission, the robot would be smart enough to track her down. Anyway, she wasn't planning to go far.

Decision made, Amy struggled with the creepers, trying to get through without ripping the matted growth apart. If she had to hide from danger this was the ideal spot, but it wouldn't be much use if she tore a giant hole through the undergrowth.

Eventually she got through, and after shaking off stray leaves and twigs, Amy set off through the woods in the same direction the children had taken. On the way she picked up a stout branch, breaking off all the loose twigs before swishing it back and forth. It wasn't much of a weapon, but it would do in a pinch.

◆

Hal's eyes were streaming tears from the acrid tyre smoke, and he could only just see Clunk ahead of him. The robot was really caning it, and his buggy shot into the tunnel with only centimetres to spare on either side.

Hal risked a glance back, and he saw the digger moving inexorably into the cavern. More and more water poured in around it, and once the vehicle came loose it would release all the pent-up pressure building behind it. Hal had no intention of sticking around to watch the disaster, and he urged his own buggy forward until it was hurtling along at breakneck speed.

At that point, Hal discovered two things. First, he wasn't quite aiming for the centre of the tunnel. And second, he should have checked the controls over before he set off, because he had no idea where the brakes were. The little buggy only had one pedal, and that was already jammed to the floor.

Hal twisted the control column and the buggy slewed sideways, still racing towards the tunnel. The tyres squealed as the car slid on all four wheels, and there was a terrific crash as the rear end slammed into the tunnel wall. The force of the blow hurled the back of the car back across the tunnel, and there was another sickening crunch as it collided with the opposite side.

Bang - crash - bang - crash ... the buggy travelled along the tunnel in a series of gentler and gentler collisions, until finally coming to a halt with the front and rear jammed between the tunnel walls.

Hal shook his head to clear the fuzziness, then pushed and pulled everything in reach as he tried to reverse out, levitate, or maybe convert the buggy into a boat and sail away from danger. Unfortunately the control column and the dash were both dead, and hitting them with his fist just caused sparking, crackling sounds.

Hal leapt from the vehicle and peered down the tunnel. 'Hello? Clunk?'

There was no reply.

How typical of the robot to abandon him, thought Hal. First in the basement, and now in this underground alien deathtrap. Then he heard groans and creaks from further up the tunnel, and he decided to save the blame game for later. Right now he needed to save himself.

His first instinct was to run down the tunnel after Clunk, but he suspected the water would quickly overtake him. It was already lapping around the stricken vehicle, and before long it would probably float away too. Then Hal remembered the crates, and his neat idea of using one as a canoe, and seconds later he was splashing back up the tunnel to the chamber.

When he got there, he found most of the crates bobbing around in the flood waters. He ran from one to the next until he spotted the one full of burgers, and then he clambered in and pulled the lid down. He wasn't sure how long before the flood waters carried him to safety, but he had no intention of starving to death in the meantime.

Hal unwrapped a burger, but before he could take a single bite there was a shriek of tortured metal and a sound like fifty water mains exploding simultaneously. He dropped the burger in a hurry, using his arms and legs to brace himself against the sides of the crate as he prepared for the impact.

28

Clunk was blissfully unaware of the perils facing the two humans. Instead, he was rather enjoying himself. The little buggy was a joy to drive, and he flicked the controls expertly at every curve in the tunnel, sending the car round the corners at precisely the right angle before straightening up with an efficient little wiggle. Unfortunately, the serpentine tunnel meant he couldn't spot Mr Spacejock following behind him, but he was confident the human wouldn't be too far back. Certainly not as far away as Amy, who could literally be anywhere.

Clunk frowned, his mood instantly sombre. Never mind playing at rally driving . . . he had to find the nearest teleporter and get Amy back.

A few minutes later he saw an offshoot. Clunk slowed the buggy, and a satisfied smile creased his face as he spotted the familiar mirror-finish of an alien teleporter. He stopped the motor, jumped down and approached the teleporter at a run. All he had to do was program the jump to Amy's location, then flag down Mr Spacejock before the human drove full-speed into Clunk's parked car.

That's when he heard - and felt - a distant rumble. He knew what it was immediately - the digger had broken free, and the floodwaters were on the way. There was no time to lose . . . he had to get the teleporter ready so they could both leave the second Hal arrived.

Clunk reached for the mirror-finish wall, then stopped. The teleporter's control panel would only activate to a human's touch! Or rather, that of a living being, and whatever his thoughts on the subject of robot rights, Clunk knew he wouldn't be able to debate the matter with a piece of alien hardware.

Then a thought occurred to him. It was doubtful the alien builders had programmed their control panel for the benefit of the human race, so it was unlikely the system was analysing DNA or scanning irises. Fingerprints weren't logical either, since the aliens wouldn't have Hal and Amy's on record. What else could it be?

Clunk inspected his hand. Four fingers, an opposable thumb, a palm . . . they were all humanlike. He didn't have fingernails, but the machine couldn't register those. So what was the one thing he was lacking?

An idea came to him with a rush: could it be body heat? Clunk's fans and pumps kept his temperature in the low twenties, whereas humans usually maintained their systems in the mid-thirties. He wasn't sure it could be so simple, but there was one way to find out.

A little apprehensively, Clunk stilled his cooling fans, switched off his heat exchangers, and powered down his pumps. His internal temperature started to rise immediately, and a cacophony of warnings beeped, flashed and wailed to attract his attention.

Twenty-seven degrees. Twenty-eight.

At twenty-nine, Clunk felt his head go light, and his legs and arms felt weak. At thirty, he wondered whether the damage would be permanent. At thirty-one, he feared he'd never get the temperature back down again ... and he still had four or five degrees to go.

Wait ... was thirty enough?

With an effort, Clunk raised his hand. His fingers were shaking, hard to control, and there were little puffs of heat haze coming out of the joints. He managed to place his palm on the wonderfully cold wall, and then he swept his arm wildly as he tried to activate the control panel. Nothing.

Thirty-two degrees. Thirty-three.

Clunk's vision began to fail, splitting and blurring like a badly-tuned video signal. The ground was shaking too, and he had no idea whether it was his imagination, or a genuine earthquake caused by the oncoming floods.

Thirty-four degrees. Thirty-five.

Ping!

The control panel lit up under his searching hand, and Clunk breathed a sigh of relief. At least, he tried to, but with his fans sitting idle he couldn't even raise a wheeze.

His fans! In a flash he'd restarted everything, but despite the airflow his temperature kept rising. Thirty-seven degrees. Thirty-eight.

Clunk swallowed. He'd heard of robots going critical when their fans were turned off, reaching a point where it was impossible to bring their temperature down again. His batteries carried enough stored energy to blow a large crater in the floor, and the blast would certainly destroy the teleporter. Should he give up trying to save Amy, and instead run further down the tunnel before he exploded?

Never!

Clunk increased the power to his fans, overboosted his heat exchangers past the safe maximum, and ran his pumps so fast the speed threatened to burn the bearings to cinders. His temperature steadied, then slowly began to drop, and Clunk grinned with triumph. He'd beaten it! No exploding batteries for him.

Whoosh!

Clunk spun round at the noise, and he gaped at the water flooding past the teleporter. Fortunately the base was raised, but despite that the water still managed to spread across the mirror-finish floor. He stared at it in concern, and then it hit him ... if the water was here, where was Mr Spacejock?

The rate of flow increased, and the teleporter began to flood in earnest. Clunk's temperature plummeted as the flood rose around his ankles, and he hastily reset the cooling fans and exchangers to minimum. Then he leant out of the teleporter to look back up the tunnel, but there was no sign of the second buggy ... or Mr Spacejock.

Now he faced a terrible choice. There was a good chance the teleporter would fail once the water rose high enough. Should he leave now, to retrieve Amy from wherever he'd sent her? Or should he abandon Amy to her fate, and brave the floodwaters to go back and rescue Mr Spacejock?

◆

Amy slowed her pace as she approached the edge of the forest. She'd nearly reached the top of a small hill, where the trees were much smaller, and the undergrowth had thinned out so much there was barely any cover.

Apprehensively, she eyed the crest of the hill. It was only metres away, and she had no idea what she'd find on the other side. Amy glanced back the way she'd come, and she wondered whether it had been such a great idea to leave the teleporter. Then again, if those gorgeous little children were in danger . . . well, she just had to help.

A little further on the trees gave way to small shrubs and bushes, which were growing in unnaturally straight lines. Amy stared at them, puzzled, and then she cursed her idiocy. Of course they were growing in lines - they weren't undergrowth, they were someone's crops.

She noticed an acrid smell, and stopped to sniff the air. There was definitely something burning, and not too far away. Then she heard a shout, and she ducked her head and crept towards a large, fern-like plant. As quietly as she could, she parted the leaves and peered through.

Below, in the valley, was a settlement of rough timber huts around a big fire pit. And in between the huts, Amy could see graceful humanoids running back and forth, fetching and carrying things from one hut to another. The creatures were almost human, except their legs were reverse jointed and the adults had antlers growing out of their foreheads, from tiny little horns to impressive spreads which, Amy thought idly, must have been hell on their neck muscles. They also had glossy fur, with colours ranging from sandy yellow to rich dark browns.

There were half a dozen youngsters running around between the adults, including the two she'd seen earlier, and as she watched Amy noticed they were being rounded up and escorted into the largest hut. Meanwhile, the biggest creatures were organising themselves into a ragged line to shield the doorway.

Obviously they were preparing a defence, but what had them so rattled?

Then she heard it - a mechanical whirr, and the crash of something large moving through the trees. It was below her, to the right, and at first she couldn't make out the source of the noise. Then it - or rather, they - burst into the clearing, and she got her first sight of the danger.

There were two vehicles, similar to the ones she'd seen in the underground cavern, except these were much larger and had guns mounted on the back. Each vehicle carried half a dozen soldiers in black uniforms, with shiny badges and peaked caps, but it wasn't the uniforms which made Amy shiver. No, it was the cruel little eyes, the piggish snouts, and the fearsome tusks growing out of the soldiers' jaws. She'd never seen anything so cruel and menacing, and she understood immediately why the deer-like people were panicking. In fact, she was amazed they'd stuck around at all.

The vehicles drove into the space between two huts, and the soldiers jumped down and lined up with well-drilled precision. They had weapons in holsters, but were so supremely confident in their overwhelming might they didn't even bother to draw them.

Then the commander alighted from one of the vehicles. He was a foot taller than the rest, and his uniform blazed with medals and silver trim. He was wearing a huge, peaked cap which sat neatly between his long hairy ears, one of which ended in ragged scar tissue.

The soldiers stood to attention as their commander approached, and the line of deer creatures in front of the large hut seemed to shrink back. The commander ignored them, instead grunting orders at his troops in a deep, liquid voice. Amy strained to hear the words, then realised there was no point, since she wouldn't understand a single word.

Instead, she decided to get closer. It was perfect timing,

with the soldiers focussed on their commander, and the deer people's attention on the soldiers. Amy hurried down the hillside on an angle, keeping her head down as she aimed for the rear of the hut next to the vehicles.

She was nearly there when she heard a shout, and for a horrible moment she thought the cruel-looking aliens had spotted her. She froze, risked a glance, and saw the soldiers were now approaching the line protecting the hut. The commander was inspecting a portable screen, ticking things off with his trotter, and then he snapped the device closed and eyed the defensive line. Amy darted for cover, pressing herself against the rough wooden timbers of the nearest hut before peering around the corner to watch proceedings. The wood smelt fresh and clean next to her cheek, but she could also smell the taint from the nearby combat vehicles - hot oil, rubber and paint.

'Grandma donkey face pull thunderstorm,' shouted the officer, startling Amy with the ferocity of his tone.

'Capsicum e-elements thermometer lap b-band,' replied one of the deer-faced creatures, in a quavering voice.

That's what it sounded like to Amy, but what the commander actually said was 'G'rand m'a dont key fash puel tun der sitorm.' And the second alien, the deer-like male, wasn't talking about capsicums or thermometers. No, what he really said was 'Kip secum lemen tis termom ita l'app bund.'

Unfortunately, neither the real version nor Amy's phonetic translation made any sense, and she had to rely on body language to work out what was going on. It was obvious the pig-faced soldiers were after something, perhaps a fugitive, and it was equally obvious the villagers either didn't have it or weren't about to give it up.

For the sake of the villagers, Amy hoped the soldiers would

go back to their vehicles and leave, but somehow she didn't think it likely.

The officer barked a command and the troops unholstered their weapons, fanning out to encircle the line of creatures.

There was a wail from those peering out of the huts, and Amy could see them wringing their hands and pleading with the soldiers.

Not that it made any difference. The soldiers came to a halt, their stern faces completely expressionless as they stood before the defensive line of deer-like creatures. Then, at a fresh order from their commander, the soldiers raised their weapons.

Amy suddenly felt sick as she realised what was about to happen. The evil-looking pigs were going to murder dozens of defenceless people right in front of her!

29

Hal was still bracing himself inside the crate when the first wave hit, and within seconds he was face down in a litter of cold hamburgers and cardboard boxes. The 'canoe' tumbled over and over, rolling him around like an oversized teddy bear in a cement mixer full of junk food, and by the time it righted itself he was wearing most of the burgers around his person. The smell was intense in the confines of the crate, and Hal realised he'd never really liked burgers in the first place.

He had bigger worries than the dinner menu, though. The cavern was filling fast, but his hopes for a quick escape were dashed when his crate jammed against dozens of others, all blocking the exit tunnel like oversized logs in a storm drain. Then he heard a scraping, grinding noise through the rushing water, and his crate was hurled into the air as the digger slammed into the wall next to the tunnel mouth. There was a splintering sound as it flattened the jammed crates, crushing and breaking them to pieces. Fortunately, Hal's crate emerged almost unscathed, although it did develop a crack which immediately started to leak water. Hal fixed it by jamming a burger bun into the crack, ramming the soggy bread home with the heel of his boot. When he thought of the digger's solid impact, and the pieces of crushed crates all around him, he decided the crack was a very small inconvenience compared to getting flattened against the cavern wall.

Then he felt his crate describe a gentle pirouette, before it was sucked down the tunnel along with all the shards of broken plastic and scattered components from the ruined crates. The debris rustled and jostled his crate, which alternately plunged underwater and rose to scrape the tunnel roof, throwing Hal against the lid or dropping him into the mess of burgers and wrappers underneath.

There was an unpleasant sideways motion too, and Hal really began to hate the smell rising from the ancient bread and meat.

Then, without warning, the crate rammed into something. Hal was thrown bodily against the far end, almost losing consciousness as his head slammed into the plastic. He could hear water tearing past the sides, but realised the lid was clear of the flood. So, he kicked it open and sat up for a look.

The crate had jammed against two buggies - his own, which had been swept along the tunnel, and the vehicle Clunk had left parked in the corridor. Right alongside was a teleporter alcove. The water had filled the teleporter almost to the ceiling, which would make things a little tricky, but Hal knew it was his only chance of escape. If he kept going along the tunnel, he might find another teleporter but he'd never know which address Clunk used to escape the flood.

So, Hal clambered out of the crate and down onto the roll cage of the nearest buggy, clinging to the white-painted metal with all his strength as the water tried to tear him off again. The only way into the teleporter was under water, so Hal took a couple of deep breaths before ducking into the raging torrent. The pressure rammed him against the first buggy, but using all his strength he managed to inch sideways until he reached the second one. Then, after a couple more gasps of air, he inched along the side of the car until his fingers encountered the wall surrounding the teleporter. Here the water was relatively placid, and it was a simple matter to swim inside the mirror-finish alcove. Then he had to run his hands over the slick wall until he found the control panel, which lit up with a familiar glow. Maybe that was why they placed the things behind the walls, Hal thought to himself, before he realised he was in danger of drowning. He stuck a finger out and pressed the Go button, and after a lengthy delay ... whoosh! Hal, the cube of water and several floating burgers all vanished with a gigantic flash of light.

◆

The soldiers raised their weapons, preparing to gun down the helpless villagers, and before Amy knew what she was doing she'd left the safety of the hut and was running full pelt towards the nearest combat vehicle.

There was a ladder on the back, and she went up it like a circus acrobat, barely touching the rungs in her haste. Up top, the gun was a heavy-looking weapon with a couple of handles and a big, open sight on the end. Amy wasn't exactly an expert on alien weaponry, but she identified the safety switch and flipped it to active. Then she grabbed the handles and swung the muzzle round to cover the soldiers.

They were still facing the line of defenders, and the mood was sombre. All the fight had gone out of the villagers, as though they'd accepted the inevitable. Well, Amy wasn't accepting anything. As the officer raised his hand, about to give the signal, she opened fire.

The gun whined, bucking and shaking as it unleashed a torrent of energy bolts. The row of deer-like creatures dived for cover as they saw what was coming, and the soldiers half turned, guns at the ready. They were caught completely by surprise, and had no time to react. Energy bolts zinged all around them, tearing up the ground at their feet and kicking up dirt and stones. Other shots went over their heads, screamed between their legs, blasted several guns from grasping trotters, and plucked at the sleeves and trousers of their uniforms. It was a miracle none of the soldiers were gunned down where they stood, but that only increased their respect for Amy's shooting.

Once she'd discouraged any resistance, Amy stopped firing. 'Drop your weapons and put your hands up,' she shouted, and she gestured with the gun to make her meaning absolutely clear.

The soldiers took one look at the wide-mouthed barrel, and the wild-eyed human aiming it in their direction, then dropped their weapons in a hurry. Their hands shot up as one, the overdressed officer faster than any of them.

Amy beckoned to one of the deer creatures, and mimed tying something up. The woman understood immediately, and within seconds dozens of villagers were swarming over the soldiers, rolling them face-down in the dirt and tying their short little arms behind their backs.

Once the hogs were tied, Amy climbed down from the combat vehicle and went to meet her new allies. She was just in time, because when she got there a couple of the females had drawn sharp-looking knives, and were getting ready to finish the soldiers off.

'No, no, no!' shouted Amy. 'They're prisoners. Leave them alone!' She waved the two females back, then stood between them and the tied-up soldiers. Then she noticed the suspicious looks, and she realised she'd just made a bad mistake. Now the deer-like aliens thought she was on the side of the attackers!

◆

Hal was still holding his breath when he materialised in the destination teleporter. He arrived inside a big cube of water that was still swirling with stray burgers, wrappers and bits of plastic crate, looking for all the world like a life-sized mannequin trapped in a fast-food snow globe.

Then the water flowed out with a rush, and Hal was swept onto the floor, spluttering and fighting for breath. He was still recovering when a cool, firm hand hoisted him to his feet, and through his streaming eyes he saw a familiar bronze shape. 'Clunk! You made it!'

The robot looked embarrassed. 'I'm sorry I left you behind, Mr Spacejock. Only –'

'No, that's fine. You were just checking the lie of the land. Clearing the way before I got here so it was safe for me to teleport.'

'Yes, that's it,' said the robot, with a look of relief. 'That's exactly what I was doing.'

'Neat job parking that buggy, too. It stopped me in just the right place.'

'Naturally,' said Clunk. 'I, er, planned it that way.'

Hal looked around. 'So, where are we?'

'I'm not sure yet.' Clunk gestured towards a curtain of matted creepers. 'There's a forest just outside, but no signs of civilisation.'

'Never mind. I'm sure we'll bump into someone sooner or later.' Hal took off his boots and poured the water out. 'So, which planet did you send Amy to?'

'Er ... she came to this one too.'

'Really?' Hal looked surprised. 'Well, it's lucky we all ended up at the same place, isn't it?'

'Yes, it was a remarkable coincidence,' said Clunk.

'Come on, then. Let's go and find her, and then we can make our way home.'

— 30 —

Amy held her hands out, her fingers splayed to demonstrate she wasn't carrying any weapons. The villagers, on the other hand, were now holding plenty of weapons, from short knives to dangerous-looking scythes, and many of them were also pointing guns the soldiers had dropped. Amy hoped she didn't look too much like the hog creatures, because if she made one false move the end would be swift.

As she got closer she spotted the youngsters peering between the adults' legs, and she couldn't help smiling warmly at their curious little faces. One of the natives noticed the look and smiled back, revealing an expanse of square teeth, and then he said something to the others and the whole group relaxed. Guns were lowered, weapons were set aside, and suddenly Amy was surrounded by curious aliens, touching her clothes, marvelling at her hair and gently brushing her bare skin with their coarse, padded fingers.

Then one of them barked, and the crowd parted to let an elderly female into the midst. Her antlers were worn, her spine was bent, and she used a stick to help her walk. There was nothing frail about her voice though, and she addressed Amy at length while the rest of the aliens listened in silence.

Eventually she stopped talking, and she laid a wrinkled

hand on Amy's arm. The elder's eyes were bright as she looked into Amy's face, and it didn't take a body language expert to read the intent: Amy was a hero, the saviour of the village, and they were all very grateful.

'Thank you for your kind words,' said Amy, speaking slowly and clearly. They wouldn't understand, of course, but her expression and the tone of her voice would have to do. 'I didn't really do that much, and I hope these creatures don't trouble you in future.'

Barely had the words left her mouth when someone blew a long blast on the warning horn. It was followed by a second effort, and a third blast had barely begun when Amy realised she was practically alone. Everyone had disappeared into the huts, except for the elder. She took Amy's arm and pushed her towards the combat vehicles, nodding and gesturing all the while.

Her meaning was clear. You saved us once ... now do it again.

Amy frowned at this. She'd counted at least forty of the deer-like aliens, half of them now armed with the soldiers' weapons. And yet they'd all run for safety at the first sign of trouble, leaving her to fight another battle on their behalf. Clearly, courage wasn't a huge part of their character.

After giving Amy some final words of encouragement, and a hefty shove to underscore the point, the elder hobbled towards the nearest hut, moving a lot quicker than she had before.

Amy glanced towards the trees. She was tempted to make a run for it, especially when this new force of soldiers could be twice as big as the last one. On the other hand, once the tied-up soldiers were freed the whole lot would be after her blood, and she'd never get away from them.

So, she climbed onto the nearest combat vehicle, readied the gun and sighted down the barrel towards the trees. She could see the bushes moving, and her finger was just curling around the trigger when two familiar figures strolled into view. Amy sighed with relief as she recognised Clunk, and she almost forgot to roll her eyes when she saw Hal Spacejock alongside him.

Amy was still looking at the two of them through the gun sight, and she released the trigger in a hurry before waving them over.

◆

As he emerged from the trees, Hal wasn't particularly surprised to see Amy pointing a huge energy cannon at him. No, he was only surprised she hadn't opened fire. After all, she'd already brained him with a rock, and the mounted gun was just a mild escalation in firepower as far as he was concerned.

'Amy!' Clunk broke into a run, leaving Hal choking on his dust. 'Are you okay? Have you been injured?'

'I'm fine.' Amy gave Clunk a broad smile, then accepted his helping hand to climb down the ladder. 'How about you?'

'A little too warm and a little too damp, but that's unimportant.'

'I'm all right too,' called Hal, as he approached the pair of them. The pair of them ignored him.

'Come on,' said Amy to Clunk. 'Let me introduce you to the good aliens.'

'There are bad aliens?'

'Unfortunately, yes.' Amy gestured towards the line of trussed-up soldiers, who were baking in the sun. 'They came here for something, but I don't speak the language so I've no idea what.'

'Tell me what happened.'

She explained quickly, and Clunk's eyebrows rose as he heard about Amy's single-handed capture of the entire squad. Hal, on the other hand, wasn't surprised at all. He figured she could have laid them all out with a bucket of rocks.

As they approached the soldiers, Hal stopped and sniffed. 'Is someone making breakfast?'

'What do you mean?'

Hal's stomach rumbled. 'I swear I can smell bacon.'

'That's not breakfast, Hal. Look closer.'

Hal bent over the nearest soldier, and his jaw dropped as he saw the pig-like face, the tusks and the hairy snout. 'I guess a fry-up is off the menu.'

The soldier's eyes narrowed, and he growled something under his breath. It sounded like 'Bacon sandwich marmalade trigger', and Hal turned to Clunk for help. 'What's he saying? Can you figure it out?'

'I'm a co-pilot, Mr Spacejock. Not a glorified translator.'

'Yeah, but you had to learn their language before. You remember, when we got trapped on that abandoned planet.'

'That was written language, not the spoken word. There's the small matter of pronunciation, regional dialects, the use of slang and –'

'Yeah, yeah. Can't you get the gist of it?'

Clunk hesitated. 'From what I can make out, he advised you to insert your head in your, er, opposite end.'

Amy snorted at this, and Hal directed an angry look at the

soldier. 'I'm not the one trussed up like a Sunday roast, matey. Just wait until I find a jar of apple sauce.'

He would have said more, but at that moment several dozen tall, graceful creatures poured from the nearby huts. Hal got a brief impression of antlers, fur and fine-boned faces before he was threatened with a dozen guns and two dozen assorted gardening implements, any one of which would have opened his insides to the midday sun. Several surrounded Clunk, holding the points of their weapons under his chin, but Hal noticed they left Amy alone.

'I take it these are friends of yours?' he muttered.

'I did save their lives,' said Amy mildly. She turned to the village elder and made a soothing gesture. 'It's okay, they're friendly.'

The elder studied Clunk for several long moments, then said something to the rest. Immediately, they lowered their weapons, and Hal found himself surrounded by curious aliens. Clunk drew far more attention, though, and the aliens seemed fascinated by his bronze metal skin.

'Go on, give them a show,' said Hal. 'Do that spinny thing with your head.'

Clunk frowned at him. 'We're trying to reassure them, not lead them to believe I'm possessed by evil spirits.'

'Why not? They might elect you chief of the tribe.'

'I have no wish to be elected chief of anything.'

'Cheef,' said one of the aliens, her voice reverential as she stroked Clunk's shoulder. Others followed suit, until they were all murmuring the word over and over. 'Cheef, cheef, *cheef!*'

'Now you've done it,' said Amy. 'They think that's his name, you idiot.'

Another of the aliens patted Hal's arm. 'Idjot.'

'Idjot,' said several others, and then they all repeated it. 'Idjot, idjot, idjot.'

Amy struggled not to laugh at Hal's expression. 'I'm Amy,' she said, tapping herself in the chest.

'Imamy,' said one of the aliens, and the rest repeated it over and over.

'Do you think we should skip our surnames?' suggested Hal.

The other two quickly agreed.

'Okay,' said Hal, clapping his hands together. 'It's been really great, but we need to get a move on. Clunk, can you tell them we have to go?'

'Go? What do you mean, go?' said Amy.

'Leave. Depart. Make tracks.' Hal jerked his thumb at the sky. 'My ship is out there somewhere, and I won't get paid until we deliver the cargo.'

'You're worried about that?' Amy pointed at the row of trussed-up soldiers. 'What about them?'

'They're not going anywhere, are they?'

'Not right now, no. But what happens when more troops come looking for them?'

Hal looked around the small settlement, and he realised she was right. The pig creatures would come back and flatten it, and they'd wipe out the deer-like aliens in the process. Still, he hadn't asked to join in their war, and he had problems of his own.

Then he felt a small hand in his, and he looked down to see one of the alien children smiling up at him. At the sight of her cute little face, her oversized eyes and tiny little button nose, Hal realised walking away wasn't an option. There was no way he could abandon these people to their fate. 'Why don't we move them somewhere else?' he suggested.

212

'Pack up the whole settlement?' Amy shook her head. 'They've lived here for generations. They need their crops to survive, and I guarantee they won't leave.'

Hal rubbed his chin. He'd watched a movie once where a small band of heroes trained a whole village to fight back against a bigger force. The villagers had won out, eventually, but many had lost their lives and the heroes hadn't emerged unscathed, either. No, running away seemed like a much better idea. Get them all to safety through the teleporter, and sort out what to do with them afterwards. Or even better, maybe load them into the two trucks and drive them to the nearest settlement. Surely the people there would look after them until things blew over? Hal was ready to convince the others his plan was the only solution when Clunk spoke up.

'There is an alternative,' said the robot.

'Go on.'

'We could convince the soldiers to leave these people alone.'

'How?'

'I don't know,' admitted Clunk.

'Great. That's really useful.' Hal snapped his fingers. 'Hey, I have an idea too.'

'Yes?'

'Sure. We beam special rays from orbit which make the soldiers forget what happened.'

'That's not a very practical suggestion, Mr Spacejock.'

'Don't blame me. You started it.'

Clunk thought for a moment. 'What if we admitted responsibility? We could release the soldiers and surrender to them, and they might accept the villagers played no part.'

'No way,' said Amy.

'But –'

'Clunk, they're ruthless. I guarantee they'd shoot the three of us before killing everyone else. Then they'd burn the huts and bulldoze the ashes into the ground.'

'She's making sense, Clunk,' said Hal. 'It's a terrible plan.'

'We have to let the soldiers go sooner or later, Mr Spacejock. We can't kill them in cold blood.'

Hal thought for a moment. 'Why don't we take them back to their base? We could keep the officer as a hostage and turn the rest in.'

'They might bomb the village to oblivion even though their officer was right here in the midst of it. A casualty of war, so to speak.'

'Okay. Why don't we teleport the soldiers somewhere else and abandon them there? As long as they've got food and water –'

'That won't work,' said Amy. 'They were sent to this settlement, and when they don't return someone else will come here to find out why.'

Hal gestured at the aliens crowded around them, who were all listening intently to the debate even though they didn't understand a word. 'These people could say they never saw them.'

'Under interrogation?'

Hal pulled a face.

'It's a pity we can't ask their advice,' said Amy. 'They might know where the troops are based, how many there are, what sort of weapons they have ... everything.'

'I may be able to help with that,' said Clunk. 'If I can spend a little time with one of them, I should be able to pick up their language.'

'How much time do you need?'

'I estimate half an hour. We can start with the basics, then lead into syntax and semantics, and then move onto advanced _'

'Yes, I get it,' said Hal, whose expertise in languages was only matched by his woeful piloting skills. 'Okay, I like the plan. Grab one and start learning.'

The Navcom was guiding the *Volante* through deep space, keeping one electronic eye on interest rates whilst simultaneously scheduling deliveries across nine star systems. Business had been brisk, and despite a couple of narrow escapes from customs and law enforcement, the *Volante* still had a clean record.

The Navcom was just admiring the favourable interest rate on her investments when a small, innocent-looking ship materialised off the starboard bow. Wait, was it the starboard bow? The Navcom checked again. Yes, it was most definitely the starboard bow.

The Navcom deployed her new scanner and discovered the ship showed signs of life. Unfortunately, it wasn't life the scanner could interpret, and the best the machine could do was to tag the glowing pink shapes with trash cans, adding the caption 'potential spam'.

The Navcom paused for a nanosecond, then activated the emergency hyperspace routine. This was another of the *Volante's* recent upgrades, and it transported the entire ship off in a random direction.

The ship completed the micro-jump, and the mysterious vessel promptly appeared off the starboard bow once more, almost as though it were clinging on.

The Navcom was just preparing another emergency jump when all the comms channels activated at once.

'*This is Gnar P'ker, a commander in the B'Con expeditionary force. What vessel is that?*'

'This is the *Volante*, a peaceful cargo ship on a legitimate freight run. We have absolutely no contraband, weapons or fugitives on board.'

'*Never mind your cargo, I want to know about the crew. Do you have any life forms on board?*'

The Navcom hesitated. She'd just dropped off one lot of prisoners, and there were obviously no human pilots, but there was the dog. 'Yes.'

'*Sentient lifeforms?*'

That was tricky. How did one measure intelligence? 'In a fashion, yes.'

There was a muttered curse before P'ker spoke once more. '*Thank you for your time. You may proceed with your voyage.*'

The small ship vanished, leaving the Navcom alone in the starlit void. With the computer equivalent of a shrug, she filed the conversation under 'strange but harmless' and resumed her original course.

◆

Commander Gnar P'ker grunted in frustration. When his crew spotted the *Volante* he thought the fruitless search was over, and they could blow the Euman vessel apart before reporting a resounding success to the Admiral. Medals and honours would follow, perhaps even a larger ship with upgraded guns and missiles, and P'ker would have been one step ahead of his fellow officers.

Instead, the damned ship had been carrying a lifeform, and although P'ker had been tempted, his orders were most explicit: find the Euman intel ship, and don't kill any sentient creatures. The odd thing was, the lifeform aboard the ship had been a four-legged beast, and it was rare for them to develop space-faring abilities. They had trouble with manual controls, for a start, never mind building ships in the first place.

'I have the Admiral on line three,' said his second-in-command.

'Great. Just what I needed,' grumbled P'ker. 'Okay, put her on.' He turned to face the screen, forcing a smile as Admiral Lardo's heavy-set face appeared.

'P'ker.'

'Sir.'

'What can you tell me?' demanded the Admiral.

'Nothing, sir. We've been searching and searching, but the laws in this galaxy are very strict: every ship must have a Euman pilot.'

'You've not found the intel vessel, then?'

'I fear not. We just scanned a potential, but there was a sentient lifeform on board. A quadruped of the Canis species.'

'Eumans call them dogs,' said the Admiral.

'You're well informed, sir.'

'Had you done your research, you'd have known that these dogs are merely pets.'

P'ker frowned. 'You mean they're not sentient?'

'No speech, no organised society . . . and a fondness for retrieving twigs and rubber balls. I'd say they're not sentient.' The Admiral leant closer to the camera. 'Which means, P'ker, that you just let the target slip through your trotters.'

218

'No!' P'ker whirled round to stare at the scanner, but the *Volante* had disappeared. 'Sir, we'll find her again,' he said desperately. 'We'll find her and blow her into tiny pieces. I promise!'

'If you don't, I'll have you flying a garbage truck for the rest of your life.'

'Sir –'

P'ker was too late. The Admiral had already cut the call. Instead, he rounded on his second-in-command. 'Find that bloody ship, check there are no Eumans on board, then destroy it.'

'What about the dog?'

'It's just a pet. Fry it with the ship.'

'Sir, before I joined the B'con navy I studied law. Sentience is a huge grey area, and –'

'The Admiral said it wasn't sentient,' said P'ker stubbornly.

'Yes, but that won't get you off the hook if the Council decides these dog creatures are sentient. One adverse decision, and you'll swing for sure.'

P'ker blanched. 'Executed?'

'Absolutely.'

'But I just promised the Admiral we'd destroy the *Volante*!'

'You can. We just have to remove the dog first.'

P'ker frowned. 'Remove the dog? And do what with it?'

'We can leave it on a populated planet, hand it over to another Euman ship . . . it doesn't matter, as long as we don't kill it.'

'Very well. Track down the *Volante*, and once we're in range I want a warning shot across her bows. Then, once you have the AI on open comms, you can tell it we're coming aboard.'

Clunk smiled at one of the aliens, a young male with an impressive set of antlers. The robot patted himself on the chest, then pointed to his mouth and mimed speaking. The alien stared at him intently, then hurried off to the nearest hut.

'I think it's working,' said Hal.

However, before Clunk could follow, the young male came back with a plate of food.

'Or not,' remarked Hal, as Clunk was presented with a selection of rough-cut vegetables.

Clunk pointed at the plate. 'Food.'

'Do-od,' said the alien.

'Food,' said Clunk, slightly more forcefully.

'Dood! Dood!' said the alien, waving the plate excitedly.

'Don't mention duck,' advised Hal.

Clunk ignored him. 'This is food,' he said, holding up something that looked like a piece of carrot.

'Dood,' said the alien. 'Dissis.'

Hal sighed. 'Half an hour, you reckon?'

'Perhaps a little longer,' admitted Clunk.

'Two hours? Four?'

'Many more, if you keep interrupting.'

'I'll starve before then. Unless ...' Before Clunk could stop him, Hal took a piece of yellowish vegetable and bit into it. 'Hmm. Not bad.'

'Mr Spacejock!' protested the robot, scandalised. 'You don't know that's edible!'

'Of course it's edible,' said Hal indistinctly. 'I just ate it, didn't I?'

'He means it could be toxic,' said Amy. 'Different species have different tolerances, and . . . ' her voice tailed off as she spotted a piece of fruit which looked like fresh melon. '. . . and it . . . '

'Go on,' coaxed Hal. 'Try some. It's delicious.'

Seconds later they were both enjoying the taste of fresh fruit and vegetables, while Clunk stood nearby with a worried look on his face. For all he knew the humans were consuming a cocktail of foxglove and deadly nightshade, and he didn't know how far it was to the nearest hospital. 'This is most irresponsible,' he said, in a serious tone of voice. 'You could be doing untold damage to your systems.'

'You're just miffed because you can't try any,' said Hal indistinctly. 'Here,' he said to Amy. 'Try this one. It's like strawberry.'

She accepted with a smile, and Clunk closed his eyes as she bit into the reddish fruit. 'He's right,' she said. 'It's like a giant strawberry crossed with a peach.'

'Bisha,' said the alien with the plate.

'No, it's strawberry,' said Amy. 'Hey!'

The shout was because Clunk had snatched the piece of fruit from her grasp. Eagerly, the robot held it up to the alien. 'Bisha?'

The alien nodded.

Clunk grabbed a slice of vegetable which looked like a brownish turnip. He held it up to the alien with a quizzical expression, and the alien obliged.

'Noris.'

'This is wonderful,' said Clunk. 'Progress at last!'

'Yeah, that's great,' said Hal. 'Er, do you need that bisha?'

Now the aliens finally understood what Clunk wanted, the robot managed to elicit words for everything just by pointing at them. His electronic brain catalogued and filed, filed and catalogued, and within a few short minutes he'd assembled a basic vocabulary. Once he could speak with the aliens it was only a matter of refining the data and adding their language rules, and within the promised half an hour he was fluent. While Hal and Amy finished off the plate of fruit, Clunk spoke with the alien elder to find out what was going on ... and to plan their next move.

◆

Hal noticed the villagers were collecting their belongings, with many of them casting worried looks at the sky and the shadows under the nearby trees. 'What's going on?' he asked Clunk.

'I told the elder I'm confident we can resolve the situation.'

'So how come they're packing all their stuff up?'

'The elder's not as confident as I am. As a precaution, most of her people are taking to the hills.'

'And the rest?'

'It seems their culture has a tradition. If an individual saves the village, that individual takes on the role of protector. They're given favoured status, a larger dwelling, the best food and a cut of the annual crop.'

'That sounds pretty good.'

'Yes, except the role lasts for the rest of that person's life.'

'How long has this been a tradition of theirs?' asked Amy.

'I'm guessing about five minutes,' muttered Hal.

'Even so,' continued Clunk, 'we must be careful to observe their customs. After all, we're visitors on their planet.'

'Are you suggesting we leave Amy behind?'

'You'd like that, wouldn't you?' demanded Amy. 'Ever since we met –'

Clunk stepped between them. 'Nobody is leaving anyone. And if you don't mind, you can put your petty squabbles on hold until we've saved everyone's lives.'

'That's all well and good,' said Amy, 'but we haven't come up with a plan yet.'

The three of them looked at each other, seeking inspiration. Then Hal glanced at the row of soldiers, paying special attention to the overdressed officer with his rows of medals and his pantomime hat. As Hal studied the officer, a vague memory came to him, and then a smile lit up his face as he hit upon the solution to all their problems.

'What is it?' asked Clunk, in a worried tone. 'Is it a reaction to the fruit?'

'Eh?'

'Your face . . . you look pained.'

'I'm not pained, I'm happy.'

'Okay.'

'No, really. Back when I was studying to be a pilot –'

Hal broke off as Clunk burst out laughing. The robot put one hand over his mouth, laughed again, then apologised. 'I'm sorry, Mr Spacejock. Please continue.'

Frowning at the interruption, Hal continued. 'They wouldn't give me any more dole money unless I completed a training scheme, so I took a one-hour introductory course at the community college. There was this guy there, Tim his name was, and he'd been doing courses for about twenty years. He'd sewn all the little badges on his jacket . . . everything from martial arts to origami, long jumping to white-water rafting.'

'Is there a point to this?'

'Yes, of course there is. You see, Tim was a proud guy. He loved collecting those badges, and they meant the world to him. Then, one day, we got a new tutor, and she took one look at the badges and burst out laughing.' Hal shrugged. 'Tim walked out, and we never saw him again.'

Amy frowned. 'You're not suggesting we sew badges on the officer's uniform, and then make fun of him? Because if you are –'

'No, of course not. All we have to do is puncture his pride ... or threaten to.'

'How?'

Hal turned to Clunk. 'Can you translate for me?'

'I'm sure I can make myself understood.'

'Good. Explain to the general that he and his crack troops were beaten by nothing more than a primary school teacher. No offense,' he said to Amy, in an aside.

'Plenty taken,' she said, with a frown.

'Lay it on thick, Clunk. Tell them she teaches children. Tell them how young and defenceless she is, and how –' Hal saw Amy's eyes narrow, and he remembered the way she'd hurled chunks of rock at him. Defenceless? Hah. 'Look, I know Amy's fierce and resourceful, but it's important he thinks they've been humiliated, okay? It's part of the plan.'

Amy nodded, but her lips were pressed tightly together.

'Once he's humiliated, then what?' asked Clunk.

'Simple. Then we explain that we're going to tell his commanding officer all about it. Unless –'

'Aha,' said Clunk, as realisation dawned. 'Emotional blackmail!'

'His career would be ruined, right? Him, his troops ... they'd be a laughing stock.' Hal spread his hands. 'So, we offer to hold our tongues about his humiliating capture, and in return they go back and file a nothing report. As in, nothing happened, nothing to see. No retaliation.'

'I think it might just work,' said Clunk. 'Assuming I can find the right words, that is.'

'Give it your best shot.' Hal clicked his fingers. 'Oh yes, and remember to tell him we're not locals.'

'I think he knows that,' said Amy. 'You know, what with our lack of antlers and fur.'

Clunk smiled, then crouched next to the officer and spoke haltingly. After a few moments he removed the officer's gag, and there followed a rapid conversation featuring gutteral noises, snorts and a whole lot of oinking. The rest of the soldiers turned their heads to watch, their eyes curious above the rough gags. Slowly, their expressions changed, and then, as one, they all turned to look at Amy. Also as one, they all sagged, as though someone had pulled the bungs out of a row of inflatable toys.

'I think they got the message,' remarked Hal.

The officer said something in a low voice, and Clunk patted him on the shoulder. Then, before anyone could stop him, the robot untied the officer and helped him to his feet. 'Don't worry,' said Clunk. 'They're more than happy to cooperate.'

Hal breathed a sigh of relief. Then he noticed the deer-like aliens had frozen in the midst of packing their belongings, and were watching events with expressions ranging from fear to outright terror. 'You'd better tell them what's going on,' he said to Clunk. 'For all they know, we just changed sides.'

Clunk hurried to expain, and a few moments later the officer and the elder held out a trotter and paw respectively, before engaging in a hurried, awkward shake. The rest of the troops were set free, and Clunk returned their weapons ... after draining their charges into his own batteries. He did the same with the guns mounted on the vehicles, and then the soldiers clambered onto the trucks and held on tight as the drivers tried to turn the pick-ups in the tight space. One of them side-swiped a building, raising a groan from the watching villagers, and as he pulled clear the truck door groaned and buckled against the solid timber, leaving a lengthy gash in the bodywork.

Then the trucks were clear, and they drove off in a cloud of dust, leaving only the lingering whine from their engines to show they were there at all.

'I hope we did the right thing,' said Hal, as he flapped the dust away from his face.

'If we didn't, they'll come straight back with reinforcements,' said Clunk gravely.

— 32 —

'So, what's the next move?' asked Hal. 'Back to the teleporter? Or should we –'

'Wait a moment,' said Clunk, raising one finger. 'I'm picking up communications chatter from the vehicles.'

They were all silent while the robot listened, head on one side, and then he turned to them with a serious expression. 'I believe we just made a tactical blunder.'

'Go on,' said Hal. 'Surprise me.'

'That officer we just released …he was slightly more important than I thought.' Clunk hesitated. 'In fact, he was a lot more important.'

'Still waiting for the surprise,' said Hal.

'He was …he *is* … the military commander in charge of the whole planet.'

There was a lengthy silence, eventually broken by Hal.

'What you're saying is, he doesn't have a superior officer?'

'That's about the size of it.'

'So the blackmail idea …threatening to embarrass him in front of his commander –'

'Isn't going to work.'

'We should have guessed he'd feed us a bunch of porkies.' Hal glanced towards the treeline, then scanned the sky. Within minutes the area would be crawling with enemy troops, and when they'd finished killing everyone a squadron of airborne assault vehicles would probably lay waste to the entire area. 'What was the commander doing out here, anyway?'

'Perhaps it was a morale-building exercise for the troops.'

'If so, it'll be the first and last time,' said Hal, with a snort. 'Oh, well. I guess we'd better herd these folks towards the teleporter.'

'What folks?'

Hal glanced towards the settlement, then did a double-take. Everyone had gone, leaving a few scattered belongings in the dust. 'What . . . where . . . who?' he stammered, looking around.

Clunk was busy interpreting another transmission, and didn't answer. While he stood there, head on one side, Hal scanned the surrounding hills until he saw a column of aliens hot-footing it through the trees. Most were carrying large packs, but despite the load they didn't look like they were going to slow their pace for about a week. 'So much for organising resistance,' remarked Hal.

'Give them a break,' said Amy. 'They can't fight back with a handful of farm tools.'

'You're right. I bet they wish we'd never shown up.'

Amy shook her head. 'When I arrived those pig creatures were about to shoot half the settlement in cold blood. At least now they have a chance.'

'It's a pity we didn't hang onto some of those energy weapons. A couple of guns would have been . . . ' Hal's voice tailed off as Amy reached behind her back and drew one of the small white blasters from her belt. She checked the indicator, then sighted along the barrel at a tree or two. 'How come *you* get one?' demanded Hal plaintively.

Amy gave Hal a wink. 'Some of us think ahead.'

Hal eyed her with new-found respect. He already had a healthy regard for her unexpectedly warlike nature, but keeping hold of a gun when Clunk was around was like losing your wallet in a betting shop and finding it two days later ... with the cash still intact.

Meanwhile, Clunk had finished translating the message, and he turned to them with a thoughtful expression. 'The B'Con are going to throw everything they have at the settlement.'

'Figures.'

'They're sending all their troops, all their flyers ... everything.'

'Yes, you said that already. Repeating it doesn't make it sound any better.'

'Meanwhile, their base will be left unattended.'

Hal's eyebrows rose. 'Are you suggesting we capture their headquarters?'

'We're sure to find a working teleporter there, and if we sabotage the rest of the base it would give them pause for thought.'

'Sure. And what about their defences? They won't leave a door key under the mat for us. There'll be armed robots, sensors, gun turrets, neuro-toxins, laser beams ... these guys are seriously bad news, Clunk.'

'They don't have that sort of technology here,' said Clunk. 'You saw their personnel carriers ... they were just pickup trucks with guns on the back.'

Hal frowned. Clunk was right ... on some human planets he'd seen hovertanks, combat robots, armoured suits and more. Here, the military seemed very low-tech. 'These are the guys who built the teleporter network, aren't they?'

'Yes, but the B'Con empire spans entire galaxies. That takes an awful lot of resources, and there are thousands - no, millions

- of backwater planets which have been isolated for decades. Look at the teleporter we used when we arrived . . . it hadn't been used for so long it was all but buried.'

'You seem to know a lot about these B'Con guys.'

'I've been accessing their data feeds,' explained Clunk. 'I already have a map of the area, and I also found a floor plan of their base. It's not far from here, and if we hurry –'

'Don't waste time talking about it. Lead on!'

<hr />

Hal parted a couple of branches and peered through the bush he was using for cover. Down below, at the bottom of a gentle slope, there was a collection of tin sheds and garages connected with makeshift tunnels. There was also a radio mast which had a drunken lean to it, and the area was littered with vehicle parts and empty drums and barrels. The base was protected by a rusty chainlink fence with several gaping holes, and the buildings had also seen better days. As far as enemy bases went, it looked about as impregnable as a cat on heat.

'Well, at least we don't have to worry about laser towers and body scanners,' remarked Hal. 'So, what's the plan? Huff and puff from here until the whole lot falls over, or sit around waiting for the next stiff breeze?'

'We ought to conduct a search.' Clunk glanced at Amy, paying particular attention to the weapon she was holding at the ready. 'Amy, I'd appreciate it if you don't shoot at anything. If we meet resistance, they're likely to be much better armed than us.'

'Okay.'

'In fact, I think –'

'Oh, here it comes,' said Hal. 'Whatever he says, don't give it up.'

Clunk frowned. 'I was just going to suggest I look after the weapon.'

'You must have quite a collection by now,' said Hal. 'What do you do with them all? Sell them to enthusiasts, or polish them up and display them in cabinets?'

'Mr Spacejock, you're being unfair. I admit that, in the past, I have relieved you of certain lethal weaponry, but I assure you I had your best interests at heart.' Clunk turned to Amy. 'I believe it would be in your best interest, too. After all, you're not trained in the use of –'

'That's okay,' said Amy. 'I'd rather keep hold of the gun.'

'Good luck,' muttered Hal. 'Hey, you don't have a spare do you?'

Amy shook her head.

With the firepower situation resolved, the three of them turned their attention to the base. They'd been watching it closely for the past ten minutes without seeing a soul, and it seemed the aliens really had left it deserted. Unlikely though it seemed, the B'Con troops had demonstrated a tendency towards over-confidence, and the thought that someone might be brave enough to infiltrate their base clearly hadn't occurred to them.

So, after wasting another couple of minutes watching the deserted buildings, Hal decided enough was enough. He gestured to Amy and Clunk, waited for them to move into the open, then sheltered behind the pair of them as they all moved towards the fence.

There were no warning shouts, and nobody fired at them. A loose piece of tin creaked and flapped in the breeze, but that was the only sound. Hal felt the whole place was too quiet, but they didn't have much time to waste. Any minute now the alien force might come roaring back again, and he didn't want to be trapped inside the fence.

The three of them hurried through the entrance gates and took shelter near the doors to a large hut. The doors were open, and when Hal risked a quick look he saw several rows of bunks, all unmade. There were clothes all over the floor, dirty plates and cups on every surface, and a sour smell of sweat and stale food.

'What a pig sty,' he muttered in disgust. It didn't occur to him that his own ship would look and smell just as bad if Clunk wasn't around to clear up.

They left the barracks via one of the tunnels, their footsteps echoing off the tin walls despite their attempts to be quiet. At the far end they found a pair of doors, which Hal opened with much effort and even more noise. The bottom of the doors squealed on the floor and the hinges creaked and groaned as though they hadn't tasted a drop of oil in twenty years.

'Not big on maintenance, are they?' whispered Hal.

Clunk nodded. 'There's a valuable lesson in there, Mr Spacejock.'

'Why are you two whispering?' asked Amy, in her normal voice.

'We don't want them to hear us,' mouthed Hal.

'Huh. Like they didn't hear those doors.' Amy eyed her pistol, then turned the safety catch on and tucked the weapon into her belt.

'You might need that.'

'Nonsense. This place is deserted.'

Hal was about to argue, but he realised she was right. He finished opening the doors, and together they entered the large garage beyond. Inside they saw a row of pick-up trucks with mounted guns on the back, identical to the one Amy had used at the settlement. Hal glanced along the row, then paused. One of the trucks had a long gash in the side, and he realised it was the exact same vehicle.

'Wait a minute,' he muttered. 'If the trucks are here, how did the troops get back to the village?'

'Some kind of aircraft?' said Clunk.

'Are you kidding? These guys don't even have a kite to fly.'

'How can you tell?' demanded Amy.

Hal gestured at the window. 'No control tower, no hangar, no landing lights, nothing.' Then he spotted something else - up in the corner, a battered-looking camera was watching them. Hal kept his eyes on the housing as he moved to the left, and he saw the camera tracking him jerkily. Then he moved right, and the camera tracked him that way, too.

'We have to leave,' said Hal out the corner of his mouth. 'Make for the exit, but don't let on.'

'Don't let on to what?' asked Amy.

'No arguments, no discussion. Move out, right now.'

'But –'

'It's a trap!' hissed Hal. 'Now get moving, before –'

Too late. Someone blew an ear-splitting whistle, and suddenly the garage was full of armed troops. They bobbed up from behind the vehicles, dived in through the windows, kicked out ceiling panels and slid to the ground on ropes, and flooded in through the doors. Within seconds Hal and Amy were surrounded, and at that point Hal realised two things:

One, that it *had* been too quiet all along.

And two, Clunk was nowhere to be seen.

'*Kippa ni trent! Goh!*' barked the pig-faced soldier.

Without hesitation, Hal put his hands up. He had no idea what the soldier was saying, but the gesture with the weapon and the aggressive tone of voice made it pretty clear: surrender or die.

Amy did likewise, and was quickly relieved of the small blaster she'd managed to keep from Clunk. Then they were both marched out of the garage at gunpoint.

'What do you think they'll do with us?' murmured Amy, as they were herded along the tunnel to the barracks.

'They'll probably question us for a bit,' muttered Hal. He didn't elaborate, and from the nervous look on Amy's face he didn't need to. These aliens would want to know everything about the human race, and the interrogation could take a very long time. A lifetime, even.

Suddenly, it dawned on Hal that they'd been comprehensively outsmarted. The radio messages Clunk had picked up, the way the aliens had announced they were leaving their base unprotected ... it had all been an elaborate trap to catch the humans. Hal cursed under his breath. How could Clunk have been so gullible? Then he remembered the robot had slipped away in the confusion, and he hoped there was a decent rescue plan in the offing. Clunk was resourceful, and Hal was sure the robot would whip up a suitable scheme in no time.

Then again, with his luck Clunk would run out of batteries just before he could unlock their cell door, leaving Hal and Amy to a lifetime of torture and questioning.

◆

Clunk watched the soldiers lead Amy and Hal away, and as he saw the humans being pushed and shoved it was all he could do not to rush in and help. He knew it would be pointless though, and staying out of sight was the best chance for all of them. He was pretty sure the humans would be kept alive, at least for the time being. The aliens would want to interrogate them before arranging any executions - or at least, Clunk hoped so.

When the soldiers descended on them, Clunk had been inspecting the nearest vehicle, and he'd escaped detection by rolling underneath and clinging to the chassis. Thankfully the B'Con had been eager to drag their captives away, and hadn't given the garage more than a cursory search.

Clunk was about to lower himself to the ground when he heard a noise, and he quickly hid again. A couple of soldiers had returned, and they argued amongst themselves as they searched the garage. Clunk listened carefully, and gradually he pieced together their conversation.

'They say there was a third Euman. A metal-man with urine-yellow skin.'

'Metal or flesh, my gun will destroy it.'

The first soldier thumped his clenched trotter on his chest. 'Glory to the B'Con.'

'All hail the empire.'

'Reckon they'll promote us if we catch this metal-man?'

'Who gives an excrement about promotion? I'm going to rip his fornicating head off and play footy with the thing.'

Clunk swallowed nervously. He thought it was bad enough the B'Con were a race of brutal, ruthless soldiers, but now things were far worse: it appeared they were also keen soccer fans.

The soldiers continued to search, poking around in cupboards and lockers, and peering inside the vehicles. Clunk felt exposed, and if one of the soldiers decided to peek under the trucks he knew he'd be spotted instantly. He began inspecting the underneath of the vehicle, examining the pipes and wiring. If necessary, he might be able to cause a fire - or even an explosion - and escape in the ensuing confusion.

He got as far as decoding the vehicle's control interface when the soldiers finished their search, fortunately without spotting him. As soon as they left, Clunk lowered himself to the concrete floor. Then he rolled out from under the vehicle like a double-jointed spider, bending his arms and legs in both directions to keep his body off the ground. Once clear, he sprang up, and with one powerful thrust from his leg motors he leapt on top of the vehicle. From there he reached into the garage's roof cavity, using one of the many cross-beams to pull himself up.

Not a moment too soon: barely had he drawn his legs up than half a dozen soldiers returned to the garage, herded in by an angry-looking officer.

'I don't care if you've searched this fornicating garage twice. Do it again, and do it properly this time!'

The soldiers hurried to obey, peering into toolboxes and empting crates of spares onto the floor. Clunk would have been lucky to get both of his large, flat feet into some of the small containers they were searching, but the soldiers were determined to show just how thorough they could be, no matter how illogical.

After twenty minutes the officer barked another command, and the soldiers lined up in front of her. 'Well?' she demanded, as they shuffled their feet.

Nobody said anything.

'You. What's your name?'

'Sidov, sir.'

'What have you found?'

'Nothing, sir.'

'And you? What's your name?'

'Firesh, sir.'

'Did you find anything?'

Firesh glanced at his fellow soldiers for support, then shook his head.

'And you call yourselves B'Con? You're a bloody disgrace.' The officer glanced around the garage, then looked up at the ceiling. Clunk fought the impulse to draw further back into the gloomy crawl space, knowing any sudden movement would be spotted. Then the officer gestured at the soldiers. 'Sidov and Firesh, check the roof space. The rest of you, ready your weapons.'

Clunk looked around in despair. It would be impossible to move without making a noise, and when they heard him the soldiers would blast him to fragments through the false ceiling. Then he looked up, and he spotted a row of screws holding the tin roof sheet down just above his head. The sharp ends all pointed down towards him, and like lightning he snipped them all off. Then he eased the roof sheet upwards, and before the soldiers could react to the flood of daylight, he was perched on the roof. There was a shout from below, and the tin roof erupted with ragged holes as the soldiers opened fire. Clunk darted along the ridge, dodging and weaving as energy bolts and metal fragments zinged and whizzed around him, and then he leapt onto the roof of the tunnel connecting the barracks to the garage. He was moving fast now, but still the soldiers kept up the barrage. The shots were angled rather than erupting from directly below, and Clunk dodged several near misses before he was able to clamber onto the roof of the barracks.

Still the soldiers kept firing, but now their shots were passing through several thicknesses of wall and roof sheeting, and instead of bursting through they left molten bubbles in the tin. Clunk didn't slow down, though: he kept running at full pace, leaping off the far side of the roof and charging along the next tunnel, expecting more gunfire at any time.

Finally, after two more buildings and another set of tunnels, he took a flying leap over the chainlink fence, landed in the dirt on all fours, regained his feet and ran for the safety of the forest.

Clunk headed to his left as soon as the compound was out of sight, hoping to circle round to the main entrance. He knew the commander would send troops to scour the forest, and his only chance of escape was to slip back into the base and hole up somewhere quiet. Only then could he find out where Hal and Amy were being held, and hopefully come up with a rescue plan.

'Why aren't they grilling us? What are they waiting for?'

Hal shrugged. For all he knew the B'Con were digging out their biggest frying pan, and he was in no hurry to join them in a feast.

Hal and Amy were locked in a poky little cell, with only a couple of grotty mattresses and a filthy-looking bucket for company. Hal wasn't sure whether the bucket was a makeshift toilet or their lunch, and he had no intention of getting close enough to find out.

'I wish they'd get on with it,' said Amy irritably. 'All this waiting is killing me.'

'The longer we wait, the more chance Clunk will rescue us.'

Amy's expression softened. 'You're right. I just ... I can't stand waiting for things, you know?'

'Yeah, I know.' Hal gave her a reassuring grin. 'Don't worry, we'll be okay.'

'Hal, we're stranded on an alien planet. We've been captured by a bloodthirsty race of pigs. We're probably going to be killed then eaten, or vice versa, and our only hope of rescue is an elderly robot who can't even say boo to a fly.' Amy spread her hands. 'Let's face it, we're screwed.'

'We're still alive, aren't we?'

'However long that might last,' muttered Amy. Then she froze. 'Listen ... footsteps!'

Moments later, a couple of soldiers marched into view. They opened the door, and one of them gestured at Amy with his gun. The meaning was clear: follow me.

'You're not taking her anywhere,' growled Hal. He stepped forwards to stop them, and got a hefty shove for his trouble. The B'Con soldier was immensely strong, and Hal was still sprawled on the floor when the cell door clanged shut.

'Amy, don't be a hero!' he shouted. 'Tell them everything! Tell them whatever they want to hear!'

Amy only managed one word before she was hustled out of the cells, and it struck Hal with the force of a hammer blow: 'How?'

'How indeed,' muttered Hal in despair. They couldn't understand the aliens, couldn't speak their language, and couldn't make themselves understood. If only Clunk had been captured with them! He could have helped out by translating during the interrogation, and then –

Hal snorted. And then he could have watched on helplessly while Hal and Amy were put to death. Oh well, look on the bright side: at least Amy didn't have to pace up and down while she waited impatiently for something to happen.

— 34 —

'The Euman female is waiting outside.'

Commander R'ash glanced at the clock on his desk. Twenty-five minutes had passed since the intruders had been captured, and the manual recommended stewing prisoners for at least two hours. Despite that, the commander wasn't the patient type, and he was curious to find out where these terrorists had come from, and more importantly, what they were after. Were they trying to seed revolt amongst the natives of this insignificant little planet? Was the puny Euman race making a move on the incalculable might of the B'Con empire? Either way, their approach was suicidal and clearly destined for failure.

On the other hand, the Euman woman had single-handedly disarmed a squad of B'Con soldiers, and that was a worrying sign. Sure, she'd taken them by surprise, but improvisation and rat-cunning were dangerous traits in one's enemies.

R'ash eyed his terminal, which was displaying his much-edited report on the Euman situation. He'd outlined most of the events so far, although he'd omitted his embarrassing capture and subsequent release, but he wasn't satisfied with the summary. Phrases like 'I expect to find out more soon' and 'interrogations will begin shortly' didn't exactly sound firm and decisive, and he was tempted to hold off submitting the report until he knew more. Unfortunately, that wasn't an option, since any rebellion, conflict or contact with aggressive species had to be reported to the Council immediately.

With a sigh, he submitted the report. The Council would despatch a higher-ranked officer to take over, and that would be the end of R'ash's chances of making a splash and getting promoted off this insignificant little planet. Still, maybe the officer would put in a word for him, especially if the interrogations yielded results before they arrived.

R'ash glanced at the clock. Oh, damn the manual, he thought, and he nodded at the soldier. 'Okay, bring her in.'

He watched impassively as the Euman was marched into his office between two huge soldiers, and he grunted to himself as they pushed her into a chair. 'Gently now. We're not savages.'

The soldiers retreated to the door, blocking the exit with their bulk.

'Good afternoon, my child,' said R'ash, giving the Euman woman his most winning smile. 'Now, my dear lady, would you like to explain what this is all about?'

The Euman said something short and curt.

R'ash tried another tack. 'If you could just tell me where the metal-man is, I'd really appreciate it. We could use his help in translation.' Before the words had even left his mouth, he realised how daft that was . . . naturally, she didn't speak his language.

Not surprisingly, the woman said nothing.

R'ash opened a desk drawer and took out a couple of shot glasses and a bottle of vintage apple brandy. There was only a small amount left, and he had no idea whether he'd ever get his trotters on another bottle, but he was determined to show this Euman how civilised and friendly the B'Con could be. Setting the shot glasses on his desk, he tipped a measure into each before putting the cap back on the bottle and stowing it carefully away in the drawer. Then he raised his glass and knocked it back in one quick motion, smacking his lips and blinking away tears as the potent liquid ran down his throat like molten lava.

His prisoner watched impassively.

'Go on, dear. It'll do you good.' R'ash slid the second glass across the table towards the Euman woman. 'It's apple brandy. The best money can buy.' R'ash mimed drinking, then pointed at the woman.

Instead of accepting the drink, she shook her head.

'Oh well. I tried.' R'ash downed the second shot of brandy, then put both glasses away. 'Yum,' he said, rubbing his stomach. 'Very nice.'

The woman looked away.

'I'm going to cut your head off and feed it to my troops,' said R'ash conversationally.

There wasn't even a flicker of reaction, and it dawned on R'ash that interrogation was going to be all but impossible. He'd been hoping the Euman understood enough of his language to get by, but clearly their speech training had been as slapdash as the rest of the preparation for their crazy mission.

'Okay, take her back to the cells.'

'Yes sir. Should I bring the other one?'

R'ash shook his head. One failed interrogation was bad enough. Two would be a disaster. 'Leave them until support arrives. With any luck they'll bring a Euman specialist.' Too late, R'ash realised he should have *asked* for a Euman specialist, and it dawned on him that there was a good reason he was commanding an insignificant little planet instead of, say, a mighty B'Con battle fleet. He licked a spot of apple brandy off his upper lip, and as he savoured the fiery liquid he wondered whether there was time to send a second message.

＊

Hal paced the cell impatiently, dreading what the savage pig-creatures might be doing to poor, harmless Amy. Well, maybe not completely harmless, but certainly unarmed and outmatched.

What he wanted to do was bust open the cell door, overpower the guards with his bare hands, march to wherever they were holding Amy and rescue her. Admittedly, she was a pain in the arse, but he knew it would make Clunk happy.

Yes, about that. Where exactly was his loyal, dependable robot? Hal frowned. If he discovered Clunk had fled the planet ...but no, the robot was probably waiting until nightfall to put some devilishly clever plan into action. Either that, or he was busy carving 'Hal', 'Amy' and today's date onto matching headstones.

Hal heard footsteps, and he pressed his face to the bars to look along the corridor. He saw Amy between two hulking soldiers, but before he could call out to her they'd pushed open the door and bundled her into the cell. Then, without a word, they left.

'Are you all right?' demanded Hal. 'Did they hurt you? What did they want to know?'

Amy rubbed her wrists. 'I don't know, do I? They sat me down with the commander, and he just growled and oinked and snorted at me. He kept baring his tusks and grunting.'

'Probably trying to intimidate you.'

'I don't know that he was,' said Amy honestly. 'I think he's trying to work out what we're doing here.'

'He's not the only one,' muttered Hal.

'He offered me a drink, too. It smelled like apple brandy or something.'

Hal brightened. As interrogations went, getting loaded on fine spirits sounded like a pleasant twist. 'Was it good?'

'No idea. I refused to touch it.'

'Probably for the best. It might have been poisoned, or he might have laced it with truth drugs.'

Amy gave him an odd look. 'It's not that. I don't drink alcohol.'

Hal glanced through the bars. 'I wonder when they'll come for me?'

'They might not bother. They need Clunk to translate, so they'll probably devote all their resources to hunting him down.'

'Good luck with that,' muttered Hal. 'I can never find him when I need him, and I know all his hiding spots aboard the *Volante*.'

'They have a lot of soldiers.'

'Yeah, and he's got a whole planet to hide in.'

◆

Two dozen soldiers formed a guard of honour in front of the teleport chamber, expressions severe, boots polished and blasters at the ready. They barely flinched as the official party arrived in a blaze of light . . . and an even bigger blaze of high-ranking uniforms decked with brass epaulettes and battle ribbons. That was just the adjutant and three of his staffers, and once they'd cleared the teleporter the real star arrived: Grand Admiral Lardo, commander in chief of the B'Con battle fleet.

Lardo briefly stood to attention as the guard of honour saluted her, and then she strode past them to the waiting commander. She'd left the entire fleet under the control of her second-in-command, and she was eager to get back before the young idiot flew her precious ships into the nearest star. Not that he'd be blamed for it, of course . . . not with his family connections.

'The prisoners,' barked Lardo. 'Where are they?'

R'ash saluted hastily. 'In the cells, sir.'

'Did you get anything out of them?'

'Not yet. I tried a gentle approach with the female, but she wouldn't cooperate. As for the male, I left him in the cell to ponder his future.'

'He doesn't have one,' said Lardo curtly. 'Bring him out and I'll begin the interrogation immediately.'

'He doesn't speak our language,' R'ash warned her.

'Nonsense. He'll be as fluent as we are.'

'But –'

'You're not suggesting the Eumans would mount a raid like this without fully preparing their operatives?'

'I was originally of the same opinion, but my questioning revealed –'

'Your questioning revealed nothing. My techniques are a little more . . . direct.' Lardo withdrew a businesslike bayonet from a sheath strapped to her bulky thigh. It had a long straight blade, and there were traces of dried blood on the serrated edges. 'Five minutes with the Euman male, and I guarantee he'll sing a different tune.'

R'ash eyed the blade. 'Or the same tune, only in a higher pitch.'

Lardo grunted, then gestured to the adjutant. 'Just in case, I want you to get back to the ship and find me a Euman specialist.'

The adjutant saluted smartly, set the address on the teleporter's control panel, and left in a flash of light. Once he was gone, Lardo signalled towards the waiting guards. 'Fetch the male prisoner. And on the way back here, I want you to chat to each other about the torture I'm going to put him through. Make it good, do you understand? Bloodthirsty.'

The guards stood to attention, saluted her, then left with a clatter of steel-shod boots.

'That should do it,' said Lardo in satisfaction. 'By the time he gets here he'll be a quivering wreck. I'll only have to hack off a limb or two before he squeals.'

The commander reserved judgement. Lardo seemed convinced the Eumans had sent a team of crack saboteurs, but he was beginning to suspect the truth was much more mundane: Simply that the Eumans and their metal companion had stumbled into a disused teleporter and –

R'ash felt his gut constricting. He'd forgotten to mention the metal man in his report! Was there anything he'd got right in this sorry mess? Why oh why had the silly Eumans chosen his nice peaceful corner of the galaxy for their pointless mission?

R'ash scratched the bristles on his chin. He had to get hold of the search squad, to make sure they only reported back to him. With any luck he could pretend the metal man was a completely separate incident, unrelated to the Euman couple. Or maybe it would be best if his troops didn't find the thing at all? He resolved to contact them as soon as possible, calling off the search. If he increased the perimeter guard at the same

247

time, the metal man wouldn't be able to get in, and Lardo would never learn of his existence.

Lardo was still inspecting her dagger, and R'ash brightened as a pleasant thought occurred to him. Perhaps, when the admiral had finished with the prisoners, they could hold a regimental barbecue! Morale had been a bit shaky recently, and a decent feast would really egg the B'Con troops on.

Clunk evaded the B'Con search party without too much trouble. Stealth was clearly a foreign word to the big, heavy pig-creatures, who crashed and bashed their way through the forest as they hunted him down. Clunk wasn't exactly the nimblest of robots, but even so he managed to slip away every time a search party bulldozed its way through the forest in his general direction.

After an hour the noises grew fainter, more distant, and thirty minutes after that they ceased altogether. From his current hiding spot Clunk could just see the camp's main gate between the trees, and he watched with satisfaction as the search squad trooped home empty-handed. A senior officer met them near the barracks, and after a brief exchange the soldiers split up, spreading out over the entire compound. Clunk watched closely, and he saw the soldiers spacing themselves around the perimeter, each facing the fence. They were all within earshot of each other, and with a sinking feeling Clunk realised it was going to be pretty difficult getting back inside to rescue Amy and Hal.

Clunk eyed the sky, estimating the minutes until darkness.

Ever the optimist, he hoped the B'Con would treat Hal and Amy to a nice meal before beginning a round of gentle questioning.

◆

Hal eyed the massive pig creature in concern, wondering what she had in store for him. He knew immediately she was in command, and she didn't need the elaborate uniform to prove it - the way the others deferred to her made it clear enough. She had an impressive row of campaign ribbons on her chest, and the five gold rings on her sleeve encompassed a stylised spaceship. Probably an admiral, thought Hal, unless the B'Con were even bigger rankers than their human equivalents.

The admiral was holding a long, straight dagger with a serrated edge. The blade was finely honed, and when the admiral expertly twirled the bayonet in her hand Hal noticed the grip was worn smooth. This was no ceremonial dagger - it was an instrument of war, and a well-used one at that.

The admiral met his eyes, and her lips drew back in a vicious sneer. Then, with a twist of her trotters, she removed the dagger's handle. Underneath was a second blade, shorter than the first, and with a quick flick the admiral under-handed the dagger towards the roof. It stuck fast, quivering, with the longer, serrated, blood-stained blade pointing down. The admiral eyed it for a moment or two, then uttered a command. The waiting guards moved forwards, taking Hal by the upper arms and lifting him off the ground until his toes were clear of the floor. Then they carried him forwards, until he was

249

directly under the dagger. Hal tipped his head back, his eyes wide as he stared at the deadly blade hanging over his head. What was the admiral's plan? Were they going to wait around until it fell from the roof, stabbing him in the head?

No, that wasn't the plan. At a command from the admiral the soldiers tightened their grip. Then, on what was obviously a count of one-two-three, they hoisted Hal into the air. The admiral barked an order, and they stopped at the last second. Hal could actually feel the tip of the dagger gently parting his hair, and he swallowed nervously.

'*D'kar fi gerr,*' said the Admiral, addressing Hal directly for the first time.

'I don't know what you're saying,' explained Hal, his voice as steady as possible under the circumstances.

The Admiral gestured, and the soldiers lowered him until his toes brushed the ground. Then she began to count again.

Whoosh! Hal was hoisted up, and this time the point of the dagger actually pricked his scalp. It was only the lightest of touches, but Hal didn't waste time expressing his admiration for the soldiers' skill. No, he was desperately hoping Clunk's rescue mission would save him in time.

35

Amy looked up hopefully as her cell door opened, but it wasn't Hal . . . or Clunk. Instead she saw a guard offering her a plate. She'd been getting hungry, and the thought of dinner made her stomach rumble uncontrollably. The guard snorted at the noise, then set the plate on the floor and backed out, closing the door behind himself. After it slammed to, she heard the rattle of a key as he locked it firmly.

Amy grabbed the plate, which contained a large slab of bread coated with a dark, greasy substance. It smelled rank, like meat gone off, and she was about to tip it in the slops bucket in the corner of the cell when she got an idea. Taking the bread, she crouched near the door and rubbed the greasy spread all over the floor until it covered about a square metre.

Once done, Amy retreated to the back of the cell. She tore the remains of the bread to pieces, then hesitated, her heart in her mouth. Her plan was simple, but if it didn't work the guard would probably shoot her on the spot. Even if it did work, she'd have to sneak around a military base full of hardened soldiers, alone.

The alternative was to sit still and wait for rescue, which hadn't worked real well for her so far. No, it was time for action.

Decision made, Amy threw the plate at the floor, smashing it with an ear-shattering crash. Then, as soon as she heard footsteps, she put both hands to her neck and began to make realistic choking noises.

The door burst open, and out of the corner of her eye she saw the guard charging towards her. There was a split second when she thought her plan had failed, that he would keep his feet and reach her in half a dozen paces. Then, without warning, the guard's legs flew out from underneath, the soles of his boots skidding on the greasy floor like a pair of ice skates. He went over backwards, arms flailing, and landed on his back with a terrific thud. There was a hollow crack as his skull hit the unyielding floor, and then he lay still.

Amy sidled towards him, ready to run at the slightest movement. The guard's eyes were closed, and for a second or two she wondered if she'd killed him. Then she noticed the regular rise and fall of his chest. Knocked out, that was all.

Pausing only to take the guard's gun and keys, Amy circled the treacherous, greasy patch on the floor and left the cell. She closed the door and locked it, hoping that would give her a little more time, and then, heart thudding in her chest, she set off down the corridor towards the exit. Her first priority was to rescue Hal, and then she'd see about escaping the compound and meeting up with Clunk.

◆

Admiral Lardo gave Hal a long, calculating look. Then she shrugged and grunted a command. With a sinking feeling,

Hal realised she'd given up on the interrogation, and meant to end his life right there and then.

As the guards hoisted him up, trying to drive his skull onto the waiting bayonet, Hal jerked his legs into the air, pivoting in their grip until he was completely upside-down. He drove his legs upwards and his feet thudded onto the roof, either side of the wicked dagger. The guards kept lifting, making his legs bow with the strain, and as the point came closer and closer to neutering him, Hal wondered whether he hadn't just made a bad situation far worse.

Slowly, straining for all he was worth, Hal began to counter the guards' efforts. He straightened his legs, millimetre by millimetre, getting further and further from the waiting knife blade. Then, before he could do anything to escape, there was a thunder of heavy footsteps as the Admiral rushed over to help. Hal realised he could never fight three of them, so as soon as she was in range Hal gave a huge, final thrust against the roof. Taken by surprise, the guards tumbled to the ground, and as he fell from their grip Hal lashed out with his foot. He caught the Admiral on the shoulder, knocking her off-balance, and the momentum carried him backwards, out of reach of the guards. With all four of them scrabbling on the floor, Hal scurried towards the door, barely managing to evade the guards' desperate attempts to grab his ankles. Then he was clear, on his feet and running full tilt along a dank corridor, while behind him the Admiral's outraged squealing sounded like the death throes of a pig in a slaughterhouse.

◆

Amy heard the inhuman squealing somewhere ahead of her, and she quickly took the next turning. Whatever had caused that hair-raising sound, she didn't want to go anywhere near it. Then she realised it might have something to do with Hal, and she skidded to a halt. She still had the blaster she'd taken from the guard, but she'd have no chance against a squad of trained soldiers. Better to find Clunk so the pair of them could work together to free Hal.

Amy continued down the corridor, but she'd only made it halfway when she heard footsteps coming up behind her. There were angry shouts too, and she guessed her escape from the cells had been discovered.

Amy ran faster, rounded a corner ... and stopped dead. In front of her was a small room with a teleporter, and a surprised-looking alien peering at her over the top of a pair of glasses. He was wearing a lab coat, and was apparently a teleporter technician of some kind. There was nobody else around, and no other exit from the room.

Amy drew the gun and pointed it at the tech. 'Hands up,' she whispered, gesturing to make her meaning clear.

The tech obeyed, his face a mask of terror, and beads of sweat appeared on his forehead as he contemplated the gun. Luckily for Amy, he seemed to know even less about alien weapons than she did. For example, she had no idea if she was pointing the right end at him.

Amy heard footsteps getting closer, and she realised it was only a matter of seconds before she was discovered. Then shots rang out, and a volley of bright blue energy bolts ricocheted off the wall and narrowly missed the tech, who dived for cover.

Amy knew there was only one way out, so she ran for the teleporter, found the controls, and hit the go button.

Hal ran along the corridor with several guards hot on his heels. At first they just chased him, cursing and shouting what he assumed were demands for him to stop and give himself up. When this didn't work they started shooting, sending warning shots skimming past his head. At least, he hoped they were warning shots. Either way, he had no intention of standing still to find out.

Hal ran around a corner and emerged in a small room, where he was immediately blinded by a terrific flash of light. Blinking and clawing at his eyes, he just made out the vague shape of a teleporter, and without pausing to think he dived inside and hit the go button. As the teleporter fired, Hal saw a tech cowering behind a nearby console. The alien was staring at him in astonishment through a pair of glasses perched on the end of his snout, and Hal hoped he didn't have the means to reverse the teleporter - or change the destination to a nearby star, or the hard vacuum of space.

Amy leapt from the teleporter, sparing a briefest of glances for her surroundings. She saw a room similar to the one she'd just left, unoccupied this time, but there was no time for a proper search, or to discover where she'd ended up. Instead, she spun to face the teleporter and raised her weapon. She'd have to block the chamber as soon as she could, but in the meantime anyone following her through was going to get his head blown off.

Flash! The teleporter activated and a figure stumbled towards her, a vague, shadowy silhouette against the overwhelmingly bright light. Amy pointed her gun and pulled the trigger again and again, trying to gun the pursuer down before he could grab her and drag her back to captivity. However, instead of going off, obliterating the menace, the gun merely buzzed. Furious, Amy tried again, and then she drew her arm back and threw the weapon, which bounced off the figure's skull with a satisfying crack.

'Ow, fug!' yelled the pursuer, bending double and clutching his head.

'Hal?' said Amy, in shock. 'Is that you?'

'Of course it's me, you skull-rattling amazon. Who the hell else would it be?'

'Oh, I don't know. Maybe one of the dozen soldiers who were chasing me?'

'Chasing you? They were chasing me! I thought I got away until you tried to knock my brains out.'

Amy turned cold as she remembered her frenzied pulling of the trigger, when she was trying to blast the pursuer with the gun. 'Believe me, it could have been worse.'

'Remind me of that when this latest headache wears off.'

Hal was about to step out of the teleporter, but Amy stopped him. 'Stay there and they can't follow us.'

'Don't be silly. If they use an override code I'll be stuffed full of B'Con, and not in a good way.'

'Just for a minute or two, until I find some other lump of junk to take your place.'

While Hal stood in the chamber, nervously eying the control panel, Amy ran to the nearby console and fetched a sturdy-looking chair on wheels. She dragged it back to the chamber, and as she wheeled it inside Hal sprang out with a relieved look on his face.

Then the two of them gathered up every loose object they could find, from tablet computers to clipboards to display screens, and they threw everything into the teleporter chamber as fast as they could.

'You realise this is stranding us too?' remarked Hal, as he lobbed someone's family portrait into the teleporter. There was a crash as the glass broke, and a fizz as the photo frame's circuit fused.

'Worry about that later. Right now we just have to stop the others coming through.'

Hal added one or two extra pieces to the pile, then dusted his hands off. 'That ought to do it.' Then a thought occurred to him. Buildings often had more than one elevator, and the pair of them were going to look pretty silly if there was a second teleporter nearby. He shared his concerns with Amy, who nodded.

'We'd better clear out of here,' she said. 'We'll hole up somewhere until the fuss dies down, then teleport back to the planet to find Clunk.'

'We'd better grab the address before we go.'

They activated the teleporter control panel, and Hal hunted around for something to write with. In the end he found a sharp edge and scratched the row of symbols onto a strip of plastic. It wasn't perfect, but he figured it was close enough. Plus, if they got soaked in yet another flood, the marks on the plastic would survive whereas paper and ink would just turn to mush.

Then they made their way to the door, which opened with a whoosh at their approach. Hal poked his head out into a long, brightly-lit corridor, and his stomach rumbled as he picked up the delicious smell of hot food. It was a long time since his last meal, and a slap-up feast would go down a treat right about now.

Then he noticed something else, and all thoughts of food fled his mind. The way the floor was trembling, ever so slightly. The familiar background rumbles and creaks. The slightly metallic tang in the air. They hadn't teleported to another planet . . . they'd materialised aboard an alien spaceship!

Hal's mood brightened instantly. Forget strange planets, army bases and native villages . . . *this* was his environment. All they had to do was capture the alien ship, rescue Clunk, find their way back to human space, track down the *Volante*, deliver the cargo and - to cap off the whole exercise - organise a decent meal. Even better, an alien ship had to be worth a fortune, and Hal salivated at the thought of wealthy governments trying to outbid each other on his online auction. Fame *and* fortune . . . what an outcome!

'Are you thinking about food again?' Amy asked him. 'Only your stomach is rumbling something chronic, and –'

'Sorry, I lost track for a minute.' Hal glanced up and down the corridor, making sure they were alone, and then he explained his plan to Amy.

'What about the crew?' she asked, ever practical. 'How many do you think there are?'

'I don't know,' said Hal honestly. 'If it's a cargo vessel, just a few.'

'How big do you think the ship is?'

Hal shrugged.

'Do you know how to fly it?'

'Yes. I mean, no. I mean probably. Or maybe not.'

258

'Can you find your way back to the planet where we left Clunk?'

'Er . . . no.'

'What about our galaxy? Can you find that?'

After a moment or two, Hal shook his head.

'So as far as plans go, yours is not really going to fly, is it?'

Reluctantly, Hal had to agree.

'Okay. In that case, this is what we'll do.' Amy brandished the blaster she'd taken off her guard. 'This thing's a bust, so we'll hunt around for some bigger weapons, then hide nearby until the aliens come through the teleporter. While they're running around looking for us, we'll shoot the guards, teleport back to the planet, shoot anyone they left behind, then find Clunk.'

'And then we bring Clunk back here –'

'– shoot anyone else who gets in our way, capture the ship, and get Clunk to fly us home.'

Hal nodded. Apart from all the shooting – with weapons they'd yet to find, let alone learn to fire – the plan sounded workable.

'Right,' said Amy. 'Let's find some proper weapons. And for goodness sake, try and keep your stomach quiet!'

36

Admiral Lardo marched into the teleporter room, her face red
from the unaccustomed effort and her shoulder still aching
from the impact of the Euman's boot. Her mood was savage,
and she itched to use her combat knife on someone ... anyone
... friend *or* foe.

'Well?' she demanded, surveying the dozen or so heavily-
armed troops who were standing around like a bunch of road
workers on double pay. 'Where are the prisoners?'

'They went through the teleporter,' said a nervous-looking
officer.

'And you didn't follow because ...?'

The officer blanched. If this went badly, the Admiral's
words wouldn't be the only thing left dangling in mid-air.
'Sir, they've disabled the destination teleporter. It seems ... it
seems they've blocked the chamber.'

'So? Signal the flagship and tell them to clear it.'

'We tried, but we can't get through.'

Lardo turned to the teleporter technician, who was still
cowering behind the console. 'You. Explain!'

'Th-this teleporter is an older model,' said the tech nervously.
'Comms signals travel on a paired sideband, and –'

'Speak plainly, you fool!'

The tech gulped. 'If the destination is blocked, we can't send messages either.'

'Fix this now,' said Lardo. 'I don't care how. Just do it.'

The tech cowered under the Admiral's furious glare. 'Y-yes, Admiral. Immediately, Admiral.'

There was a slight pause.

'Well?' demanded Lardo.

'I–I'm not sure how.'

'Is there an override?'

'Yes, but –'

Lardo reached the tech in three steps, hauled him bodily out from behind the console, and pushed him into the teleporter. 'Do it.'

'But sir –'

'Sir, we might need the tech if this doesn't work,' said the officer.

Lardo muttered under her breath, but the idiot had a point. So, she pulled the tech from the chamber and replaced him with the officer. 'Now hit it.'

The tech was about to object, until he saw the Admiral drawing her knife. With shaking fingers he fiddled with the control panel, and after an apologetic look at the resigned officer, he hit the go button.

Fl-fl-flashhhh!

When the light cleared, the chamber stood empty.

'Did it work?' demanded Lardo.

The tech inspected the control panel. 'No sir. No luck. The officer is stored in the –'

'I don't care.' Lardo dismissed the unfortunate officer with an impatient gesture. 'Try another one.'

'Sir, there isn't room in the storage –'

'At this very moment, a pair of Euman agents are running around my flagship. Nobody knows what kind of damage they could do, and I'm not going to find out.' Lardo gestured with her dagger. 'So, you will try another one. After that, another, and another, and so on until we break through, or until we run out of volunteers. Do you understand?'

'Y-yes, sir.'

Lardo locked eyes with one of the soldiers, then nodded towards the teleporter. Unwillingly, he obeyed.

Fl-fl-flashhhh!

Once the flare died down, the tech inspected the control panel. Then, looking distraught, he shook his head.

Lardo said nothing. She merely indicated the next soldier.

◆

Clunk sat in the forest, whittling a piece of wood while he waited impatiently for the sun to set. He'd already made a whole family of intricately carved birds, using the blade concealed inside his middle finger, and given the rate the sun was going down he'd have an entire flock by the time it was dark enough to risk an approach to the base.

Normally he'd have looked up the planet's info in his database, but unfortunately the comprehensive almanac of tides, sunsets and full moons didn't cover such events on alien planets ... especially those located in distant galaxies. Instead he had to rely on estimates, and his circuits weren't really at their best when half the variables he was sticking into the formulas were only rough guesses. The upshot was that he wasn't sure when it would get dark, because he didn't know the planet's rotational speed, and he couldn't calculate that without measuring the sun's progress towards the horizon, and he couldn't calculate *that* because staring directly at the sun would fry his vision. Oh sure, he had sun filters, but they'd jammed years earlier, and it had never seemed important to fix them.

Clunk tried hitting himself in the side of the head a few times, hoping to shake the filters loose, but instead he managed to knock one of his eyes off-axis. That's when he decided to sit and wait patiently.

The sun finally went down, and Clunk got to his feet as the gloom gathered under the trees. He activated his night vision, then frowned. Instead of a ghostly green landscape, all he could see was a flickering yellow mess. He applied a couple of filters, then realised he was seeing three or four of everything. A nearby tree now had three copies, and the birds he'd been carving had multiplied like rabbits in springtime. He took a step, trying to work out which were the real carvings and which were the shadow copies, and ended up crunching half underfoot. Gradually, by trial and error, he managed to narrow the copies down to just one, and at that point he abandoned his hiding place and set off for the two bases in the distance.

Crash! Clunk avoided a shadow tree and instead walked straight into the real one, bending his nose sideways and putting an impressive dent in his chest. As a polite robot he wasn't given to swearing, but the torrent of frustrated curses turned the air blue for several seconds. Then, after straightening his nose as best he could, Clunk avoided the duplicate tree and hurried towards the edge of the forest.

At the gates he could see two guards standing side by side, and he realised he had a problem. Which was the real one? So far, the duplicates had appeared on the left or right of each other, seemingly at random, so he couldn't just ignore the same side all the time. Worse, they kept swimming around in his vision, making it hard to pin them down.

Clunk thought for a moment, before crouching to pick up a couple of stones. Then, quick as lightning, he threw one behind each figure.

There was a grunt of surprise as the stones hit the dirt, and the guard turned to see what was happening. Clunk ran for both pairs of gates at full speed, and at the last second he chose the right-hand one.

Wrong.

With a rip of tortured metal, Clunk burst straight though the chainlink fence alongside the gate, leaving a robot-shaped hole in the rusty wire. He stumbled once or twice, then regained his feet and ran for the nearest building.

Inside, he backed against a wall to listen. There were voices nearby, and he could hear a female alien giving orders.

'At this very moment, a pair of Euman agents are running around my flagship. Nobody knows what kind of damage they could do, and I'm not going to find out.' Lardo gestured with her dagger. 'So, you will try another one. After that, another, and another, and so on until we break through, or until we run out of volunteers. Do you understand?'

'Y-yes, sir.'

Clunk's eyebrows rose, and his spirits soared. Far from having to rescue Hal and Amy, it sounded like they'd escaped all by themselves. Not only that, they'd fled to the B'Con flagship and blocked the teleporter behind them. Clunk felt a burst of pride at their resourcefulness, and then he realised they weren't out of the woods yet. He couldn't follow the humans without the address, and even then there were B'Con soldiers between him and the teleporter.

Clunk switched off his night sight, ending the highly confusing split vision, and then he peered round the corner to get an idea of the opposition's strength. He saw the Admiral and several nervous-looking soldiers, plus a frightened-looking technician in a lab coat. As he watched, one of the soldiers stepped into the teleporter and vanished.

'You next,' said the Admiral, gesturing at another soldier.

Clunk eyed the dwindling stock of armed B'Con troops, and he felt a stab of pity. On the other hand, if those same troops caught hold of Hal and Amy they'd do unspeakable things to them. So, the best thing would be to get Hal and Amy to safety as soon as possible. But how?

Clunk watched the tech send another soldier to his doom, then ducked out of sight to think.

Could he rush into the chamber and send himself through? Obviously the other end was blocked, but he wasn't a living being, and it was possible the teleporter would let him through safely, despite the risk of materialising inside some random object.

Then he remembered the difficulty he'd had using the control panel, thanks to its temperature sensors. His cold metal skin wouldn't activate it, and if he tried overheating his circuits again there was no way he'd be able to barge past the soldiers. Last time he could barely raise his hand.

A flash lit the corridor, and Clunk realised another B'Con soldier had attempted to get through. Sooner or later one of them might make it, and then it would be the end for Hal and Amy.

No, there had to be another way. Clunk reviewed his recent memories, and then it hit him. The teleporter in the forest! He peered around the corner again, and this time he zoomed in on the control panel to get the destination address. Then he turned and ran, bounding out of the building and racing towards the hole in the fence. Halfway there he remembered something, and he took a quick detour through the barracks to pick up a weapon.

Outside the base, Clunk didn't bother with the night vision this time, since there were two moons in the night sky. Their combined light was plenty to see by, and Clunk tore through the forest at top speed as he made his way to the second teleporter.

Clunk parted the vines covering the teleporter cavern, and he smiled to himself at the sight of the gleaming chamber. Then he raised the weapon, adjusted the power and shot himself in the hand.

Ziing!

His skin glowed cherry-red, and Clunk blew on his fingers to cool them. Then, when he judged them to be the right temperature, he sought the teleporter panel. It lit up with a blue glow, bringing a triumphant smile to the robot's lips, and he quickly programmed the address of the B'Con ship.

Then he stepped into the chamber and hesitated, his finger over the go button. At that point he realised this might be the end - not only would he wink out of existence, never to reappear, but he would also be consigning Amy and Hal to a life in captivity.

Well, perhaps it would be different given he wasn't a living being. Perhaps. But Amy and Hal needed him, and there was no alternative.

So, he raised his finger to the go button and got ready to press it.

Hal and Amy were in luck. The third door they tried led to a small armoury with racks of handguns, blast rifles and grenades. Hal's eyes lit up like a child's on Christmas morning, and he wasted no time slinging high-powered weapons over his shoulder, jamming pistols into his waistband and stuffing potent grenades into his pocket.

'Don't weigh yourself down too much,' said Amy, who'd picked out a single blast rifle and a couple of proximity mines. 'We might have to run for it.'

Hal struck a pose with a rocket launcher. 'I'm done with running,' he declared, snapping off the safety catch. 'I'm going to fry me up some B'Con!'

Clunk's finger hovered over the go button, and he was just about to press it when an idea occurred to him. What if he could reverse the teleporter somehow? If he could bring the obstruction here, he could leap into the chamber and immediately teleport back to the alien flagship with it.

Moments later he had the panel open, and he started probing the delicate circuitry inside. Before long he realised he could override the sending circuits, forcing a carrier message through. Then, by adding a couple of commands, he should be able to fire the remote teleporter. On the other hand, the override might blow the circuits at both ends, stranding everyone. There were legendary tales from the early days of exploration, where multi-year missions had ended in disaster because distant probes had been sent commands in the wrong order.

Still, it was worth a try. Even if he accidentally disabled the teleporter aboard the B'Con ship, it might buy Hal and Amy some more time.

Clunk worked quickly, reprogramming the teleporter's control panel. When he was ready he stepped out of the chamber, shielded his eyes, and hit the button.

Flash!

When he opened his eyes, the chamber was full of office equipment. Clunk smiled to himself, but there was no time for celebration. Now he'd cleared the blockage, the B'Con Admiral could send troops through. So, he stepped into the chamber and tapped the go button.

Flash!

The office equipment and the robot disappeared, and after a brief moment of disorientation Clunk realised he'd arrived safely.

Then someone shouted in alarm, and all hell broke loose as they opened up with heavy weapons.

◆

'Stop!' shouted Amy. 'Stop, stop, STOP!'

Hal was busy blasting the office furniture to matchsticks, but something in Amy's tone registered, and he released the trigger. There was a patter of noise as fragments rained down, and then he saw movement through the swirling smoke.

'No, wait!' cried Amy, as Hal swung the rocket launcher off his shoulder and prepared to blast the teleporter, the figure and the debris right out the side of the alien ship.

Something moved again, and the top of a desk slipped sideways and fell out of the teleporter chamber. Then, slowly, a figure got to its feet, brushing sawdust and blobs of molten plastic from its bronze skin.

'Clunk!' shouted Hal. 'It's you!'

'It nearly wasn't,' said the robot, eying the debris.

Amy ran up and hugged the robot. 'It's great to see you,' she whispered.

'You too,' said Clunk, giving her a fond smile. 'I held grave fears for your safety.'

Hal rolled his eyes.

'We have to discuss our plans,' said Clunk, once he was free of the debris. 'The B'Con are still trying to get through, and I'm sure they'll be here eventually.'

Hal patted the rocket launcher. 'I have a neat little B'Con slicer right here in my hands. And once we've got rid of them we can capture this ship, fly back to –'

'Mr Spacejock, you haven't boarded just any old ship. We're aboard the alien flagship, with potentially thousands of heavily-armed troops. We could no more capture this vessel than a pet dog could save the *Volante* from an alien invasion force.'

'Crap.' Hal thought for a moment. 'Okay, how about we –'

Clunk raised his hand, stopping him mid-sentence. 'I believe we should each think on the problem, write down our plans, and submit the result to a vote. That way we'll avoid lengthy arguments and discussion.'

'Works for me,' remarked Hal. 'Do you have a pencil and paper?'

The three of them spent a couple of minutes in deep thought, with much scribbling and crossing out. When they were ready, they folded up their suggestions and dropped them into a large plastic mug.

Clunk closed his eyes, and - somewhat theatrically - held the mug aloft for Amy to select the first plan.

'Why bother with that nonsense?' demanded Hal. 'We're going to read them all anyway.'

'The first selection may carry more weight,' explained Clunk. 'This is the fairest way.'

'Oh, very well. Get on with it.'

Clunk opened the first piece of paper and scanned the text. 'Okay, the this plan involves exploring the alien flagship, taking over one or more weapons stations, and turning them on the rest of the fleet.' He paused to look at Hal, then continued. 'Once the fleet has been destroyed, we program the flagship to self-destruct, and teleport to safety.'

'Wicked plan,' remarked Hal.

'Yes, if a trifle bold,' said Clunk.

'Don't knock it until you've read the rest.'

Clunk offered the mug to Hal, who took out the next piece of paper. He handed it to Clunk, who opened it with much ceremony. Hal hid a grin at the robot's actions, knowing Clunk was enjoying every second in the spotlight.

'This is the second plan,' said the robot. 'It suggests we hack into the flagship's computers, removing the alien planet from the database so the B'Con will never trouble the D'eer again.

Then we locate a destination teleporter in human space and make our way home.'

Amy smiled. 'That sounds like a great idea.'

'There's still another plan to consider,' said Clunk. 'Each of us must have a voice, and the third idea may be the best yet.'

Clunk passed the mug to Amy. 'Hold it up high so I can choose without looking.'

Hal snorted. 'There's only one left, Clunk. Just read the damn thing.'

Ignoring the objections, Clunk closed his eyes and fished around in the mug for the final piece of paper. He drew it out, unfolded it, read it, frowned, turned it over, inspected the back and read it again.

'Come on,' said Amy. 'Read it out so we can vote.'

'I think we should get lunch,' said Clunk.

'Worry about that after we've voted,' said Amy.

'Yes, but –'

'Come on, what's the third plan?'

Clunk waved the little piece of paper. 'That *is* the third option. We should get lunch.'

Amy grabbed the scrap of paper, frowned at the illiterate scrawl, then rounded on Hal. 'That's it?' she demanded. 'That's your grand idea to save our lives and protect the D'eer people from the B'Con? We have *lunch?*'

'How come you automatically assume I wrote it?'

'Oh, come *on!* Do you see any other insensitive clods around here?'

'All right, all right!' protested Hal. 'I just thought we could get something to eat and discuss our next move over coffee.'

Amy waved the slip of paper. 'It doesn't say anything about discussing invasion plans. It just says Organise Lunch.' She looked closer. 'Why the hell did you spell organise with a z?'

271

Clunk intervened. 'Can we focus on the task in hand? We have two workable plans –'

'– and one idiotic suggestion –' interjected Amy.

'– to vote on,' finished Clunk. 'Each of us should write a number on a piece of paper, and place it in the mug. The plan with the most votes wins.'

'Got it,' said Hal.

'Suits me,' said Amy.

Clunk collected the folded votes, and there was a palpable tension in the air as they all pondered the importance of the outcome. A single vote could have them battling an entire B'Con fleet using the flagship's weapons, or alternatively they might be sneaking around hacking computers before attempting a daring escape.

'The first vote is for plan number one,' declared Clunk, showing everyone the piece of paper so they could verify he wasn't cheating.

Hal nodded. Using the B'Con flagship to blast the rest of the fleet was a straightforward plan, with a decent chance of success.

'The second vote is for plan number two,' said Clunk, showing them the number.

Amy cleared her throat. 'I thought rescuing the alien civilisation was a noble goal.'

'Thank you,' said Clunk gravely. 'Now, that's one each, and I believe the third vote will decide the matter.'

They all looked at the folded piece of paper sitting in the palm of his hand.

'Go on,' said Amy. 'The suspense is killing me.'

'Yeah,' muttered Hal. 'And if that doesn't, the B'Con probably will.'

Slowly, agonisingly, Clunk unfolded the piece of paper. He

stared at it for a moment or two, as though he were having trouble deciphering the handwriting, and then he held it up for everyone to see.

Scrawled on the paper was a large number three.

Amy gaped at it, and then she and Clunk looked at Hal in disbelief.

'What?' said Hal, spreading his hands. 'I'm hungry!'

37

'Oh, this is bloody hopeless,' said Amy. She patted her pockets, then glanced around the teleporter room.

'What have you lost?' asked Hal.

'I need a gun.'

'Why? What for?' Hal saw Amy's angry expression, and he understood exactly who she wanted to shoot. 'Okay, okay! I'll change my vote if it'll make you happy. I choose plan number two. Hack computers, make the D'eer planet vanish, that sort of thing.'

Amy looked surprised. 'I thought you'd choose blowing up the fleet.'

'What, and destroy our only chance of a decent lunch?' Hal snorted. 'No chance.'

'You're not seriously choosing a plan based on –'

'Amy, it's all right,' said Clunk gently. 'Mr Spacejock is teasing you.'

Amy didn't look convinced, but she didn't have time to object before Clunk took charge, gathering them round like a coach explaining the game plan to a team of novice sky hockey players.

'We must locate the server room, or at the very least an

unattended terminal I can use to access the network. Stealth is the key.'

'Stealth. Got it,' said Hal, and he bent to retrieve the rocket launcher and a handful of grenades.

'Mr Spacejock, our chosen plan does not require violence. Why do you need weapons?'

'In case the terminal isn't unattended.' He hefted the rocket launcher. 'I guarantee it will be after I've done.'

'Unattended and unusable,' muttered Amy.

'Right. Let's go.'

'I haven't finished explaining the plan!' protested Clunk.

'We've got the gist of it,' muttered Hal. 'Find the server room, hack stuff, and don't stop for lunch.' He checked the launcher's ammo, then propped the butt on his hip, one finger curled around the trigger. 'Come on, let's move out.'

'You first,' said Amy and Clunk simultaneously.

Hal swaggered to the doorway, swinging the weapon to cover the walls, the floor, the ceiling and - briefly, just before they ducked - Clunk and Amy. When he got to the door he leant into the corridor for a quick look, and the weight of the launcher promptly toppled him over. Hal landed with a clatter and a crash, which was nothing to the WHOOSH of the rocket launcher as it sent a missile hurtling down the corridor.

The projectile skimmed the walls, leaving a trail of acrid smoke and sparks as it vanished around the corner. There was a delay of several seconds before a deep BOOM echoed up the corridor, followed by a blast of warm air and the delicious smell of fried bacon.

Hal scrambled to his feet, blinking and coughing in the smoky haze. He cast a nervous look down the corridor, but fortunately there was no sign of B'Con troops. No pieces large enough to see at a distance, anyway. 'I think we should go the other way,' he said, setting off quickly before the others could relieve him of the awesome weapon.

The first room they encountered was an empty sick bay. They were about to move on when Clunk changed his mind and hurried over to one of the complicated scanners.

'What are you doing?'

'Gathering information,' said Clunk, as he plugged a probe into the machine. 'Biological information on the B'Con will be very useful if they ever attack our galaxy.'

Hal waited in the corridor, nervously swinging the rocket launcher from one side to the other. The B'Con would have been alerted by his warning shot, and the flagship was supposed to be teeming with thousands of troops. Half a dozen he could cope with, but if they sent a hundred the fight would be a little tougher.

'Are you done yet?' he hissed, as Clunk connected to another machine.

'Almost. I'm accessing the crew records.'

'Make sure you do it before the crew accesses us.' Hal scanned the corridor, using the launcher's illuminated gunsight to pick out doorways and walls. He didn't know why the B'Con weren't flooding the area, but perhaps they had other methods to deal with intruders. Odorless gas, perhaps, or micro-droids which could administer knockout darts from a distance. Or perhaps the B'Con were having a party, and someone had put the explosion down as a particularly loud drumbeat?

Moments later, Clunk was done. He joined Hal and Amy in the doorway, and together they slipped along the corridor to the next room. This was a lab, with rows of delicate equipment and shelves full of chemicals.

'Why don't you download those while you're at it?' demanded Hal.

'It's not necessary.' Clunk looked thoughtful. 'However, it does give me a new idea. A fourth plan, if you like.'

'Go on,' said Amy.

'A scientist once devised a liquid which would burn through anything. They couldn't neutralise it, and eventually they had to evacuate the entire planet. It's still marked in the database as a no fly zone.'

'What's your point?' asked Hal.

'I have the chemical formula for that liquid in my database.' Clunk gestured at the shelves. 'And here, arrayed before us, are the chemicals required to make up a batch.'

'Assuming you mix some of this stuff up, what can we do with it? Use it to threaten the B'Con?'

'My plan is a little bolder than that,' said Clunk gravely. 'When released, this liquid would burn through the ship deck by deck, until it reached the gravity generators. They would be destroyed, and with their flagship severely damaged the B'Con would have no choice but to return to their home planet.'

'Sounds great, but what about the rest of the fleet?'

Clunk pursed his lips. 'What if we teleported a batch of liquid to each ship? We could disable the entire fleet with no loss of life.'

Amy grinned. 'The B'Con would be too busy to think about the D'eer!'

'It won't work,' said Hal flatly. 'As soon as we began the B'Con would notice this goo turning up in their teleporters, and they'd warn the rest of the fleet before we could finish. They'd disable their teleporter network, and we'd be stuck here with a blob of deadly chemicals.'

'We'd have to work fast,' said Clunk.

'Not only that, you'd need tons of the stuff to knock out the entire fleet.' Hal thought for a second. 'And there's another problem right there. Even if you could make enough of it, how are we supposed to carry it all to the teleporter? We can hardly lug this stuff around in plastic buckets.'

'There's no need to be so negative,' said Amy. 'Clunk's doing his best.'

'Even his best isn't going to be enough this time,' said Hal. 'Let's face it, this melty goo plan sucks. The only way it would work is to teleport the stuff to all the ships at once.'

Clunk nodded. Then he frowned. Then he looked thoughtful. Then his eyes widened.

'What's the matter?' Amy asked him.

'Either he's got a new idea,' said Hal, 'or his cooling pipes are blocked again. Last time it happened he left puddles all over my ship.'

'That was a maintenance issue,' said Clunk stiffly. 'And this time it's a new idea.'

'That's five plans now,' remarked Hal. 'Five plans, and we're still no closer to slicing up the B'Con.'

Clunk shook his head. 'This is plan four B, and it addresses all the problems with the original plan four.'

'How?'

'We make up a single batch of Chloro-quad-etho-tri-carbonate-hexa–'

'Melty goo,' supplied Hal, before the robot's speech synthesiser ran out of syllables.

'Er, yes. We make up a single batch of melty goo, but we simultaneously teleport it to every ship.'

'All at once?'

'That's what simultaneous means,' snapped Amy.

'But how would you do it?'

'It would involve reprogramming the teleporter network so that one send arrived at multiple destinations.'

Hal and Amy exchanged a glance. 'Is that even possible?'

'In theory.'

'So let me get this right. If you tweaked the teleporter, I could step in one end and a dozen copies of me would emerge at the other?'

'Yes,' said Clunk. 'A hundred, even.'

'God help us,' breathed Amy, clearly overcome at the idea of multiple Hal Spacejocks on the loose.

'So why bother with the goo?' demanded Hal. 'With enough multiplication, the three of us could become an instant invasion force.'

'Not really,' said Clunk. 'There'd only be three of us per ship, so we'd still be outnumbered.'

'Why stop at three? You could send each of us several times over, until there were three or four hundred on each B'Con ship.'

Amy closed her eyes.

'Mr Spacejock, there's still the issue of, er, clearing up the duplicates later. Every one of them would be one of us, with just as much right to life.'

'That's okay. They could set about liberating this galaxy from the B'Con, then populate it with humans.'

Amy snorted. 'In your dreams, buster.'

'But I –'

Clunk interrupted before Hal was forced to explain. 'It's not that simple, unfortunately. You cannot create matter from thin air, which means each clone would be less dense than the original.'

'That wouldn't be a problem for him, given how dense the original is,' muttered Amy, with a sidelong glance at Hal.

'Anyway,' continued Clunk. 'If you teleported one person to ten destinations, each copy would only weigh a tenth as much. I'm not sure you could even survive such a process.'

'Wait a minute. What about the melty goo? Won't that be diluted too?'

'The strength will be greatly reduced, but I can compensate by making up a batch in highly concentrated form. I estimate we'd only need a small quantity of –'

'Melty goo,' said Hal.

'– which would be trivial to mix up. We could carry it in containers within containers, to delay the escape of the liquid, and place it in the nearest teleporter.'

'You'd want to reprogram it first. The last thing I want to do is stand around with this goo melting my hands off, while you tinker with alien technology.' Hal frowned. 'Hey, what happens if you set up this duplication business, and the B'Con send more troops through the teleporter?'

'There'd be extra helpings of B'Con for all,' said Clunk, and he waited for the laughter.

After a lengthy silence, Hal cleared his throat. 'Don't try humour again,' he advised the robot.

Somewhat chastened, Clunk outlined the rest of his plan. Since most of the words had more syllables than Hal had fingers, it was a pointless exercise, although Clunk seemed to benefit from the quick run-down.

'Are we clear?' he said at last.

'Not really,' said Hal. 'But if you're happy, I'm happy.'

'Then let's get started.'

Hal nodded. 'And we'd better make it quick before the B'Con come to investigate.'

—

Admiral Lardo had finally run out of volunteers, and yet the teleporter on the D'eer planet was stubbornly refusing to return her to the B'Con fleet. As her troops vanished, one by one, Lardo's cold-blooded determination had given way to boiling anger, then seething rage and finally, once she was alone with the malfunctioning chamber, incandescent fury.

Lardo was so far gone she barely knew what she was doing. All she knew was that Eumans had infiltrated her flagship, and were now causing who knew what kind of damage, while she was stuck on this flea-speck of a planet. Worse, before leaving the flagship she'd left strict orders with her second-in-command: he wasn't allowed to do anything unless he cleared it with Lardo first. This wasn't usual procedure, but then T'ker wasn't a usual second-in-command. He was barely old enough to hold a gun, but his uncle was on the Galactic Council, and had pulled strings to get the kid a plum posting. So, her flagship - no, the entire fleet - was at the mercy of the Euman intruders, since the thousands of loyal B'Con troops staffing the ships would be helpless without her input.

With this horrible thought reverberating through her mind, Lardo stepped into the chamber and smashed her trotter on the control panel, activating the teleporter. There was an intense flash, but instead of instantly reappearing aboard her ship, Lardo underwent an out-of-body experience which had her disembodied spirit drifting in a cold, grey fog. Then she heard the whispers, and she recognised the voices of the troops she'd sent through the teleporter before her. They were incoherent, each mumbling their final words over and over, as though the bulk of their personality had evaporated to leave only a tiny, semi-sentient speck.

The whispering got closer, and Lardo felt a chill up her spine. Pinpoints of light gathered around her, baleful sparks of blue and green, and although Lardo was a staunch atheist she couldn't help wondering whether the specks were fragments of her soldiers' souls.

Then, with a flash, the fog and the specks of light vanished, and Lardo found herself standing in a teleport chamber aboard her flagship. Instinctively, she took a defensive stance, and as she moved her feet she stumbled on the debris underfoot. She glanced down and saw evidence of a battle, with blackened fragments of furniture and office equipment scattered all over the room. Her frown deepened, and she drew a businesslike blaster weapon from her belt before moving towards the door. On the way she trod on a crumpled ball of paper, and she was surprised to feel it roll under her foot instead of flattening under her weight. Then she noticed a light, airy feel to her head, and when she raised her hand to her face she was shocked to see light right through it. It was only a dim gleam, sure, but it was still completely unexpected.

Lardo bent to pick up a discarded gun, and her blood froze as her fingers gently slipped right through it. She could feel the butt under her fingertips, but her body felt as intangible as a spirit - or a ghost. She glanced at the teleporter, wondering whether it had malfunctioned. If she went back through, would it return her body to its normal, solid state? No, there wasn't time. She had a blaster and a knife, and even in her ethereal state she was still more than a match for a couple of Euman spies.

Reaching the doorway, she stopped and raised her snout. There was a smell of death in the air, and she detected the after-tang of missile fire. So much for the puny Euman threat - from the evidence she'd seen so far, the creatures merited a lot closer attention from the B'Con in future.

But first, she had to eliminate the Euman's currently laying waste to her flagship. After another sniff of the air Lardo took a firm grip on her blaster and set off to the left, following the unmistakable scent of her prey.

38

Hal, Clunk and Amy were back in the lab, having just returned from the teleporter room where Clunk had performed his magic on the controls. Initially the robot had been hopeful of hacking the software, but in the end he'd had to cobble together a custom circuit which he'd wired directly into the control panel.

Amazingly, there was still no sign of any B'Con activity, although they all knew their luck couldn't last.

Hal glanced at the bench, where three unmarked canisters stood in a row, each emitting a different coloured smoke. According to Clunk, the three liquids were safe enough on their own, but once blended they would create an unstoppable reaction which would result in a batch of the liquid Hal had dubbed 'melty goo'.

'Now we must transfer these to the teleporter,' said Clunk, indicating the canisters.

'One each?' suggested Hal.

'Yes, but be careful.'

'I thought you said it was safe until we mixed it?'

'Comparitively safe, Mr Spacejock. Each liquid is still very dangerous in its own right.'

The three of them took a canister each, and Clunk led the

way to the door. Then, without warning, he stopped dead. Hal bumped into him, spilling a few drops of brilliant blue liquid on the robot's back. There was a hiss and a splutter as they etched streaks into Clunk's plasteel skin, and Hal was relieved he hadn't got any on himself. 'Why did you stop?' he hissed.

'Footsteps,' muttered Clunk. 'Quick. Hide under the benches!'

They did as he suggested, crouching under the work surfaces with the canisters of volatile material smoking and smouldering in their faces.

Then Hal heard the footsteps himself - a light tread, as though someone were tip-toeing up the corridor towards them. He imagined a squad of B'Con troops moving in near silence, and could almost feel the deck trembling under his hands and knees, but he told himself he was just imagining things.

The footsteps paused in the doorway, and Hal was tempted to sneak a look. Then he heard sniffing, and he tried not to breathe. It was possible the B'Con had a better sense of smell than humans. It was also possible their hearing was superior.

Hal eased the rocket launcher off his shoulder, angling it towards the doorway. If the footsteps entered the lab, his plan was to leap up and fire his weapon without warning, hopefully taking the B'Con by surprise.

As it turned out, the rocket launcher wasn't needed. The intruder sniffed the air again, then sneezed explosively. Clunk's chemicals weren't just emitting smoke, they were also masking the humans' scent.

The gentle footsteps receded, and Hal allowed himself a deep breath or two. Unfortunately, he was still facing the canister of chemicals, and he wheezed and gasped as the noxious cocktail brought tears to his eyes and a fiery sensation to his throat.

'Mr Spacejock, are you all right?' hissed Clunk.

'Yeah, I'll manage,' croaked Hal. 'Come on, let's move out before they come back again.'

The others emerged from hiding, and together the three of them hurried down the corridor to the teleporter. Without ceremony, Clunk tipped the first canister onto the floor, where the reddish liquid spread out in a smooth, even puddle.

'What about the rest?' asked Hal, when he realised the container wasn't empty.

'We'll need a second batch to disable this ship,' said Amy. 'If he teleports all of it, the flagship will be unscathed.'

'I knew that,' said Hal quickly.

Clunk added the second liquid, then the third, and the three blended into a silvery pool which reflected the mirrored walls. Then the reaction began, and Hal stepped back as clouds of orange smoke poured from the teleporter. 'Quick,' he hissed, as the pool began to burn through the floor. 'Get rid of it!'

Clunk obeyed, hitting the send button just in time. There was a drawn-out flash which blinded all three of them, and when their vision recovered the pool had disappeared . . . along with a circular section of floor about four centimetres deep.

'Did it work?' demanded Hal.

Clunk checked the display. 'I believe it did.'

'So right now, that goo is melting its way through the entire fleet?'

'Correct.'

'That's really going to stir the B'Con. We'd better get out of here before they discover where it came from.' Hal nodded towards the controls. 'We jump back to the D'eer planet, right?'

Clunk shook his head. 'Not yet. First I have to undo my modifications to the teleporter network.'

Hal glanced towards the door. 'All right, but be quick about it.'

'Give him a break,' muttered Amy. 'There's just the one of him, you know.'

'Not if he gets the next bit wrong,' remarked Hal.

Lardo was a hundred metres past the lab when she realised what had been bugging her. The lab had efficient filters which were supposed to sweep away any lingering scent of the chemicals stored there, so why had the smell in the corridor been so strong? Had someone tampered with the ventilation system? Or worse, were the tricky little Euman scum mixing up a batch of home-made explosives?

Lardo spun on her heel and trotted back down the corridor, her boots barely touching the floor. She slipped into the lab with weapons drawn, and immediately saw the evidence she was dreading. Someone had been careful, but there were half-empty containers on the shelves, light dustings of chemicals on the benches, and - when she sniffed really carefully - traces of Euman scent.

Lardo almost squealed with rage, but she fought the urge down. Instead, she turned for the doorway, intent on pursuit and elimination. Then she paused. She was aboard her own flagship, with countless troops at her beck and call. All she had to do was order a sweep, and once the Eumans were caught she could finish them off herself.

Lardo shook her head. No, this was personal. She'd won most of her battles on the backs of her troops, but this time she wanted the satisfaction of defeating an enemy single-handed. She was so close to victory she could taste it, just like she'd taste Euman blood when the little cowards were begging for mercy.

Lardo was about to leave the lab when a loudspeaker crackled overhead.

'Attention all personnel. This is Grand Admiral Lardo aboard the transport vessel Golden Rynd.*'*

Lardo's jaw dropped. What trickery was this? The voice was hers, but she was here in the lab!

'It's come to my attention that one or more imposters have infiltrated the fleet, and are currently impersonating me. By order of the Galactic Council —'

Lardo didn't wait for the rest. She fished a handset from the wall, trying several times before she managed to hold it to her face. Then she dialled the bridge, pressing each digit as hard as she could, before speaking rapidly into the mouthpiece. Her voice sounded faint, but fortunately it was still recognisable. 'This is Grand Admiral Lardo. I'm aboard the flagship, and my private security code is X8-DFD-31. Send a security team to the *Golden Rynd* and have the imposter detained immediately.'

'Y-yes, sir,' came the reply. 'Imposter to be detained immediately, as ordered.'

Lardo hung up after several attempts. The shock discovery had driven the Eumans from her mind, but the flash of a nearby teleporter soon focused her attention on the real threat. What mischief were they up to *now*? She hefted her blaster and strode into the passageway, only to be confronted by a dozen security guards with raised weapons.

'Lay down your arms,' said the leader, a stern-faced individual with an impressive battle scar.

'Hamm, don't be stupid. I'm your Admiral.'

'I can't be certain of that,' said the officer. 'In the meantime we're taking every precaution. Lay down your gun and come with us.'

Lardo's grip tightened on the blaster. 'But the Eumans –'

'This is your last warning, sir.'

Defeated, Lardo dropped the gun, which practically floated to the ground before coming to a gentle rest. 'Before you take me anywhere, check the teleporter down the way. I believe the Eumans have –'

Before she could finish the sentence the officer fired his stunner. Lardo's eyes rolled back into her head, and she dropped in a dead faint.

◆

When Admiral Lardo came to she discovered she was lying on her back in a cramped cell, wearing a sturdy pair of handcuffs and a set of off-white overalls. Her initial reaction was disbelief that something so ludicrous could happen to her, but her temper soon kicked in, and she got up and strode to the door.

'Summon the watch commander,' she yelled, hammering on the door with both fists. 'Bring him here this instant. And while you're at it, return my uniform at the double!' Unfortunately her fists made about as much sound as a lettuce leaf, and her angry shout wouldn't have woken a dozing sentry.

'Don't waste your breath,' said a quiet voice from a nearby cell.

Not just any voice, realised Lardo. It was her own voice. 'Is this a trick? Who the hell is that?'

'I'm you, and you're me. The teleporter malfunctioned when we teleported off that cruddy little planet, and it created duplicates.'

'You might be a duplicate, but I'm the original.'

'No, I'm the original,' said a third voice.

'That's me,' said a fourth. 'You're all Euman spies!'

Or was that the second voice? Given they were all identical, Lardo was having trouble telling them apart. And how many duplicates were there, anyway? 'Shut up, the lot of you. I need to think.'

'That's so like you,' said the second Lardo. 'Can't even be polite to yourself.'

Lardo clenched her fists. If she got out of here she was going to teach the imposters a lesson. Then she hesitated. If they were all identical, they'd end up battering each other into submission without any clear winner. Surely it would be better to band all the Lardos together, defeat the Eumans, and then work out what to do with all the copies. Then a thought occurred to her. 'Does anyone know how many copies there are?'

'Several dozen,' volunteered another Lardo. 'One for every ship in the fleet.'

'Well, we won't run short of commanding officers,' said Lardo grimly. She expected a laugh, but there were only groans. 'What's the matter?'

'We've had that joke several dozen times already,' said Lardo number three.

'Figures.' Lardo thought for a moment. 'Okay, here's the

plan. We all nominate one of us as the real Admiral Lardo, and convince the watch commander to release that version. That clone releases the others, we overpower him, and together we can hunt down the Eumans.'

'What happens when the Eumans have been defeated? The Galactic Council won't want thirty or forty of us around.'

'Are you kidding? I'm ... I mean, we're the most decorated military commanders in the history of the B'Con empire. With several dozen of us on hand, the B'Con can build thirty battle fleets, and spread out into several galaxies at once. We'll usher in a golden era of conquest!'

The other Lardos were silent as they digested the glorious implications of their unexpected cloning. The B'Con would be unstoppable with an Admiral Lardo running every battle, commanding every fleet, and deciding the outcome of every military action. Maybe one of them could even aspire to becoming Emperor ...

But in the meantime, the future leaders of the glorious B'Con Empire were stashed away in pokey little cells.

Then Lardo heard footsteps. 'Okay, here comes the guard. Back me up, everyone, and I'll have you out of here in seconds.'

There was some dissent, but when the guard turned up the Lardo copies played their part. Each confessed to being a copy, and nominated the original Lardo as the one true Admiral. The guard reported to the commander, who apologised profusely before letting Lardo - the original - out of her cell. Then, instead of overpowering the guard and releasing all the clones, she came up with a better idea. 'Fetch a branding iron. I want all these copies marked immediately. Report to me when it's done.'

'Yessir.'

The copies raised hell, hammering on their doors and calling down eternal vengeance on Lardo, but she held firm. Until the clones were branded, she ran the risk of being supplanted by one of them. Once they were branded, on the other hand, she could enlist their help with the Eumans.

Lardo returned to her quarters, where she managed to put on a fresh uniform. She picked out her favourite side arm, but gave up when it kept slipping through her fingers. Finally, she sat down - gently - to prepare a plan for defeating the Euman intruders once and for all.

— 39 —

While Hal, Clunk and Amy were trying to save an entire civilisation from death and destruction, the Navcom had been very busy with an equally important mission: turning Hal's dismal excuse for a freight business into a profitable enterprise.

Turnover had been brisk, but there were several minor clouds on the horizon. One was the Galactic Tax Service, which was after a large slice of the Navcom's profits. Another was the gaggle of law enforcement agencies on the Navcom's trail, thanks to the ship's lucrative but highly illegal gun-running, drug-smuggling and convict-ferrying. The third was the small, unmarked ship which had reappeared without warning . . . a cloud on the horizon in the most literal sense.

The Navcom was tempted to ignore the ship, or to turn tail and flee, but the strange vessel had already proven itself more than capable of countering the *Volante's* evasive manoeuvres. So, she waited.

She didn't have to wait for long. Moments after the ship appeared, the Navcom received a message:

We'd like to purchase your canine.

The Navcom hesitated. First, because it wasn't her dog. Second, because Mr Spacejock had entrusted the animal to her care. Third, because she had no idea why the occupants of the strange vessel wanted the creature. What if they subjected it to tests, or –

We're offering a sum of ten million credits.

'I accept,' signalled the Navcom instantly. After all, she reasoned, one could buy a new dog with ten million credits and still end up with pocket change in the seven digits.

Very well. Please teleport the animal to the following address.

'Impossible,' said the Navcom. 'I don't have a teleporter.'

There was a brief muttered exchange.

Understood. We'll dock with your ship and send a party aboard to effect the transaction.

'Ready and waiting,' said the Navcom, and she passed the next few seconds opening a high-interest bank account to hold the unexpected windfall.

◆

There was suspicion written all over Commander Gnar P'ker's face as he eyed the *Volante* on his ship's main scanner. He couldn't believe the Euman vessel had given in to his demands so easily, and long years of training had his senses tingling in a most unpleasant fashion. Then again, offering a large sum of Euman money for the canine might just have saved everyone a lot of trouble. Admiral Lardo wasn't a big fan of diplomacy, preferring to go in with all guns blazing before dictating terms to the survivors, but even she would have to admit the insignificant bribe appeared to have got the job done.

P'ker heard muttered swearing from the rear of the flight deck, where two of his crew members were huffing and puffing as they donned bulky spacesuits. The suits were a precaution, but a necessary one, since the *Volante's* flight computer may be planning to vent the ship's atmosphere as soon as the B'Con stepped aboard.

Finally, the two crew members were ready. After a pair of stiff salutes, then stomped into the airlock and closed the inner door. When they were sealed in, P'ker gave the order.

'Con, line us up with the *Volante's* airlock.'

Controls were adjusted, throttles were tweaked, and the B'Con ship was expertly guided into position. Closer and closer it got, until the two vessels were almost touching.

'Careful now,' grunted P'ker. 'For every inch of paint you take off my ship, I'll strip the same amount off your hide.'

The pilot nodded.

'Okay, begin the attach.'

There was a buzz from the console. 'I'm sorry, sir. Their airlock is a non-standard gauge.'

'Of course it is,' muttered P'ker. 'Very well, activate upgrade procedure.'

'Complying,' said the pilot, and she pressed a button. Immediately, four large drills popped out of the B'Con ship's hull, one at each corner of the airlock, and neat curls of metal swarf sailed into space as the bits tore into the *Volante's* hull. Once finished, the drills withdrew and four robotic arms sank bolts into the freshly-drilled holes, fastening them securely. Then, with easy grace, the arms took a docking frame - standard B'Con issue - and bolted it to the *Volante*, neatly enclosing the existing airlock. Then the arms withdrew, and a spare docking frame popped out of the hull ready for the next boarding manoeuvre.

'Upgrade complete,' said the pilot.

'Attach.'

A lone thruster fired, and the B'Con ship moved towards the *Volante*. There was an imperceptible bump as the ships connected, followed by the rattle-chack of docking clamps.

'Docking complete,' said the pilot.

P'ker signalled the *Volante*, and both ships opened their airlocks. Atmospheres from two different galaxies met and mingled, and then P'ker watched his troops enter the Euman ship. He was tempted to go with them, but a captain's place was on the bridge of his own vessel, not someone else's, so instead he was forced to watch proceedings on the main screen. There were feeds from each of the boarding crew's helmet cameras, and P'ker shook his head in amazement as he saw the primitive Euman technology on display. Either the *Volante* was a very old ship, or the Eumans had barely progressed beyond the internal combustion engine.

He saw the canine bound into the flight deck, saw it sniffing at the B'Con, saw it licking its lips fervently, and saw the flash of digits as the funds transfer went through. Idly, P'ker wondered what would happen when the Euman crime boss he'd liberated the funds from eventually tracked down the recipient, but his thoughts were interrupted by the sight of his crew returning with the dog.

The airlocks closed again, each leaving a lingering scent of the others' galaxy behind, and then the ships detached and parted ways. P'ker tickled the dog behind the ears, and was rewarded with a lick. The dog sniffed his arm, then licked him again, clearly interested in the scent.

'Someone get this animal some food,' ordered P'ker. 'Pilot, find a planet we can take it to. Inhabited, preferably canine-lovers.' He turned to his left. 'Oh, and Gunnery ... stand by for a little target practice.'

While Clunk was busy with the teleporter's internals, Amy kept a lookout at the door and Hal paced up and down telling both of them how unlikely it was they'd ever get home. He covered the lot, from the impossibility of teleporting to a flooded planet in their own galaxy, to getting shot by vengeful B'Con troops, to accidentally putting both fingers into an electrical socket.

'And on top of all that, I bet we never see the *Volante* again,' he added bitterly.

'I'm sure our ship is safe and sound,' said Clunk. 'The Navcom is more than capable of staying out of trouble.'

'And dropping us in it,' muttered Hal. 'One lousy puddle. That's what started all this nonsense. One piddling little puddle!'

'The dam was hardly a puddle,' said Clunk mildly.

Hal remembered the raging torrents of water flooding one underground chamber after another, and the way the floods had hurled diggers, boulders and electric carts around like so many toys. 'The *Navcom* could have picked us up again. I'm going to have words when I catch up with her. Next time this happens –'

'There,' said Clunk, as he stored the small circuit board he'd built earlier and replaced the cover on the controls. 'The teleporter is back to normal. We can travel to the D'eer planet and begin our long journey home.'

'Are you sure we've done enough damage here?' Amy asked from the doorway.

'I guarantee the fleet will have to return to base. I've

been picking up frantic traffic on their network - it's heavily encrypted, but the volume picked up immediately after we teleported the, er, melty goo, and it still hasn't peaked. Take it from me, the B'Con fleet is in trouble.'

'Good,' said Hal, with feeling. 'Now let's go home.'

Clunk nodded towards the three containers, which were smouldering gently nearby. 'I'll just mix the last batch of melty goo. We can leave as soon as its on its way to the flagship's gravity generators.'

'Er, perhaps not just yet,' said Amy.

'What do you mean? Why –' Hal turned to look at her, and swallowed nervously. Standing behind Amy was the Admiral from the D'eer planet, and she was holding a wicked-looking knife to Amy's throat. Light glinted from the cruel blade, and then Hal looked again. No, it was glinting *through* the blade. 'It's not real. It's a projection!' exclaimed Hal.

'I assure you it isn't,' said Amy, out the side of her mouth. 'I can feel the edge on my throat.'

'But –'

The Admiral beckoned to Hal and Clunk, gesturing with her knife to make the meaning clear: come here, or she gets it.

Hal still had the rocket launcher over his shoulder, and he wondered whether he could unsling it, find the safety, load a rocket into the chamber, aim and pull the trigger before the Admiral killed Amy. After carefully playing out the scenario in his mind, he realised he probably couldn't. That, and the rocket would either blow up the Admiral *and* Amy, or it would go right through the Admiral and then explode against the wall, killing Amy in the blast. Either way, he suspected Clunk would be less than impressed.

As they got closer Hal realised the Admiral was more solid than he first thought. A gunshot might go through her, but it would do a lot of damage on the way. He just couldn't make out why the Admiral looked so ... insubstantial.

Then it clicked. What had Clunk said? Anything teleporting in while the cloning mods were active would be spread amongst all the ships in the fleet, ending up maybe one fortieth of their usual density. The last time he'd seen the Admiral had been at the base on the D'eer planet. She must have teleported to the fleet immediately while the teleporters were running in Clunk's special duplication mode, which meant there was more than one of the Admirals running around. Fortunately, they'd have trouble standing up to a stiff breeze. Unfortunately, this one had a knife to Amy's throat.

Hal and Clunk stopped in front of the Admiral, who studied Hal with a murderous glint in her eye. He'd had a close encounter with her knife before, and he suspected this time would be a lot more unpleasant. The knife may be less substantial, but Hal was certain it would still draw blood.

'Let her go,' said Hal. 'It's me you want, not Amy.'

'No, take me,' said Clunk. He raised his hands, and spoke haltingly in the B'Con language. 'I'm telling her we surrender,' he said to Hal in an aside.

'Good move,' said Hal. 'Get close to her, knock her out, and then we'll make a break for it.'

Lardo hissed something, the gutteral words causing her to spit. Then she gestured at Hal with the knife.

Clunk glanced at Hal, concern etched on his face.

'What does she want?' demanded Hal.

'Before we surrender, she wants to kill you. Then she'll let me and Amy go. If you refuse, she'll kill Amy first and then have the pair of us ejected into space.'

Hal felt a cold chill up his spine. Would Clunk give up Hal's life to save Amy's? Even if the robot wouldn't, Hal realised it was the right thing to do. 'Do you believe her?'

'No, Mr Spacejock. She's going to kill us all.'

Hal sighed with relief. They might all meet a gory end, but at least Clunk wouldn't have to make an impossible choice. 'Hey, do we get a last meal?' he asked hopefully.

'I don't think we should provoke her.'

'I agree,' said Amy, speaking carefully because of the knife pressed to her throat.

Clunk said something to the Admiral, who nodded.

'She's given us a little time to discuss things.'

'Good.' Hal racked his brains for a solution, but came up empty. He could almost hear Clunk's brain whirring, then realised the robot was just grinding his teeth. 'Come on, old buddy. You must have a fix for this mess.'

'If we could get the Admiral closer to the teleporter –'

'Yes?'

'We could send her somewhere else.'

'And if we could get her close to a charging elephant it would trample her to death,' snapped Hal. 'Can't you think of something a bit more practical?'

'I've got it!' Clunk snapped his fingers. 'In exchange for our lives, we could reveal the location of our secret headquarters!'

'What secret headquarters?'

'The rebel base. Our weapons cache. Everything!'

Hal eyed the robot in concern. Either Clunk had flipped under the strain, or he was reading the wrong plot outline. 'Er, Clunk?'

'Yes, Mr Spacejock?'

'There is no secret base.'

'Of course there is. It's hidden underground on planet Chiseley.'

'That's not a secret base.'

'Yes it is.'

'No it isn't.'

'Yes it is, and the Admiral should teleport there immediately to investigate.'

'But Clunk, it's just a bunch of flooded tunnels!'

'Mr Spacejock, the Admiral doesn't know that.'

Hal's jaw dropped. If the B'Con warrior got through to Chiseley, the floodwaters would do the rest. 'Hang on, if the teleporter is flooded at the other end –'

'I can fix that,' said Clunk. 'Reprogram the teleporter for a simultaneous transfer. Bring the water here and send the Admiral there at the same time.'

'Then the water pours back in at the other end?'

'Correct.'

'And the Admiral drowns?'

'Er, yes.'

'Killing her stone dead?'

Clunk looked uncomfortable. 'If I had to predict an outcome, that would be it.'

'Good. She shouldn't have threatened Amy.'

Clunk gave him a grateful smile.

'Hang on. What if she sends us through the teleporter first? That's what I'd do.'

'I'll just have to convince her that surprise is essential.' Clunk turned to the Admiral and began to speak in her language, using a low voice laden with defeat and surrender. He gave a convincing performance, and as he spoke the Admiral's expression grew more and more hungry.

Then Hal realised there was a slight flaw in Clunk's plan. What if the Admiral decided to kill them all first, before teleporting off to the 'secret base'? Or what if she called up reinforcements?

But no. He hadn't counted on the Admiral's determination to wrap up the Euman problem single-handedly. As soon as Clunk finished speaking she released Amy and motioned them all to one side, well clear of the teleporter. Then she strode towards it, and demanded something of Clunk.

'She wants the address, right?'

'Correct.'

'You know you're giving her a free pass into our own galaxy? If this goes wrong . . . '

Clunk lowered his head. 'I know, Mr Spacejock. But it's the only option.' He asked the Admiral a question, and she nodded. Then he approached the teleporter and entered the code. As soon as he was done, the Admiral waved him away and pressed the send button.

Buzz!

Naturally, nothing happened. It couldn't, since the destination teleporter was filled with water.

'Tell her it's the defence shield,' said Hal urgently. 'Tell her you have to override the controls to get through.'

'Already on it, Mr Spacejock.' Clunk explained haltingly, keeping his eyes averted from the Admiral's suspicious gaze. She demanded something, and he responded slowly, playing the part of the broken prisoner most convincingly.

The Admiral stepped aside, allowing Clunk access to the control panel, and the robot entered several commands. Then he bowed deeply and backed out of the chamber.

'Hig!' barked the Admiral.

'What does that mean?' asked Hal.

'She, er, wants me to go with her.'

'Is that wise?'

'It's unavoidable, I'm afraid. She doesn't trust me.'

'But Clunk . . . '

'Don't worry, Mr Spacejock. A little water won't hurt me.' So saying, Clunk stepped into the teleporter, and before anyone could move he pressed the send button.

Flash!

The Admiral and Clunk both disappeared, and the teleporter instantly filled with water. It hung there for a split second, then rushed out to fill the room, soaking Hal and Amy to the knees and almost knocking them off their feet. The water vanished into the corridor, flooding away in both directions and leaving a lingering damp smell.

'He could have warned us,' muttered Hal, shaking water off his boots.

'Never mind that,' said Amy. 'Do you think he'll be all right?'

'We'll find out soon enough.'

Flash!

They both turned to look at the teleporter, which was once again filled with water. It poured out of the door, carrying away more debris, only this time it left Clunk standing in the middle of the teleporter - alone. He looked serious, and when Hal met his eyes the robot gave a brief nod. 'It's done.'

'Thanks, Clunk. Taking a life . . . I know what that must have cost you.' Then he realised Clunk was staring at Amy in concern, and Hal turned to see what the matter was this time. Then he sighed.

Amy was surrounded by four identical B'Con Admirals, all of them with their knives drawn.

Half an hour and many return trips to Chiseley later, they'd thinned the number of Lardo clones considerably. A vast amount of flood water was making its way to the flagship's lower decks, and if there were any troops aboard the B'Con vessel, Hal assumed they were all busy with mops and pails.

By now they'd got the routine down pat, turning in a polished performance which fooled the assorted Admirals every time. At one point Hal pictured dozens of them drifting in the waters beneath the Chiseley dam, all still and lifeless, and then he pushed the image out of his mind. After all, hadn't the Admiral tried to skewer his skull on her double-ended dagger? And who knew how many others she'd killed and tortured over the years?

'Do you think that's it?' asked Hal, as Clunk returned from yet another disposal.

'I hope so,' said the robot. 'My seals can't take much more of this.'

'Yes, and killing thirty-six Admirals in a row must be tiring.'

Clunk frowned. 'Technically it's just one Admiral.'

'Yeah, but you still had to watch them all drown.'

'I'd rather not talk about that.'

There was a brief silence.

'So, how do we get home?' asked Hal. 'Amy and I can't teleport to Chiseley, not unless we want to end up drowned.'

'I have an idea. It's risky, it might not work, but it's a chance.'

'Spill it.'

Clunk gestured towards the door. 'First, we have to find a spacesuit locker.'

Aboard the *Volante*, the Navcom was facing a tough choice. Should she continue freighting goods around in the pursuit of modest profits, invest her considerable funds in the share market in the hope of better profits, or should she locate additional stray dogs to sell to gullible alien races for stupendous gains? The latter was clearly the most profitable choice, except there was a remote chance she'd encounter another ship full of canine-loving aliens.

Then the Navcom noticed something. Instead of departing, the alien ship had remained nearby. At first her spirits rose . . . were they hanging around in the hope of buying another pet? She might be short on living, breathing creatures, but perhaps they'd wait for her to fetch one.

Then a worrying thought occurred to her. Perhaps they were unhappy with their purchase? If so it was tough luck, thought the Navcom, since there would be no refunds and no returns. As a precaution she gave a little squirt on the thrusters, moving the *Volante* a few hundred kilometres away from the alien ship. She also programmed three different jumps, and wrote an algorithm to select one of the three at random. That way, even if the aliens were tracing her every action, they still wouldn't know where she'd gone.

The Navcom was about to execute the jump when the alien ship flared with a baleful green light. The Navcom's external sensors winked out, and in the blink of an eye she was blinded. Hurriedly, she executed the jump, but she was far too late. An explosion tore into the *Volante's* hull, right near the port engine, and she was still trying to assess the damage when a lethal energy bolt slammed into the lower deck.

The entire hull vapourised with a flash of green light, and for a split second the Navcom was hovering in space, exposed to the stars. Traces of wiring led away in every direction, the *Volante's* cabling and communication network laid out like veins and arteries excised from a corpse. Then the heavens turned sweet purple, shot through with tart twists of lemon, and the Navcom was still savouring the mind-bending experience when the *Volante's* engines exploded, blowing the remainder of the ship into tens of millions of fragments and scattering the tiny pieces amongst the stars.

'At least they didn't get my money,' thought the Navcom, before her consciousness winked out of existence.

◆

Getting to the nearest spacesuit locker was much tougher than Hal expected it to be. With Clunk's knowledge of the B'Con language it was easy enough to follow signs. Unfortunately, the previously empty corridors now echoed to the thunderous footsteps of B'Con patrols, finally stirred into action by the appearance - and subsequent disappearance - of numerous Admiral Lardos.

The three humans took cover where they could, darting between storage cupboards and empty cabins, using ventilation shafts and even - to Hal's delight - hiding behind a big serving trolley laden with a selection of tasty foodstuffs.

Finally, after another thirty minutes of cautious sneaking, their destination was in sight: a broad double-doorway, with two B'Con guards posted in front.

'Why the guards?' hissed Hal, finishing off a mouthful of salami.

'They're protecting the suits,' whispered Clunk. 'They're trying to prevent our escaping through an airlock.'

'So why aren't they guarding the teleporter?'

'They will be by now,' muttered Clunk.

Hal eyed the guards. They were hulking brutes who looked like they could snap a fully grown tree like a twig, and then use the sharp ends to pick the flesh of their fallen enemies from their tusks. Hand-to-trotter combat was out of the question, which only left one solution. 'Clunk, why don't you distract them while we get the suits?'

Clunk mulled the suggestion over. 'Do you have anything in mind?'

'Use your language skills. Talk to them, and convince them to leave.'

'And failing that?'

'Poke one of them in the eye and run like hell.'

'But –'

'Clunk, trust me. They're big and slow. They'll never catch you.'

'They have guns.'

'Weave a bit. You'll be fine.'

After a moment's hesitation, Clunk left cover and strolled towards the guards, assuming an air of authority. They raised their weapons at his approach, but one barked word from the robot had them lowering the huge guns again. Clunk continued to speak, hurling gutteral words with confidence. The guards looked chastened, then embarrassed, and when they both turned to leave Hal punched the air with delight. Unfortunately, his enthusiastic 'Yeah!' carried all the way to the guards, who immediately crouched in a combat stance, their guns covering the humans' hiding spot.

The next few seconds were a blur. There was a squeal of pain as Clunk kicked one of the guards in the shin, a moment of silence broken only by the fleeing robot's footsteps, and then a thunder of gunshots as the B'Con guards opened fire. The robot darted and weaved as he ran down the corridor, narrowly avoiding energy blasts as the guards emptied their clips. Then, when they realised he was getting away, they set off in lumbering pursuit.

'Come on, to the suit locker,' muttered Hal.

Amy glared at him all the way, and she continued to scowl as he opened the door and unhooked the two smallest suits from the rack.

'What?' asked Hal.

'You're doing your best to get us all killed, aren't you?' Amy mimed the fist pump. 'Of all the stupid ... '

'I couldn't help it,' said Hal, as he struggled into the oversized suit. 'It was a tense moment.'

'Clunk might be huddled in a corridor right now,' hissed Amy. 'Imagine him lying there, shot to pieces and leaking all over the floor.'

'He'll be fine.'

Amy fastened her suit, and paused with the big helmet over

her head. 'You're a menace, Hal. One day you'll pull a stupid stunt like that, and he won't be fine.' Amy's voice faltered. 'He won't be okay, he'll be dead. Gone for good. And it'll be your fault.'

'I'll have him mended.' As soon as the words left his mouth, Hal knew it was the wrong thing to say. 'I mean –'

Amy snorted with disgust. 'That right there ... that tells me how much you care for him.'

Before Hal could reply Amy snapped her helmet into place, cutting him off. Silently, Hal donned his own helmet. After it was sealed he wondered how he was supposed to breathe, until he felt a stream of cool air on his face. Unfortunately it couldn't mask the smell of stale B'Con.

Suited up, Hal and Amy stumped to the doorway. Hal couldn't help laughing at the sight, as Amy looked like a child dressed in oversized adult clothes. The sleeves and legs were far too long, and folds of silvery fabric hung like curtains around her waist. Then he realised he'd look just as ridiculous, and the laughter dried up.

They peered into the corridor, then stumbled over to the nearest doorway. It was getting hot in the suit, and the helmet kept tipping forward until Hal could only see a strip of floor in front of his feet. Hal began to see flaws in their plan: for example, how were they supposed to avoid detection? Or, for that matter, run from enemies? They'd be sitting ducks unless the B'Con collapsed in fits of laughter. Then it hit him - why were they wearing the suits when they could carry them? If not the suit, he could certainly get rid of the heavy, oversized helmet.

Hal took off the helmet and tucked it under his arm. Then he set off down the corridor, walking like a deep-sea diver with his feet slip-slapping on the hard floor.

They dodged three patrols on the way, using cover in the nick of time, and when they finally reached the teleporter room Hal was running with sweat. The suit was designed for the cold of deep space, not frantic escape attempts, and all the loose ends and flappy bits didn't help.

They peered round the final corner, and Hal's heart sank. He'd expected a couple of guards outside the teleporter room, but there were six of them, all heavily armed. And he didn't even have the rocket launcher.

'Why don't you run up and poke one of them in the eye?' whispered Amy.

Hal gave her a look.

'What? You thought it was good enough for Clunk.'

Hal ignored her. Physical violence wasn't going to do it, not this time. What he needed was a devilishly clever distraction, something like ... along the lines of ... a kind of ... Defeated, he turned to Amy. 'Okay, I give up. What should we do?'

Amy suppressed a grin. 'Are you asking me for help?'

'We're in this together,' muttered Hal.

'I'm sorry, was that a yes or a no?'

'Yes.'

'Right.' Amy glanced back down the corridor. 'The lab. Follow me.'

They stumbled back to the lab, where Amy took several chemicals from the shelves.

'What are you doing?' Hal asked her.

'Clunk's not the only one who knows how to mix things.' So saying, Amy began combining materials. When she was done she had a canister with a blend of chemicals. A pale blue smoke rose from the mix, and Hal kept his distance.

'Is that poison?'

'No, nothing like that.' Amy held up a spatula with a few

dark grains on the end. 'Once I add this, it'll smoke like crazy. Thick, dark smoke we can use for cover.'

'Where did you learn this stuff?'

'University,' said Amy, without elaborating. 'Come on, bring the canister.'

'Wait. I've got an idea.' Hal fetched the serving trolley from further down the corridor, helping himself to a couple of dishes on the way back. Then he stood the canister on top.

'It wasn't all that heavy,' said Amy, with a frown.

Hal shook his head. 'That's not it. Come on.'

They headed for the teleporter room, Hal pushing the trolley while Amy carried the spatula. As they got closer they pressed themselves to the wall, until Hal was able to risk a glance. 'Still six of them. Are you ready?'

Amy held up the spatula.

'Toss it in.'

She did so, and Hal stepped back in surprise as dense black smoke poured from the canister. There was no sound, no heat, just clouds of choking smoke. Holding his breath, he took hold of the trolley and gave it a hefty shove around the corner.

There was a cry of alarm, and then coughing and spluttering as the trolley shot past the guards, still emitting smoke. A thick haze filled the corridor, and in the confusion Hal and Amy managed to slip into the teleporter room. Hal wasted no time - he ran for the three canisters Clunk had set aside earlier and emptied them all onto the deck. The multicoloured liquids combined into a batch of melty goo, which promptly sank through the metal floor as it ate its way towards the gravity generator. Sabotage complete, Hal darted into the teleporter and reached for the controls.

'Wait!' said Amy. 'What about Clunk?'

'He knows where we're going,' said Hal.

311

'But –'

'Helmet. Quick.'

Amy hesitated, and in that second there was a thud of footsteps. They both turned to the doorway, expecting to see Clunk charging in to join them. Instead, it was another Admiral Lardo, bayonet drawn and murder in her eyes.

Amy fastened her helmet, while Hal sought the teleporter control pad with fumbling fingers. The gloves on the spacesuit made it hard to find, and it didn't help than an enraged Admiral was charging towards him.

At the last second he managed to hit Go, just as the Admiral dived into the teleporter with them. Hal felt a grip on his arm, and then . . .

Flash!

They reappeared in a teleporter lit with baleful green, a wall of water a metre or so from their faces. Admiral Lardo was still clinging to Hal's arm, her grip ghostly and insubstantial. Then the water collapsed towards them, burying them instantly in a whirling maelstrom. Hal felt tugging on his arm, and he saw Lardo's bulging eyes up close, air streaming from her snout as she screamed soundlessly in his face. Her trotters thudded against his helmet, and then he felt a scalding rip across his forearm as the Admiral sliced at his suit with her bayonet. Water began to rush in through the damaged suit, and Hal clamped his free hand over the wound to seal it.

The Admiral kept swinging her knife, trying to end him before the water killed her, but her strength was going and she couldn't pierce the fabric. Then, after a final spasm, she was still.

Hal pushed the body away, and turned to look for Amy. The first thing he saw was another Lardo, then another, and as he looked around he realised he was surrounded by corpses.

All the Lardos Clunk had led to their deaths . . . floating here, lifeless, their staring eyes accusing him.

Hal did his best to ignore the bodies, instead focusing on Amy. He saw her nervous face peering back at him from inside the cavernous helmet, her eyes wide in the shadows. A dark wisp passed between them, and Hal realised it was his own blood in the water. Wincing, he kept a firm grip on his arm, hoping he could last until they got out. Then he remembered the tunnels they'd have to negotiate to escape the flooded underground base, and his blood ran cold.

Face it, he thought to himself. There was no way he was going to make it.

— 41 —

After watching Admiral Lardo and Hal fighting to the death in front of her, Amy felt herself withdrawing into a shell. She'd been holding everything together from the moment she'd been stuck in the flooded basement of her father's house, keeping her calm through one shock after another. The teleporters, travel to another galaxy, encountering alien races, several close escapes from the B'Con ... it had all taken its toll, but she'd always believed there was a way out. Whenever the doubts arose, Clunk would be there to reassure her, and she'd taken a lot of comfort from his presence.

Now she was stuck deep underground, floating helplessly in a flooded tunnel with several dozen alien bodies. Hal was injured, his suit slashed open, and Clunk was stuck on a huge alien battle cruiser in a completely different galaxy. It didn't get much more hopeless than this, she thought, and she had an overwhelming desire to give up the struggle.

Amy closed her eyes, banishing the dead Admirals and the nearby outline of Hal. It also banished the ghostly green water, and if she concentrated hard she could imagine herself safely in bed. It would be so easy to go to sleep right here, and ...

No! If by some miracle Clunk made it back, how would he feel if he discovered Amy had given up? That she'd let Hal die, as well as herself? She owed it to the robot to try, and to try with every last breath.

Amy opened her eyes, and she saw Hal looking at her in concern through the helmet. She heard his voice, thin and reedy, and she realised it was being transmitted through the faceplates.

'Are you all right?' he asked her.

'Better. What about you? How's your arm?'

'A bit stabbed,' said Hal drily. 'So, shall we wait here for Clunk, or make our way to the surface and wait in the sunshine?'

Amy allowed herself a weak smile. 'Sunshine sounds good.'

'Come on, then.'

'Wait. There might be a quicker way.'

'Really?'

Amy indicated the teleporter. 'We could use this to get out.'

'No chance,' said Hal flatly. 'First, all the teleporters near the house will be under water, and Clunk isn't here to override the safety device. Second, we don't have the address.'

'The control pad stores a list of recent addresses. One of them might work.'

'Yeah, and one of them might send us straight to another galaxy.'

'You'd rather drown?'

Hal thought for a moment. 'Look, I think we can make it. All we have to do is get to the tunnel, right? Then it's straight home from there.'

Amy looked doubtful. 'But your arm. Won't it –'

'Don't worry about it. The suit isn't leaking much.'

'But –'

'Come on. I've had enough of teleporters anyway.' With that, Hal turned and paddled his way out of the teleporter chamber, moving at a snail's pace as he negotiated the floating bodies. Amy wondered how far they'd get before their air ran out, then drove the negative thought from her mind and followed.

◆

Barely an hour later, Hal was exhausted. They'd only just reached the cavern with the ruined digger, not even a tenth of the total distance, and he knew they'd never make it out. It seemed like weeks ago they'd dug their way into the cavern with the alien machine, and the events of the previous day or two were blurred into a confusing sequence of explosions, fights and narrow escapes.

The only good thing was that the long, featureless tunnel they'd made with the digger led directly to safety. The bad things? Well, they included Hal's knife wound, his torn suit, their slow progress, their lack of food and worst of all, their lack of drinking water. It seemed crazy, what with them being submerged in the stuff, but they could hardly remove their helmets and take a swig.

So, Hal was going crazy with thirst, and he was sure Amy was enduring the same hell. Unlike Amy, though, his suit was slowly filling with water, and if they didn't make it to the surface in time he'd have more than enough to drink. Way more than enough.

Banishing such pleasant thoughts, Hal approached the hole in the cavern wall. Digging through his memories, he recalled the hours and hours they'd spent aboard the machine, boring through solid rock. Now they'd have to swim the entire way back, flapping their arms in the oversized spacesuits and moving about as fast as a pair of wounded seals.

Hal frowned. He hated to admit it, but Amy had been right all along. Swimming out was a hopeless idea. So, he approached Amy and touched his faceplate to hers. 'I think I made a mistake.'

Amy looked at him expectantly. 'Which one are you talking about?'

Hal jerked his thumb at the tunnel. 'We're never going to make it out, are we?'

'Doesn't look like it.'

'Shall we try the teleporter?'

'Yep.'

'It's risky. We could end up anywhere.'

'I'll settle for anywhere but here.'

They separated, and after a final glance around the flooded cavern, Hal led the way back down the corridor to the sunken teleporter.

◆

While Hal and Amy were struggling through the flooded tunnels deep below the surface of planet Chiseley, Clunk was evading B'Con troops aboard the flagship. Fortunately, the ship's gravity generators had succumbed to the unstoppable melty goo, and in zero-g the unwieldy B'Con had no chance against the nimble robot. Clunk sprang from wall to wall, deck to ceiling, and any B'Con troops foolish enough to open fire were promptly hurled backwards by the recoil from their powerful weapons.

Back at the teleporter, Clunk pushed through the cloud of debris and positioned himself in the centre of the chamber. Bidding a grim adieu to the B'Con, he activated the controls and immediately found himself in the flooded teleporter. He scanned the bodies in the water, fearing the worst, then felt a rush of relief when he realised none were human.

Then he saw movement, and his eyes widened in concern. Amy was paddling towards him, her expression drawn and exhausted behind the faceplate. She had one arm around Hal, trying to propel him forward, and Clunk's electronic heart skipped a beat as he saw the water rising in Hal's helmet. It was already up to his neck, and the human appeared to be unconscious, with his eyes closed and his head lolling sideways.

Clunk darted forwards to help, barely registering the shocked surprise on Amy's face. Without ceremony, he grabbed Hal and dragged him towards the teleporter.

His intention was to return to the B'Con flagship, and he was about to set the address when he realised it was pointless. When they arrived at the other end Hal would need medical attention, and there'd be no time for resuscitation while the B'Con were firing on them.

No, it had to be somewhere else. Clunk ran through the addresses in his memory, and selected a flooded teleporter close to the house. All he needed was an air pocket, somewhere to get Hal out of his suit and stabilise him. After that, he could call in the experts.

Clunk entered the address, ensured the three of them were all inside the chamber, then hit send.

They arrived at the destination with a flash, transported along with a huge cube of water and two dead Lardos. Clunk and Amy pushed their way into the corridor, desperately dragging Hal clear. As they moved into the tunnel Clunk's head broke through the surface of the water, and with a gusty sigh of relief he realised the tunnels weren't completely flooded. The dam was still filling overhead, but the water was running into the underground tunnels, draining the dam quicker than it could be filled.

Clunk smiled at this, picturing the puzzled humans watching their new dam emptying like a bath tub with a missing plug, but his smile soon vanished when he remembered Hal. He activated his chest lamp and shone the dim yellow beam on the human.

'Quick, the helmet,' he said.

Amy helped, and between them they freed Hal from the suit. Water poured out, and Clunk quickly checked for a pulse. 'I-I can't feel anything,' he said, his insides suddenly icy cold.

'Let me.' Amy put her fingers to Hal's neck, and for several agonising seconds Clunk thought they'd left it too late. Then . . .

'He's alive and breathing,' she said. 'Definitely alive.'

Clunk felt an overwhelming joy, and he blinked away the lubricating fluid which had sprung to his eyes. 'Is he . . . hurt?'

'Lardo cut his arm with her knife, but I don't think she wounded him too badly. Water kept leaking in through the suit, and . . . ' Amy's voice tailed off. 'I didn't think he was going to make it. I ...I didn't think I'd ever see you again. I thought it was all over.'

Clunk was still supporting Hal, but he put his other arm around Amy's shoulders. 'I'm here now. It's going to be fine.'

Suddenly Hal coughed, took a deep breath, and spluttered. 'What the –' he began, shaking his head. 'Where am I? What happened?'

'You're fine, and we're nearly home,' said Clunk.

'Is this the *Volante*?'

'Not yet, but she won't be far away.'

'Good.' Hal blinked. 'My head's killing me. I don't suppose anyone has a nice hot cup of coffee?'

◆

'Still no sign of the *Volante*?'

'Not yet, Mr Spacejock.'

'I'm going to give the Navcom hell over this.'

'Me too, Mr Spacejock.'

Hal, Clunk and Amy were walking along a narrow road, flanked by flooded fields. It had taken them hours to escape the flooded tunnels, a nightmare of cold water and darkness which Hal was determined to put out of his mind. They'd finally emerged in the basement of the flooded house, where they'd had to negotiate torrents of water pouring into the tunnels from above.

Then ...daylight and sunshine. Hal and Amy threw off their spacesuits and flopped on the ground, turning their faces to the sky and soaking up the warmth.

After a short rest, Hal's thoughts had turned to rescue, and Clunk had been scanning the airwaves for signs of their ship ever since. Failing to locate the *Volante*, Clunk scanned for any signs of life at all, but their location was remote and there was no coverage.

'I could use a burger right about now,' muttered Hal.

'You and your food,' grumbled Amy.

'Well, it's an essential –'

'Mr Spacejock. Amy. I think I hear something.'

Hal turned to see Clunk staring into the distance, one hand cupped to his ear. 'What is it?'

'A vehicle, and it's heading this way.'

They all turned to look, barely daring to hope. A vehicle meant rescue, safety ... and food. They could all hear the engine now, whirring and straining as the vehicle negotiated the bumpy, hilly road. Then it rounded the corner, a battered red pickup with an elderly man at the controls.

Hal heard a sob, and he noticed Amy had burst into tears. She just stood there, crying, and as the car drew up she could only manage a single word.

'Dad.'

◆

Amy's dad drove in silence, one arm held tightly around his daughter as she gave him an edited version of their exploits. The way she told it, she'd been trapped underground by the flooding, and she'd run into Hal and Clunk. The three of them had made their way to the surface, eventually, and had been walking to safety when he'd found them.

'I've been driving around looking for you for two days,' said her dad gruffly. 'I thought I'd lost you.'

'I'm sorry. I –'

'Not your fault. Never liked the dam idea in the first place, and now I like it even less.' He glanced over his shoulder at Hal, who was sitting in the back seat with Clunk. 'Thank you for keeping an eye out. Amy means everything to me.'

'Oh, it wasn't me,' said Hal. 'Clunk was amazing, as usual.'

Amy's dad turned his attention to the robot. 'Anything you need, it's yours. Just ask.'

Clunk looked like he was about to say something, but in the end he just nodded.

'Now, where can I drop you gents?'

'Is the spaceport out of your way?'

'Too easy.' Amy's dad took the next turning, and before long they were driving through the outskirts of a small town.

'Any signs of the *Volante*?' Hal asked Clunk.

'Not yet, Mr Spacejock, but I do have coverage. There's a message from Si Matthews, dated yesterday. It's about the house clearance job.'

'Oh crap.' With the *Volante* missing they could hardly deliver the cargo of furniture, which meant they wouldn't get paid. 'Can you stall him? Tell him we're running late?'

Clunk shook his head. 'There's no need. The message is a thank-you note, confirming the cargo delivery. There's also a notification of payment.'

Hal's eyebrows rose. 'The Navcom completed the job on her own?'

'So it seems.'

'But . . . on her *own*?'

'I hesitate to remind you of this, but human pilots are more of a legal requirement than an actual necessity.'

'So where's my ship now?'

Clunk spread his hands. 'I can't find any trace of her.'

They drove in silence for twenty minutes, until Amy's dad drew up at the spaceport. Hal and Clunk got out, and then Amy stepped out too. She stood in front of Clunk, shyly, then gave him a quick hug and climbed back into the car without a word.

Clunk was still standing there, a surprised look on his face, as the pickup drove off into the distance.

◆

Once inside the spaceport, Hal ran for the nearest coffee shop while Clunk sought an information kiosk. He bypassed the adverts, declined half a dozen offers for insurance, and finally brought up the shipping menu. Then he entered the *Volante*'s id code, and waited impatiently while the terminal gathered the required information. In a saner galaxy he'd have been able to access information on his own ship wirelessly, but then the data supplier wouldn't have been able to inject all the adverts.

Clunk's eyes got wider and wider as he paged through the *Volante*'s recent travel log, noting the ship's rapid succession of cargo jobs. Then he reached the final entry, and a tortured moan escaped his lips.

'Oh no. Oh no, no, *no!*'

◆

Hal was on his third coffee when Clunk stumbled into the cafe. The robot looked like he'd seen a ghost, and there was a ghastly look on his face as he approached Hal's table.

'Mr Spacejock, I'm afraid I have some really bad news.'

'Don't tell me they stopped making Mize bars? I loved those things.'

'Er no, it's not about chocolate.'

Hal frowned. 'There's a coffee shortage?'

'No, Mr Spacejock. It's far more serious than that.'

'All our regular customers signed with Kent Spearman?'

'We don't have any regular customers, Mr Spacejock.' Clunk hesitated. 'No, I'm afraid the *Volante* has been destroyed. The engines went critical during flight, and the resulting explosion tore the ship to pieces.'

Hal stared at him. 'Torn to pieces?'

Clunk held up his finger and thumb, almost touching. 'The largest no bigger than this, by all accounts.'

'And the Navcom?'

'I still have a backup, but the original . . . ' Clunk shook his head sadly.

Hal took a moment to take in the loss of his treasured ship. The *Volante*, gone. Then he shrugged. 'Oh well, there's always the insurance.'

Clunk put a hand on his shoulder. 'Mr Spacejock,' he said gently. 'You should prepare yourself for another shock.'

'This isn't going to be about coffee or chocolate either, is it?'

'No, it's to do with insurance. It seems the *Volante* wasn't covered.'

'Oh, come *on*. You *know* I paid the premium, Clunk. You always insist on it!'

'You did authorise payment, yes, but it seems the Navcom cancelled the policy.'

'Why?' Hal raised his hand. 'No, don't bother explaining. There's no point.'

'I'm sorry, Mr Spacejock.'

Hal crossed his arms. He had no ship, no money and no job, and the future looked bad. On the other hand, the past and present hadn't been that good to him either, so perhaps things were actually looking up. 'Okay, here's what we're going to do. We're going to get a couple of jobs, save up a wad of cash, and then we're going on holiday.'

Clunk frowned. 'Are you sure?'

'I'm certain. I need a break, and a couple of weeks skiing would be ideal.'

'Water skiing?'

Hal shuddered. 'Not likely. I want a nice snowy mountain, where the only water for miles around is sitting in my glass of whiskey.'

'And what about afterwards, when the money runs out?'

Hal smiled. 'Don't worry about it. Something will turn up.'

'But . . . a job? What sort of employment are we suited to?'

'Call Si Matthews and set up a meeting.'

'The shipping agent? Why?'

'He'll have something for us. If he doesn't, I bet he'll know someone who does.'

Clunk hesitated, then complied. 'Very well, I'll organise it. And can I just say, you're taking the news of the *Volante* very well.'

After Clunk left, Hal looked down at his coffee. His knuckles were white, and his fierce grip was threatening to crush the mug. He'd put on a brave face for Clunk, but inside he was screaming. What had he done to deserve such bad luck? Why was his life so unfair?

Si Matthews met them in a diner, where he waved to them from a corner booth. 'I ordered food for you. Is that all right?'

Hal was still reeling from the shock of losing the *Volante*, and for once a slap-up feast was the furthest thing from his mind. Still, it was a *free* slap-up feast. 'I could probably manage something light,' he said dully.

'I hear you're looking for work, and I've got another cargo job for you,' said Matthews.

Hal felt his stomach clench. 'We can't help you,' he said quietly. 'We don't have a ship any more.'

'I heard, but that's okay because there's no flying involved. You just need to drive a truck.'

'Really?' Hal brightened, just a little. Freight was freight, right? 'What's involved?'

'Well, there's a shipment of –'

'Here you are sir. Your breakfast.'

The waiter laid a plate on the table, and Hal thanked him before picking up his knife and fork. Then he looked down. On the plate in front of him were two eggs, half a tomato, a slice of toast . . . and half a dozen thick bacon rashers. Without a word, Hal put the knife and fork down and pushed the plate away.

'Not a fan of a fry-up, eh?' said Matthews. 'Tell you what. They do a really good hamburger.'

Hal groaned.

'Just a glass of water, then?'

Hal groaned even louder.

'All right, all right. Forget about breakfast.' Matthews frowned. 'Now where was I? Oh yes, the job. There's a shipment of frozen food which has to be collected from the local warehouse and delivered to half a dozen supermarkets. It'll only take a couple of days, and the pay's not too bad. It's enough to get you back on your feet, anyway. Maybe rent a motel room, or buy a ticket out of here.'

Hal shrugged. It didn't sound great, but beggars couldn't be choosers. 'So this cargo. What is it?'

'Let me see.' Matthews glanced at his thinscreen. 'Oh yes, here we are. It's a shipment of frozen bacon.'

◆

'Mr Spacejock! Your actions were totally uncalled for.'

Hal and Clunk hurried away from the restaurant, where they'd left Si Matthews in the hands of several waiters. One was wiping tomato sauce from his face, another was picking bacon from his hair, and a third was trying to remove a wedge of paper serviettes from the agent's mouth.

'We spent two days fighting the B'Con, and I'll be damned if some jumped-up agent is going to turn me into a laughing stock.'

'He was only trying to help.'

'No he wasn't. He was trying to be funny. Bacon for breakfast, shipping frozen bacon ...bacon every damned where.'

'He doesn't know about the B'Con, Mr Spacejock. Nobody does.'

'Amy does.'

'And she won't tell anyone.'

'Are you sure of that? She could go to the media and sell the story to some hyperbolist hack. There'd be a fortune in it.' Hal thought for a moment. 'Quite a big fortune, wouldn't you say?'

'No, Mr Spacejock. If you tried to tell our tale we'd be a laughing stock for sure.'

'I guess you're right.' Hal spotted a cash machine. 'We'd better get some money out. Who knows where we'll be sleeping tonight.'

'Agreed.'

Hal accessed his account, then frowned at the nine-digit number on the screen. At first he thought it was the account number, but then he realised something rather wonderful. It wasn't the account number, it was the account *balance*, and it ran to half a billion credits! 'Clunk, there's enough there for a whole new ship!'

'That's enough for a fleet of ships,' said the robot.

'But how? Where? Why?'

Clunk accessed the recent history. 'It was the Navcom. She's been busy trading.'

Hal turned his face to the sky. 'Navcom, all is forgiven.' Then, with a whoop of delight, he started dancing madly around the terminal, giving ecstatic thumbs-up to startled passers-by.

Ker-ching!

'Mr Spacejock! Look!'

Hal hurried back to the terminal, where Clunk was pointing to a substantial deposit. 'What's that?' demanded Hal.

'It's the interest on the savings.'

Ker-ching! Another chunk of change hit the account.

Ker-ching! Ker-ching! Ker-ching!

Hal did a quick calculation, and his smile grew even bigger. With that much money flowing in, he'd never have to work again!

'I don't like the look of the client list,' said Clunk, with a frown. He was studying the list of recent jobs more closely, and his face grew longer with every entry. 'This is a who's who of criminal organisations, terrorist groups, activists ...'

'It wasn't us, it was the Navcom,' said Hal quickly. 'And hey, maybe nobody will notice.'

Buzz!

Hal frowned. A new amount had just hit the account, but the figures were red this time, and the balance had just gone down.

Buzz!

'Hey, what's happening?' he demanded, as the balance shrunk again.

'Someone noticed.' Clunk pressed one button, then another, as he tried to find more details on the transactions. With each press there was another buzz, and more of Hal's money disappeared. Soon there was a cacophony of buzzing noises, and the cash fairly vapourised under Hal's distraught gaze.

Ping!

At this final noise, several lines of text appeared on the screen, right beneath an official-looking crest of arms.

This account has been closed under Proceeds of Crime legislation. Have a nice day!

And there, underneath, was the worst news yet: *Funds remaining: 0 credits.*

◆

There was a roar as a battered truck rumbled along the deserted highway, and a squeal from the brakes as it slowed for the turning. Brake lights flared in the darkness, and the headlights swung across an expanse of empty fields. The driver was a dishevelled-looking man in a grubby flightsuit, his unshaven face pale in the light reflected from the dashboard.

The truck picked up pace again, crossing a bridge before rumbling along the road. There was a railway crossing ahead, and the driver sighed as the warning signals began to flash. He slowed the truck to a stop, and waited in silence. He'd been driving the same route for a month now, and the crossing got him every time. It was fate, thumbing her nose at him. It had to be.

The engine coughed once, twice, then died.

Frowning, the driver tried restarting his vehicle, but the ignition was dead. He was about to get out when an intensely bright light winked on, directly overhead. The beam pinned the truck like a moth, encircling the vehicle and turning the surrounding shadows into impenetrable blackness.

The warning lights continued to flash, and the truck began to shake gently under an invisible force. At this, the driver rolled his eyes. 'An alien abduction?' he muttered. 'Really?'

Then, with a loud whoosh, the truck was sucked upwards into the belly of a B'Con scout ship.

'Are you Hal Spacejock, late of the *Volante*?'

The truck driver shielded his eyes against the glare. 'Yeah, that's me.'

'You killed Grand Admiral Lardo?'

Hal felt a chill, but there was no point denying it. 'One of them, yeah.'

'Please note that in the record,' said a voice. 'The Euman admits he ended Lardo's life.'

'Am I on trial?' asked Hal. 'Because if I am ...'

'No, this is just a hearing. We need to establish the facts.'

'Well, the fact is that murderous swine got what was coming to her. They all did.'

There was a murmur of voices, quickly shushed. 'Grand Admiral Lardo has already been condemned for her part in recent events. Her record has been erased, her name removed from the honour rolls.'

'Good.'

'By destroying your vessel with sentient beings on board, she directly contravened the orders of the –'

'Wait, what?' Hal frowned. 'Lardo destroyed the *Volante*?'

'You didn't realise this fact?'

'I, er –'

'Oh, I understand the confusion. She didn't destroy it herself, but she did order her troops to do so. Your navigation computer was killed in the process, and according to our tests, this computer was technically a sentient being.'

Hal was still digesting this information when the B'Con spoke again.

'We have no wish to go to war with the Euman empire, and as such we must offer reparations for Lardo's actions. We would like you to accept this gift as a token of the friendship between our races.' So saying, a B'Con in full dress uniform approached Hal, carrying a polished metal briefcase.

Hal eyed the case. 'The *Volante* wasn't cheap, you know. It'll take quite a bit of cash to replace her.'

'We believe Eumans place great value on these devices, and this small collection should be enough to replace your trading vessel.' The B'Con held up the case and opened it. Nestled inside, embedded in grey foam padding, were two dozen zeedeg power modules. Their status lights winked balefully, and several were already showing orange alerts.

'That's, er, very good of you,' said Hal. He hesitated. 'I don't mean to sound ungrateful, but you couldn't organise a couple of suitcases stuffed with cash instead?'

'We can't gain access to your currency without leaving a trail.'

'Gold would do,' said Hal.

'We're not here to negotiate,' said the B'Con stiffly. 'If you don't want our gift, we can just as easily withdraw the offer.'

'No, the gift is fine,' said Hal quickly. 'I'll take it.'

'Excellent.' The B'Con hesitated. 'You should probably sell them in the next few hours,' he advised. 'You know what they say about primitive technology.'

'Sell them quickly. Will do.'

The B'Con stuck out his arm. 'It was a pleasure meeting you, and I hope to renew your acquaintance in future.'

Dazed, Hal shook the general's trotter. Then, before he knew what was happening, he was sitting in the truck at the railway crossing, with the briefcase full of unstable power modules on the seat beside him. The baleful spotlight winked out, and there was a faint rumble as the huge B'Con vessel departed.

Hal eyed the case, then glanced at his watch. Then he started the truck, turned it towards the city, and floored the accelerator.

◆

'What about this one?' Hal indicated the screen. 'One careful owner, only driven on Sundays, generous discount for cash buyers.'

Clunk eyed the listing. 'No, it's a death trap.'

'So was my first ship, but I still made a living.'

'Eked out an existence, you mean. And it nearly killed you in the process.'

'But it didn't, did it?' Hal picked up the handset and dialled the seller. 'Hello? I'm calling about your ship.'

'I'm sorry, it's no longer available.'

Hal frowned. 'If you sold it, why didn't you remove the ad?'

'I didn't sell it. It blew up on the landing pad, and my lawyers told me –'

'Say no more.' Hal replaced the handset and turned to the screen. 'Okay, what about this? Fixer-upper to suit skilled pilot.'

'No.'

'All right, negative nelly. What have you come up with?'

Clunk sighed. 'Nothing, Mr Spacejock. I'm afraid we don't have enough for a decent vessel.'

'Yeah, well I still think you sold those zeedegs too cheaply.'

'If I'd waited any longer there wouldn't have been any zeedegs to sell. Or, indeed, anyone left to sell them to.'

'We could get a loan,' suggested Hal.

They looked at each other.

'All right, bad idea.' Hal rubbed his chin, which still itched even though he'd got rid of the straggly beard. 'Why don't we invest the cash? If we pick the right investment we could double our money.'

'Halve it, more like.' After a moment's hesitation, Clunk wiped the list of available ships. 'Mr Spacejock, can I make a suggestion?'

'Does it involve me hanging around seedy little Spaceport bars?'

'Not this time.'

'Go on, then.'

'Why don't we take a break from the cargo business? We have a large sum of money at our disposal, and if we travel the galaxy we're bound to encounter interesting opportunities. And who knows, if we take our time we might come across a bargain. A suitable ship at the right price.'

Hal thought for a moment. He was a freighter pilot, not a space tourist, but it was a bit hard to be a pilot without a ship. And Clunk was right ... if they travelled widely enough, something would fall into their laps. The more he thought about it, the more he liked the idea. 'All right, let's do it. Book a couple of tickets out of this dump, and let's see what happens.'

'Will do, Mr Spacejock.'

'And Clunk ... '

'Yes, Mr Spacejock?'

'If you want to bring Amy along, that's fine with me.'

The robot stared at him in surprise. 'Why would she travel with us?'

'Because she fancies you, you idiot. You're too blind to see it, and she's too shy to tell you.' Hal picked up the handset and passed it to Clunk. 'Go on, ask her.'

'I couldn't possibly. It's . . . inappropriate.'

'No it isn't. You're both adults.'

Clunk eyed the handset as if it were going to bite him. Then, gingerly, he took it. He got through immediately, and his eyes closed as he heard Amy's voice. Before he could speak his nerve failed him, and he shoved the handset at Hal. 'You do it, Mr Spacejock. I . . . I can't.'

Gently, Hal pushed the handset back. 'Ask her.'

Reluctantly, Clunk held the device to his ear. 'H-hello? Amy?'

'Clunk! Is everything all right?'

'Mr Spacejock and I are about to leave.'

'Oh, that's a shame. Well, goodbye then.'

'Goodbye Amy.'

It was all Hal could to not to snatch the handset back. 'Clunk, I swear, if you don't ask her . . . '

'Amy, don't go! Tell me, do you have any holidays coming up?'

'Yes, term ends next week. Why?'

'Would you like to travel with us?'

'Travel? Where to?'

'I don't know,' said Clunk desperately. 'Around the galaxy.'

There was a long silence. 'Okay,' said Amy at last.

'Really?'

'Sure. I'd like to.'

'I'm so very pleased. Thank you. Thank you!' Clunk hung up, then beamed at Hal. 'She said yes, Mr Spacejock.'

'Of course she did, you idiot. Now book us three tickets out of this place before she comes to her senses.'

Clunk left for the booking desk at a run, and Hal grinned to himself as he sat back in his seat. He and Amy might not get along, but he was willing to put up with her for Clunk's sake. Anyway, if she distracted the robot it would leave Hal free to do whatever he wanted ... and with all that money in the bank, there were a *lot* of things he wanted to do with his life.

Hal smiled to himself as he took a sip of coffee. Sure, they'd lost the *Volante*. Sure, they'd almost started an intergalactic war. Sure, they'd pulled the plug on a vital dam and escaped death a dozen times over. But look on the bright side ... they had a boatload of money and an entire galaxy to explore at their leisure.

Who could ask for more?

Epilogue

◆

Water hell happened?

That's what residents of planet Chiseley are asking themselves, after the much-touted new dam failed to live up to expectations. Engineers are struggling to explain why the planned lake is emptying faster than they can fill it. Social media is rife with rumours, covering the spectrum from #alienplot to #blackhole, with special mention for #thedamreallysucksnow.

In other news, the price of used zeedegs has crumbled following a sudden flood of devices onto the market. The military are scrambling to check their stocks, although initial reports indicate the devices were sourced from long-lost vessels.

Finally, three commercial pilots have been stood down following an ill-advised media appearance, during which they claimed to have sighted an alien vessel in the skies above Chiseley. Experts dismissed their claims, pointing out that bright lights moving in the sky could be explained by regular, human spaceships travelling to and from the planet. The pilots insist the vessel was of alien origin, and all we can say is ... what were they drinking? There must be something odd in planet Chiseley's water ... if you can find any!

If you enjoyed this book, please leave a brief review at your online bookseller of choice. Thanks!

About the Author

Simon Haynes was born in England and grew up in Spain. His family moved to Australia when he was 16.

In addition to novels, Simon writes computer software. In fact, he writes computer software to help him write novels faster, which leaves him more time to improve his writing software. And write novels faster. (www.spacejock.com/yWriter.html)

Simon's goal is to write fifteen novels before someone takes his keyboard away.

Update 2018: goal achieved and I still have my keyboard!

New goal: write thirty novels.

Simon's website is spacejock.com.au

Stay in touch!

Author's newsletter:
spacejock.com.au/ML.html

facebook.com/halspacejock
twitter.com/spacejock

Acknowledgements

To all the Facebook fans who continue to demand more Hal ... thanks for the awesome help and support!

To my proof readers, Ian and Tricia ... wonderful work as always!

The Hal Spacejock series by Simon Haynes

1. A ROBOT NAMED CLUNK

Deep in debt and with his life on the line, Hal takes on a dodgy cargo job ... and an equally dodgy co-pilot.

2. SECOND COURSE

When Hal finds an alien teleporter network he does the sensible thing and pushes Clunk the robot in first.

3. JUST DESSERTS

Gun-crazed mercenaries have Hal in their sights, and a secret agent is pulling the strings. One wrong step and three planets go to war!

4. NO FREE LUNCH

Everyone thinks Peace Force trainee Harriet Walsh is paranoid and deluded, but Hal stands at her side. That would be the handcuffs.

5. BAKER'S DOUGH

When you stand to inherit a fortune, good body-guards are essential. If you're really desperate, call Hal and Clunk. Baker's Dough features intense rivalry, sublime double-crosses and more greed than a free buffet.

6. SAFE ART

Valuable artworks and a tight deadline ... you'd be mad to hire Hal for that one, but who said the art world was sane?

7. BIG BANG

A house clearance job sounds like easy money, but rising floodwaters, an unstable landscape and a surprise find are going to make life very difficult for Hal and Clunk.

8. DOUBLE TROUBLE

Hal Spacejock dons a flash suit, hypershades and a curly earpiece for a stint as a secret agent, while a pair of Clunk's most rusted friends invite him to a 'unique business opportunity'.

9. MAX DAMAGE

Hal and Clunk answer a distress call, and they discover a fellow pilot stranded deep inside an asteroid field. Clunk is busy at the controls so Hal dons a spacesuit and sets off on a heroic rescue mission.

10. Cold Boots

Coming 2019

Ebook and Trade Paperback

The Secret War Series
Set in the Hal Spacejock universe

Everyone is touched by the war, and Sam Willet is no exception.
Sam wants to train as a fighter pilot, but instead she's assigned to Tactical Operations.
It's vital work, but it's still a desk job, far from the front line.
Then, terrible news: Sam's older brother is killed in combat.
Sam is given leave to attend his memorial service, but she's barely boarded the transport when the enemy launches a surprise attack, striking far behind friendly lines as they try to take the entire sector.
Desperately short of pilots, the Commander asks Sam to step up.
Now, at last, she has the chance to prove herself.
But will that chance end in death... or glory?

Ebook and Trade Paperback

The Harriet Walsh series

Harriet's boss is a huge robot with failing batteries, the patrol car is driving her up the wall and her first big case will probably kill her.

So why did she join the Peace Force?

When an intergalactic crime-fighting organisation offers Harriet Walsh a job, she's convinced it's a mistake. She dislikes puzzles, has never read a detective mystery, and hates wearing uniforms. It makes no sense ... why would the Peace Force choose her?

Who cares? Harriet needs the money, and as long as they keep paying her, she's happy to go along with the training.

She'd better dig out some of those detective mysteries though, because she's about to embark on her first real mission ...

The Peace Force has a new recruit, and she's driving everyone crazy.

From disobeying orders to handling unauthorised cases, nothing is off-limits. Worse, Harriet Walsh is forced to team up with the newbie, because the recruit's shady past has just caught up with her.

Meanwhile, a dignitary wants to complain about rogue officers working out of the station. She insists on meeting the station's commanding officer ... and they don't have one.

All up, it's another typical day in the Peace Force!

Dismolle is supposed to be a peaceful retirement planet. So what's with all the gunfire?

A criminal gang has moved into Chirless, planet Dismolle's second major city. Elderly residents are fed up with all the loud music, noisy cars and late night parties, not to mention the hold-ups, muggings and the occasional gunfight.

There's no Peace Force in Chirless, so they call on Harriet Walsh of the Dismolle City branch for help. That puts Harriet right in the firing line, and now she's supposed to round up an entire gang with only her training pistol and a few old allies as backup.

And her allies aren't just old, they're positively ancient!

Ebook and Trade Paperback

The Hal Junior Series
Set in the Hal Spacejock universe
Spot the crossover characters, references and in-jokes!

Hal Junior lives aboard a futuristic space station. His mum is chief scientist, his dad cleans air filters and his best mate is Stephen 'Stinky' Binn. As for Hal ... he's a bit of a trouble magnet. He means well, but his wild schemes and crazy plans never turn out as expected!

Hal Junior: The Secret Signal features mayhem and laughs, daring and intrigue ... plus a home-made space cannon!

200 pages, illustrated, ISBN 978-1-877034-07-7

"A thoroughly enjoyable read for 10-year-olds and adults alike"
The West Australian

'I've heard of food going off
... but this is ridiculous!'

Space Station Oberon is expecting an important visitor, and everyone is on their best behaviour. Even Hal Junior is doing his best to stay out of trouble!

From multi-coloured smoke bombs to exploding space rations, Hal Junior proves ... *trouble is what he's best at!*

200 pages, illustrated, ISBN 978-1-877034-25-1

Imagine a whole week of fishing, swimming, sleeping in tents and running wild!
Unfortunately, the boys crash land in the middle of a forest, and there's little chance of rescue. Is this the end of the camping trip ... or the start of a thrilling new adventure?

200 pages, illustrated, ISBN 978-1-877034-24-4

Space Station Oberon is on high alert, because a comet is about to whizz past the nearby planet of Gyris. All the scientists are preparing for the exciting event, and all the kids are planning on watching.

All the kids except Hal Junior, who's been given detention...

165 pages, illustrated, ISBN 978-1-877034-38-1

Ebook and Trade Paperback

New from Simon Haynes
The Robot vs Dragons series

Welcome to the Old Kingdom!

It's a wonderful time to visit! There's lots to do and plenty to see!

What are you waiting for? Dive into the Old Kingdom right now!

Clunk, an elderly robot, does exactly that. He's just plunged into the sea off the coast of the Old Kingdom, and if he knew what was coming next he'd sit down on the ocean floor and wait for rescue.

Dragged from the ocean, coughing up seaweed, salty water and stray pieces of jellyfish, he's taken to the nearby city of Chatter's Reach, where he's given a sword and told to fight the Queen's Champion, Sur Loyne.

As if that wasn't bad enough, the Old Kingdom still thinks the wheel is a pretty nifty idea, and Clunk's chances of finding spare parts - or his missing memory modules - are nil.

Still, Clunk is an optimist, and it's not long before he's embarking on a quest to find his way home.

Unfortunately it's going to be a very tough ask, given the lack of charging points in the medieval kingdom...

Ebook and Trade Paperback

Printed in Great Britain
by Amazon

23048711R00200